James Inglis

The Humour of the Scot

'Neath Northern Lights and Southern Cross

James Inglis

The Humour of the Scot
'Neath Northern Lights and Southern Cross

ISBN/EAN: 9783337258337

Printed in Europe, USA, Canada, Australia, Japan

Cover: Foto ©Andreas Hilbeck / pixelio.de

More available books at **www.hansebooks.com**

THE

HUMOUR OF THE SCOT

'NEATH NORTHERN LIGHTS AND

SOUTHERN CROSS

BY

JAMES INGLIS

'MAORI,'

AUTHOR OF 'OOR AIN FOLK,' 'SPORT AND WORK ON THE NEPAUL FRONTIER,'
'TIRHOOT RHYMES,' 'OUR AUSTRALIAN COUSINS,' 'OUR NEW ZEALAND
COUSINS,' 'TENT LIFE IN TIGER LAND,' ETC. ETC. ETC.

Hear, Land o' Cakes and brither Scots,
Frae Maidenkirk to Johnny Groat's,
If there's a hole in a' your coats,
        I rede ye, tent it ;
A chiel's amang ye takin' notes,
        An' faith he'll prent it !

EDINBURGH

DAVID DOUGLAS, 10 CASTLE STREET

1894

DEDICATION

I dedicate this book to my dear Aunt Margaret,

Mrs. DAVID INGLIS, of Murlingden, Brechin,

the sole surviving representative amongst my relatives of that older generation about which most of these random recollections and jottings have been written.

PREFACE

In collecting the materials for a former book, *Oor Ain Folk*, I noted down from time to time many Scotch stories, which, although scarcely perhaps applicable to the more restricted scope and personal character of that volume, were yet, in my opinion, worthy of publication in some permanent record, as bearing on the always interesting story of the evolution and growth of any marked type of national character. Beyond a doubt the Scottish character *is* one of the most marked, yet most piquant and interesting, in the wide range of complex diversities that make up the sum total of our common humanity. It is trite, but true, that the study of individual character, and how that merges into the growth of national character, has always had a deep human interest, not only to the ordinary rank and file, but certainly to every thoughtful and observant man. Now in the illustrations which are afforded by current anecdotes, by individual peculiarities, by odd customs, by phases of thought or habit, even when these are accidental and transitory, it is recognised that in these the historian, the politician, the philosopher, and the moralist,

may oft find his richest material, so that even the mere
story-teller and gossip-monger, the retailer of anecdote
received at second-hand, finds his appropriate place—
humble, yet, perchance, more useful than even he himself
may realise—in the great temple of human history, the
vast, complicated fabric of man's development and destiny.
Well, I pretend to no higher *rôle* than that. In this volume
I do not put forward any claim to originality—I am
but a humble scribe ; and I am led into this train of
thought by the reception accorded in the Press to the
simple record of family life, which, under the homely
title above alluded to, jumped at once into a popularity
which was to me as grateful as it was unexpected. Nor
has the appreciation been confined to my own countrymen. Commendations of the most cordial and kindly
nature have come to me from all quarters ; and I have
been asked to lose no time in furnishing to apparently
troops of expectant readers, my promised further budget
of Scottish story and reminiscence. This let me try to
do in my own unpretentious way. Now that suggests
an illustration.

My father, the old minister, was a good musician and
a clever fiddler, and he was waited on by a humble
'wricht' one day with a home-made violin, which he
wished the minister to try. It was certainly a *unique*
instrument—a rare fiddle, in fact, but scarcely a Stradi-
varius. The complacent builder was asked, referring to
the material :—

' An' hoo did ye mak' it, Davie ? '

'Oh, minister,' responded the beaming artist, 'I made it a' oot o' my ain heid.'

'Ay, Davie,' was the dry rejoinder, 'an' I've nae doot there's eneuch wid left, tae mak' anither.'

On another occasion my father had been announced to preach in the Masonic Lodge at Tarfside, up in Glenesk. Nearing the building, he met the custodian, old Peter Duncan, and asked :—

' Are there mony fowk come, Peter ? '

' Oo ay,' said Peter, 'there's a gey pucklie ; but I'm thinkin' there'll be nae fun till ye gang in an' begin.'

And now for the application.

I found, as I have said, that after writing *Oor Ain Folk* I had enough material left in my head for another book ; so in the humble hope that the gentle reader may find the present volume not altogether 'wooden,' but possessed of some interest and not a little harmless 'fun,' and under the encouragement of former leniency and kindness, let us, acting on Peter's hint, without further preface, just 'Gang in and begin.'

JAS. INGLIS.

Murlingden, Brechin, *August* 1894.

CONTENTS

CHAPTER I

INTRODUCTION—SCOTTISH HUMOUR, AND THE FORMATION OF THE NATIONAL CHARACTER

CHAPTER II

BIBLICAL AND THEOLOGICAL

CHAPTER III

Minister and Manse

CHAPTER IV

Minister and People

CHAPTER V

PRECENTORS AND PSALMODY

CHAPTER VI

KIRKYAIRDS, SEXTONS, AND BURIALS

CHAPTER VII

FUNERAL CUSTOMS, EPITAPHS, ETC.

CHAPTER VIII

RUSTICITY OF THE OLDEN TIME

CHAPTER IX

RUSTICITY OF THE OLDEN TIME (*continued*)

CHAPTER X

OLD-FASHIONED SERVANTS AND SERVICE

CHAPTER XI

DISTINCTIVE FEATURES OF SCOTTISH HUMOUR

CHAPTER XII

ODDITIES OF SPEECH AND OLD-TIME BLUNTNESS

CHAPTER XVI

NAITERALS

Modern methods in treatment of the insane—Danger of overdoing even philanthropy—The old-time village life—'Finla' o' the Gun'—Too literal an answer to prayer—'Jock Brodie'—'Singin' Willie'—'Jock Heral''—'Gude, gude wirds'—Stories of 'The Laird'—'Johnnie Maisterton'—A queer old parish minister and some stories about him—A cautious Scot—A tight place for Abraham—Rustic simplicity

CHAPTER XVII

STORIES OF HIGHLANDERS

The Celtic temperament—Difficulties of the English tongue to the Gael—Examples of Gaelic-English—'News from Tulloch'—An Australian illustration—Two Highland hotel anecdotes—The Skye barometer—Old John M'Leod and the Oban porter—Distinguished company—The first recorded eviction—A *mal de mer* experience—A Highland grace, from *Blackwood*—Curious marriage customs

CHAPTER XVIII

THE SCOT ABROAD

Pride of country—Scottish generosity—The Struan Highlander—A Sydney matron's experience—An Antipodean beadle—A typical Scot in Calcutta—Characteristic stories about him—A close-fisted Scot in Melbourne—A Sydney alderman—Two new-chum Scots in Sydney—A disillusioned grazier—A robber despoiled—'Walkin' on the Sawbath'—'Shooin' the cat'—Angling in New Zealand—A pawky Scot in the East—An engineer's estimate of classic music

CHAPTER XIX

THE HUMOUR OF THE SCOT

CHAPTER I

INTRODUCTION—SCOTTISH HUMOUR, AND THE FORMATION OF THE NATIONAL CHARACTER

What the early records tell—'The rugged Scot' of early times—
The clan era merges into the national—The Reformation : its
material aspect—The pretensions of the Presbyter—Influence
on the national character of the new repressive *régime*—
Illustration : the Aberdeen waiter—The origin of 'pawkiness'
—Illustrations : the two drovers—A plethora of pease brose—
Recipe for acquiring the English tongue—'Paisley Tam' an'
cauld watter—An effectual prayer—An English description
of a Scotch dish—The auld wifie's pet pig—Grumblin' Jessie
—Quaint definitions—'Needin' a rest'—Effects of 'gowf'—
The Corstorphine wheelwright.

IT is not necessary nowadays to use much effort in the
attempt to demonstrate, even to the scoffer and the
cynic, that 'oor ain fowk' possess even more than an
ordinary share of that faculty which Lowell somewhere
speaks of as 'the modulating, restraining balance-wheel,
a sense of humour.' But it is very difficult to define it
in such lucid terms as will meet general acceptance.
We have all such different ideals of what constitutes

B

it. It is such a Protean and elusive thing, that mere
set, formal phrases, seem all too rigid and inelastic to
properly describe it. Of all the attempts to elaborately
analyse or dissect this much-spoken-of thing, Scottish
humour, I have seen no two alike, and not one which
seems to me to do complete justice to the theme. I do
not certainly intend to attempt a task which has been
handled by masters, with whom I do not presume to
compare myself; but if I can make some friendly
doubter even dimly discern that there is indeed a fund
of genuine undoubted humour in the Scottish nature, I
feel that I will best achieve a success by simply giving
my gathered illustrations, my jottings here and there—
contributions from many sources, noted down under
many a strange circumstance of time and place—and
let these speak for themselves. If after reading my
budget any one is still determined to maintain that the
Scotch have no humour, then I opine it can only be from
some strange lack in the story-teller, and not the want
of humour in the stories themselves.

A word or two of exposition on the causes that led
to the formation of the peculiar Scottish character
might not be out of place, as these afford a clue to the
wholly unique manifestations of typical Scottish humour
which most writers on the subject love to cite. One
writer has said that Scottish humour plays like an
electric current between the two opposite poles of
'releegion and whusky.' This is but another way of
saying that the national character exhibits the sudden
alternations between a deep, abiding, ever-recurring
tendency to metaphysics, and the rebound to hilarious
relaxation.

But if we think of the formative influences at work through the long procession of centuries of national growth, we cease to wonder, and can, I think, trace cause and effect clearly and reasonably.

The history of the people is one of incessant struggle. First with nature. The climate always has been rigorous : the natural configuration of the country was wild and rugged, the soil by no means fertile ; the surrounding seas treacherous and stormy. There are few broad rivers. The early records tell of fierce fights with wolves and wild beasts ; of battles with no less wild and aggressive foreign invaders. There were imperfect means of communication ; no real corporate life ; an utter absence of national solidarity. What few towns there were, were for the most part under the dominance of foreign ideas and learning. Next, the whole country became a prey to faction : inter-tribal feuds, cruel onslaughts, and fierce reprisals raged. Husbandry and all the peaceful arts were consequently neglected. The clansman's hand was ready to grasp stilt of plough, or handle of claymore, as quickly vary-ing emergencies dictated. During the 'lang fore nichts' in the rude baronial castles or in the squalid huts of the peasantry, there were few intellectual resources. There were practically no books. Art was not yet born. The fare was scanty as the manners were un-couth. The atmosphere of tribal estrangement — of mutual distrust, of incessant vigilance, of reckless aggression and hereditary hate—as well as the natural environment of morass and forest, swift stream and 'craggy fell,' the savage grandeur of rocky pass, or the trackless loneliness of upland moor, all acted on the character of the people; and so 'the rugged Scot' grew up, stern, suspicious, hardy, self-contained, undemonstrative.   In times of peace, slow, meditative, poetic, superstitious, dreamily speculative; in war or sudden emergency, quick to resent an injury, ready to plan, swift to execute, cruel, dogged, determined, hard to conquer, resourceful, resolute and daring in action, implacable in his revenge.

In fact the Scot of the ancient records was more or less of a barbarian: wild and untamed, like the winds that whistled round his rugged mountains; cruel and unbridled as the treacherous seas which hissed and beat upon the beetling cliffs that confront the surges of the wintry wild Atlantic.

Coming down to only a few short centuries ago, we find scenes of lawlessness, rapine, and bloodshed, daily occurrences in the very metropolis itself.   Society was not homogeneous; the nation had not yet been crystallised.   There was no middle class such as we know now. True, there were powerful guilds in the towns, but these as a rule maintained an attitude of watchful suspicion, and armed truce against the powerful barons and nobles with their hordes of ruthless retainers.   The influence of the laird or chief in rural parts was paramount.   Fealty to the chief or clan was the one supreme virtue.   The bond of kinship or clanship was, however, becoming a living political as well as a natural force.   A community of blood, traditions, interests, cemented the various units of the clan together; and gradually by alliances, intermarriages, and other softening, consolidating, and elevating influences, this feeling of clannishness from being tribal, grew till it merged into the national, and now there is perhaps no more intense national spirit under heaven, than that which is the common bond and heritage of 'brither Scots.'

It was a long road to travel though, and the study is interesting; but I can only dash in the main outlines in this necessarily hurried fashion.

When the feudal power began to wane; when military tenures and service were no longer the rule; when the cities and towns with their guilds began to wrest privilege after privilege, and charter after charter, from the turbulent nobility; when one central authority began to put down inter-tribal strife with the strong hand of paramount law;—then the currents of national life began to move in the moral and spiritual domains of the national mind.

The ancient historic Church of Rome had got a good grip on the Scottish collar; but its methods of sub-jugation and domination had been too nearly allied to the rough-and-ready methods of baron and earl and chief. And so in the growing spirit of independence, in the strengthening of the bonds of corporate action, in the awakening of the critical and questioning faculties of the people, it was inevitable that the revulsion and the protest should come.

From very authentic sources we are able to see that the mere material and mechanical aspect of the Reforma-tion, quite apart altogether from the undoubtedly higher, holier, and purer phases of the question, must have exerted a by no means idle influence on the ultimate issue. What I mean is this: the tax of raising the enormous revenues of the old Roman faith, of keeping up the pomp and pageantry of the ritual and hierarchy alone, must have been a terrific drain on the naturally poor resources of such a people and such a country. So the principles of the Reformation must have commended themselves to the stern, hard, practical, and frugal nature of the Scot.

Doubtless there were other causes at work, for the movement was a complex one. The greed of the nobles for the church lands, for instance, was a potent factor in overturning the sacerdotal supremacy, but I cannot help thinking, that the people groaned under the burden of oppressive exactions in the name of the Church, which must have sorely tried their limited resources.

They had seen so much of the luxury, the arrogance, the licentiousness and greed, of abbot and prior, and prelate and priest, that naturally when, after heroic efforts, they succeeded in freeing themselves from what had come to be looked on as an incubus, a rebound to the other extreme was naturally to be looked for.

Hence the studied simplicity, the almost painful bareness of the succeeding ritual of ultra - Presbyterianism. Hence that harsh pragmatic Puritanism, that somewhat gloomy Calvinistic estimate of life and duty, that cast-iron pessimistic theology which has cast such a shadow over some of the finer attributes of the national character. But in all fairness let it be noted, too, what is seldom sufficiently pointed out, that Calvinism as commonly railed at, is not the philosophy or theology of John Calvin himself—a fine heroic soul he !—but the metaphysical refinements and accretions of the seventeenth century theology, which is but a vile travesty of the system of Calvin. When I speak of Calvinism therefore, I mean the adulterated and not the pure, the spurious and not the real original system of John Calvin.

Bigotry, and intolerance always accompany extreme views either in religion or politics, and the history of 'oor ain fowk,' alas ! shows much of both.

The Presbyter, in some respects, tried to assume a power almost as arrogant and irresponsible as that of the priest, over the spirits of his flock ; but there were certain notable differences. For instance, the Presbyterian clergy fully recognised the value of free and popular education. All honour to John Knox for that imperishable boon ! They stoutly upheld the inalienable and inestimable right of private judgment; the liberty of the individual conscience ; the right to search the Scriptures for oneself. They allied themselves, too, with the people in all the popular movements for more freedom. They battled nobly and well for popular rights ; and with all their faults, mistakes, and failings, Scotland will never cease to cherish with loving gratitude the memory of the sturdy heroes of the Reformation.

But what has this to do with Scottish humour ? the impatient reader may ask. Well, just this. The conflict was so momentous, the change was so thorough, the swing of the pendulum was so wildly to an opposite extreme, that the national character was doomed to feel the depressing influence of the somewhat distorted and soured *régime*, which now began to take the place of the old laxity, the easy formalism, and the spiritual enslavement which had obtained under the former priestly system. Under the repressive rigour of Calvinism and the Puritan movement all expression of natural joyous feeling was sternly subjected to restraint. It was looked on as sinful to even betray natural innocent emotion at all of any kind. The Sabbath, especially, from being 'a delight' became 'a weariness.' The ordinances of public worship appealed only to the conscience and intellect, and left the emotions and affections pretty well out of the computation altogether. All this of course begat a smug Pharisaism, an unctuous hypocrisy, on the part of many; and a hard rigour, a pragmatic harshness of judgment, on the part of others. In fact the standards of duty, of obligation, of everyday action, were suddenly changed. So it was that the free, unrestrained exuberance of youthful feeling was scowled down by the 'unco guid,' and a settled standard of gloomy self-restraint became the common attribute of the common people. To dance, or sing, or laugh heartily, was heinous in a common person; but for a minister or an office-bearer to dance, or play the fiddle, for example, was as the seven deadly and unforgivable sins rolled into one.

Doubtless the sour, depressing shadow is lifting, but the feeling still lingers. For instance, this illustration may for the moment suffice. It happened in Aberdeen. My friend Francis Murray and myself, two returned indigo-planters, who after some twelve years in India had desired to look on the old land again, happened to be, for the time, quartered in one of the leading hotels in the Granite City. It was a calm, quiet Sunday morning, sunny and warm. Murray was coming downstairs, not thinking of the day particularly, and he was whustlin'. Only fancy! what unpardonable levity! A white-haired old waiter of the rigid,

inflexible, granite-featured, emotionless type, happened
to be coming up the stair, bearing a tray in his hands.
At the ungodly sounds of mirth and levity he paused,
and his face assumed the rigidity of a Gorgon's. He
literally glared at the Sabbath desecrator, and in tones
of dreadful severity asked if he 'didna ken that this was
the Sawbath.' Murray was amused. I fear it must be
recorded he was even in a scoffing mood. At any rate
he not only continued to whistle, with even greater
animation, but he began to execute a sort of *solo nautch*
or *pas seul* on the stairs. The old man perceiving this
unregenerate attitude, slowly took up his tray, which he
had laid down in a recess while administering his rebuke,
and then with a withering look, in which contempt quite
overcame any lingering pity, he said, in words that cut
like a whip-lash: 'Eh, man! ye're no funny; ye're jist
wicked!'

Poor Murray collapsed, and no doubt he deserved the
rebuke; but let us, just for one moment longer, resume
our argument and try to work it out.

Of course it was not in the nature of things that the
free, innocent play of feeling and emotion could be
absolutely and entirely stifled, but under the new
standards, and in obedience to the new judgments, it
could not fail to manifest itself differently than it was
wont to do.

So it begot, as it seems to me, that peculiar sly,
pawky, half-apologetic, half-shamefaced enjoyment of a
joke, which is so truly characteristic of most ebullitions
and illustrations of purely Scottish humour: that
restrained attitude of mind, which deals in hint and
innuendo—which ofttimes only places half an incident or

some salient point before you, and leaves the rest to be inferred—which seeks to give even the broadly ludicrous a solemn, semi-sacred twist, and which is responsible for making Scottish jokes so often seem laboured, ponderous, and indeed quite incomprehensible to the bewildered and uninitiated outsider.

Bearing this then in mind, let us now proceed to enjoy with what appetite we may, a few of the contents of my well-filled wallet, illustrative of the fun and humour of 'oor ain fowk'; and if the gentle reader come across here and there 'a chestnut' of the wormy kind, let him eschew it and crack the next. Let me instance, first, a few taken at random, illustrative of various phases of Scottish character and humour, before I proceed to classify the more salient characteristics under their respective heads as I shall attempt to do.

It is improbable that some at least of my readers may not have heard the following illustration of Scottish humour, but for the sake of those who have not heard it, and because it is so thoroughly characteristic of certain of these traditional phases of Caledonian character which we have just been considering, I make no further apology for reproducing it here.

Scene—Banks of Loch Katrine. Jock and Wullie, two cattle-dealers, muffled in their plaids and breasting the sharp breeze, walking alongside the Loch. *Wullie loq.:* 'Ay! Jock, an' so ye've sell't yer coo, I'm hearin'.'

'Ou ay!'

'Imphm, an' hoo muckle did ye get for her?'

'Oh, I did fairly weel—I got twal' pounds!'

'Twal' pounds!' ejaculated Wullie (affecting a somewhat contemptuous depreciation, pretending to be

indignant, but in reality jealous, and wishing to lower
Jock's estimate of his own cleverness). 'Twal' pounds?
Hech, man, what for did ye no gang tae Lunnon? for I'm
hearin' there's a gran' market there, an' ye micht hae
gotten auchteen pounds for her at least. *Jock* (testily,
quite seeing through Wullie's tactics, and resenting the
implied doubt of his business capacity). 'Ay! ay!
nae doot, nae doot! Ye're a vera clever chield, Wullie!
Ay, awfu' clever! Losh man! if I cud only tak' Loch
Katrine doon to—ahem!'—with a significant downward
jerk of the thumb—'I could get saxpence a gless for
the watter, ay an' more!'

Of the droll, kindly sort of humour which lies more
in the picture presented and the ideas suggested to the
mind than in anything said, is the following: A young
artisan, who had a great liking for feathered pets, had
married the lassie of his choice, but she, poor girl, had
been a mill-hand nearly all her life, and had never
acquired much knowledge of housekeeping; least of all
did she understand anything of the art and practice of
domestic cookery. She had seen her Wullie, however,
often mixing his pease meal for his birds, and with artless
induction she thought that what was good for them,
could not be bad for him; so the first day Wullie came
back from the shop, she had a generous bowl of pease
brose ready for him. Nothing loath, he supped the
homely but filling fare with relish, and Maggie was
delighted at the success of her first attempt at catering.
Wullie having to go early to work, generally took breakfast at a stall on the way to the works, and coming home
the second night, anticipating 'a tasty bit denner,' he
was again confronted with pease brose! He judged

that possibly Maggie had not got properly 'fixed up' yet in the kitchen, or something had happened to prevent her providing a different dish, and so said nothing. But on the third day, finding the same delicacy again set down, he having now perhaps some faint glimmering of the truth, said very good naturedly: 'Od bless me, Maggie, dae ye think ye've mairried a mavis?'

The humour of the following is of that kind which is not perhaps readily understood by 'the Southron.'

A servant girl in Edinburgh, who spoke Scotch with such a broad accent as at times hardly to be comprehended even by her mistress, who was herself a native of Ayrshire, the county of classic Scotch, on being asked how she contrived to make herself understood in England where she had previously been for some time in service, replied: 'Oh, it's easy eneuch to speak Englitch; ye've naething tae dae bit leave oot a' the Rs, an' gie ilka wird a bit chaw i' the middle.'

The next is an illustration of the pawky sly sort, and, one might almost say of course, is connected with the drinking habits of the people, and introduces the minister.

A reverend D.D. had been calling on a 'Paisley body' in his parish—Tam by name, and a very well-known character. The Doctor found Tam with 'a broon pig' (an earthenware jar) on the table beside him, and observing the vessel, asked Tam what he had in it. 'Ow it's jist a sowp o' yill!' said Tam. 'Ay! and how much may you have taken to-day now?' asked the minister. 'Oh weel!' replied Tam, 'this is jist my fourth pint!' 'Your fourth pint?' quoth his reverence. 'I don't believe I could drink four pints *of water* in a whole day !' 'Na, naither could I !' dryly responded Tam. (Tam was evidently of the same mind as another worthy who, as an excuse for his bibulous proclivities, said : ' He didna like cauld watter in his shoon, far less in his stammick.')

Here is another in which the minister also plays a prominent part. He had been paying his visits to sundry of his flock, and among others had encountered a man who seemed very depressed and despondent, and evidently nourishing morose and resentful feelings against some one. The minister soon elicited the information that John had received notice from his landlord to quit, and that a certain chimney-sweep whom he named was taking the house 'ower his heid'; giving in fact a higher rent. John was very downhearted, for the house suited him, and he had been at considerable pains to make it cheerful and comfortable. The minister of course sympathised, and administered what comfort he could, but laid especial stress on the efficacy of prayer as a universal solvent of all difficulties. ' Jist tak' yer trouble to the throne of grace, John,' he said, as he took his leave, ' and no doubt your path will be made plain to you !'

Some short time after he again called, and found John still in occupancy of the old home, and this time looking blithe and whistling like a lintie. The usual conversation ensued, and John began to thank the minister for having given him such good advice on his former visit. The worthy man felt delighted that John had proved so amenable, and that his pious admonitions had seemingly found so receptive a soil. He expressed his satisfaction, and hoped that John had found much

peace of mind from the exercise of prayer and that he
would continue the practice. 'Ou ay!' assented John.
'Man! I'm rael gled ye gied me yon advice!' 'Yes?
How so?' said the pleased minister, eager for details.
'Eh, man, the sweep's deid!' chuckled the unsophisticated cobbler; but it is not said how the surprised
minister took the unexpected announcement of how
poor John had interpreted the advice he had given him.

There is 'understandable' humour to a Scotchman in
the following English definition of a well-known Highland
dish. An English sportsman having become belated on the
moors, found his way to a retired sheiling, where he was
hospitably entertained by the old wifie who there abode.
Knowing him to be hungry and tired, she made him a
nice tasty dish of sowens which he enjoyed. Describing
his experiences afterwards, he said : 'The old woman put
some dirty water and dust into a pot, but thank goodness it came out a pudding.' Sowens, it may be explained, is simply the dust and fine siftings of the meal,
that is swept up in the mill and sold to poor folk.

The humour of the following, lies in the utter in-
congruity of the ideas suggested by the acts and words
of the principal character, and the total unconsciousness
on her part of any approach to the humorous. This is
a very common kind of Scottish humour, and clearly
shows if you appreciate it, that you are capable of
dramatising a situation, so to speak, and of being
impressed by the humour of it. She was a poor, artless,
old woman, whose sole treasure, a pet pig, had died.
She was telling the story of its sufferings, and expatiating
on its many virtues to a sympathetic visitor. 'Eh, mem,
but it wis a bonnie wee bit grumphie, an' when it first

took ill I couldna sleep for thinkin' o't, an' as the nicht wis cauld, I gaed oot an' rowed it in an' auld flannel petticoat o' my ain, deed ay, mem! But aye it grew waur, and keepit gruntin' and pechin', so I gaed oot again, an' poured some whisky doon its throat, an' that did nae gude'; then sobbingly, 'Weel, mem, I gaed oot again, when it wis near mornin', an'—an'' (bursting into tears, and dropping into a congenial and appropriate strain) 'its saul wis wi' its Maker, mem!'

A clever vivacious friend, Miss B—— of Edinburgh, who visited us some time ago in Sydney with her brother, told me the following, which is simply delicious, as illustrating the captious, self-justifying spirit, of one very common type of 'oor ain fowk.'

Miss B—— had been visiting in her district, and had called on this particularly querulous old pensioner, and the following colloquy ensued.

'Well, Jessie, how are ye the day?'

'Oh, no vera weel.' And then followed a torrent of grumbling complaints, to which Miss B—— kept up an accompaniment of pleasant little speeches and bright cheery words of comfort. On leaving, she said :—

'Well, Jessie, good-bye, an' God bless ye!'

Jessie, somewhat mollified by the bright visit and kindly attentions, as well as a nice little gift from her cheerful visitor, mumbled out in a grudging, grumbling sort of assent :—

'Oh, He's dune that already!'

'Ay, Jessie,' said Miss B., wishing to impress the toothless old crone with a still deeper sense of what she owed to the divine beneficence, 'ay, Jessie! an' for many a lang year He has blessed ye!'

'Ou ay,' at once retorted Jessie, 'but ye ken I hinna provokit Him ony !'

What a commentary on the old hidebound theology of the ancient time—'Justification by works !' and what a speaking instance of the widely prevalent though unacknowledged Pharisaism of the present day !   Jessie is no solitary type.

The following is another of these humorous definitions which it would be difficult to find out of Scotland.

During the Queen's Jubilee year two old wives were discussing the matter, and one evidently did not have a very clear understanding of what a jubilee really was. The other undertook to enlighten her.   'Ye ken it's this w'y !' she said.   'Whan ye're marriet for twenty-five years, it's yer silver waddin'.   An' whan ye're marriet for fifty years it's a gowden waddin'.   An' syne whan yer man dees, that's yer jubilee !'

A still better definition is that given by an old wrinkled bodie, to one of her cronies, who had been told by the doctor that she was suffering from sciatica. 'Skyatticka, 'umman, the doctor said.'   'Fat's that ?'   'Oh, 'deed, Marget, it's jist a new lang-nebbit wird for teethache i' the sma' o' the back !'

Of the quaintly satirical, yet without one spice of bitterness, take this.   A congregation perceiving that their minister was a bit 'run down,' and would be all the better of a holiday, presented him with a considerable gift of money, arranged for 'pulpit supply' during his absence, and sent him off to the Continent for a holiday.   A tourist just back from a ramble through the Rhineland, happened to meet rather a prominent member of the congregation, and during conversation casually mentioned that he had met the minister during his tour in Germany. He continued : 'I had heard that he was quite broken down, but he was looking very well indeed when I met him. He didn't look as if he needed a rest.' 'Na!' said the church member, very calmly, but with a lurking gleam of suppressed drollery in his eye. 'Na! it wisna him ; it wis the congregation that wis needin' a rest.'

How droll too the unstudied exaggeration of the recent convert, but devoted zealot to the seductions of golf, that most fascinating of Scottish games. The staid, rotund, and eminently respectable sportsman, had just driven the ball into an utterly impracticable 'bunker,' and his fruitless endeavours to extricate it had caused him quite to forget his long-acquired propriety. In fact, he had just indulged in the hitherto rare luxury of 'a good round sweir.' Pausing a moment, while his pricking conscience accused him, he blurted out with most comical contrition and self-justification : 'Weel, sirss, I couldna help it ! I began gowf a Christian man, but, hech me, it's fair turnin' me intil a blaspheemin' sinner !'

Another good specimen of sly humour is that told of a certain wheelwright of Corstorphine. He had been waited on one day by Dr. Anderson, a quaint old village oddity, who ordered him to make a flail or two, and casually happened to let fall a remark in an irrelevant sort of way, but with a certain significant intonation, that 'he had seen some fine ash sticks for flails up in the Laird's plantin'.' By and by in comes the minister, Dr. Simpson, who said : 'John, I hear ye are goin' to mak' some flails for the doctor, ye had better jist mak' twa or three pair for me at the same time. I hear there's some fine ash sticks jist sootable, up in the Laird's plantin'.'

Presently, John accordingly wends his way up to the plantation to cut down the ash sticks, thus significantly suggested to him, and while right in the middle of his job, who should come on the scene but the Laird himself?

With some asperity he accosted the interloper. 'What are ye doin' here, sir ?'

'Od, sir,' was the ready answer, 'I'm jist cuttin' doon some ash sticks to mak' flails for the meenister an' the doctor !'

'But are you not aware, sir, that this is my property ?'

'Hoot ay ! I ken that weel eneuch !'

'Well, sir, am I to understand that the doctor and the minister told you to come here and steal my property ?'

'Weel no, sir ! But they baith tell't me there wis fine sootable ash sticks up here, an' they baith weel kent I hed nae wud o' my ain !'

CHAPTER II

The sense of individuality peculiarly Scottish—World-wide influence of Scottish humour—Power of laughter—The Scottish
humourist in Australia—In an Indian camp—In the haunts of
commerce — 'Blessed gift of humour' — Need for delicate
treatment in many typical cases referring to matters theological—The tombs of David and Solomon—Satan 'on the
chain'—Adam's state of innocence—The 'klatt' in Eden—
A christenin' story—An Aberdeen estimate of the conduct of
Joseph's brethren—A boy's idea of 'being born again'—An
old evangelist on Enoch—The deacon's prayer—An old maid's
estimate of Solomon — Prayer of a W.S. — The colonial
minister's difficulties—Inestimable value of the Bible Class
and Bible teaching — Catechetical troubles — 'Pearls before
swine'—The dogma of 'total depravity' — How 'the Fall'
might have been avoided—Kirsty's idea of 'the Prodigal Son.'

ONE of the chief charms of the old Scottish manner
from a modern point of view, seems to me to consist in
its fresh, breezy unconventionality, its unstudied directness. There was a frank yet not over-weening recognition
of one's individuality : what has become proverbial, in
fact, in the oft-quoted saying that the Scotchman's
favourite prayer is, 'Lord, sen's a guid conceit o' oorsels.'
Some unfortunate 'furriners, puir craeters,' imagine

that in this there is an implied jibe or reproach. There
is really no element of reproach in it. It but expresses,
though possibly in a somewhat exaggerated way, the
sense of one's individual value. There is a hearty, manly,
virile sense of the value of one's own opinion, the deep
significance of one's own inner consciousness, the responsibility of one's deliberate freewill, which is as far
removed from fussy, obtrusive self-consciousness, as the
swagger of the pomatumed recruit is, from the lithe yet
stately swing of the veteran of a score of campaigns.
Now, in a smug, sleek, conventional age, when our news-
papers frame our opinions for us in the main, when
minds have all to go through the crank-mill of a leaden
system of cram, when we are girt round and hemmed in
with a rigid code of priggish prescriptions, extending to
the very minutiæ of the daily round of our duties and
pleasures alike, these delightful revelations of a different
order, when men and women indulged in, nay insisted
on, their individuality, and were content to be natural,
appeal to the inherent, the latent Bohemianism that lies,
I think, at the back of all true love of humour ; and
they come to us like a whiff of caller air off the heather,
when we may have been for a time stifling in the
heavy languorous atmosphere of the hot-house or trim
conservatory.

    This partly, though not wholly, explains the keen
pleasure most Scotchmen take in these pawky sayings
and racy incidents which form the never-ending subject
of Scottish reminiscence. There are complexities, I
admit, which go far deeper than I have yet tried to
indicate—and indeed the delight in a humorous situation
is not confined to 'oor ain fowk' by any means—for,

thanks to such men as Dean Ramsay, Mr. Barrie, and others, Scottish humour has now become a world-wide heritage, and forms the spice for many a dish in which not one other distinctively Scotch national ingredient may form a part.

It is a common boast that though 'Britannia may rule the waves,' our Scottish engineers control the motive forces of the world; and like the pre-eminence of our engineers, the sway and influence of Scottish story and reminiscence has now become universal. Just let me illustrate.

You hear the hearty burst of ringing laughter from the shearers' camp in sunny Australia after the arduous day's toil is over, and the gleam of the fragrant gum-wood fire lights up the tanned and bearded faces of the sinewy shearers. Depend upon it Old Sandy, 'the boss of the shed,' has been detailing some droll illustration of the quaint humour of his kith and kintra, which begins in some such dry, undemonstrative fashion as, 'I mind yince, whin I wis a callant,' and gradually works up to a culmination of delighted tickling of the risible faculties, evidenced by the broadening faces, the widening grins, until at length the climax comes, in the exuberant, unrestrained, full-mouthed Ha! ha! ha! Ho! ho! ho! of health-giving, care-dispelling, devil-defeating, hearty laughter. I do believe the devil hates a hearty laugh. Humour is not demoniac, and the hypocrite, the cynic, the sensualist, the envious man, the cruel and greedy man, seldom or ever laughs heartily. Their laugh is 'from the teeth outwards,' never from the chest.

Or again, beneath the flooding radiance of the full, round moon, showing white as samite against the dark mass of heavy, shaded mango-trees, with yonder tall, plumy palm, sentinel-like, guarding the glistening temple of white marble that shelters the grim and hideous idol with the many arms in the dark, mysterious chamber beneath—see the ordered array of snowy tents from whence ever and anon come the sounds of jollity and ringing mirth. The long day's hunt is over : the tiger skins have been pegged out by the dusky camp-followers ; the watch fires are twinkling in an irregular circle round the camp ; the elephants are swaying their never-resting trunks and bodies, and swishing their ever-moving tails against their leathery flanks ; while sub-dued by distance come the monotonous pulsations of the village tom-toms on the drowsy air, or the long-drawn, echoing cry of the jackals in the distant jungle, or the sighing, mysterious whisper of the swift, treacher-ous Indian river, as it seethes along under the crumbling sandbanks. The red dust that has been whirling aloft all the brazen day, in the furnace-blast of the burning March westerly gale, is now settling down on forest leaf and jungle grass and village thatch like a thin gray pall. The blistering sun made it all day look like a blood-red veil. The glamour and the mystery, the spell and the witchery, of the gorgeous East is around and about us ; but we rise superior to it all. The dust and glare and heat are forgotten. The punkah may wave above us, and the carpet snake and centipede and scorpion may crawl around the tent, but we are far away, back in the braes of Angus, or amid the heather of Strathconan once again ; and out upon the startled air, heavy with oriental scents and laden with the clinging mists and exhalations of the Eastern night, rises again that free, unrestrained, spontaneous, hearty, ringing laugh, dominating every sound else, as the kingly race dominates the multitudes that sleep beneath the full-orbed moon. What is it? Simply this—'Old Mac' has been telling a Scottish story, and Scottish humour has once more been victorious over every disability of climate and exile, and every drawback of discomfort, danger, and savage environment.

Again, see that group of gray-bearded men pause in the middle of the crowded, bustling, city street. But now, each was intent on some pressing concern of the moment. There was a keen look of calculation in each quick-glancing eye. There was decision in each firm step, and the alert, shrewd, trained intelligence of each, was wide awake to all that was passing in the busy haunt of commercial activity amid which they moved. They pause at the sight of a merry-featured, genial-looking man, with a quaint suggestion of drollery and humour lurking in the crow's feet about his eyes, and the mobile twitchings of his slightly ruddy nose. As if impelled by a common motive, the busy men of commerce and finance begin to converge round this man as to a common centre. Note, too, as they approach, the rigid lines of their facial expressions begin to relax, the hard, firm-set lips insensibly soften, the features imperceptibly assume a more youthful, kindlier mould, and in a few moments, as if assisting in some rite of worship common to the whole group, they bend their bodies forward in the attitude of strained attention. The heads and shoulders gradually gather closer together. You can almost fancy the ears are elongating as the bodies assume every instant a more acute dorsal angle.

The centre man with the merry look and the mellow voice seems to be chanting or intoning something. Perhaps some portion of a litany! Who knows? Suddenly, as if touched by a simultaneous electric shock, the heads are thrown back, the hands vigorously smite the knees or thighs as the former angle is reversed, and the back is now curved inwards while the region of *embonpoint* is thrust violently forward, and from the assembled cluster, while timid wayfarers and scurrying hurrying passers-by cast looks of wonderment, derision, or envy at the coterie, there bursts a loud, long-sustained cacophony, a reverberating, ringing, roaring Ha! ha! ha! Ho! ho! ho! that brings dancing tears to the eyes, brightens the sooty gloom of the sordid street, and actually for one brief, joyous moment, puts to flight the hosts of Mammon and the imps of that demon of our modern civilisation that men call 'Unrestricted Competition.' And what has brought it all about? What is the meaning of it all? Ask that old gentleman who is now wiping his eyes and brow, while his fat sides still shake with the delicious sensations of gratified humour, and he will probably tell you, 'Oh, it's that deil's buckie Jamie, or Wullie, or Geordie So-and-so's been tellin's a new Scottish story he's got haud o'.' Note, the old gentleman has unconsciously fallen into a mode of speech which is part of his boyhood. He has reverted to his native vernacular. For a brief moment in the heart of busy London, or Liverpool, or Sydney, he is back again 'amang the heather,' and for one brief, blissful moment he is a boy once more. O blessed gift and power of humour! What bright, inspiring, cheering impulses and emotions canst thou not stir and quicken into noble, elevating life and energy? And, alas! too, like every human faculty, to what swinish depths and to what 'base uses' mayest not thou be put?

One of the most difficult and delicate gradations or manifestations of our native humour is undoubtedly that which plays round the treatment of sacred subjects It may be like a harmless lambent flame, lighting up and scorching not. It may be like a ruddy glow, heating, warming, comforting, and cheering, yet still innocent and non-destructive. In rude or reckless hands it may be a blasting, scathing, wholly subversive and destructive influence.

Considering the peculiar discipline of the nation in matters controversial and polemic, which was a direct effect of the Reformation; throwing open the Book of Books to the eager study of the common people, and issuing in the long, stern, but victorious struggle for the right of private judgment; we who are of the soil and the race need feel no surprise, that so many of the good old anecdotes of humorous speculation, of pithy expression, of whimsical interpretation and droll experience, should cluster round matters biblical and beliefs theological; but as my aim in this collection is more to use illustration than homily, perhaps I may be pardoned if I pass from the didactic, once more to the reminiscent and descriptive.

One very esteemed neighbour of mine in New South Wales, a well-known leading banker, not himself a Scotchman, but more enthusiastic, I think, than any Caledonian I have ever met, in his appreciation of Scottish humour, writing me from Aden, of all places on the face of the earth, says : 'I send you the enclosed two stories

for your book if you care to have them.   They are said
never to have been hitherto published, and I certainly
have never heard them before.'

'On his wedding tour, many years ago, a well-known
medico and his wife joined a party of sight-seers who
were being shown over the departed glories of "far-
famed Holyrood." After they had gone through the
interior of the Palace, they were conducted by the old
custodian to the small burying-ground adjoining, where
quite a number of celebrated historic personages have
been laid to rest. "And this," said the guide, "is the
tomb of King David." An elderly lady of the party
seized his arm with much fervour, and with a deep
tremor in her voice, and tears in her eyes, exclaimed, to
the no small amusement of the rest of the party, and to
the astonishment of the guide, whose imagination had
never risen to such a flight : "Eh, sirs ! d'ye mean tae
tell me that that's the place whaur the blessed Psaw'mist
lies ?   Oh, jist to think o't !   That my puir een shuld
have ever gazed upon a spot sae sacred." Evidently
desirous of still further emotional excitement, however,
she again turned to the attendant, and with deep
intensity she asked : "An' whaur may Solomon lie ? "

The second story, according to my friendly correspondent, is even better. He thus gives it ; and I am, of
course, not responsible for any theological bent it may
be thought to betray.

'A teacher in a Scottish Sunday School, who was
more given to preaching at, than to teaching his scholars,
took as his subject one Sunday the afflictions of Job—
in connection with which it behoved him to expound,
very emphatically, the limitations that were imposed

upon Satanic power. He complacently demonstrated, at least to his own satisfaction, that Satan could go no farther than God permitted him. In short he affirmed that "God had Satan on a chain," and that "the arch enemy of mankind" was thereby completely under divine control. On the following Sunday, the subject happened to be a sort of sequel to the former lesson, the text for the day being, "Be sober, be vigilant, for your enemy the devil, like a roaring lion," etc. On this occasion it behoved the worthy teacher to fittingly illustrate the wandering and predatory character of Apollyon, and in order to impress on his class, as deeply as possible, the dangers they were exposed to by night and by day—but especially by night—he urged them not to rove far away from their homes, so that they might always have a place of ready refuge from his demoniac assaults. With much wealth of imagery and illustration, he had driven this nail surely home, and felt satisfied from the countenances of the class that he had put in a clencher. Just then, however, one little sceptic—some ten years of age —with a logical turn of mind evidently, propounded a bit of a poser : "Didna ye tell us last Sunday, sir," said he, "that God had Sawtan on a chain? Hoo can he be gangin' stravaigin' aboot in siccan a fashion as ye have been tellin's if that be the case?" The teacher, quite unused to having his theology challenged in this fashion, and yet feeling that some plausible explanation was demanded, braced himself up and thus delivered himself. "Ou ay ! ou ay ! nae doot it's *pairfeckly true* God HAS Sawtan on a chain ; but, ye see, it's a gey an' lang yin. It's sae lang, in fac', that God can haud him fast an' yet lat him gang up an' doon through the length an'

breadth o' the warld ! "   "Humph ! " responded the uncon-
vinced and wholly irreverent precocity, " if that's the w'y
o't, the deevil micht jist as weel be gangin' aboot lowse ! " '

The above reminds me of a capital story which has
possibly been published, but which I believe originated
in my native village, in the time of Mr. Hutton, my
father's predecessor.

A young clerical friend, who was notoriously hen-
pecked, had taken charge temporarily, of old Mr. Hutton's
duties. He had been warned by the venerable incumbent,
to beware of the sharp wit of one old fellow, whom he
had described, and whom the young *locum tenens* would
have to meet during his customary catechising itinerary.
The young minister, sure enough, in the course of his
duties, soon found himself in the very position as to which
he had received the friendly caution from Mr. Hutton.
Confident, however, in his own powers—just perhaps a
little over-confident—he, after he had questioned nearly
all the members of the group gathered in the spacious
farm-kitchen, turned rather sharply to the pawky plough-
man, being in fact conscious of, and rather irritated by,
his shrewdly observant and self-possessed manner, and in
his loftiest and most patronising tone said : ' Can you
tell me, my good man, how long did Adam continue in a
state of innocence ? ' ' Ou ay ! I ken that brawly ! ' said
the humorous misogynist. ' It wis jist till he got a wife,
sir ! But can ye tell me hoo lang efter that ? '

The catechist had inly to confess that he would have
done well to have paid more heed to his wise senior's
shrewd advice.

Not less characteristic and, I think, delightfully racy
of the soil, was the purely professional reply of another

bothy hand in the Mearns, who on being asked by the minister : ' For what purpose were our first parents put into the garden of Eden ? ' answered : ' Tae keep it clean, and klatt it, sir ! '

Poor Jock's duties being those pertaining to the important office of cattleman, in which the ' klatt,' or muck rake, is the indispensable instrument of use, his rough-and-ready interpretation of the ban of Eden— labour as a penalty for rebellion—led him to adopt the heavy burden of his daily toil as the fittest illustration, though probably the ' klatt ' belongs to a later era than the time of the first gardener.

My friend Mr. Morrison, the well-known publisher and bookseller of Glasgow, told me recently a laughable christening story, very characteristic of the Bœotian sim-plicity of some of the old-time farm hands, and their direct bluntness of expression.   It was new to me, although I fancy it has already been published.   Jock had been sent by Tibbie his wife to see the minister, preparatory to making arrangements for the baptism of their first-born. Having stated his message, the pastor, following the usual custom, proceeded to put a few questions to Jock, with a view to test his fitness to stand sponsor, and to gauge his doctrinal knowledge on the subject of this particular sacrament.   The only immediate result of his catechising, however, was to demonstrate Jock's utter and hopeless ignorance.   The minister sadly shook his head.   Jock looked eager and alarmed.   At last the good man said : ' John ! John ! ye're no FIT to hold up your child ! ' ' No fit,' said the swarthy, brawny giant, complacently survey-ing his own athletic frame.   ' No fit ?   Losh, sir, I cud haud him up altho' he wis a bull stirk ! '

This reminds me of another capital catechising story from my neighbouring granite county, Aberdeen. The class had been reading the story of Joseph and his brethren, and it came to the turn of the visiting minister to examine the boys, with a view to test their recollection of the main points of the narrative.

With much unction and unnecessary prolixity, he had expatiated on the cruelty and treachery of the wicked brothers, the grief of the bereaved old patriarch, and so on. The replies had been quick, intelligent, and correct to all his questions. Such as—

' What great crime did these sons of Jacob commit ? '

' They sold their brother Joseph.'

' Quite correct. And for how much ? '

' Twenty pieces of silver.'

' Quite right '; and then wishing to impress on them the added heinousness of their conduct in the lie they told to their aged father, he asked—

' And what added to the cruelty and wickedness of these bad brothers ? '

A pause.

' What made their treachery even more detestable and heinous ? '

Then a bright, little fellow stretched out an eager hand.

' Well ! my man ? '

' Please, sir, they sell't him ower cheap.'

The following is not new. It has been attributed to Norman Macleod and at least a dozen other prominent Scottish divines. I think, however, it is good enough to bear repetition, as, although well known to Scottish readers, it may be new to some of those who hail from ' the ither side o'. Tweed.'

The minister had been examining the class on the Shorter Catechism, and the subject was Regeneration. He had been gravely trying to illustrate and explain what 'being born again' meant. He spoke of the new life—the new birth—the upspringing of a new principle in the inner man—and so on ; and then with his good heart welling with tenderness, he addressed a bright-eyed little chappie, who had been manifesting great attention and interest, and he said to him, expecting an immediate, hearty response :—

'Noo, my wee mannie, wadna ye like to be born again ?

'Na, sir!' came the answer, prompt and emphatic, much to his surprise and disappointment.

'What! I am surprised! Would ye no like to be born again ?'

'Na, sir !' again came the reply, no less decided and prompt.

'Dear me, how's that ? *Why* wad ye no like to be born again ?'

'Because I micht be born a lassie, sir,' said the little theologian, much to the good minister's relief, and not a little to his amusement.

Somewhat after the same state of mind as Jock was in, when he thought of the 'klatt' being used in Eden, was that of an old evangelist on the east coast among the 'fisher fowk,' and which I have got 'first hand' from my dear old friend, the Rev. James H——, now in Sydney, New South Wales.

'I had a missionary for a time in my old church,' he writes, 'who used to say some strange things. One day he happened to have been preaching on Enoch, and no doubt desiring to illustrate his subject in such a way as to appeal to the immediate comprehension of the simple folk among whom he ministered, he told them in his quaint, homely fashion that—" In Enoch's time the kintra hed so feow fowk intill it, that there wud not be more than two faimilies atween Aberdour an' Dumfries." Further—" That sairvants in Enoch's time were not to be had for love nor money, consequently Enoch had to be his own baker, and moreover he hed to darn his own stockings.'

'Preaching one day on spirits,' continues my friend, 'he attempted to prove that a spirit had no *corpus*, by saying that "Mary Magdalene, out of whom seeven deevils hed been cast, did not require a coffin one whit the less on that accoont." '

In this connection I might cite the case of a cautious old deacon, who had acquired some very liberal or, as his compeers would have said, 'latitudinawrian' views of salvation. He was offering up a petition one night at a prayer-meeting, when in a temporary moment of forgetfulness, he thanked God for the 'salvation of all men,' but immediately qualified the sweeping admission by a true touch of genuine Scottish casuistry, adding, 'which, O Lord! as Thou knowest, is true in one sense, but not in another!'

As further illustrating the shrewd, practical estimate of the characters of biblical biography, of which I have given some rare examples in *Oor Ain Folk*, I might cite the following :—

A rather flippant, young, self-sufficient fellow had been discussing the questions of women's rights, and the status of woman in our modern social order, with a shrewd old village dame, who was evidently an advanced Radical, and he had found that the old lady carried argumentative guns of no mean range and penetration. With a certain spice of mischief, wishing to pique her, he instanced the dictum of Solomon, the wise monarch of Israel, who, he said, must beyond a doubt have been a competent judge of the ways of women, their character, and capabilities. Thinking thus to silence her with the weight of an appeal to Scripture, he said :—

'You know what Solomon said '—referring to his many wives—' "That amid the multitude he could not find one good woman." '

With a contemptuous toss of the head and a swift intuition which, however inconsequential and illogical, was splendidly feminine and spirited, the incensed old maid said : ' Hech, man ! nae wumman, nae dacent wumman ony w'y, wud hae haen onything tae dae wi' sic a character ! '

Somewhat akin to the old deacon's prayer above mentioned, but differing totally in the mental attitude of the suppliant, is the following. Nothing could, I think, more graphically portray the ineffable condescension and complacent self-righteousness of the modern Pharisee. He was a precise, formal, snuff-dried, ' perjink ' Writer to the Signet, in Edinburgh, and an elder in one of the leading churches there. At one church meeting, he was called on to lead in prayer, and he opened his petition mincingly and patronisingly in these words, spoken with an affected English accent :—

' O Lud ! we are pooah sinnahs, at least some of us, comparatively speaking.'

D

As may have been seen from some of the foregoing examples, the hard-worked, conscientious, country minister had oftentimes rather a disconcerting experience during his annual round of catechetical visits to his flock. Let it not for a moment be inferred from the samples I have given, of what were after all abnormal incidents, that I am out of sympathy with the good old-fashioned custom of testing the knowledge of the flock in sacred lore by the pastor. On the contrary, I think it was a custom which is now most regrettably falling into desuetude as far as my information goes. I have been so long away from my native land that I really know not how far the old custom is adhered to or departed from, but this I know, that in the Colonies the younger generation have not the same intimate knowledge of Scripture that their forefathers had, and the oftentimes hard-worked and under-paid minister has not the same opportunities for testing the knowledge of his flock that are afforded by the closer settlement and more circumscribed areas of parishes at home. In the Colonies it is no uncommon thing for a Presbyterian clergyman to have charge of a cure of souls, small indeed in numbers as measured by home standards, but scattered over a territory bigger far than many a Scottish county. In my New England electorate I know of one dear old ' brither Scot,' from the Borderland, who for wellnigh twice a score of years has ministered to the spiritual wants of scattered, isolated, little communities of Presbyterians, and in all weathers has nobly done his duty of visiting, ministration, and the hundred and one kindly offices of the pastorate, which the scoffing outsider knows nothing of, with a rare fidelity and honest thoroughness that have won him the true respect and affection of every class of the community. He is only one of many. The clerical brethren at home, surrounded with amenities which are the outcome of generations of hallowed associations and memories, may in those moments of depression and lowered vitality which come to every worker in the intellectual and spiritual planes, indulge in a momentary envious thought of the broader horizon and wider sphere which he thinks belongs to his colonial fellow-worker. Alas! 'Far birds have fine feathers,' and the colonial office of the ministry is not by any means so devoid of cares and *désagréables* as the occupant of the quiet, humdrum country manse may think. The conclusion of the whole matter, so far as my own humble judgment and observation go, is that, next to preaching, the Bible Class—the steady, constant, unwearying, faithful inculcation of the great truths and facts of Bible history—is the most precious and profitable work that a Christian minister or any Christian worker can undertake. The plain, simple presentation of Bible truth is what I mean. Dogma and doctrine will come later on, when 'the man has put away childish things'; but the 'childish things' themselves, the leading facts, that is, of Bible history, are in themselves a liberal education, and when the Scottish nation sits down to reckon up all its advantages, and the things that have made for its truest and best progress, let it not forget the Bible lessons in the parish schools, and the faithful ministerial catechisings in the homes of the people.

Sometimes certainly, as I have shown, the experiences of the catechist were humorous and grotesque enough,

and I have only room for one or two more of the sort.
It was in 'the black country' of the west of Scotland, and
the minister, on such a round of duty as I have been
describing, entered the lowly dwelling of one of the
pitmen. The presiding *genius loci* was a rather fiery-faced
virago, who, with arms akimbo, and her flaming hair
in wild disarray, gave the man of peace, as he thought,
but a chill welcome. However, duty called, and he was
not to be daunted by appearances however untoward and
discouraging. After the usual conventional prelimin-
aries of talk, he proceeded to his pastoral task, and
began operations by asking the good wife—what he
thought was a safe and easy question :—

'What are you made of, Janet?'

'Ow jist flesh an' bluid, sir! what else?'

'Oh no, Janet! you are made of dust!'

'Dust, sir? I'll dust yer lugs for ye!'

And in spite of protestations and explanations, the
worthy minister had to beat an undignified retreat.

It might have been the same minister, but at any
rate it was under somewhat similar circumstances in
a small town in Clackmannanshire, that the worthy
pastor had occasion to visit the long, unlovely row of
pitmen's cottages or cabins built near the pit, and
generally known in local parlance—*par excellence*—as
'THE RAW.' The housewife was not such a Tartar
as the one last referred to, for she had bidden the
minister a kindly welcome ; and in the exercise of a
rude hospitality had produced the whisky bottle
and a rather dingy-looking glass. While leaning on
the rickety table and conversing, the glass was
unfortunately upset and broken. The collier's wife, in

great concern, unconsciously disclosed the communal element in this primitive society by exclaiming : 'Eh ! wae's me, sirss ! an' there's no anither haill gless in a' the Raw !'

Some subtle association of ideas when I get on the topic of ministers, brings yet another biblical anecdote to mind.

The story was told me by a gallant officer on my late voyage from Australia, and the subject was a gentle, meek-tempered pastor of a rural parish in Rox-burghshire. The good minister, while a perfectly lamb-like Arcadian in ordinary times, became sometimes a very Boanerges in the pulpit. He liked to thunder forth 'swelling words' of sesquipedalian length, and one day having fallen into a perfect fervour, 'his soul waxed wroth within him' as he noted the evident drowsiness of the bulk of his bucolic hearers. Smiting the sacred volume before him, he rolled out : 'But what is the use of my speaking thus? It is but casting pearls before swine.' Suddenly he paused, and, with a deprecatory cough behind his hand, he added : 'Brethren, the ex-pression is strictly scriptural.'

While on this subject of theological belief I cannot refrain from reproducing a delicious extract I cut from *Blackwood's Magazine* some time ago. It is so delightfully Scottish. An ardent Presbyterian was discussing with a brother churchman, the character and religious belief of X their common friend. The first of them thought X was going all wrong ; that his life was well enough, but on questions of doctrine and faith he was very shaky. 'Oh, not at all ! I don't agree with you,' said the other. 'X is all right, I am sure ; he thoroughly believes in total depravity!' 'He may believe in it,' was the answer, 'as a dogma; but the question is, Does he act up to it in his life? I am afraid he does not!'

A quip which was as orthodox as it is witty is the following:—

A minister passed one of his flock on the high road, and the good man kindly bade the minister 'Good-mornin',' remarking at the same time that it was 'verra cauld.' 'Ay, ay! Sandie,' said the jocular cleric, making an obvious pun on the sound of the word 'cauld,' 'Many are called, but few are chosen.' 'Aweel, minister,' was Sandie's dry retort, 'if ye're no chosen, I'm thinkin' ye'll no be lang cauld!'

Equally characteristic was the following. The anecdote is not new, but thus it goes:—

A popular English Nonconformist divine was residing with a farmer near Glasgow, while on a visit to that city, whither he had gone on a deputation from the Wesleyan Missionary Society. After dinner, in reply to an invitation to partake of some fine fruit, he mentioned to the family a curious circumstance concerning himself, namely, that he had never in his life tasted an apple, pear, grape, or indeed any kind of green fruit. The fact seemed to evoke considerable surprise from the company; but a cautious Scotchman of a practical, matter-of-fact turn of mind, and who had listened with apparent unconcern, dryly remarked: 'It's a peety but ye had been in Paradise, an' there michtna hae been ony fa'!'

Let me be pardoned if I venture just to add still another which has not been before published. It shows the quaint realism and somewhat prosaic imagination of the simple folk of the older generation. My cousin,

Mrs. Harkness, had an old faithful servant from Harris named Kirsty. Kirsty knew but very little English, but showed her good upbringing, and good example too, by never neglecting the duty of attending public worship, although it was often but little of the English she could understand. One night, however, she came home looking very pleased, and said in reply to the usual question, 'Well, Kirsty, how did you get on to-night?' 'Oh, mistress, I likit ta minister so weel ta nicht. I could follow nearly efery word.' 'Ay, and what was he preaching about, Kirsty?' 'Deed, I canna richtly tell you. |It will pe what they caa' *Cumstrohl* in ta Gaelic. Sorra tak' it; I dinna know in the worl' what they will caal him in ta Englitch. But,' her face lighting up, 'it wass ta laad that went awaay an' aāte ta peelins!'

Poor Kirsty's idea of the Prodigal Son eating out of the trough of swine husks, may not have been an oriental one, but suggested by home conditions. Yet it was graphic, and there is just a touch of pathos in it too.

CHAPTER III

MINISTER AND MANSE

Their influence on the people—The Presbytery dinner—Critical
attitude towards the minister—John's criticism of the new
minister—A Montrose hearer—The sick fisherman—A punning
text—Caustic advice—Salient features of Presbyterianism :
its merits and drawbacks—Belief in democracy—Free speech
—Instances of pulpit criticism—Droll descriptions of ministers
—Wholesale plagiarism—Au'ra the critic—Dr. Aird's story—
Hope even for a bishop—Reluctant emotion—A dream and
the interpretation thereof.

It is a genuine tribute to the quiet power and widely
prevalent influence of the pulpit and the manse upon
the life and character of the people, the peasantry
especially, that so many stories of Scottish life and
character find their inspiration and their rallying-point
in the occupant of both.   There are quite as many
Scottish anecdotes about ministers, their sayings and
doings, as about whisky, and that is saying a good deal.
Nor indeed need this be wondered at.   In the length
and breadth of rural Scotland, at all events, the manse
and the kirk were always a living centre of intellectual
and spiritual life.   In the cities, of course, there were
plentiful channels of activity and numberless distrac-

tions, but not so in the country. Farmer and hind alike, old and young, rich and poor, all had in turn, at some time or other, to come into personal contact with, or come under the influence of, the minister. Then too he was generally one of the people themselves. He had graduated in the common school. He belonged to no narrow, exclusive, sacerdotal caste. He was essentially 'a minister,' not 'a priest.' Added to this he was, from the very fact of his being a minister of the Presbyterian Church, a man of solid attainments and of considerable culture. If not a brilliant scholar, or a profound theologian, the high standards of education so wisely set up by the Church, ensured at least that the Scottish minister should be the equal in scholarship, if not the superior, of any ordinary man over whom he ministered. Indeed to a genial, earnest, whole-souled man, and such they mostly were, there were a thousand kindly, tender ties being constantly formed, which served to make the connection between the manse and the parish a very real and a very enduring one. But all this I have detailed at length in *Oor Ain Folk*, and it is dwelt upon by every writer on Scottish character from John Galt downwards.

Some of the very best illustrations, in fact, of the oddities and drolleries, the quaint quips and funny conceits, the angularities and crannies, the strongly-marked and ever-varying individuality of that strange compound the rural Scot, are to be found among the rich treasure-trove of anecdote and observation, which almost every country minister had at his command in my young days. I well remember at the Presbytery dinners what a rich flow of humour would be let loose ;

how story would succeed story in endless procession.
And to have seen and heard these reverend gentlemen
when a good dinner had mellowed their frame of mind,
and toned down for a time the professional rigidity of
their general demeanour, was an introduction to *Noctes
Ambrosianæ* of a most enjoyable order indeed.   Nor
was the refreshment provided, always such as would
have suited an ascetic, although I never remember it
to have been on so lavish a scale as is implied in the
remark of a Church of Scotland clergyman the other
day to a young clerical friend of my own.   Speaking of
old times, and the changes that have taken place in
public sentiment, the subject of Presbytery dinners
happened to come up.   The old gentleman's eye kindled
at the bare recollection, and he racily said : ' Eh, man,
I mind fine whan the Presbytery denner was jist like
the washin' day, wi' the steam o' the toddy.'

Of course the minister was, in his parish, like 'a city
set on a hill.'   ' He could not be hid.'   If it was his
office and duty to chide the careless, to reprove the
thoughtless, to rebuke the erring, or to denounce the
hardened and obdurate, depend upon it his own conduct
was most narrowly watched and freely criticised.   The
watchful scrutiny, too, extended to his wife and family,
and even to distant relations and the very servants.
The manse, it was thought, possessed 'great preveeleges,'
and these carried with them corresponding duties and
responsibilities.   As a rule, the bluff, frank independence of the sturdy Scottish nature, had a certain manly,
chivalrous strain in it, so that while the parishioners were
perfectly well aware of the limits within which clerical
authority could be exercised,—and indeed with a lazy

or inept, a grasping or autocratic, or above all a worldly minister, they would very often 'show their teeth,' as the saying is, and manifest their independence in a way that was very peremptory and often startlingly efficacious, —yet, the general attitude was one of much personal regard and genuine lovingkindness towards their minister, and they were not disposed to be too exacting if the good man were at all possessed of ordinary tact and transparent honesty of purpose.

Perhaps, however, the few selected illustrations I have to give, will best show the relationships that existed between the minister and his people in the fast-vanishing olden time, and the unique position of the minister himself, in the days ere Agnosticism and Theosophy had become fashionable with the dilettanti.

Here, for instance, is a gem in the way of rustic criticism, worthy of a Greek philosopher, and showing most tellingly the shrewd estimate of the relative positions of shepherd and flock on the part of the parishioner. A very studious, scholarly minister, of nervous, sensitive, retiring nature, had lately been inducted into a parish by the patron of the living, and while delivering erudite discourses he was not very attentive to his pastoral duties. One of his hearers, a bit of a Diogenes in his way, was asked, 'How he likit the new minister.' John's reply was delicious: 'Weel, I canna jist a'thegither say; for throw the week he's inveesible, an' on the Sawbath he's incompreehensible!'

The next shows the kindly, genial nature of the old-time pastor.

A venerable divine in Montrose was accosted by an

old wifie one day—one of his most attentive and appreciative hearers—with a remark after this sort: 'Eh, doctor, I div like richt weel to hear yer ain sel' preech, for what *ye* say jist gaes in at the yae lug an' oot at the tither!' The poor old bodie really meant that the good doctor was clear and easily understandable. With a humorous smile the worthy minister replied: 'Ah, my gude wumman, I'm fleyed there's only ower mony like yersel'!'

As showing how purely professional a view of certain clerical duties was taken by some of the simple rustic folks, and the queer association of ideas suggested by certain ministrations, the following is decidedly quaint. It happened, I believe, to the parish minister of Inverallochy, who had gone to visit a sick fisherman. The poor fellow was pretty cheerful, but when the minister after a little conversation proceeded to kneel down by the bedside, intending to offer up prayer, the startled patient was apparently aroused all at once to a consciousness that his condition was possibly more dangerous than he had even himself suspected, and with an outburst that was pathetic, yet irresistibly ludicrous, he blurted out: 'O Lord! has it come to this?'

Of punning texts there have been numberless instances published, but probably this is one of the best. It was on the occasion of the Laird bringing home his third wife, and the old minister took for his text: 'There will be abundance of peace so long as the *moon* endureth!'

For quiet, dry irony the following, too, is worthy of record. 'What will I preach about?' said a conceited young fellow, who had rather an exaggerated estimate of his own gifts of extemporary speech, as he chatted with the elderly brother in the vestry, previous to beginning the service. 'What *will* I preach about? It is nearly time to go into the pulpit, and really I do not know what to preach about?' 'Jist preach aboot a quarter of an 'oor!' was the caustic reply.

I fancy there can be little question of the claim made for the Presbyterian form of church government, that it has fostered and strengthened the critical faculties of the people. It certainly deepens the sense of individual responsibility; and although the system of Presbytery, and Synod, and General Assembly undoubtedly affords ample scope for the ambitious, the gifted, and the daring among both clergy and laity to make their mark, and display their capacity for debate, for administrative ability, or for bold initiative, yet the genius of the system, as it appears to me, lies more in the constant recognition of the worth of the individual—the inalienable privilege of the individual member to exercise his own private right of judgment; and enjoying as they do the widest franchise in all essential matters pertaining to the temporal government of the Church—to the selection of ministers, for instance, and appointment to all minor offices—thanks to the Disruption movement—it is little wonder that we find the critical faculty so keen, the sense of one's own importance so active, and the spirit of breezy independence so manifest, as becomes very evident so soon as you begin to tackle a Scottish Presbyterian on any point of doctrine, practice, precedent, or discipline, in connection with church affairs.

Doubtless there are drawbacks. Some pragmatic, self-assertive, combative being in a church, may disturb for a time the corporate serenity ; some 'thrawn,' lop-sided individual, with a mental or intellectual twist or kink in him, may act for the time being as a moral blister ; but even that surely is better than the unruffled stagnation of an inert indifferentism, the torpor of meek acquiescence in priestly decrees, the tame subservience to the dominance of a sacerdotal or aristocratic caste, or that benumbing thraldom of the human spirit, begotten always by a costly and complicated system of ritual and ornate worship, in which the mere form, and the personality of the hierophant, tend invariably to supplant the spirit and the divine object of worship.

In church government as in politics, I believe in trusting the people—in allowing them the widest and freest franchise possible, and in encouraging and cultivating to the utmost, the sense of individual responsibility and the sacred right of free, private judgment. I am optimist enough to believe that the corporate good-sense of an educated people, trained to exercise their judgment and to weigh their responsibilities, will, in the main, suffice to prevent any glaring or long-continued abuse of such freedom. And in any case, I fancy even the mistakes and excesses of such a free system, are preferable to the wild outbursts of fanatic fury and unreasonable rage perpetrated by helots or thralls—whether spontaneous, or directed by dictator or demagogue, aristocrat or plutocrat, king or priest.

I have culled one or two pithy instances of this free criticism, which illustrate the points I have touched upon, and which I value, too, as being capital specimens of the pithy, terse expressiveness of the Scottish tongue.

What could be more pointed, terse, and forcible, for instance, than the following ?

Two old cronies had been hearing the famous Dr. Chalmers, and in exercise of the freedom I have been referring to, were discussing the merits of the preacher after his performances in the pulpit. One of the two was distinctly and declaredly appreciative, almost effusively so for a cannie Scot ; but her praises did not seem to find much echo from her companion. Wishing to evoke some encomiastic criticism from her reticent fellow-hearer she said :—

'Weel, Marget ! an' what thocht ye o' oor doctor the day, than ? '

' 'Deed, no muckle ! '

'Toots, 'umman ! Surely he wis unco deep ! '

'Umph ! He wisna deep, he was drumlie ! '

The subject of the next was a pretentious young preacher, whose complacent conceit had made him quite oblivious of the fact that he was addressing as coldly critical, and, to one of his calibre and methods, as unresponsive and perhaps cynical an audience as could be found in all Christendom. At length, having essayed an oratorical flight quite beyond the strength of his callow intellectual pinions, he found himself tangled in an inextricable and incomprehensible jumble of mixed metaphors. One old wife, sitting in the body of the kirk beside her gudeman, and who had been listening most intently, with her hand behind her ear, bent over and appealed to her grim consort, in a tone loud enough to be heard for several seats around :—

'Fat's his grund, John?'

John replied with a most expressive grunt, and in a tone even more widely audible:—

'Hech! he his *nae* grund. He's soomin'!'

A specimen of rather shrewd and semi-contemptuous criticism was that on a Congregational minister of decidedly mediocre powers and low spirituality, who had forsaken his own connection to join the Establishment. He was appointed to the charge of S—— parish, and on the occasion of his first appearance in his new pulpit, a number of his old hearers, impelled by curiosity, went to hear him make his *debut* in his fresh environment. Among them was an old fisherman—a strong Independent—and he made the following comment after the service on the way home:—

'Ay, ay! he'll nae doot mak' a gude Moderate minister!'

'How so?'

'Oh, he jist prayed aboot the craps, an' the weather, an' the cattle baists; in fac', a'thing aboot a fairm-yaird!'

Similarly Dr. Mason relates a good anecdote, illustrating the strange vagaries of pulpit criticism. One old woman, he tells, after having heard a newly-placed minister preach, was heard to exclaim: 'Eh! weel, sirss! he hisna a divertin' coontenance!'

As an unconscious association of ideas by which reading the sermon was classed as a bad habit, the following is characteristic:—

An old coach-driver, who was an enthusiastic admirer of the reverend Dr. Welsh, minister of Old Deer, was expatiating to his box-seat passenger on the virtues of his favourite. He was very loud and very emphatic on the merits of the learned doctor. 'He wis a graund scholar; he wis a fine, poo'erfu' preacher; he wis a magneeficent theeologian,' and so on, and so on. The passenger innocently asked : 'Does he read ?' With an accent of deep disgust the driver replied : 'Feech, na ! He jist bites his nails an' claws his croon i' the poo'pit.'

Somewhat akin to this was the terse but telling description, by a country servant lassie, of a well-known clergyman in my native county, Forfarshire. His appearance is not a little remarkable, as he affects a clean-shaven face, which is 'sicklied o'er' possibly with the 'pale cast of thought,' though some of his clerical brethren doubt if it be that. The pale face is surmounted by a *chevelure* of frizzed hair, something after the manner of a chief of the Solomon Islands, and he has a Boanerges-like voice, which he tries to model on the style of Henry Irving. This was the occupant of the pulpit on the evening in question ; and the lassie, on her return home, was of course asked about the minister and the sermon in orthodox Scottish style. She replied :—

'Oh, it wisna oor ain minister the nicht; we hed a strainger.'

'Oh, who was it? what was he like?'

'I didna hear his naime, mem ; but he had a face like a wumman, a vyse (voice) like a lion, an' a heid like a heather besom !'

An old minister in Aberdeenshire on his deathbed bequeathed a bit of worldly wisdom to his only son in these words : 'Jock,' he faintly said, 'dinna mairry for siller ; ye'll can borrow cheaper.'

To another of these sturdy farmer-clerics of the old school who was rather an indifferent preacher, and who was conducting his 'veesitations,' a decidedly disconcerting answer was given by an old maiden lady, with whom, as it happened, the minister was not a *persona grata*. She was just preparing to partake of her afternoon tea when the minister arrived, and of course, in obedience to the universally recognised and practised laws of Scottish hospitality, she proffered him a share of the fragrant, steaming decoction.

The poor man was under some constraint, knowing full well that he was no great favourite with Miss Jean. He was, besides, utterly devoid of that pleasant social tact which is such a valuable endowment. Remarking that there was some obstruction in the spout of the teapot, and for want of anything better to say, he stupidly hazarded the remark :—

'Yer teapot disna rin, Miss Kennedy.'

'Ah, minister,' dryly retorted the spinster, 'it's jist like yersel'. It has an unco puir delivery.'

The Rev. Mr. L—— of M—— was accosted one Monday morning by a member of his congregation—a quiet, pawky weaver—and after the usual interchange of pleasant salutations the weaver said :—

'Thon wis a fine sappy sermon ye gied 's yesterday, minister !'

'Weel, John,' said the gratified preacher, 'I'm sure I'm gled if ye were pleased.'

'Ay,' said John, with dry significance ; 'but it wisna yer ain !'

'Weel, ye see, John,' somewhat sheepishly replied

Mr. L—— —and making the best of it—'we ministers are sometimes overworked just like other workmen; and after a hard week of extra duties we are sometimes not in a fit state to attack original composition, and so we have just to read up, and are forced to borrow ideas occasionally.'

John's reply was deliciously professional and very Scottish: 'Oo ay, sir! nae doot! I wadna min' if ye only took a pirn or twa occasionally, but ye suldna tak' the haill wab, sir!'

Doubtless this free, plain-spoken criticism had its advantages. It kept the occupant of the pulpit up to the mark, and was an evidence both of the blunt independence and the keen intellectual attentiveness and mental alertness of the hearers. The mutual relationship was, so far as I know, quite peculiar to the Scottish people. Here is another homely illustration.

In a certain congregation near Glasgow there was one of the class of hearers I have been referring to, named Andrew Hutton, generally spoken of as 'An'ra.' A nervous, emotional young preacher named M'Lean had been occupying the pulpit for a time during the summer, and though a scholarly, eloquent man, his nervousness made him very rapid in his utterance. An old friend of mine, who told me the story, after the sermon one day, had overtaken An'ra, and as usual they began criticising the preacher and the sermon. Mr. M—— said: 'He is a clever man, An'ra, but I thought he spoke rather fast.' 'Ow ay, sir,' responded An'ra, in a dry, matter-of-fact tone, 'the fac' is, I've chackit him twae-'ree times for the same faut masel'.'

Dr. Aird, a venerable ex-Moderator of the Free

Church of Scotland, told a good story about a minister
who in the old days of patronage had been forced upon
a congregation at Alness.   The anecdote has already
seen publication, but it is good enough to bear repetition.   As may easily be imagined, the new minister
was but coldly received ; but he took possession of
manse and pulpit, began to visit the people, and one
day called upon an old elder, who however greeted him
very gruffly.   Nothing daunted, the minister seated
himself, began conversing, and in a little while took out
his snuff-box.

'Oh,' said the elder, 'ye tak' snuff, div ye ?'

'Oh yes.'

'Weel, that's the first mark o' grace I've seen in ye.'

'How do you make that out ?' asked the minister.

'Div ye no read o' Solomon's temple,' replied the
elder, 'that a' the snuffers were o' pure gold ?'

The following also is second-hand, but is, I think,
very characteristic of an old-fashioned, narrow, rural
type of rustic sectarianism, which, however, is not
exclusively Scottish or Presbyterian.   A well-known
Anglican bishop, while paying a visit at Taymouth
Castle during the lifetime of the last Marquis of Breadalbane, a devoted adherent of the Free Church of Scotland, was taken by Lady Breadalbane (*née* Baillie of
Jerviswoode) into one of the cottages on the estate
occupied by an old Highland woman, a 'true blue'
Presbyterian, who was greatly pleased by the bishop's
frank and friendly manner.   A few days afterwards
the bishop left the castle, and Lady Breadalbane paid
another visit to her humble friend, when the following
conversation took place :—

'Do you know who that was, Mary, that came to see you last week?'

'No, my lady,' was the reply.

'The famous Bishop of Oxford,' said her ladyship.

On which the old Highland crofter, with a tolerance and discrimination rising superior to the traditions of her ancestral faith, quietly remarked :—

'Aweel, my lady, he's a rael fine man; an' a' I can say is, that I trust an' pray he'll gang to heeven, bishop though he be !'

The same attitude of somewhat unwilling admiration towards any person outside the narrow circle of one's own familiar ken, is exemplified in the following :—

A raw, rustic youth came to visit his friends in Glasgow, and, with. the proverbial hospitality of the Clydeside capital, they spared no pains to make his stay agreeable. On the Sunday they took him to hear one of St. Mungo's most able and renowned preachers, who happened to deliver, even for him, an exceptionally moving and pathetic sermon. Returning from church, in answer to a query how he liked the service, he revealed his feelings thus :—

'It wis a rare discoorse ! A' the fowk near me wis greetin'; an', feth, I wis gey near't masel'. But I didna like tae gie w'y, seein' he wisna oor ain meenister.'

A clerical friend sends me the following, which he characterises as a 'made-up story, but quaint.' There is humour in it, certainly of the conventional kind, but it also affords an illustration of the way in which the rustic mind was wont to regard the professions and their distinguishing characteristics. The story was told my friend by an old Carnoustie man of eighty-six summers,

who asked him if he had ever heard of the perplexing
dream a certain man had, and its interpretation. 'No,'
was my friend's reply; 'let me hear it.' 'Aweel,' said
the patriarch, 'it's aboot a man that had a terrible
dream. He thocht he had three sons, and yin turned
oot a beggar, yin a thief, and the third a murderer.
He was sore perplexed, and tell't his dream to a friend.'
According to the story, the friend must have been a bit
of a cynic, for his advice was to 'mak' ane a minister,
an' he'll ha'e to do plenty o' begging; mak' anither a
lawyer, an' deil a fear o' him but he'll thieve eneuch;
an' if ye mak' the third a doctor, sorra tak' him, but
he'll kill plenty!'

CHAPTER IV

MINISTER AND PEOPLE

Feudal monopolists—The Scottish Universities—The training for
manse life—Dry, clerical humour—The Apostle of the Highlands performs a queer christening—The minister of Birse on
snuff-taking—Anecdotes of 'Wattie Dunlop'—Deducing a
doctrine—Auld Jenny on preaching—A dubious compliment
—Unemotional hearers—The elder's presentation speech—A
lapsus linguæ—Dr. Eadie on the Speerit—Patrick Robertson's
'convairt'—Dunkie Demster's enemy—Pawky clerical puns—
An electioneering prayer—Dr. Lindsay Alexander's beadle.

THE picture would be incomplete, however, were we
only to consider the attitude of the lay mind toward
the cleric. To an ambitious, strong-minded, or gifted
man the office of the ministry always afforded splendid
scope for the exercise of his best energies. Doubtless
in the majority of cases, the Scottish clergy obeyed deep
spiritual impulses and a clear call from the unseen, in
the choice of their sacred profession. Under feudal
institutions, however, and a clan system, which, however much it may have been in its origin founded on a
community of kinship and territory, and embraced all
classes of the community, yet became increasingly aristocratic as it developed, the best positions in the

higher professions were thus more and more monopolised by the rich and powerful, and the common people were largely excluded from a participation in the prizes of political and professional careers. This is much what has happened under a strong feudal system everywhere. The son of a poor man could not aspire to an officership in army or navy. Parliament and the Bar were for the most part beyond his reach. The younger cadets of titled or rich families, plucked the plums in commerce and adventure. But happily the avenues of learning were open to the humblest and poorest of Scotia's sons. So the ranks of the learned professions were constantly being reinforced by the strenuous Spartan sons of farm and manse and humble cottage, and especially so in the noble healing professions— healing in the broadest sense—healing the maladies of human flesh and human spirit, the cure of both bodies and souls of men. The world at large owes a debt of gratitude to the grand old Scottish Universities for their splendid armies of earnest, well-trained sons in both physic and divinity. The roll of their distinguished graduates is indeed legion.

From following the plough to filling the pulpit or the professor's chair, was thus quite a common achievement to the persevering, tenacious, ambitious students of the very humblest origin ; and having to exercise self-denial and determination of the most strenuous kind, having to overcome difficulties that would have daunted any less determined race, having gone through the hard discipline of an exacting, keenly competitive collegiate course, little wonder was it that the men who emerged victorious from such an ordeal and with such a training, were able pretty generally to hold their own, to render a good account of their stewardship to even the most critical and contumacious; and so the rural records of Scottish manse-life teem with illustrations of racy wit and manly independence, of heroic endeavour and noble self - abnegation, of fervid zeal and lofty patriotism, of quiet endurance and 'patient continuance in well-doing,' and, in a word, many of the brightest examples of 'plain living and high thinking' among all the crowded pages of human biography.

But I am dealing more with the humorous side of Scottish character, and my own disposition perhaps naturally draws me in that direction; so I must content myself and, I trust, please my readers by transcribing from my note-book now, some of the specimens I have gathered, in which the worthy minister himself appears to more or less good advantage.

A good instance of dry, clerical, caustic wit is that told of an old divine, who was of a genial disposition, but liked to be met in the same spirit. A young minister of the new-fangled ascetic school, had been filling the old gentleman's pulpit during the evening service, and after a fervid and fiery discourse he was disrobing in the vestry. The old gentleman had made some pleasant complimentary speeches, and was pressing the hospitality of the manse on the younger brother, whose response had been somewhat of a frigid character. The old man, however, on hospitable thoughts intent, said : 'Hoots, man, ye've preached a good sermon an' ye'll be nane the waur o' a sma' refresher efter yer day's wark. So come awa' and ye can share a tumbler of good toddy wi' me.' The younger man responded to this : 'That

he was much obliged, but really he did not drink, nor
did he approve of drinking.' 'Aweel, aweel,' said the
kindly old man, 'I'll no press ye. "Let every man be
fully persuaded in his own mind," ye ken. But ye can
surely come inbye, and we can share a pipe and a quiet
crack together.' Still more frigidly came the disclaimer,
'That really he did not smoke!' whereat the old minister
suddenly changed his tone and sharply asked : 'Ay, man,
do ye eat gerse ?' 'Eat grass ?' asked the youth, quite
surprised at such a question. 'Eat grass ? No ! What
makes you ask that ?' 'Weel, weel,' came the dry
retort, 'ye can gang yer ways ; for if ye neither smoke
nor drink nor eat gerse, yer naither fit company for
man nor beast.'

Innumerable are the good stories told of that fine old
Highland gentleman and minister, the Rev. Mr. M'Intosh
of Ferintosh, called from his zeal and noble Christian
activity 'the Apostle of the Highlands.' Perhaps one
of the most characteristic and least known—although
I am afraid it has already been published—is that
wherein he turned the tables on a knot of rather supercilious, scoffing, young English sportsmen. It occurred
on one of the boats coming from Skye, about the time
of the General Assembly's annual gathering, and
Ferintosh was accompanied by a young clerical brother,
whose zeal and temper would seem to have been greater
than his discretion. At all events, he had become
entangled in rather a heated argument with the young
gentlemen aforesaid—a hilarious party, who had been
'doing' Skye, and who had become possessed of an
idea that the young cleric was fair 'game' for their
Cockney wit. One of them was the proud possessor of a

fine little Skye-terrier puppy, and being a little elevated
with the wine they had taken, they were annoying the
young minister by requesting him to bestow a fitting
baptismal appellation on the wee doggie.   They had been
rather uncomplimentary in their remarks about the
Scottish ritual—had indulged in some ill-bred sneers
about the churches and ministers generally—and the
fiery young Celt, minister though he was, had lost his
temper, and was indulging in an unprofitable wrangle
with the graceless young scamps.   Just then Mr.
M'Intosh came up to the party, and his keen eye
and ready wit at once took in the whole situation.
Shouldering his way into the very centre of the group,
he good-humouredly effected a diversion in his youthful
colleague's favour by demanding if it was 'according
to the ethics of English sport for half a dozen to set on
one ?'   The young fellows, seeing in the venerable old
divine but a fresh target for their coarse wit, winked at
each other, and turned their attention to the new-comer.

'Oh ! we were simply wanting the parson to exercise
his vocation,' said the ringleader.

'Ay,' dryly replied the old minister, ' as how ?'

'Well, we simply wanted him to baptize this puppy
dog,' said the chief tormentor.

'Oh, ye want yer puppy dog bapteezed, do ye ?'
said M'Intosh.   'Well, I have no objections to do that
for ye.'

At this the young fellows nudged each other,
guffawed, gathered closer round, and imagined they
saw a good joke well on the way, and that they would
have some ripe fun at the expense of the veteran
preacher.   By this time nearly all the passengers,

attracted by the unusual proceedings, had gathered round the group.

Still apparently good-humoured, and perfectly self-possessed, the old man addressed the assembly. In a few well-chosen words of quiet, manly dignity, he told them that this young *gentleman*—putting a peculiarly scornful emphasis on the word—had asked him to administer the sacrament of baptism, and as a humble minister of the Scottish Church he felt no hesitation in complying with the request. 'But,' said he, 'it must be done according to the formulas of that Church, and I will accordingly invite you to accompany me in prayer.' Then baring his venerable head, while his silver hair streamed in the breeze, he offered up an eloquent petition; and being a man of rare eloquence and fervour, he administered a scathing rebuke to the scoffers and completely subdued the feelings of all around.

Next, with a proud glance, and in ringing accents, in which those who knew him best might have detected a lurking trace of grim, defiant humour, he asked the rather chapfallen and now hesitating scoffer to 'stand forward.' The magnetic force of the old apostle compelled instant obedience.

Addressing him in crisp, clear-cut tones, he said, with a sharp Highland accent :—

'Now, sir! you want your puppy dog bapteezed? Well, sir, I can only, as I have said, perform the ceremony in accordance with the regulations and formulas of the Scottish Presbyterian Church of which I am but a humble and unworthy minister. In accordance with our custom it is necessary that I should ask you a question.' (There was a movement of interested expectation among the audience, and the culprit in the midst wriggled rather uneasily.) 'Hold up your puppy dog, sir.' There was something in the stern command which permitted of no refusal.

Clear and ringing now swelled the voice of the old minister, as amid the wonderment of the gaping crowd, quickly to be followed by peals of laughter, he thundered at the head of the abashed and disconcerted fop : 'Now, sir ! will you swear in the face of God and of this congregation that you are the father of this puppy dog ? '

The 'biter was bit,' and for the rest of the voyage the crestfallen Cockneys gave the Scottish clergy a very wide berth indeed.

As showing the homely familiarity which the friendly footing between pastor and flock engendered, and the quaintness of some of the pulpit utterances occasionally one comes across, in pursuing this course of inquiry, I am tempted to chronicle an incident told of the minister of Birse, the Rev. Joseph Smith. He was rather a quick-tempered but a kindly man ; and one hot, close, muggy Sunday he had to undergo an incessant accompaniment to the delivery of his sermon, of a rap-rap-rap, tap-tap-tapping on the lids of the snuff-boxes, with one of which it would have seemed nearly every male worshipper in the congregation was provided. Nor was this all. The snuff-takers did not assimilate the titillatory and fragrant powder *à la Versailles*, but with a directness and energy, accompanied by snorting, inhalatory sounds—if that be a permissible expression—which filled the sacred building with reverberations, and almost drowned the voice of the preacher. His irritated nerves could stand the maddening strain no longer. Suddenly he paused; and then he abashed the noisy votaries of the pungent weed by saying in his severest and most indignant manner: 'My freens! it would be a blessin' to me, an' I'm sure a blessin' to yersel's, if ye wad leave a' yer sneeshin' mulls at hame.'

As an instance of that theological dogma which Burns describes as

<blockquote>. . . a hangman's whip,</blockquote>

I might instance the following.

A boy belonging to Leochel-Cushnie was apprenticed to a joiner at Fettercairn, and one day had been sent to the ironmonger's to buy a pund o' nails. The minister happened to be in the shop, and the following dialogue took place.

Boy. I want a pund o' nails.

Ironmonger. Oh, ye want a pund o' nails, div ye? Ye'll be a strainger tae Fettercairn, ah'm thinkin'? Whaur div ye come frae?

Boy. Frae Leochel-Cushnie.

Minister (in a deep grave voice). Ay, ye come frae Leochel-Cushnie, div ye? Are there mony that fear the Lord in Leochel-Cushnie, na?

Boy. I dinna ken, sir; but there's a gey pucklie o's richt feared at the deil.

Many good stories are told of that famous but eccentric divine the Rev. Walter Dunlop of Dumfries, better known by the affectionately-meant familiarity of 'Wattie Dunlop.' He said one evening by way of homely warning at a service largely attended by young

women : 'A' you young men an' young wimmen, jist
gang straucht hame and read yer Bibles, for remember
Judas betrayed oor Saviour wi' a kiss.'

One of the best-known instances of his ready wit is,
of course, that retort to the three would-be clever cits,
who, thinking to make fun of the parson, asked him if
he had heard the news. 'What news?' said the un-
suspecting Wattie. 'Oh, the deil's deid.' 'Ah, in that
case,' instantly responded the old man, with a roguish
twinkle in his eye, 'I maun e'en pray for three
faitherless bairns.'

An old minister in the same county, Dumfries, was
much annoyed by one of his hearers, a great theologian
in his own opinion, who always would insist upon him
deducing '*doctrines*' from all his texts, as well as the
usual 'heads' and 'particulars.' One day he was pro-
voked to protest, and said to his troublesome friend :—

'But, John, ye canna deduce a doctrine from every
text.'

'I wad like to hear yin that I cudna deduce a doctrine frae!' replied John, very bumptiously.

'Well, now, what doctrine would you deduce frae
this text, John? "Jesus I know, and Paul I know; but
who art thou?"'

John's reply has not been chronicled.

Of a somewhat similar character is my next. The
theologian this time, however, was an old wifie who,
discussing matters with her minister one day, said:
'Toots, minister, ye mak' a great fash aboot preachin'
twa bits o' sermons; od onybody cud dae that; hech,
I wad undertak' that masel'!'

'Well now, Jenny,' good-humouredly replied the

minister, 'I'll just gie ye a text, an' see what ye'll mak'
o't; an' it's this : "It is better to dwell in a corner of
the house-top, than with a brawling woman, and in a
wide house." '

'What do ye mean, minister?' said Jenny, instantly
bridling up; 'do ye mean onything personal?'

'Ah,' laughed the minister, 'ye wad never do for a
preacher.'

'An' what for no, sir?'

'Oh, you come ower sune to the application.'

Away up in the north there was a parish minister
who was notoriously the prosiest and dullest of preachers,
but who was a fine character and a good pastor. One
day a cattle-dealer met him in the train, on his way to a
near market, after having heard something derogatory
to the powers of the minister as a preacher. Wishing
to pay his favourite a compliment, he said : 'Weel,
Dr. ——, they may say what they like, but ye're the
finest man in a' the pairishes roond aboot; and '—with
fine scorn—'efter a's said an' dune, wha cares for
preachin', man?'

The Rev. Mr. Haldane, on his first visit to Scotland,
was a guest of the Earl of Kintore, and preached for
the first time in his life to a Presbyterian congregation.
Having ministered most of his time in Cornwall, where
the people are most demonstrative, he was chilled by
the aspect of the congregation. Do what he could, he
could rouse no responsive emotion, and the people while
looking and listening attentively, seemed utterly cold
and impassive. He felt much discouraged, but on his
way home, in company with the Earl, they overtook an
old Scotch bodie creeping home to her humble cottage.

The Earl spoke to her a few kind words, and she said in her earnest, homely way : ' Eh, sir, but I wis dreidfu' weel pleased wi' yer Englishman the day ! '

This comforted and encouraged Mr. Haldane much, and gave him an insight into a phase of character he had not before been familiar with. But how thoroughly Scottish !

Not so complimentary was that brilliant remark of the elder who had been chosen as spokesman by a deputation to make some presentation or other to their minister in token of their regard. After stammering confusedly through various bald platitudes, and wishing in his peroration to be particularly impressive and eloquent, he said : ' In short, sir, to use the bewtifu' wirds o' Scripter, you are, sir, in truth, a soondin' bress an' a tinklin' cymbal ! '

Not less ridiculous was the *lapsus* of the reverend lecturer who, dilating on the evils of intemperance, and wishing to say that 'Drink was bad for both soul and body,' convulsed his audience by saying : ' It's bad, ma freens, for baith bowl and soddy ' ; but fairly brought the house down when, in attempting to correct himself he said : ' Tuts, I mean soddy an' bowl.'

The following witty equivoque is told of the venerable Dr. Eadie of Glasgow. He was called one evening to the house of one of his parishioners to baptize ' a bit bairnie,' and among the witnesses to the ceremony was a crotchety, officious, old maiden lady who had determined in her own mind she would take advantage of the opportunity to ' speir ' at the doctor when he was likely to finish with a rather prolonged course of lectures he had been giving on the subject of ' The Power of the Spirit.'

F

Accordingly after the christening, and when the usual hospitality common to such occasions was being exercised, the old lady sidled up to and somewhat imperiously addressed the doctor in these words : 'Ay, doctor, an' whan are ye gaun tae be dune wi' the Speerit, na?' The old doctor seizing the decanter which was within reach, and purposely misapprehending her, rejoined very coolly : 'Hoots, wumman, it'll stan' anither roond yet brawly.'

Of Patrick Robertson of Craigdam, a well-known evangelist, a good story is told, which may appropriately be introduced here.

Going home one night, he spied a drunken man prostrate in the gutter, and under the impulse of his natural kindliness, not knowing at the moment but what the poor man might be ill or even dying, he raised him up. The presumably worthy object of this solicitude, however, soon revealed the real cause of his prostration. Glowering up at his 'Good Samaritan' with bloodshot eyes, and recognising the features of the eloquent evangelist, he hiccuped out :—

'Eh, Maister Robertson, is that you? Losh, man (hic), d'ye no ken (hic) I wis ane o' yer first convairts?'

'Ay,' says Patrick dryly, and with a significant shake of the head, 'vera like *my* handiwark!'

An old minister tells this story of a Sunday School experience. The teacher had been reading the portion about 'praying for one's enemies, and doing good to those that despitefully use you,' etc. Desirous of seeing whether the boys really understood what 'enemy' meant, he began to illustrate acts of friendship, detailed acts of kindness, and so on, and then asked the class if they

could name any one who was their 'friend.' Out went
the little hands, and he appealed to one bright little
fellow, who promptly replied by saying, 'Ma Uncle.'
'Quite right,' said the teacher. Next he began to
expatiate on acts of hostility, unkindness, and so forth,
and seeing an unwonted look of intelligence on the face
of a poor suppressed sort of a neglected waif, named
'Dunkie Demster,' he asked: 'Now can any of you, if
you have such a thing, name me an enemy?'

Out went poor little Dunkie's emaciated little orphan
hand and arm.

'Well, Dunkie, who is your enemy?'

'Ma Auntie,' was the tearful answer.

Alas! what an innocent, unconscious disclosure of
cruel neglect, and the pitiless blighting of a young child's
budding affection, was contained in the artless and
pathetic reply.

An example of pawky, clerical wit, is the following :—

An old farmer in the parish was about to be married
the second time. His bride-elect had been his housekeeper. She was credited with a shrewish disposition,
was at all events a woman of no refinement, and she
simply detested the minister, who in some way or other
had managed to incur her active dislike. The farmer,
however, had completely fallen under her influence, and
she, seeing the approach of her clerical *bête noire*, told the
poor farmer that he was 'not to ask that man intill the
hoose.' The poor man scarcely knew how to account
for his lack of customary hospitality, but he lamely
excused himself to the ready-witted and shrewdly-
observant minister by saying: 'I'll no be askin' ye inbye
the day, sir, for ye see I'm aboot tae be marriet again, an'

we wis jist haein' the hoose pentit' (the usual Scottish
pronunciation of 'paint' is 'pent'). 'Ah, Robert,' said
the waggish minister, 'I houp ye'll no vera sune hae to
Re-pent it.'

But perhaps no better instance of good classic clerical
wit has ever been recorded, than the following. I do
not myself remember to have seen it in print, but I can
scarcely venture to hope that it is new to all my readers.

The dominie had taken to absent himself from church,
and being accidentally met by the minister was pressed
to give some reason for his abstention from ordinances.
The minister, douce man, had a pretty shrewd suspicion
what way the dominie's proclivities had been going of
late, from certain rumours that had reached his ears.
However, the dominie's excuse was the plea that ' he was
always so wearied on the Sunday mornings, that he
always slept in.'

'Ay, an' what div ye do with yoursel' on the
Saturdays, then ?'

'Oh,' was the plausible answer, 'we hiv startit a
leeterary club, ye see, an' we meet at ilk ither's hooses,
an'—an'—we hiv a little whisky an' discussion, read an
essay, an' so on.'

'Ah,' said the pawky pastor, 'an' I've nae doot *Esse*
has the same case efter it that it has before it.'

One more instance of the many-sidedness of the old-
time minister, and the keen, vital interest he took in all
popular and current movements, while it also illustrates
the simplicity of the women-folks in regard to politics,
is as follows :—

At an election for East Aberdeen on one occasion,
Hope of Fentonbarns was a candidate. Mr. Hope was by

belief a Unitarian, and it is just possible that the then parish minister took rather an active part in canvassing for Mr. Hope's opponent who, it may not be unfair to assume, was more orthodox. One farmer who was a regular attendant at church had pledged himself to vote for Mr. Hope, and the minister took occasion to call, in hopes of getting the pledge recalled. Notwithstanding all his persuasions and blandishments, his arguments and protestations, however, he could not get the sturdy yeoman to change his mind.

'Aweel, aweel,' at length said the astute cleric, 'jist lat's pray for guidance.' So they prayed. When they had risen from their knees the farmer's wife said : 'Noo, John, ye can shairly never vote for Fentonbarns efter sic a bee-yow-ti-fu' prayer as that !' rolling the adjective over her tongue in an ecstasy of appreciation. The result is not chronicled, but I venture to think Mr. Hope got the stalwart and loyal farmer's vote, in spite of both ministerial and conjugal influence.

A good story is told of Dr. Lindsay Alexander's old beadle. The doctor was one of the most famous and eloquent preachers of the Independent or Congregational body, and always attracted large audiences of casual hearers. A certain Sunday had been set apart to make a collection on behalf of some special object, outside the immediate personal church concern. The deacons had met in the vestry to arrange the matter, and the old beadle was busy about the fireplace cleaning it up. A discussion arose about the best time for taking up the collection—whether it should be in the morning or at the evening service. Several were for evening service, but the doctor himself thought the forenoon service would be best.   He was in a minority, however, and the deacons had decided for evening, when the old beadle effected a striking diversion, by suddenly inter- posing with a very emphatic commentary.   He said : 'Ye're quite richt, doctor, quite richt to hae't i' the mornin', for whae'll ye get i' the evenin'?   Jist a wheen Presbyterians, an' they're only worth about 3d. a dizzen.'

CHAPTER V

PRECENTORS AND PSALMODY

A defiant precentor—The old style of psalmody—A precentor's paradox—A parody of the old metre—Examples of the old, wooden, halting measure—A saintly minister's defence of the old style—The old conservatism—Examples—Dr. Roxburgh's story—A competitive breakdown—Rural high notes—Questionable punctuation—A self-possessed cantor—'The Stickit Precentor'—A ludicrous paraphrase—Auld Chairlie Broon—Stories from the *Brechin Advertiser*—The other side of the shield—Opinions of Burns and Sir Walter Scott.

FROM the pulpit to the precentor's desk is an easy gradation, and I am reminded of the anecdote of a precentor who had a very wholesome horror of the fierce, imprecatory psalms, that some of the older generation loved to roll as a sweet morsel under their tongues. The minister was of the stern, protesting, Puritan type, and in these fiery outpourings of the old Jewish patriotic spirit he no doubt saw personified in his own mind the particular individuals within his own ken who dared to hold theological opinions different to his own. So he had given out the psalm and had read with great unction and fervour :—

> His children let be vagabonds,
> His wife a widow make, etc.

With a defiant toss of the head the more humane precentor uttered a practical protest, by singing out in stentorian tones :—

> God's mercies I will ever sing, etc.

To their credit the congregation, whose practice, as was not uncommonly the case, was gentler than their creed, most heartily followed the precentor, much, no doubt, to the stern, old, Calvinistic minister's chagrin.

What a tribute to the sheer dourness and dogged thrawnness of the Scottish character, has been the persistence with which they have clung to those in large part most wooden and prosaic versions of the psalms which, with unconscious irony, they call metrical. The Sternhold and Hopkins, the Tate and Brady style of metrical architecture, is surely the most wattle and dab, lob-sided and inartistic jumble of halting numbers that has been perpetrated in the whole range of literature. How the noble imagery, the lofty and sublime diction of these inspired Hebrew singers has suffered at the hands of these most prosaic and unimaginative 'mud-daubers,' as Mark Twain would call them ! Take, for instance, the rendering of the fine oriental figure of speech, 'As he clothed himself with cursing like as with his garment,' etc. It is thus caricatured :—

> As cursing he like clothes put on,
>   Into his bowels so,
> Like water, and into his bones,
>   Like oil, down let it go.

No doubt by sheer force of association, and the intense fervour of the faith of the old Scottish people, which associated with these abortive parodies, their revolt against liturgy and ritual, and the proud asser-

tion of their own independence of thought and free right
of private judgment, the old metrical version of the
Psalms possessed charms to the older folk, which we
of the younger generation may not perhaps perceive.
Still, even the old folks are beginning now to 'thole' the
chants and renderings of the grand old psalms in their
original setting ; and the more frequent use of our rich,
poetic hymnal, and appreciation of its beauties, is a
grateful and encouraging feature in the gradual evolution of a better service of the sanctuary so far as praise
is concerned, which is fast supplanting the old, bare,
ugly, unyielding type.

It used to be positively painful, even to my young,
untrained ear, to hear the mechanical, wooden way in
which some country tyke of a precentor used to murder
the magnificent ideas enshrined in the grand old psalms,
and which even the most mechanical versifiers could not
wholly destroy.

One illustration of how a neglect of ordinary punctuation used to mix the meaning and confound the sense,
comes to me as I write. The passage properly rendered
reads thus : 'The Lord will come, and He will not keep
silence, but speak out,' etc. Reading it line by line, in
a high, nasal, snuffling drawl, our precentor used to
bellow forth :—

> The Loard wull come an' he wull not—

This would be sung in every variety of time, and with
every latitude as to tune and 'curlie-wurlie quavers.'
Then came the completion of the paradox—

> Keep silence, but speak out.

Of course the utter ugliness and naked stupidity of

some of the worst examples, gave an opening which the
irreverent and the scoffers were not slow to accept.
Parodies of an unpardonable kind were rife among the
rude, bothy hands, many of which are perfectly unread-
able; but here is one which is not so bad, as it contains
a certain ironical humour of its own. Rendered in the
old style by a jovial company, line by line, and to the
accompaniment of one of the old, quavery, minor,
drawling tunes, the effect is irresistibly ludicrous :—

> Thee langer that a Ploom-tree grows,
> Thee blacker grows thee Ploom ;
> Thee langer that a Souter shoos [sews],
> Thee blacker grows his thoom.

Hech, sirs, we had muckle to thole wi' thae auld-
farrant and most unmelodious compositions. I, for one,
dinna want to revert to the old order, in that particular
at least.

It was Dean Stanley, I think, who used to call Tate
and Brady's version not the Psalter but the 'drysalter'—
and dry enough it certainly was. What, for instance,
could be finer by way of antithesis, and from merely a
literary point of view, than the picture drawn by the
inspired songster of the uprearing of the old temple,
when all ranks and classes vied with each other in
rendering willing service towards supplying materials
for the erection of the national sacred shrine? Then
with what a fine burst of poetic fervour he depicts the
rage of the invading and alien iconoclasts, wrecking the
sanctuary in their hate and fury ; ruining the fine
carved - work on which such reverent care had been
expended ; tearing down the rich hangings, and dese-
crating the very Holy of Holies. One can almost fancy

they hear the great heart-sob of a nation's agony and shame, as the Psalmist laments over the sacrilegious and humiliating outrage.

But what do these prosaic rhymsters, who are answerable for the Scottish version, make of the picture? Can any one imagine anything so halting, so uncouth, so utterly devoid of imagination or poetic feeling? Think of it being drawled at funereal pace, in long-drawn nasal wailings, such as would have put a broken-winded bagpipe to shame, and you will have some faint idea of what our grandfathers no doubt considered the very sublimated essence of exalted praise. You must try to imagine it being sung in the old style to one of the 'curlie-wurlie' tunes. The precentor probably a note or so above the congregation, and either a yard ahead or behind it. Some fine, independent-souled possessor of a piping treble, or a basso tremolo, determined, even in the 'sacrifice of praise,' to show his right of private judgment, is probably nearly a line behind everybody else. And at the end of the verse, a few scattered solos from various parts of the church roll their quavering volume in melancholy procession and mixed pattern down the aisle. Oh, it was awful! The pronunciation, too, was of the same independent and archaic pattern, and the tunes were composed so as to give the full value of each syllable. If spelling can give any idea of how the psalmody was conducted, it was something like this :—

> A-mudst thy Coan-gree-gaa-she-oans
> Thine enneemees do-o-o-o roar ;
> Their ennsigns they set up for signs
> Oaf treeiumph thee-e-e-e befoar.

But this is the bright, particular gem :—

> A maan waas faamous, and waas haad
> In ees-stcem-aaa-shee-oan,
> Accordin' as he lufted up
> His aaxe thick trees upon.

Just think of the utter parody of the splendid poetic idea that these wooden, jolting lines suggest.

Or to give only one more sample of this archaic, almost barbarous style, let me just cite one verse which is given me as from the famous 'Zachary Boyd' version, written, presumably, with the laudable intention of bringing the Bible story down to the level of the meanest comprehension. A historic fact is thus rendered :—

> Jaacob hed a fav'rite son,
> Caa'ed by his brethren Josey ;
> The pawtriarch made a tartan coat
> For tae keep him warm an' cosy.

Now I would not for the world write anything that would seem irreverent, or would wilfully hurt the feelings even of the most sensitive, but I have had it in me to make my protest, and, after all, my feelings are shared by nearly every one of my own generation to whom I have ever spoken on the subject. I remember only one exception. He was my own cousin, the Rev. Lindsay Mackie, of the New High Church, Dunedin, N.Z. He was, I think, one of the saintliest men I have ever been privileged to know. The pure, radiant spirit within, shone through the weak veil of flesh, and he was simply beloved by every one who came within the gently compulsive spiritual power of his personality. He was our loved and honoured guest for a few of the last weeks of his stay on earth, and we had many pleasant talks together on this and cognate subjects. He had an intense love for the old metrical psalms, but when one probed and analysed the feeling, even he himself had to confess that it was all, or nearly all, due to the power of association. It was because he had learned them at his loved mother's knee principally, I think, that they so commended themselves to him. He could not with any great heart defend the metre or the setting of the noble ideas, and I noted that in his reading he always fell back with apparent relief to the much more poetic rendering of the prose version.

Well, we are a persistent race, and in some things— chiefly those that concern the emotions and round which sentiment has gathered—we are about the most unyielding conservatives among Western peoples; but I am glad to see the change that has come over the service of praise, and the use of music and poetry in the public worship of Christian people since I was a boy, and I would not now be content to revert to the old order.

As an instance of the hidebound, obstinate, old conservatism, the dogged unwillingness to accept any innovation, no matter how reasonable, I think the following is very characteristic.

An evangelistic meeting was being organised in an Aberdeenshire parish, at which the conductors wished to introduce a few hymns, which at that time were quite a novelty and considered by some an ungodly innovation. Printed papers containing the hymns had been circulated among the worshippers, but they had been accepted with an icy frigidity and a suspicious sort of thrawn aversion. As soon as the first hymn was given out, a voice from the audience cried out in the broadest vernacular : ' Fat's wrang wi' the Psawlms o' Dauvit ?'

Another illustration of the same feeling is as follows:—

In a drowsy parish not very far from Lochnagar, a new precentor strove to raise the standard of the old drawling, slovenly psalmody, by introducing newer and livelier tunes, and organising among the younger members of the congregation, an effective choir. The innovation was looked on with sour disfavour by the elders and the minister, who was one of the old unyielding school. One morning the precentor and choir had sung the portion of psalm given out, to one of the new tunes, in which, either from inability or perverseness, not any of the congregation had joined. The rugged old minister after it was finished rose, and said with cutting sarcasm : ' The precentor and his choir having sung, nae doot, to their ain satisfaction, let *us*, ma freens' (laying tremendous emphasis on the *us*), ' now unite in singing to the praise and glory of God in the Hundert Psawlm.'

The Rev. Narayan Shashadri, an Indian native missionary, who visited Scotland some time ago, gave a friend of mine a striking instance of this same feeling—this dogged aversion to change. He had been speaking on this very subject to a good old Scottish elder, telling him the natives of India could really never derive any spiritual good from such objectionable metre, judged from a modern literary standpoint ; and he very frankly confessed his own preference for hymns. The old fellow slowly shook his head, pursed up his lips, and a dogged look came into his eyes, as he said rather ungraciously, but very emphatically: ' Humph ! Dauvit's no deid yet, for a' that !'

The late Dr. Roxburgh of Free St. John's, Glasgow, used to tell a most ludicrous story of a hot-tempered man named Andrew Bell, who sat pretty far back in the

gallery. One Sabbath it would seem he had been
offering some sweeties to two young women between
whom he had got seated, and he had not perhaps been
very attentive to the minister's intimation of the Psalm.
Psalm 45th and 9th had been given out—

> Among thy women hon'rable
> Kings' daughters were at hand ;
> Upon thy right hand did the queen
> In gold of Ophir stand.

But it was when the precentor, who in his private
capacity was a spindle-shanked tailor, began in his broad,
drawling Doric to read out line by line, as was then the
custom, that Andrew's face began to grow red, and a
sulky look to come into his eyes ; and no wonder, for
this is exactly how the first line sounded as the precentor
intoned it :—

> Amang thy weemen Aun'ra Bell !

The people sitting around tittered, and the lassies
tittered, but Aun'ra looked wrathful. After service he
interviewed the precentor, clutched him by the lugs, and
as he ' dauded ' his head on the wall he hissed out with
concentrated fury : ' That's tae ye, an' that's tae ye, for
pintin' me oot amang the weemen ! '

My hearty, hospitable, and humorous friend of George
Square, Edinburgh, several of whose contributions I have
already given, narrates a most ludicrous episode, of which
he and his wife were actual eye-witnesses, and which
most graphically illustrates the old free-and-easy style
of conducting this most important element in public
worship. It was in a kirk in 'The Lothians,' presided
over by the Rev. Dr. S——, who was perhaps more
of an antiquarian and geologist than an ecclesiastic ;

but on this particular occasion there happened to be in
progress a contested election for the post of precentor.
It had come to the turn of one candidate who evidently
did not know the difference between long and short
metre, or perhaps he simply had no long-metre tunes in
his *repertoire*. At all events the reverend doctor gave
out the 145th Psalm, second version, and somewhere
near the end of the psalm. The precentor started with
a short-metre tune, and of course managed the first and
third lines all right. At the second and fourth lines, however, the exigencies of the metre were too much for his
melody ; but he was in no way abashed, and very coolly
just left out the two extra syllables, and ignored them as
if they were non-existent. When he came to the 20th
verse he sang it thus (I leave out the two excised syllables
at a little distance apart from the body of the verse) :—

> The Lord preserves all, more and less,
> That bear to him a lov—— ing heart :
> But workers all of wickedness
> Destroy will he, and clean—— subvert.

When he came to 'clean' it was too much even for the
easy-going minister. Leaning over the pulpit, he tapped
the songster on the head, and said : 'Sit doon, man ! sit
doon ! that'll no dae ava'.'

My friend also tells me a most ludicrous episode of
which he too was an eye-witness. It happened in the
parish church of Kirkmabreck, a secluded parish in Kirk-
cudbrightshire, on the shores of Wigton Bay. Mr. I——
happened to be attending the church on this particular
morning, and being a trained musician himself, and for
more than thirty years past, a leading member of the
choir in one of our prominent Edinburgh churches, he

was at once conscious that the rural precentor had pitched the opening tune much too high, and was not a little curious and concerned to see how he would get out of the difficulty. With sublime unconcern, however, the singer held on 'the even tenor of his way,' and as soon as he came to a note that was fairly beyond his register, he simply looked up to the roof, set his mouth into the form the lips assume when one wishes to emit the soft whistle of surprise, and then with a sickly smile he would just go on as if he had some invisible choir behind him, who had taken up the high notes for him, and passed them safely into circulation. My friend added, 'The whole thing was so irresistibly comic that I had to leave the building.'

Another function of the precentor was analogous to that of the clerk in an English church, I suppose—that is, he had to make announcements if any one were ill, and in relation to matters of that sort—but even here it would seem there was the same sublime and wholesale disregard of the ordinary rules of punctuation — at least so we may judge from the famous and oft-quoted example, in which the precentor wishing, on behalf of a poor sailor's wife, to ask the prayers of the congregation for her husband, who was about to begin a long voyage, gave it out as if it read thus: 'A sailor going to see (sea) his wife, desires the prayers of the congregation.'

Occasionally, however, the precentor proved himself quite equal to any emergency, and, as in the following case, showed admirable *sang froid* and imperturbable self-possession. It was a stranger minister who was occupying the pulpit, and he gave out and read the 148th

Psalm, second version, which is one of the few constructed on what is known as peculiar metre.   It goes thus—

> The Lord of heaven confess,
> On high his glory raise, etc.

The precentor was for the moment a little non-plussed, but in a few minutes his native good-sense and coolness came to his succour, and he solved the difficulty and relieved the suspense of the congregation by calmly saying : 'Ay, sirss, I've nae tune for this, so we'll jist sing the first vairshon.'

Mr. G—— a distinguished student of St. Andrews, and who has since more than confirmed the promise of his student days by making a famous name for himself as a ripe scholar and *litterateur*, details a ludicrous episode of his college days, by which he earned the title of 'The Stickit Precentor.'   He had gone to a meeting with a fine, earnest, young companion, who was doing a good work among the fisher folk, and who had pressed Mr. G—— into the service as he had a good voice.   Mr. G—— willingly consented to do all he could in the way of starting the tune.   A suitable psalm was accordingly given out, and quite forgetting the then usual custom of reading line by line, Mr. G—— started the tune, and imagined he had nothing but plain-sailing ahead of him.   At the conclusion of the first line, however, and just as he was gathering breath for a continuation of the melody, a gruff voice at his elbow almost 'made his heart leap into his mouth,' and completely put all memory of the tune out of his head, by ejaculating : 'Young man, just read oot the seecont line ; I'm blin'.'   G—— read the line, but for the

life of him could not continue the tune, and that was
the first and the last time he ever essayed the task of
trying to be a precentor.

Another ludicrous story *in re* the reading of the lines,
is told of an absent-minded precentor, slightly dull of
hearing, who had somehow failed to catch the opening
intimation of the psalm, and, to make matters worse,
had forgotten his spectacles. Trusting to memory, and
to the minister reading the lines, he was, however, to all
appearance, quite up to his usual pitch of proficiency.
The minister read out very impressively—

> Like pelican in wilderness
> Forsaken I have been.

The poor precentor, whose ornithological knowledge
must have been sadly dubious, startled the congregation
considerably, and awoke their sense of humour, by
gravely taking up the response thus—

> A paitrick in a wild-deuk's nest,
> The like wis never seen !

I am told by my dear old aunt Margaret, the last
surviving now of her generation, but as full as ever of
the kindly humour and gentleness which have endeared
her to three generations of kinsfolks and neighbours,
that my grandfather had an oddity in the shape of a
servant named Auld Chairlie Broon. Chairlie was the
minister's man *par excellence*, and performed all the duties
appertaining to that onerous office ; but in addition,
when my grandfather went over to Birse to hold an
occasional service there, Chairlie was the vessel chosen
to officiate as precentor. His *repertoire* being limited,

and knowing the value of hearty co-operation, and the
device even of a notice-board not having been hit upon
in that primitive community, Chairlie used to walk up
the aisle after the minister, and nudge the sitter at
the end of each pew, notifying his tune to each, in some
such fashion as this : ' Mawthers, billies, Mawthers,'
which signified 'Martyrs, lads, Martyrs !' that being his
favourite and almost only tune.

I may dismiss the subject of precentors and psalmody
fitly, however, by a short extract from a very interesting
and readable article in that most ably conducted and
always lively provincial journal, the *Brechin Advertiser*,
which reached me after I had written this chapter.
Among much that is capitally told, and was to me
deeply interesting, the author of the article writes as
follows :—

'The length of the psalms often render curtailment
necessary, and at the present day it is very seldom that
a composition is sung without some verses being omitted.
The longest of the translations is, as is well known, the
119th. It is related of one minister that he once gave out
this particular psalm, and then, without announcing how
many stanzas were to be sung, sat down in the pulpit and
fell asleep. The precentor, faithful to his duty, struggled
bravely on until one hundred and twenty-two lines had
been reached, when he sank exhausted. His heroism,
however, did not go unrewarded; he was known ever
afterwards as "the leather-lunged precentor." [I am
sorely afraid, however, this story is apocryphal.]

'It was, possibly, the reward meted out to that
musician which made his brother precentor call a halt
at the fourth verse. The worthy divine, in intimating

the psalm, announced a portion (running to a rather large number of verses) to be sung. The "Master of the Song," however, considered the thing preposterous, and closed with the fourth stanza. The minister, noting the occurrence, leaned over the pulpit and remarked : "Man, Jamie, if ye mak' sic a wark aboot skirlin' oot four single verses, hoo d'ye think ye're to manage to sing psawms thro' a' the ages o' eternity ? " '

I am certainly free to confess, in summing up the matter, that amid much that is wooden and stilted, there are many noble verses, that rise to the height of true poetry, even in our Scottish metrical version. In the modern collection of Sacred Song, happily coming into almost general use in Presbyterian churches all the world over, and known as 'Church Praise,' there has been a most laudable attempt to winnow the chaff from the wheat and to exercise a judicious selection, although even in this, there are many that are namby-pamby and otherwise weak. The first fatal error seems to me to have been due to the old clinging idea, amounting almost to a superstitious sort of fetichism, that 'all Scripture' was of equal spiritual value. So it was considered necessary that every scrap of the Jewish Psalter which, as most folks know now, is a collection of at least five books, written by numerous authors and covering a literary period of centuries, should be rendered into the metrical—shall I say tag-raggery ? that has so excited my possibly too outspoken disapproval.

In common fairness, however, I should put on record, side by side with my adverse criticism, the fact that the old metrical version has afforded deep spiritual delight to thousands of the noblest and saintliest of Scotia's sons. And indeed there are scattered, here and there through the collection, many gems of rare poetic merit. What, for instance, could be finer than the stately, solemn sweep of 'The Old Hundredth'? 'All people that on earth do dwell'; or that special favourite, wedded to the fine sonorous measure of 'French'? 'I to the hills will lift mine eyes'; or the grand Old 103rd? 'O thou my soul, bless God the Lord,' etc.; and perhaps one of the most exalted of the whole, also wedded to a magnificent tune, 'Invocation'? 'O send thy light forth and thy truth,' etc.

Even Burns, whose wayward genius was not as a rule much influenced by pious emotions, gives a touching tribute to the old psalms in the memorable lines—

> When noble 'Elgin' beets the heav'nward flame,
> The sweetest far o' Scotia's holy lays.

Sir Walter Scott, too, called for the Scottish version when on his deathbed, and his opinion of its merit and beauty is recorded in his Journal, and in his letter to, I think, Principal Baird, was it not? when he was asked to assist in preparing a new version.

Nor is his, the only name of note among the admirers of what I have found so little provocative of tender emotions, as compared with many of our ancient and modern hymns, but these honoured names may well be set off against my possibly bad taste and unappreciative ear.

CHAPTER VI

KIRKYAIRDS, SEXTONS, AND BURIALS

The old-time neglect—Modern changes—Slack trade for the sexton
—'Little daein' i' the yaird'—Wounded vanity—'A sair
time'—A philosophic widower—'The cold grave'—A
phlegmatic pitman—'Beelzebub's bosom'—The Inverarity
grave-digger—The sexton's grievance—'Dangerous to meddle
wi' the kirk'—The old-time callousness—'A sair hoast'—
'Thae Kidds'—A too rapid hearse—'Steady wark'—'A
respeckfu' distance'—A dry retort—A 'popular' functionary
—A story from *Punch*—Dr. Kidd and his beadle—The rival
bells and betherals.

NOTHING perhaps illustrates more forcibly yet pleasingly
the change in social custom during the present century,
than the usages observed at funerals and in connection
with bereavement, the care of cemeteries, and the various
ceremonies and customs consequent on, and associated
with, the last sad common lot of poor humanity. In
former times public sentiment in regard to these matters
was certainly at a very low pass. Indeed, it might with
truth be said that sentiment in the modern sense apparently did not exist. Cemeteries were shunned as if they
were plague-spots. The mural adornments—save the
mark—were of the most repulsive and ugly character.

There was no attempt made to adorn the enclosure with flowers and shrubbery.   The surrounding wall was generally a tumble-down, rickety structure, half hidden in rank nettles and docks, and the same rank, unsightly herbage ran riot all over the sacred enclosure.   Possibly this callous, almost ostentatious, disregard of the commonest sentiment for adornment, or even for cleanliness and neatness, was part of the austere Puritanic reaction against the excessive luxury and overdone ornamentation of monkish times, to which I have already alluded, when ritual, pomp, display, and mere formality, had almost smothered all spirituality out of worship.   Be that as it may, it was undoubtedly a characteristic of the times of our grandfathers, this callous, seemingly hard, matter-of-fact, and certainly unlovely treatment of death and sepulture.   Let any one compare the stories that are preserved in every collection of Scottish anecdote, bearing on this point, with the care and reverence and tender regard we bestow on our cemeteries, and manifest in connection with bereavement nowadays, and the comparison is all in favour of the modern methods as against ' the times of former years.'

And if the popular sentiment was thus harsh and callous and cold-blooded, what must have been the mental attitude of the mere professional, the hireling, whose office it was to attend to the purely mechanical duties attendant on the disposal of the dead?   So it is that many of the stories about betherals and sextons, are of such a character that in the light of our humaner and more refined present-day sentiment, they appear almost incredibly cruel and cold-blooded.   Funeral stories seem almost brutally irreverent and heartless,

and yet ever and anon a gleam of grim humour breaks
through, which irresistibly betrays the peculiarly paradoxical side of the Scottish character, and makes these
stories tell as in a photograph, the true minute elements
and effects, which go to make up the complete picture of
the complex character of the old-time Scot. In this, as
in most things else, example has been found better than
precept. Sweet and gentle natures had mourned over
the slovenliness and ugliness of the old *régime ;* fiery-
tongued 'sons of thunder' had denounced the blemish
from many a pulpit ; pamphleteers and pressmen had
lampooned and satirised and tongue-lashed the hoary
iniquity ; but still the nettle and the dock held possession
of the kirkyaird, and the sexton and undertaker between
them, outraged all decency in their treatment of the
dead, and added 'burdens grievous to be borne' to the
already sad load which weighed down the weary heart
of the lonely and the bereaved. Gray in his *Elegy* spoke
truly when he described the churchyard as 'this neglected
spot.'

Slowly reforms, however, made their way. Hand in
hand with municipal and sanitary reforms, improvements
in the disposition and laying out of cemeteries became
increasingly manifest. As is customary, the old abuses
lingered longest in the rural districts ; but even here,
let any one remember or look back, as I can do, to what
the ordinary parish kirkyard was some forty years ago,
and see what the same solemn spot is now. Instead of
rank vegetation and the abomination of callous neglect,
there are trim paths, close-cut sward, the exquisite
glow of flowers, and the sweet, solemn shade of suitable
foliage, to say nothing of the artistic monuments and

the simple, tasteful headstones; and though there is still much room for improvement, one cannot fail to note the wondrous change that has made almost all things connected with our burial customs new and better.

A story which 'went the rounds' some time ago about the Inverarity grave-digger's wife serves to illustrate some of the points I have just touched upon. The minister had called in to see the sexton, but he happened to be away from home. The wife was there, but she looked very sad and depressed. Asked if there was anything the matter, she answered 'No,' but with such a heavy sigh and woe-begone expression that the kindly man pressed his inquiry, and insisted on knowing the trouble that was so evidently oppressing her. Was it 'onything ado wi' the weans?' 'No, they were a' richt.' 'Onything ado wi' John, then?'

The poor wife, being quite won over by the sympathy which was so rare yet so softening, was at length induced to unburden herself. In quite a burst of confidence she disclosed the source of her discomfort by saying :—

'Weel, ye see, minister, there's been sae michty little daein' i' the yaird lately' (referring to the unpardonable healthiness and longevity of the people) 'that John's clean doon-herted. Wad ye beleeve it, sir, he's berrit naethin' for the lest sax weeks but joost a wee bit scart o' a wean?'

Some time afterwards a worthy leather merchant of Edinburgh happened during a business tour to call on the 'betheral' of, let us say, Crossmyloof, who was by trade a shoemaker. My friend had booked his order (I had the story from his own lips), and over the mild refreshment with which they were sealing the compact, he said jocularly, referring to the above story :—

'Aweel! is there onythin' daein' i' the yaird the noo?'

'No, man! naethin' ava'!'

'What? No even the "scart o' a wean"?'

'No! Not even that muckle!'

'Toots, man! ye maun be ahint the times. Ye canna be keepin' up yer style, I'm thinkin'. Ye see, a'body wants a fine-got-up kirkyaird noo, wi' flooers, an' graivel walks, an' gran' ornymints, so you may depend they're gaun past ye!'

'No, no, min! 'Deed no! I assure ye we've dune a' that—an', 'deed, if they're no pleased wi' Crossmyloof, we can e'en tak' them past it in a new hearse, an' on tae ——' (naming the next parish), 'if they *maun* hae a chainge.'

How thoroughly Scottish! What other people on the face of the earth would have managed to be jocularly pawky on such a subject?

A whimsical illustration of wounded vanity and pettishness comes to me from a Brechin correspondent. A leading member of a respected family in the Damacre Road had died, and through some inadvertence the members of one family of neighbours had not received the usual formal invitation to the funeral. This was resented bitterly as a deliberate social slight, and in confiding their trouble to the minister some time afterwards, one offended old lady of the family said: 'Hech! we wisna askit tae Mr. ——'s funeral; but ne'er mind, sir, we'll hae a funeral o' oor ain some day, and then we'll ken fa tae speir.'

Another is about a man who had lost three wives,

and was being made the subject of some commiseration by a friendly gentleman. He very quaintly expressed his sense of his losses, by saying querulously : ''Deed, sir, fat wi' the bringing o' them here, and the pittin' o' them awa', I've haen a sair time o't.'

This recalls a somewhat similar anecdote told me by the Rev. A. Osborne, our much-esteemed neighbour for some years at Burwood, Sydney, N.S.W., and now the respected minister of Martyrs' Church, Dundee. He used to tell of an old Highland farmer, who at the burial of his first wife had had, with the mourners, to trudge a long distance through the heather, to the ancestral burying-ground on a sweltering hot day. What with the intense heat, their heavy burden, and the grief natural to the occasion, the poor man had narrowly escaped an attack of heat-apoplexy. Some years afterwards he had to perform a similarly mournful function on the occasion of the burial of his second wife ; but the physical conditions were entirely altered this time, as the ceremony had to be performed in the midst of a raging snow-storm, when the party of mourners had been nearly smothered in the drift, and almost paralysed by the icy grip of the terrific frost. The minister attempted some kindly consolation as the grave was being filled in, and said very sympathisingly : 'Really, John, you have had more than the usual share of sorrow in your lot.' To which the philosophic widower replied : ''Deed, sir, ye may weel say that, for fat wi' bein' yae time near burnt up wi' the heat, an' the neist time nearly smored i' the snaw drift, I'm thinkin' if I hae anither errent o' the kind, I'll hae tae treat masel' tae a hearse.'

Yet another rather shocking story illustrative of this

apparent callousness on the part of a bereaved husband, but which after all may have been the cool, philosophic way of making the best of a bad business, which is certainly part of the practical, matter-of-fact, Scottish character so frequently met with on the East Coast, may be given here.

An old fisherman had lost his wife. She had long been ailing, and indeed at her best had never been a very sweet consort. Her death might therefore have been looked upon as a happy release for both parties; but the minister, as in duty bound, felt it incumbent upon him to call on the bereaved one to offer the stereotyped condolences. On the way he called in upon an old woman, and in the course of conversation stated that he was going up to see Sandie Gillespie to condole with him on the loss of his wife.

'Hech!' said the old bodie with a snort of derision, 'ye needna fash yersel', for, gin a' stories be true, Sandie's gaen tae be mairriet again almost immediately.'

'Toots, havers, wumman!' said the minister. 'He surely cudna be sae far lost tae decency as that? Why, his wife canna be cauld in her grave yet!'

'Aweel, meenister, that is jist fat I hear, onyw'y.'

Away then sped the good minister on his kindly mission, and drawing near to Sandie's cottage he spied him sitting at the door mending his nets, and thus accosted him :—

'Weel, Sandie, so poor Kirsty's gone.'

'Ou ay, meenister,' responded the fisherman.

'It'll be a sair loss tae ye, nae doot?'

'Weel, I dinna ken,' said Sandie. 'She's maybe as weel awa'.'

The minister thought to himself that the bereavement was sitting very lightly on his phlegmatic friend, and having a slight feeling of indignation at the remarks he had heard, he said :—

'Surely there can be no truth in what I have been hearing, that you're contemplating another marriage shortly ? '

'And fat for no, sir ? '

'Why, bless me,' said the minister, 'you could surely never outrage public sentiment in this fashion ? You could not surely be so callous as to take to yourself another wife, while the mortal remains of your faithful companion for so many years are scarcely cold in the grave yet ? '

'Och ! ' said Sandie, 'that disna bather me. Ye see, sir, I've made up ma mind. But I'll no be mairriet yet for anither fortnicht, an', in the meantime, ye ken, Kirsty can aye be coolin'.'

But the same phlegmatic resignation (if such apparently heartless unconcern can be called by such a name) is evidently not altogether confined to Scotchmen, though it would seem to be a characteristic of the north-country folk, as the following Tyneside episode would seem to exemplify. A rough old tyke of a pitman had lost his bairn, and one of his mates had dropped in to condole with him, over a pot of beer.

'Weel, Dan, so ye've lost wee Danny ! Weel, weel, he wis a bonnie baarn ! '

'Ay, George, laad, he wis a fine wean. Man, gin it hedna been agin' the laaws, me an' the mither wid a' hed 'im stuffed ! '

To modern sensibility such grim matter-of-factness, if I may coin the substantive, seems truly shocking, and yet it was quite characteristic of the old-time pit folk. Indeed, I am not so very sure if they are much better even now.

The same calmly philosophic attitude of mind, while betraying a somewhat dubious and mixed knowledge of Scripture characters, is evidenced by the next anecdote which comes uppermost. It was at a funeral in my native county. All the old gossips of the clachan had gathered in the house of mourning. Just as the coffin-lid was about to be screwed down, an officious old busybody called out to the poor depressed father :—

'Come awa', John Duthie, an' kiss yer deid baub ; it's in Beelzebub's bosom noo.'

' Na, na, 'umman !' interposed another beldam, wishing to show her superior knowledge, 'it's Awbraham's boasom.'

' Oh, nivver mind, it mak's na. It's ami' them !' was the cool reply. (It makes no odds; it is among them ; it is one or the other.)

I but now referred to the wife of the Inverarity sexton, but quite as characteristic an anecdote is told of the worthy man himself.

It seems he had been waited upon by a neighbouring laird, who wanted to arrange for a plot in the churchyard, or as John thus put it—

' Oh ay ! ye'll be wantin' a lair ?'

' Yes ; just so.'

' Od, man, there's no mony left to wale noo.'

' Hoo wad ye like tae lie, sir ?'

' Well, John,' said the laird, amused and interested, 'I'm no very parteeclar. There's nae rule in the maitter, is there ?'

'Oh, nane ava'. Ilka ane can suit themsels. It's a' a maitter o' taste. There's oor lest minister ower there, for instance. He lies east an' wast. His wife lies here. She's nor' an' sooth. Ay, ay, they wir coonter a' their days, an' they're coonter yet.'

'But ye'll hae chosen a gude spot for yersel', John?'

'Ou ay! I'll be laid doon there, jist closs by the yett.'

'But that's surely a rather exposed sort of place? What made ye choose that?'

'Weel, ye see, sir, by a' accoonts, at the uprisin', there's like tae be a michty swatter o' fowk, an' if I lie here, I'll mebbe hae some chance o' gettin' oot afore the thrang.'

The sexton was, indeed, a character of no little importance in the old Scottish rural economy, and he generally lost nothing by want of self-consciousness. It was his wont 'to magnify his office,' and not unfrequently he would sourly resent any interference by either session or minister, with what he chose to consider his exclusive domain and functions. One such had bitterly resented some fancied invasion of his rights and privileges by the minister, who, as it happened, was a preacher of the 'gey dreich' kind. At any rate, John was one day confiding his grievance to a sympathising friend, who, wishing to administer comfort, ventured to remark: 'Never mind, John, mebbe he'll get a call tae some ither pairish.' 'Na!' snapped out the 'man o' mools,' 'deil a call he'll get, till I get a grup o' him.'

But even better than John's shrewd estimate of the minister's chances of preferment, was the smug estimate

of his own importance, which is illustrated by the next
on my list.

He, too, was beadle and sexton, for pluralists were
not unknown even in the days of old; and like not a
few modern pluralists both in church and state, he was
rather 'a loose fish.' Multiplied official duties do not
always mean added moral excellence. Well, at all
events, John's peccadilloes had become so flagrant, that
the session had felt it to be their painful duty to
summon him before their august tribunal, and had there
and then administered a rebuke of a length and severity
commensurate with the heinousness of the offence, and
the high official rank of the offender. You may depend
upon it this was for long a 'fly in the ointment' of
John's otherwise peaceful and uneventful career.
Poor John thought he had lived down the painful
episode; but what merit was ever proof against 'envy,
malice, and all uncharitableness'? One unlucky night,
John found himself in the village 'cheenge hoose.'
He got seduced into a heated argument with a scoffer,
'a Son of Belial,' and, sad to say, he lost his temper
and misca'ed his opponent with much vigour. Naturally this led to reprisals, and what is called in the
Mearns 'back-chat.' So it was not long ere John
was twitted with a whole catalogue of carefully-
treasured and well-remembered errors and delin-
quencies. 'The unkindest cut of all' was administered
when the unblushing opponent hissed out: 'At ony
rate ye canna say that ever *I* wis hed up afore the
session.' But great natures rise to the emergency when
the testing time comes. Suddenly John became
bland, then a look of impressive dignity took the

H

place of passion, as he solemnly delivered judgment thus : 'Ay, ay, man ! nae doot. But ye see it's no sae safe mebbe tae meddle wi' the kirk as ye think. Man !'— then a solemn pause—'Man, sin that day I've happit five o' them.'

Dozens of instances might be adduced in proof of my assumption that we have gentler, humaner, and altogether more refined manners than were common, at all events among the common folks, some two or three generations ago. For instance, it was not at all thought uncommon or unfeeling for an affectionate daughter to say of an aged parent : 'Ay, his flannens are gettin' geyan frail ; it's aboot time he wis deid.'

Another instance too of dry, pawky humour on the part of one of these beadle folk may not inaptly come in here.

Saunders was troubled with 'a sair hoast,' was, in fact, a victim to chronic asthma, and like another of the craft of whom I have spoken, he was not on very affectionate terms with his minister. One day while Saunders was digging a grave, the worthy clerical incumbent came up, and just then Saunders was seized with a violent paroxysm of coughing. He was forced for the moment to suspend operations, and as he was leaning on his spade wiping his eyes, the minister said : 'That's a very bad cough you've got, Saunders !' 'Ay, it's no vera gude,' answered Saunders very dryly. 'Still there's a hantle fowk lyin' roon' aboot ye there, sir, that wud be gey gled to hae the like o't.'

A curious instance of that tendency of habit and custom to blunt the feelings, and give a professional sort of twist to our way of looking at things, to which

I have already referred, is the reply of the old sexton to a visitor who had entered into conversation with him about some of the inscriptions on the headstones. Noticing the weather-beaten appearance of the old man, the visitor, having been led into a sort of sadly reflective train of thought, said :—

' Ye'll have been a long time here, I daresay ? '

' Ou ay ! ' said the chirpy old gossip, ' I've been beadle and saxton here, for mae nor thretty years.'

' Dear me ! what changes you must have seen ! I suppose, now, you must have buried at least one member or more out of every family in the parish in that time ? '

' Ay, gey near't. A' but yin.' This was said quite cheerily. Then, as if with a sense of some slight injustice, and somewhat complainingly, he added : ' But there's thae Kidds, noo. They hivna sae muckle as brokken grund yet.'

A much coarser instance of this almost brutal callousness, was told me by a friend who assured me he had himself been present when it occurred. He gave me name and date ; but it may suffice that it was at a funeral in Rutherglen. The chief mourner was a very fat, short-winded man, not very refined, and they were burying his wife. It was a hot, dusty day, and the cortège had insensibly quickened its funereal pace after leaving the precincts of the town, and the hearse was now rolling along at an accelerated speed, much too quick for the corpulent and perspiring widower, who was pounding along, blowing and snorting like a grampus—wiping his bald head, and almost ' larding the lean earth ' as he walked. Even his fellow-mourners, with a sense of humour which could not be restrained, were disposed to

be decorously and slyly mirthful at his expense. At
length he could stand the pace no longer. To a friend
walking beside him, whose girth and condition were
much akin to his own, he said savagely : 'Hech ! I'll
sune stop this.' Then hailing the utterly oblivious and
unconcerned driver of the hearse, he called out : 'Hi !
hi ! hi ! man ! What the —— *your* hurry ? D'ye think
we stealt the corp ? ' The Edinburgh folk dearly love to
tell this story, as an instance of west country experience.
Of course the decent Glesca bodies stigmatise it as
viciously apocryphal.

A good story is told in this connection, of the
late Rev. Mr. Barty of Ruthven. He was a fine
specimen of the pawky, hùmorous, Scottish minister
of the olden time. A vacancy had occurred in the
office of sexton, and one Peter Hardie had made
application for the appointment. Ruthven is a very
small parish, consisting then, at all events, of only
five farms. The rate per head having been duly
fixed, and the minister and Peter having just about
closed the agreement, Peter, with a keen eye to number
one, ventured the query : 'But am I to get steady wark,
sir ? ' 'Keep's a', Peter,' answered Mr. Barty, 'wi' steady
wark ye'd bury a' the pairish in a fortnicht ! '

Of the beadle's sense of his own importance perhaps
no more telling instance could be given, than that related
by a well-known and eminent divine not so very long
ago. He happened to be officiating for one of his
clerical brethren, and naturally felt somewhat diffident
in a strange church. He had duly undergone the
searching, and, as he fancied, somewhat sour scrutiny
of the solemn old beadle, and as that important function-

ary was about to leave the vestry with 'the books,' preparatory to placing them on the pulpit cushion, the preacher asked whether he should come on at once, or wait for a few further minutes.

John was pleased to give his directions thus :—

'Weel, sir, ye can jist follow at a *respeckfu'* distance.'

This reminds me of yet another, in which the good old democratic spirit of sturdy independence as well as the dry, acrid, plain-spokenness of the Scot appears.

A clergyman of notoriously unpunctual habits had made an engagement to supply the pulpit of a neighbouring parish. As usual with him, he arrived about ten minutes after the proper time, and bustling in, he said to the old beadle whom he found in the vestry :—

'Ah, Peter, I'm afraid I am late.'

'Oh, nae waur than usual!' was the dry response.

But perhaps one of the very best of the multitudes of beadle stories, is that in which the minister came off second best from the rencontre with his bibulous officer. Indeed these stories all have a family resemblance in this respect: it is generally the poor minister that gets the worst of it. The story goes, however, that on this occasion, John had been sent round the parish to distribute 'The Monthly Visitor,' and returning from his perambulatory office, it became abundantly evident to even the most casual observer that the hospitality of the parish had been partaken of 'not wisely, but too well.' In fact, poor John, in a confused, obfuscated sort of way, seemed to be conscious of this himself, and he was endeavouring to slink into his usual quarters behind the manse, when, as ill luck would have it, he came full tilt

against the minister himself, who had been to the back of
the house to break up some kindling wood for the study fire.
The worthy man was wroth. He had been out a dozen
times looking for John, whose duty it was to provide
fuel, as well as distribute tracts, dig graves, and do other
odd jobs. John tried to assume an attitude and a look
of dignified sobriety, but the unsteady gait and a most
pestilent and ill-timed hiccup, betrayed his weakness.
The wrathful cleric, finding his worst suspicions confirmed, and mindful of half an hour's arduous and
enforced toil with a blunt axe, which should have been
part of John's heritage, at once opened out on the
blinking, swaying tract-distributer, and treated him to a
regular jobation. He was admonished in most minatory
terms for showing such a pernicious example. He was
reminded of his official position and what was due to
that. He was preached at, and charged, and chidden,
till at length the dourness and underlying thrawnness
of his character was roused, and when at length the
worthy minister had about exhausted the vials of his
wrath, he again asked John what possible excuse he had
to offer for the disgraceful state he appeared in.

Amid intervening hiccups, John was understood very
sulkily and somewhat defiantly to say, that acting on the
mistress's instructions he had 'been taken frae his wark.
It was nae job o' his seekin'. But he hed been roon'
the pairish wi' the monthly tracks, and he micht mebbe
confess till haein' hed a dram, or mebbe twa, but surely
naething to mak' sic a michty wark aboot.'

This lame and unsatisfactory defence with its under-
note of defiance but added fuel to the minister's flaming
indignation, and after another vigorous outburst he

wound up by saying it ' was a burning shame and a disgrace to see a church-officer in such a state.'

'Roond the pairish, forsooth !' spluttered the indignant minister. 'Roond the pairish ! That, sir, is but
an aggravation of your offence. That, sir, but circulates
the knowledge of your backsliding, and advertises and
proclaims your wicked self-indulgence. Roond the
pairish, indeed. Ye see *me* gang roond the pairish often
eneuch, but did ye ever see *me* come home in such a
state ?'

Really this was too much. John's patience was
exhausted ; rebellion reigned ; prudence was stifled ;
the old Adam raged. But just then the saving salt of
native humour rushed to the rescue. Mastering the
first defiant impulse, and with truly Scottish pawkiness,
he made his protest thus : 'Ah, minister,' he said—and
with such a comical, pawky leer, that even in spite of his
sincere displeasure, the worthy minister could not refrain
from an inward chuckle which disarmed all his wrath—
'Ah, minister ! (hic) but YE're mebbe no a'thegither
(hic) jist sae popular as I am.'

Dear old *Punch*, the ever-green fountain of wit and
wisdom, has caught the same idea of impudent yet
humorous *insouciance* in the memorable sketch of John
and the beadle. Said his reverence :—

'John, this is a very dreadful thing. You have
heard that there is one pound missing from the box ?'

''Deed, sir, so they war tellin' me.'

Minister (very solemnly)—'But, John, you and I
alone have had access to that box.'

John (coolly)—'It's jist as ye say, sir. It maun lie
atween the twa o' us. An' the best w'y'll be for you tae

pay the tae hauf an' I'll pay the tither, an' we'll say nae mair aboot it.'

The next instance is one, however, in which the minister, contrary to the usual wont, gets rather the best of it.   The story is told of that doughty and devout old servant of God, the late Dr. Kidd of Aberdeen, and his beadle.   The kirk-officer, it would appear, was a victim, like so many of his brethren, to the national vice. He had often been severely censured, as often forgiven, and yet again would he fall into ' temptation and a snare.'   One day the worthy doctor was confronted by Jeems, so fou that all his customary caution and sleek humility had flown, and in a defiant, reckless, pot-valiant mood he challenged the burly old doctor to come and drink with him.   Recognising, with his usual ready wit, the utter futility of trying to reason with a man in such a state, and desirous of avoiding a scene, which a refusal might have precipitated, Dr. Kidd with practical good-sense at once humoured the drunken man so far as to say : ' Oh ay, Jeems, I'll come wi' ye, an' I'll drink like a beast to please ye.'   ' Hooray ! ' hiccuped the befuddled beadle, 'come along.'   So they entered the inn—the strangely-assorted couple the centre of observation to many a keen and curious pair of eyes.   Jeems hiccuped out an order for 'a mutchkin,' and when the liquor was produced, he with a very shaky hand filled out a portion for himself and greedily gulped it down.   The reverend old doctor carefully filled out a glass of cold water as his share, and quaffed that.   'Hoots !' expostulated the Bacchanalian beadle, ' ye said ye wad drink like a beast, doctor ! '   ' Ay, Jeems, an' so I have,' was the dignified reply ; 'for ye

ken a beast never drinks mair than is gude
for 't.'

I may fitly finish this chapter anent beadles, by retail-
ing an anecdote in which the trial of wit was between
two rival members of the fraternity.   It was not long
after the Disruption, and a Free Kirk had been built
fairly opposite the Auld Kirk.   The beadles of the two
rival establishments were overheard once comparing
notes.   Said the Free Kirk champion : 'D'ye ken, Davie,
what yon deavin', ding-dong, great muckle bell o' yours
aye minds me o'?   I aye think it's jist sayin' "Cauld
kail het again! Cauld kail het again!"' The other, without any seeming resentment at the implied slur on his
minister's originality and industry replied : 'Ay, Jeems,
but dae ye no ken what your wee bit tink-tinklin'
bell's aye claverin'?'   'Na ; what is't?'   'Ou jist
"C'lection ! C'lection ! C'lection ! "'

CHAPTER VII

FUNERAL CUSTOMS, EPITAPHS, ETC.

But not alone in the ranks of beadledom, and the
domain of the dead in churchyards, have reforms to be
chronicled. The besom of change has been busy in
every department of social custom ; nor, indeed, need the
reverent student of the past and the fond antiquary mourn
much that this is so. 'The old order changeth.' 'Tis
the law of growth, of progress. The old-fashioned treatment of the sick, for instance, from a modern point of
view, how heartless, how verily brutal it now seems.
The awful concoctions and boluses of our childhood ;
the fearful compounds of every vile-smelling and abom-

inably-tasting drug. Assuredly it did need a strong
constitution to weather the fierce showers of pills and
potions, blisters and blood - lettings, draughts and
drenches, that were literally rained upon any wretched
sufferer in 'the brave days of old.' The doctor was a
despot, but 'the howdie' was a veritable Star Chamber
and Grand Inquisition combined. When one thinks of
the stuffy rooms, from which every breath of free, health-
giving ozone was as rigorously excluded as if it had
been fire-damp ; of the awful box-beds with frowsy linen,
and sometimes a whole wardrobe of wearing apparel
sharing the cramped space with the sick occupants ; of
the chaff or straw mattresses, in many cases dank with
exudations from a fever-stricken frame—but why pile on
the agony ?—when one thinks of those and other nameless concomitants of ignorance and sloth and perverted
solicitude—for, after all, real kindness and concern for the
sick lay at the back of all this,—then one can begin
properly to appreciate the blessings of wire mattresses,
cheerful, airy wards, and well-ventilated sickrooms, of
trained nurses, antiseptic surgery, and the thousand and
one beneficent appliances, blessed ameliorations, and
soothing mitigations that the present generation of
sick and suffering humanity enjoy, as compared with
their immediate ancestors. Perhaps in no department
of human effort has so much been done to vindicate the
claim for man's divine nature, than is presented to us in
the deeply interesting page of patient experiment, self-
denying, unwearied research, and heroic self-sacrifice
which tells the story of modern hygienic, sanitary, and
hospital reform, and the progress of the healing art
generally. As a class, with but very very few exceptions,

the modern doctor is one of the noblest and most heroic figures of our time.   I could dilate on this topic, for I have seen them at work—often wretchedly over-worked and under-paid—in the crowded slums of great cities; in sparsely-peopled wastes on the outskirts of civilisation where the conditions of life are hard and repugnant; in the midst of plague and pestilence, and amid the gory carnage of war.   Wherever there is disease and death, and human misery and suffering; wherever his divine art can relieve and heal; wherever the sacred touch of science, and the pure flame of unselfish investigation and research for the sake of humanity, and the pure love of learning leads—there, the modern doctor, the Bayard of our puling, pessimistic age, is to be found : the paragon of pure unselfishness ; the heroic figure that relieves the dull, dead level of cynical unbelief and crass self-indulgence, which marks the low-water line of modern fashionable society.

I do not forget that there are, thank God, other noble types of character, that are leaven centres, in this *blasé, fainéant,* and largely good-for-nothing, so-called fashionable *fin-de-siècle* world of ours; but the modern doctor, I must confess—and perhaps because I have been privileged to come much in contact with many noble specimens of the profession—has always seemed to me to typify some of the best virtues and the finest attributes of our race.

But I must not forget that my theme is not modern society, but auld fashions and auld folk.   Let the kind reader pardon this digression, and let us hark back to our budget of old-time recollections.

A good story about physic just comes to me as I

write. The hero was a stolid, stingy old farmer of the old school, upon whom the minister had called. After the usual interchange of conventional remarks, the worthy pastor asked how the wife fared. The farmer, in a very nonchalant way, replied :—

'Oh, she's deid.'

'Dead?' said the minister, quite shocked. 'Dead? Dear me, it must have been very sudden. Was there an accident? How did it happen?'

'Weel, ye see, minister,' very composedly explained the bereaved one, 'she took gey onweel, an' syne she grew waur, an' some o' the neebors said I suld send for the doctor; but losh, sir, I mindit 'at I hed a bit pootherie i' the hoose, an' so I gied her the poother.'

'Well!'

'Weel, sir, she dee'd!' and then with unctuous feeling he continued: 'But eh, sir, I'm rael gled noo I didna tak' the bit poother masel'.'

It is beyond a doubt that the poor wife would have been better served had she been doctored Jedburgh fashion. What that was, may be surmised from the following true story.

A stranger came to Jedburgh one day—or, as the natives prefer to call it, Jeddart. He looked somewhat of a valetudinarian, and he asked one of the casual inhabitants to direct him to the chemist's shop.

'The what, sir?'

'The chemist's shop.'

'Ay, an' whit kin' o' a shop's that na?'

'Why, the place where ye can buy medicine!'

'Eh, sir, we've nae sic shop as that in Jeddart.'

'No? What do you do then when any one falls ill?
Do you take no medicine?'

''Deed, no! Deil a drap! We've jist whisky for the
folk, an' tar for the sheep, an' that's a' the feesick we
deal in.'

But to hark back to my reminiscences of funerals
and funeral customs.

One of the best descriptions ever written of a funeral
of the olden time, is that so graphically told by John
Galt in *The Entail;* and of course allusions to the quaint
old customs that are now fast dying out, are scattered
here and there in nearly every book relating to Scottish
history.

The hearse, for instance, is quite an innovation of
recent times, and I have myself known many worthy
old people who held it in as much contempt and repro-
bation as they held the church organ.

Christenings, weddings, and burials were all alike
opportunities for so much unwonted social intercourse,
for the meeting of kinsfolk and neighbours, and they
not unusually terminated in rough, rude, and riotous
conviviality and regrettable excess. In the Highlands,
at all events, the Celtic impulsiveness and impression-
able emotional nature of the people, often betrayed the
mourners into extravagant excesses.

An old friend, Mr. Murray, tells me of a funeral at
which he himself was an invited guest, and which, he
assures me, was a fair specimen of what was customary
in his young days. There had been the usual ceremonial
washing and streekin' of the corpse, the vigils corresponding in some degree to the Irish wake. Unstinted
supplies of refreshments had been provided, and par-

taken of with true Gaelic fervour, and at length the
funeral procession had been marshalled, and had set out
on its long, devious way. The family burial-place
happened to be at Struan; the abode of the deceased
was in Badenoch. It was too great a distance to carry
the coffin by hand, and so a farm-cart, with a pair of
plough horses harnessed tandem-fashion, had been requisitioned for the mournful transit. Alongside the
coffin in the cart a big wooden chest was placed. This
was packed with provender such as the means of the
family afforded : cakes, bread, cheese, ham, even beef,
and, above all, whisky on the most generous scale.
Some one, generally a closely-related clansman, was
deputed to act as chief steward on the occasion. His
function was to dispense whisky to every living soul
that the cortège might encounter on its way to the
graveyard. Mr. Murray met the long procession at
Dalnacardoch in Athol, and he and his companion had
at once to partake of whisky, and taste the provisions.
Of course others, nothing loath for friendship's sake, had
to see that they did not 'drink alane.' Two or three
miles further on they met the Royal Mail, at that time
running between Perth and Inverness ; but perhaps I
had better let Mr. Murray tell the tale in his own
fashion.

'Well, sir, we cam' up wi' the Mail—the train cam'
nae farrer north than Perth at that time—an' I mind
fine on the yae coach there was a fine, douce, steady
driver an' an awfu' drucken gaird ; an' on the ither
coach they had pitten a sober gaird wi' a drucken driver.
Aweel this was the sober driver an' the drucken gaird,
an' there wis a wheen passengers, an' yae Londoner sort

o' bodie. Of coorse the Mail drew up, an' the man in
the cairt boot tae hae oot the whisky, an' it was haunded
roon'.   The bit Lunnon bodie seemed fair horrifeed
whin he wis tauld he wad hae tae tak' aff his gless to
avoid giein' mortal offense.   Aweel efter a gey wheen
stoppages o' a like sort, we got to Struan.   At that time
it wis aye a near relation that baith howkit the grave
an' filled it in.   That wis coontit an honour, ye ken.
Weel, efter the puir man wis berrit, an' the grave filled
in, an' happit doon, the big aik kist wis brocht oot o'
the cairt, and it was set doon fair on the tap o' the
new-made grave, an' syne ilka body jist sat roond an'
begoud upo' the provender an' the whisky, an' jist keepit
at it as lang as they could haud oot.'

Frequently, too, old feuds were reopened, and the proceedings terminated in simply a drunken brawl. Indeed,
I am told that one funeral would very often prove the
occasion of successive ceremonies of a like kind ; but I am
not now speaking from personal knowledge, and would
fain hope that possibly my friendly informants may have
somewhat unconsciously magnified the more objectionable
episodes connected with what nowadays, at all events,
is generally so solemn and touching an office.   The old,
rude habits and excesses may still linger in some out-of-
the-way sequestered spots, but the gentler amenities hold
undisputed sway over the greater part of our, in this
respect at least, better regulated and more highly civilised
country.

Up in Glenesk I know of a certainty, from my own
boyish recollections and the corroboration of my old
kinsfolk and kentfolk, that very much the same rough-
and-ready procedure obtained, until within a very recent

period. A death was an occasion for a regular clan gathering. It was a point of honour for all the kith and kin to meet, if it were at all within the bounds of possibility. A ceaseless vigil was held over the corpse, relays of watchers succeeding each other. The hospitality was as profuse as it became unwise. Away up in the Forest o' Birse a favourite compound was considered *en règle.* It was a decoction of hot tea and whisky, and was known as Birse tea. Potations were deep and prolonged. Indeed, I have heard of one minister, who was heard to give his consent to officiate at the funeral, dependent on the condition that there should only be 'nae mair than yae browst.' The evening, however, after the minister had left, would generally see the 'one browst' mightily multiplied.

So little were the most ordinary modern sanitary conditions observed, that I can record it as a fact that in one case in the Highlands—I could name the locality, but I will not—the sheet which had covered the dead body of the poor child that had been buried, was used after the funeral as a table-cloth, on which were spread the funeral meats and cakes which had been provided for the refection of all the old women in the parish, who had, as was usual, attended at the ceremony. What makes the statement all the more significant, and more clearly accentuates the welcome change that has taken place in this particular at all events, is the fact, solemnly stated to me by one who actually witnessed the scene, that the poor child had died of diphtheria, and that no fewer than seven deaths from the same fell disease, had taken place in the same family within the preceding three months.

I

One of the notable characters at all 'the Glen' funerals, was a tall, old farmer with grizzled locks, and a curious impediment in his speech. He was generally known as 'Tirly Birly,' that being the name of his little farm. 'Tirly' somehow generally managed to get himself installed as master of the ceremonies ; and some captious critics used to slyly suggest that this was done to avoid the necessity, which lay on all and sundry, to take their due share in the burden—often a truly irksome and weighty one—of carrying the corpse. Many a time the poor dead neighbour had to be carried weary miles over the blushing heather, through quaking bogs and across trackless moors, in the sweltering heat of summer, or through the blinding drift and howling storms of an icy winter. No matter what the season, Old 'Tirly' was pretty sure to be there. He brought the 'spokes' with him, that being the synonym for the staves which were put under the coffin, and to which four carriers were apportioned. As the first four began to fag under their depressing load, Old 'Tirly's' strident voice would be heard crying out, 'Ither fower'; and the fresh relay from the accompanying band of mourners would take the place of the wearied ones, who were no doubt glad to relinquish their post of honour. Even in such a secluded corner of our island, however, as Glenesk, the old customs are fast falling into desuetude, and the ubiquitous hearse has almost entirely done away with the old-fashioned 'spokes' and 'carriers.'

It was in illustration of these old customs that the story is told of one 'Sandie Drew,' of 'The Yoker,' a small village near Glasgow. Sandie was a rough, stolid, coarse-grained 'cairter,' utterly devoid of imagination or any approach to refinement, but quite typical of the prosaic, uneducated, lower class of the town-bred Scottish men of the last generation. He and his son had been asked to attend the funeral of a neighbour lately deceased. The son was, if possible, even coarser in grain than the sire, and when asked by Sandie if he ' wis gaun,' gruffly replied :—

' 'Deed no, feyther, deil a fit ah'm gaun. What's the use ?'

' Hoots, min !' said Sandie, ' ye'd better k'wa' wi' me. Ye'll aye get a gless o' wine at ony rate, an', forbye, ye'll no hae tae cairry.'

One of my cousins, who has settled in the Lowlands, brought with him from far-away Shetland, a simple, faithful soul as gardener and 'orra man,' named Robbie. Naturally, Robbie who had never before been beyond the unsophisticated bounds of his native isle, found much food for wonder when he first was brought into contact with the more advanced civilisation of a manufacturing town ' doon sooth.' One day he returned from a walk, and said to his master : 'Losh, sir, I've seen the day, the graundest kerridge I've ever set my een on !' 'Ay, Robbie, an' what like was't ?' ' Oh, sir, it wis a great muckle black coach, an' a' mounted wi' black fur an' feathers.' It turned out to have been the first hearse poor Robbie had ever seen.

Following the country custom of providing all sorts of conveniences and refreshments for sympathetic friends and mourners, it was long a custom in the chief towns in Scotland, and indeed may yet be so for all I know to the contrary, to hire mourning carriages for the behoof of mourners who accepted invitations to the funeral. It was generally notified by advertisement inserted by the undertaker, and charged for at rates corresponding with the supposed quality of the deceased, that carriages would be in waiting at such and such a place to take mourners from the city to the place of interment. In Glasgow, I believe, a long row of such carriages generally used to stand near St. George's Church. A certain canny Scot of the famous city had, it seems, been ordered carriage exercise by his doctor for some ailment that oppressed him, and being of a frugal and an ingenious turn of mind, he had hit on an expedient which enabled him to save his pocket and obey his doctor at one and the same time. A friend had seen him in one of these mourning carriages, and later on in the day had accosted him, mentioning the circumstance, and asked, ' if it hed bin a near relation.' 'No, nae relation ava'!' was the complacent reply; 'bit, ye see, I've been ordered kerridge exercise by my doctor, an', man, I've been twice at the Toon Heid the day already.'

The strange vagaries of Highland custom as exemplified in Mr. Murray's account of the Badenoch funeral above given, would seem not wholly to have been confined to the period subsequent to death. Some confused sense of the majesty of the King of Terrors, and the need for observing due decorum at his approach, would seem to have been the actuating motive in the following strange scene, vouched for by the narrator as having been witnessed by himself in the Perthshire Highlands.

The minister, a recent arrival from the Lowlands, had gone to see a dying parishioner, and when he reached the cottage he found several of the family bathed in tears. 'Is he worse?' he asked. 'Oh, sir, he's jist deein',' was the sobbing reply. Looking towards the 'box-bed,' where the sufferer was lying almost at the last gasp, he was astonished to see two men bending over the body engaged apparently in some mysterious ceremonial.

'What are these men doing there?' he demanded.

'Eh, sir, they're jist shaivin' him.'

'Shaving him?' echoed the minister, in sheer amazement. 'Can they not let the poor man die in peace?'

'Ah, sir, it's far easier noo!' was the strange reply, given with a genuine outburst of unaffected grief.

I would be glad to know from any reader, if this was a common custom in the Highlands, for I confess it was new to me when I heard it first.

There was less emotion, if greater humour of the dry, cynical character, in the next instance I have to cite. It was in one of the old-established mercantile houses in Edinburgh, and the head of the firm had just died. An attached old *employé* who had been in the service of the house the greater part of a lifetime, and perhaps presumed a little on that fact, to occasionally perform his duties with what might appear to an outside critic, almost exaggerated deliberateness, was, as might naturally have been expected, much overcome by the sad event. Mr. Jardine the manager, now the ruling power, came upon the old fellow in a small retiring-room, crying bitterly and perhaps just a trifle ostentatiously. On being asked rather sharply what was the matter, he referred to the loss the house had just sustained, and rather affectedly whimpered out :—

'Ah, Mr. Jardine, I canna be lang efter him.'

'Aweel, Robert,' came the dry response, 'ye'd jist better gang back to yer wark i' the noo.'

Quite as devoid of emotion or sentiment was the expression used by a rough working-man in one of the Lanarkshire mining towns, and which vies with the Tyneside pitman's cool unconcern. The poor man had lost one child out of a pretty large family. He had made all the survivors members of a burial society, by paying up the requisite fees and instalments. On some neighbour expressing condolence with him for the loss of the child he had just buried, and which had not been a member of the burial club, he said, pointing to the other bairns: 'Oo ay, but if it hed hae bin ony o' thae yins, it wudna hae been sae muckle missed.'

Many a good anecdote might be chronicled of things said after the funeral. That was a bit of pungent satire overheard after the burial of a leading citizen in Glasgow, who had been notoriously grasping and miserly. Said one, referring to the contents of the will, which had just been made public: 'Well! I would have thought he'd have left more money.' 'Ah, indeed!' was the bland but witty retort, 'I did not hear how much he had taken away with him.'

Better still was the grim evasiveness illustrated by the following. It was after the funeral, and a party of the mourners, seated in a third-class carriage, were waiting for the train to start on their homeward way. Some were filling their pipes, the aroma of whisky was distinctly discernible, and there was a subdued sort of relieved feeling after tension, a kind of moral and intellectual stand-at-ease attitude of mind, which betrayed itself in every tone and gesture. Only one occupant of the carriage was an exception to the general complexion of the group. Gaunt and erect, clad in deepest mourning, voluminous crape on his rusty hat, and inflexible austerity visible in every angle of his iron countenance and steel-like starched collar—he sat bolt upright in a corner, nor suffered his cold gray eye to wander from the straight line of horizontal exactitude in which he had cast it. At length the tobacco cutting, pipe filling and lighting came to an end, and one of the company after an exchange of sundry nods and nudges, made bold to address the Gorgon-like figure in the corner.

'Ay, Maister Macdonal', this has been a sair loss to ye, nae doot?' No notice beyond a momentary glare was taken of this advance.

Another now took up his parable and said : 'She wis yer only sister, wisna she, Maister Macdonal'?'

The iron lips opened and snapped like a rat-trap as the monosyllable 'Yis!' was jerked out rather than spoken.

'Whit wis her age?' asked another.

'Fufty-three,' was shot like a pellet in reply.

'An' whit was the naiter o' her complaint?' was the next query.

'A complicashun!' was the ambiguous rejoinder, while the severity of the iron man's expression deepened.

Nothing daunted, the first interlocutor now approached the crucial question to which all this had been but the mere skirmishing prelude. All heads bent nearer as the question was put : 'An' whit did she leave, Maister Macdonal'?'

A gleam of sardonic humour, like a warm sunbeam on a winter day, shot athwart the rugged visage, as raising his eyes to the roof of the carriage in real or assumed emotion, he answered with a deep, choking sort of voice: 'She left this warl'!'

Somewhat similar was the colloquy at the church-yard gate between the stolid old betheral and an inquisitive stranger. The cortège of homeward-bound mourners was just disappearing amid the distant 'stoor,' and the grim old man was wiping his heated brows with his red spotted 'naipkin,' when the stranger came up, and said with a note of interrogation in his voice :—

'Funeral ?'

The old sexton assimilated his suspended pinch of snuff, and bowed his head in token of assent.

'Who's dead ?'

The old man wiped the superfluous pungent powder from his scrubby upper lip, and gave the required information.

'What complaint ?' persisted the inquisitor.

Leisurely putting away his 'sneeshin' mull,' and deliberately placing his cotton handkerchief in the crown of his old hat, which he slowly placed on his bald pate, he oracularly replied : 'There's nae complaint. A'body's pairfeckly setisfeed !'

Was it not a relative of Lord Brougham's who being asked to propose some toast at the feast which followed on some funeral at which the company had been present, rose to his feet, and with due solemnity but suppressed slyness proposed: 'The health of the faimily physeechian, the founder of this feast' ?

While on this sepulchral strain I may as well jot down another story still further illustrative of the apparently callous and unfeeling nature of the people, which I have already touched upon. At the marriage of a certain young couple, one of the wedding presents had been a pair of beautiful glossy white waxen candles, and these had for many years remained in 'the aumrie,' carefully wrapped in flannel, and were only brought out on great occasions to show to favoured visitors. It had long ago been settled between Marget and John that the candles would be kept intact until death should overtake one or other, when the candles would be used to add a lustre and dignity to the funeral proceedings; and many a time when the guidwife was 'redding-up,' in her annual house-cleaning, she would take out the candles, and gloating over their beautiful waxen-polished whiteness, now, alas! turning to a dull, creamy, ivory yellow, she would speculate whether John would predecease her, or whether she would be taken away first; and she would allow a thrill of pride to possess her sometimes, when she reflected what an air of distinction the burning of real waxen candles would give to the funeral ceremonies. In fact, she would often mentally rehearse the scene thus pictured to herself: the looks of surprise and envy with which the neighbours would greet her as she ushered in her splendid candles in the brightly-polished brass candlesticks. To those who know the immense significance attached to the funeral customs in rural Scotland in bygone days, this peculiar idiosyncrasy of the old lady will not be wondered at. However, poor John was at length seized with a wasting sickness. For a long time he had been confined to the box-bed in the kitchen, and the vision of an imposing funeral ceremony loomed still more largely and nearly than ever in Marget's mental introspections. Two or three times it had been 'touch and go' with John. Indeed, more than once, Marget had laid in the necessary stock of 'wines an' speerits, shortbreid and cake,' but John had ever and again rallied, and at length poor Marget began almost to feel aggrieved at such obstinacy on the 'pairt o' a deein' man.' At last, however, surely the critical climax had arrived. Poor John, after terrific fits of hectic coughing, lay gasping for breath; and the neighbours and near kindred, drawn partly by curiosity, and surely some of them from a feeling of sympathy and blood affection, had gathered together to witness the end of the departing saint. The doctor had been in, and gave his verdict that the end was near. Marget had ushered her visitors and sympathisers into the best room, and there on the table she had arrayed the customary supplies of creature comforts demanded by the strictest conventionalism; and then with a feeling of elation and gratified self-esteem she had produced the long-treasured candles, with a sigh of renunciation as she thought that at last their immaculate purity was to be sullied by the touch of flame. The crowning, triumphant moment of years of possession was at hand, and still (it was really too bad of him) poor John lingered on. A deathlike silence reigned in the guest-chamber, broken occasionally only by a deep, pious sigh or unctuous cough, as one more glass of whisky was assimilated by the grief-stricken yet 'drouthy neebors.' Marget flitted from the deathbed to the parlour with a conscious air of importance. Presently the clatter of hoofs was heard without, and the good old minister lit down from his trusty 'auld

white meer,' and reverently, with a professional look
suited for the occasion, joined the assembly; and in
obedience to the silent summons from Marget he, too,
partook of 'jist a wee drappie speerits,' with a manner
which lifted the simple custom almost into the dignity
of a solemn act of ritual. Still poor John's reluctant
spirit lingered in its worn earthly tenement. Marget's
patience became almost exhausted. It seemed really
too bad of a 'deein' man' to offer, even unconsciously,
any hindrance to the consummation of such perfect
arrangements as had been made. So the poor distracted
wife, torn by a conflict of emotions, doubtless with a
tender though sternly repressed regard for the husband
of her youth, and yet with an intense desire that every
due observation demanded by high tradition and ancient
custom should be scrupulously observed, bent low over
the dying man. She shook up his pillows, brushed back
the damp hair from the pallid brow, and then as his
sunken eyes heavily lifted, and looked through the
glazing film of gathering death into the hard-set face
whereon lay many lines of care and toil, and which now
bent over him, she whispered in his ear : ' John ! John !'
and there was a sobbing pathos in the homely words.
'Ah, John,' she said, 'the fowk are a' here, the table's
set oot, and oh, John, the wax can'les are lichted.
Dinna linger ! dinna linger !'

Of quite as practical, though not so pathetic, a character, was the conduct of a rather penurious Highlander,
of whom it is recorded that on his father's death in the
Highlands, much to the astonishment of his friends, the
dutiful but close-fisted son hired a hearse to bring the
honoured remains of his parent down to Glasgow

Cemetery.   Some one of his cronies afterwards ventured to express surprise that he had gone to such an extraordinary expense; but Tonal, with an indescribable leer in his eye, said: 'Och, man, it cost me naethin'; for, ye see, I procht doon as muckle whisky i' the hearse as buried the auld man.'

The point of this story of course lies in the fact that the whisky was smuggled, and the duty thus filched from the Crown paid all the expenses of the funeral.

While I am on the subject of funerals, Sir Alfred Roberts, of Sydney, New South Wales, told me a good story one day a poor patient who was lying in Prince Alfred Hospital, the magnificent institution over which Sir Alfred so ably presides.   The medical superintendent sent a telegram to the wife, who must have been of mixed Celtic blood, probably a north of Ireland woman. The telegram read as follows: 'Husband very ill; may die at any moment.'   No reply was received by Sir Alfred, but the dying husband received one, which read thus: 'If you die, see that you are buried by the Oddfellows.'

The next on my note-book is rather a good specimen of caustic Scotch humour.   In one of the finely-laid-out city cemeteries in the west a rich citizen who was a notorious sceptic and scoffer had erected a massive mausoleum on what he was pleased grandiloquently to call 'his ancestral plot,' with a view to perpetuate his somewhat worthless memory.   One day he met a worthy, douce elder of the kirk, a devout, simple-minded man, coming away from the vicinity of the imposing mass of masonry, and the infidel said:—

'Weel, Dauvit, ye've been up seein' that graund erection o' mine?'

' 'Deed have I, sir.'

'Gey strong place that, isn't it? It'll tak' a man a' his time to rise oot o' yon at the Day o' Jeedgement.'

'Hech, ma man,' said the elder, 'ye can gie yersel' little fash aboot risin', fin that day comes. They'll tak' the boddom oot o't tae lat ye doon!'

Yet another illustration of that curious apparent disregard of all feeling, to which I have already alluded, has, I think, been in print before; but it is very characteristic. The officiating minister at a funeral was about to offer up prayer, and wishing to have some clue to guide him to a seasonable and befitting utterance, he asked in a whisper of the man nearest to him, a stolid, wooden-faced sort of man: 'What occupation did you say the deceased followed?' 'Od, I dinna ken!' said the man; then raising his voice he said, in the most matter-of-fact way, to a friend opposite: 'Fat wis the corp to trade, John?'

Very similar was the calm, philosophic explanation of a bereaved wife to a visitor, in a fishing village near Montrose. With a view to condolence, the friendly gossip said :—

'Eh, sirss! an' so John's deid?'

'Ow ay,' said the widow, 'John's deid, puir man!' And then, as if in explanation of her composed resignation, she added somewhat deprecatingly: 'Ye ken, although nae doot he's the feyther o' the bairns, he wis, efter a', nae drap's bluid to me.'

Quite different was the feeling manifested at the humble funeral of a poor old woman near Tain. It so happened that as the meagre cortège reached the churchyard it was met by a returning crowd of the well-

to-do burghers of the town who had just been attending
the funeral of a well-known man of substance of the
neighbourhood.   Touched with a very laudable feeling
of compassion and courteous pity, they turned back
again in neighbourly and kindly spirit to convoy the
poor humble coffin to its last resting-place.   The bereaved husband could not conceal his gratification and
his added sense of importance.   Beaming with smug
complacency, he said to one of his friends, with a jerk
of his thumb towards the coffin: 'Eh, Tam, winna
Kirsty be prood o' this na?'—meaning the poor dead
wife would be proud of the large though accidental
attendance at her funeral.

The Rev. A. Osborne, a dear old friend to whom I
am indebted for many a racy story, wrote me last
November thus :—

'I have not forgotten your love of a good Scotch
story.   Here is one which I can vouch to be no
chestnut.   I have an old uncle, the U.P. minister of
S——, Glasgow, but many years ago of West L——.
Well, it seems in L—— there is a kindly-natured bit o'
a dressmaker bodie, slightly deformed, a former member
of my uncle's congregation, and still a great lover and
admirer of her old minister.   Lately she came through
to pay him a visit, and on leaving L—— she remarked
to some of her cronies : "Eh, if it war only the Lord's
wull, there's naething I wad like better than tae dee
near ma auld meenister ! "

'It so happened that in S—— she did indeed take
a bad turn, and what did she do but scuttle home
again to L—— as fast as she could?   When her friends
expressed surprise at her speedy return she naïvely said :

"Weel, the fac' is, sirss, I wis fear't the Lord wis gaun tae tak' me at ma word ! " '

Another good old U.P. minister, who has gone to his rest—the Rev. Mr. Russell—used to tell a story illustrative of the canny frugality, or, as some may call it, stinginess or parsimony, of certain of 'oor ain folk'; and it comes in not altogether inappositely while I am on the subject of the present chapter.

He had an old farmer in his congregation who lived in an outlying portion of the parish several good Scotch miles from the manse. The farmer's wife had been stricken down with sickness, and Mr. Russell made many visits to encourage and cheer the poor bodie, and ungrudgingly trudged many a weary mile over hill and moorland to administer comfort to the dying woman. The farmer was a well-to-do man for his station in life, but the love of lucre had eaten into his nature as a canker, and the dying woman's surroundings were not notorious for a superfluity of luxuries, to put it mildly. Thus Mr. Russell all the more made a point of being frequent in his visits, as these seemed to brighten up the weary tedium of the poor sufferer's lot. At length the end came, and very shortly after the funeral, the annual seat-letting of the church pews came round. The recently bereaved farmer came in his turn to secure his accustomed pew for the year, but he evidently had something on his mind. He fumbled with his hat, scratched his head, had the grace to look red and uncomfortable, but at last blurted out, as he proffered *half* the usual contribution : 'Ye see, sir, Jessie's deid, an' I wisna thinkin' o' keepin' on her seat.'

Speaking of funerals, here is a good specimen of a

genuine Scottish 'bull.' Two cronies passing by a graveyard, the one said : 'Losh, man, I wad rayther dee than be berried there !' 'Ay,' said the other, 'wi' me noo it's jist the vera revairse, for I wadna like to be berried onywhere else, if I'm spared.'

Just as much of a bull in its way was the unconscious contradiction used by one of the unemployed in Edinburgh, who had got a temporary job to sweep a heavy fall of snow from the streets. Accosting another of the gang, as he stopped to beat his arms, he said : 'Eh, Jock, man, it's as cauld as blazes !' Jock possibly did not know that with the West India nigger the place of eternal torments is located in hyperborean regions.

While on the subject of funerals one is tempted to quote the two delicious samples of unconscious humour which, however, have, I think, seen print before somewhere, they are so illustrative of the callous or maybe philosophic way of looking on bereavement, which characterises a certain class of rustic minds in Scotland, and of which I have already been giving examples.

The one is the querulous outburst of the thrifty goodwife, who, in reply to a condolence by the minister on the death of a third husband, petulantly exclaimed : 'Was ever a wumman sae plagueit wi' deein' men ?'

The other, after much the same pattern, was the reply given by an old farmer who had seen his third wife 'weel happit,' as they would call it in my county. With cheery complacency he answered the newly-arrived minister's inquiry as to how the wife was, with the guileless information : 'Dod, meenister, I'm oot o' wives the noo !'

An irreverent epitaph, which I have heard attributed

to Robbie Burns, may be chronicled here, as being somewhat akin to the subject of funerals and deaths. I do
not remember myself to have seen it in print, though no
doubt it is well known. It runs thus :—

> Here lies the body of Doctor Gordon,
> Teeth almichty, an' mooth accordin' !
> Stranger, tread lichtly on this wonder ;
> If he opens his mooth yer gone, By Thunder !

Another, which commemorates the besetting sin of
an old miser, is as follows :—

> Interred beneath this churchyard stone
>   Lies stingy Jimmy Wyatt ;
> He died one morning just at ten,
>   And saved a dinner by it.

I was told not long ago, of another epitaph, which was
said to have been written under somewhat curious
circumstances. A typical, energetic, enterprising Scotsman in foreign parts, having amassed considerable
wealth, sent home, as many of his countrymen have
done, a commission to find out the circumstances of his
old mother, if still alive, with a view to minister to her
comfort. If dead, the instructions were to provide a
headstone, with a suitable inscription, to place over her
tomb. Alas ! for the tardy good intentions. The poor
old mother had long ago filled a nameless grave, and the
very spot where she was interred was unknown. One
version says it was in St. Cyrus graveyard, and the
encroaching sea had cut away many of the graves ; but
be that as it may, the instructions were specific and
express—Expense was not to be allowed to stand in the
way. Rather than lose the profitable job, the village

K

mason therefore provided a stone, which was put up in
a corner of the churchyard, and on it were chiselled the
following lines :—

> The place where Kirsty Machir lies
> Is here or here aboot ;
> The place where Kirsty Machir lies
> There's nane can find it oot.
> The place where Kirsty Machir lies
> There's nane on earth can tell,
> Till at the Resurrection day,
> When Kirsty tells hersel'.

For pithy irony, however, commend me to the following,
composed upon a rather notorious lawyer in Aberdeenshire, about the end of the last century. With a
keen appreciation of the certainty of retribution for evil
living, the pungent scribe wrote :—

> In the last day, when others rise,
> Lie still, Red Rob, gin ye be wise.

It is extraordinary the fascination funereal literature
has for some minds. In rural Scotland the funeral and
everything pertaining to it has seemingly at all times possessed some powerful attraction for the ordinary run of
our country folk. Possibly it may have been part of the
unspoken protest, against that hard repression of natural
emotion — the stern and almost universal interdict
against gaiety and amusement which came in with the
Calvinistic standards of doctrine and discipline after the
Reformation, and about which I have spoken at some
length elsewhere.[1] In the excitement and bustle and
stir of a funeral, with its quaint customs, there was felt

---

[1] *Oor Ain Folk.* Edinburgh, 1894.

to be some legitimate excuse for social communion, and the exercise of almost unbridled excess under the guise of hospitality, which powerfully appealed to the 'natural man.' You cannot compress human nature into a mould as you can clay, and in this little commonplace fact, lies the explanation of much that seems so curious and unique in one's survey of the quaint, paradoxical, and deeply-interesting story of the evolution of Scottish national character.

How droll, yet how thoroughly Scottish, for instance, the complaint of the querulous old fellow who had migrated from Nithsdale to London, and to whom his friends used regularly to send the local paper. The first thing of course that John would look at, was the obituary column. On one occasion he was heard grumblingly to say, in a tone of displeased disappointment : 'What's the use o' sendin' a paper like that? There's no a leevin' sowl deid that I was acquant wi'.'

But the old customs are fast dying out. The old order, with all its crudity and much that was regrettable, had yet an element of the picturesque and uncommon about it. We are falling into the uniform and the prosaic more and more. Our faculty of wonder, of admiration, of awe, of spontaneity, is becoming compressed into a sort of machine-made sameness of pattern. We no longer follow our individual bent as the old folks did. The tawdry, inartistic, Socialist paint-brush, is splashing us all over with a dead gray distemper, and light and shade are vanishing from the landscape of social custom and national character. We are approximating to the unemotional, prosaic type of mind of the draper's apprentice in classic Ayr. He was fresh from the country, and the worthy draper, wishing to set the lad somewhat at his ease, said :—

'Ay, ma man, an' whaur div ye come frae ? '

'Frae Sorn.'

'Sorn !   That's a healthy place.   Folk'll no dee often there ? '

(Apprentice) ' Jist aince ! '

Before I close the chapter, and while on this subject, I would like to append one or two quaint and rather touching epitaphs we copied in the old graveyard beside Loch Lee when up in Glenesk the other day.

One is over the grave of ' Donald Nichol, age 85, who died in 1799,' and runs as follows :—

> The Grave, Great Teacher, to one level brings
> Heroes and Beggars, Galley Slaves and Kings.

Donald's birth would be in the year 1714, and no doubt the allusion to galley slaves, which sounds so strange to modern ears, and suggests such far-off historic recollections, would be perfectly appropriate at the time it was carven on the crumbling gray slate, where it now stands half eaten away by Time.

Another reads thus :—

> Here is reposed the dust of David Christison,
> Farmer in Auchronie, who died 20th Decc[r].
> aged 61 years.
>
> A man of integrity and veracity,
> And charitably disposed to the Indigent.

What a simple and yet what a splendid record to the man's nobility of character !   It is pleasant to think that

'Auchronie,' a snug little farmhouse, close behind my grandfather's old manse, is still in the occupation of David Christison's descendants, and that the good old character for hospitality and kindness to the needy and indigent, is still nobly maintained.

The last I shall give is from a quaint old tomb near the handsome memorial stone that has been erected over the grave of Alexander Ross, the famous Glen Poet. The inscription reads thus :—

> Stop, passenger, incline thine head,
> And talk a little with the dead.
> I had my day, as well as thou,
> But worms are my companions now.
> Hence then, and for thy change prepare
> With bent endeavour, earnest care ;
> For death pursues thee as a post,
> There's not a moment to be lost.

The allusion to the 'pursuing postman' is very quaint, and takes one a long way back. It irresistibly reminded me of my old Indian days, and the running *dak* men or Indian postmen among the jungles and waste places there.

There fell into my hands after *Oor Ain Folk* was published, and too late, of course, for inclusion in that family record, a copy of the last will and testament of my grandfather, the old minister of Glenesk. It affords a curious glimpse into the character of a fine typical 'farmer-cleric' of the old school, and a few brief extracts may perhaps not be uninteresting. There is a tone of deep piety and living faith in it, relieved with an odd gleam or two of the old man's habitual humour, which is, I think, very characteristic of a special phase of the old Scottish type of mind.

He begins by stating that 'being in full possession of all my mental powers, but considering that life is short and uncertain,' he provides for payment of all his debts. Then leaves to his wife and unmarried daughters 'as many beds, furniture, bed blankets, bed and table linen to furnish a house for their accommodation, and every article of furniture for that purpose,' for their sole use. All the rest that they did not require, and his other effects, such as live stock, crops, etc., were to be 'sold by public roup,' the interest to be paid to the widow and unmarried daughters during their lifetime, or if any of the daughters married, to the remaining unmarried ones; and at the marriage or death of the last, everything was to be realised and divided equally among the whole of his family or their descendants share and share alike. After various directions as to certain shares and moneys, he proceeds : 'I leave a few of my books to my son Robert'—that was my father, who succeeded him in the ministry of the parish—'and my thermometer to my son David, and my old worn-out watch to David Inglis, my grandson. *She is worn out with years and infirmities like myself.* I leave my two razors, who have served me so long and so faithfully, one to David and the other to Robert; any other small articles as a remembrancer to each of my five daughters.' What a picture of the kindly, compact, old manse home-life do not these quaint, pathetic touches present !

After constituting his two sons and two of his old elders executors and trustees, he proceeds : 'I regret it was not in my power to leave more to my family. I wish that they should all share equally as far as possible. I commit my soul and body to the holy keeping of

Almighty God, hoping and believing that when the wise purposes are served with me here on earth, my body shall rest in the hope of a glorious resurrection, and my Immortal Soul, through the merits, righteousness, and mediation of Jesus Christ our Blessed Redeemer, shall be exalted to Heaven to enjoy the Beatific Presence until the morning of the resurrection, when my body shall be raised from the grave by the Voice of the Son of God, and soul and body shall be exalted to the King-dom of Heaven, to celebrate the praises of Redeeming Love throughout the endless ages of eternity.' What a splendid confession of triumphant faith! The fine old man then concludes thus : 'I fervently pray that God in His mercy may spare me a little longer in the world for the benefit of my family, and while I live may I live to His praise, and prove a useful and faithful minister in His church, and may I at last die in His favour through merits of Jesus Christ, my Lord and Saviour. Amen.'

There is a postscript which gives a very graphic presentment of the kindly old man's state of mind. 'I most earnestly recommend to my two sons, David and Robert,' he writes, 'be as attentive to their mother and their unprovided sisters as you possibly can be. Recol-lect what I did for my mother and sister, and also an aunt died long before any of you were born. I have no power to enjoin this duty on any person, but I most earnestly recommend it to you, and all of you who may have ability, to be assisting to those of your sisters who may stand in need of assistance. Your affectionate father,

'DAVID INGLIS.'

I am sure little comment is needed. The old man may have left little worldly gear—indeed with his poor stipend, his large family, and his open, generous hospitality at all times to all comers, it was wonder he left any provision at all—but he left a priceless heritage in his honest name, his deep piety, his earnest faith, and his warm, affectionate, kindly Christian character. The story I have been privileged to write of his son's life proves, I think, that the fine old Glen minister's example and precepts had not altogether been vainly given.

CHAPTER VIII

RUSTICITY OF THE OLDEN TIME

Modern progress and old-time customs: a contrast—'The change-less East': a retrospect—The law of change—One of the old school—The old-time shell-fish sort of existence—Instances—The old farmer and the silver spoon—'Clean beats Fittie'—'A naiteral deith'—A luxurious dinner—The pawky weaver—Peter's rat case—No a maisterpiece—'The wonnerfu' works o' natur''—Poverty of expression—The pawky shepherd and the barber.

SOME of the anecdotes I have already given, may have appeared to some of my readers almost apocryphal, and for this reason: Changes have been so rapid in not only the realm of thought and feeling, but in the very outward aspect of things, that it is hard to bring one's mind to realise that such a primitive state of society existed within the compass of an ordinary lifetime, as some of these stories disclose. To my younger readers especially, will the humour often seem strained, the manners uncouth, and the incidents forced and exaggerated. Those who are older, and more of my own age, will however bear me out if they tax their recollections, and summon up boyish memories of the older stock as I have done. To young folks nowadays who have, comparatively speaking, travelled about, and seen the world; who have enjoyed the advantages of modern education and rapid transit; to whom the daily Press brings nigh 'the ends of the earth' almost every hour, and to whom scientific research and the abounding wealth of modern art, literature, and invention, have opened new worlds of thought, speculation, and experience, it is very difficult indeed to enter into these quaint, bygone attitudes of mind and expressions of emotion, which are characteristic of this class of reminiscence.

We are accustomed to speak of 'the changeless East'; of the iron-bound conservatism of the Chinese; of the rigid trammels of caste that exist in India; of the unalterable customs of Persian or Arab; but even in these proverbial illustrations, we often fail to realise the terrific 'pace' that modern progress has 'put on.' Look at Japan. Go to any large city in India, or even China. What do you find? Modern hotels, Western dress, modern municipal management, the daily local Press, the ubiquitous policeman and police courts. Railways, telegraphs, telephones—typewriters even, and 'tinned salmon.' Away in the back villages of Behar, on the frontiers of native states, or among the thick jungles of the Terai, you may still come across the old primitive customs; but even there, change is apparent, and the old village arts and handicrafts, the old village laws and usages, the old traditions, worship, and standards of life and thought, are fast becoming modernised.

In Scotland it has been the same. Here and there in some secluded lan'ward parish, or remote Highland glen, you may yet come, now and then, on some simple primitive community, where the modern abomination of a tourist hotel, with its sleek, snub-nosed tribe of splay-footed waiters, has not yet upreared its hateful presence, with the concomitants of bad whisky, and greasy 'made-dishes'; but such idyllic nooks are now rare.

I sit writing this in my own dear old Glen. I smell the fragrant sweetness of the birks round Ardoch, and the crimson heather is bursting into bloom. I have been away for thirty-two long, eventful years. The hot Eastern sun and the desiccating Austral winds have tanned my cheeks; and though tender emotions swell within me, and at every turn some fond recollection is stirred at the sight of the familiar hills and burns—at the sound of the old familiar names of places that I have not heard for more than half a lifetime, yet—yet—how *can* I express it?—things are not the same. There is some subtle change. There is a feeling of incompleteness—a jarring note somehow; an undertone of extreme sadness—sometimes almost dejection; a dim, half-expressed, half-denied feeling of dissatisfaction and disappointment. Are the great swelling hills really smaller and barer-looking, or is it only my fancy? The Esk and the Mark and the Tarf are the same; the tawny, yellow waters come bounding and foaming over the gray rocks as of yore; and yet, somehow, the channels seem narrowed and the volume decreased. Ah! the dear old faces, too! how many are gone! The peat stacks seem fewer. There are no thatch houses now left in the Glen, save one or two that are mouldering to decay. Stone cottages have taken their place. Trim, neat, substantial? Yes, with tropæolum climbing like embracing flames about the front, and honeysuckle running riot over the enclosing dykes of the kailyards.

As cosy looking? as 'canty and crouse' and 'bien-like' as the lowly theek hoosies of old? No! I do not think so !

And the old kindly, hearty, frank, simple, spontaneous loving-kindness and large-hearted generous hospitality of the dear old days, seems, too, to have for the most part passed. Not altogether. Some of the essentially 'hame ower folk' are still left, and oh! what a charm to enjoy their unaffected, warm - hearted, unstudied directness. Here at a humble farmhouse, for instance, behind the old manse where once my grandfather and my father dwelt, overlooking the quiet kirkyaird where reposes the dust of generations of my forbears, under this hospitable roof of Auchronie, in converse with the dear, gentle-mannered old lady, who presides so sweetly over the well-furnished tea-table, in quite the old unstinted style, a leaf out of the past is turned back, and the visions of boyhood return again.

But this is the exception. Elsewhere it is much on the 'naething - for-naething, and michty-little-for-sax-pence' plan. You are warned beforehand, long ere you may have made any request, that you must not expect this, and you need not look for that, although you are quite prepared to make ample, nay handsome allowance for any little service that may be rendered. There are now limitations, restrictions, conventionalities, rates, scales, regulations, petty greedinesses, affectations, red tape, and disillusionment, to a large degree, where formerly the all-pervading, warm, comforting feeling of communion, of kinship, of home warmth, and the glow of kindness, unstudied, unaffected, and disinterested, reigned supreme.

But so it had to be. And, after all, there are no
doubt compensations, and so the world progresses. But
how few were the wants, how uneventful the lives, how
restricted the horizon of these old times, the page of
Scottish anecdote and reminiscence forcibly reminds us.
The smallest incidents were invested with an importance
and a significance which made up to these simple primitive folk for the more agitating sensations of the present
time. How admirably Barrie has portrayed this, in
that masterpiece of his, *A Window in Thrums !* 'Jess'
and 'Leeb' and 'Hendry' are photographs from the life,
yet invested with such a subtle charm from the genius of
the author, that they become real to us—generic types—
and they are set for ever among the great masterpieces—
those living creations of the immortals, which adorn the
long and splendid gallery of English literature.

It is really a work of the rarest difficulty to empty
oneself of one's own personality, as it were, and enter
into the very mental being of one of these simple
primitive folk ; and this Barrie has done. For instance,
what is all your varied experience to one of the type
I met but yesterday. Frail in body, rheumatic and
tottering in his gait, but the eye is still bright, the
voice hearty and resonant. The locks are 'lyart,' but
the beard is thick and strong. He puffs vigorously at
an old and very short cutty, and from very pronounced
indications on the summer air, we can surmise that his
nerves are still strong, for the tobacco certainly is.
Pulling up the pony, we accost the old fellow :
'Weel, Jock, an' how are you ?' He peers up at us,
takes out his 'cutty,' knocks the 'dottle' out on his
thumb-nail, gets quit of some saliva, wipes his lips with

the back of his hand, and as we have been curiously watching the process of cogitation, and the appeal to recollection going on all the time, we are prepared for his first utterance :—

'Dod, na ! ye hae the better o' me. Fa is't ?'

'D'ye no mind me ?'

'No, min ! no i' ye noo, at ony rate, bit I'll mebbe min' in a whyllie. I ken yer face tōō.'

'Aweel, Jock, ye kent me fine fin I wis a lathie.'

Slowly a look of pleased recognition and awakened memory begins to play over the rugged features. The mouth opens, the shoulders straighten, the eyes blink with a sort of merry twinkle, then smiting his stick with both hands on the ground, he says, 'Ye'll no be fae foarin' pairts, are ye ?' 'Oh yes,' we answer, 'I've been abroad for a long time.'

Then comes the ripened certainty. With an emphasis and a heartiness that go very near raising a lump in my throat, the old man says : 'Dod, than, ye're Jeems !' Then my hand is grasped and pressed, and eager query after query is poured fast upon me ; and just for a brief minute one feels how deep and true a thing is kindly human affection after all, and a meeting like this makes amends for many, many a rebuff and disappointment.

Now there are men like that, dozens of them yet alive, who have perhaps never had service with more than probably two or three masters during the whole course of their three or fourscore years. They are shrewd judges of character, they have good store of native common-sense ; but their wants are few, their ambitions have never been stirred, they are not what you would call refined or educated, but they are true, honest, sincere, faithful. Oh, if with the modern accomplishments and learning, the modern breadth and culture and mental activity and intellectual quickness, we could only more increasingly and tenaciously keep a hold, too, of these fine old homespun cardinal virtues, what a world this would be!

However, the point I wish more immediately to illustrate, is the extreme simplicity, the restricted experience, of 'the rude forefathers' of these secluded 'hamlets.' I met another old resident, a sort of replica of 'Jock.' He had been over threescore years in the same house and on the same farm. Asked if ever he had been out of the parish, he responded with quite sprightly alacrity: 'Ay, aince, fin I wis a young chap.'

'Where did you go?'

'Man, I wis aince i' Montrose!' (about twenty miles distant).

I happened to be going up to call at a farm some miles away, and was not very sure of the road, so never doubting but that this old, old inhabitant, would know every path and every soul within the radius of ten miles at least, I asked: 'Div ye ken where I turn off to So-and-so?'

'Fa bides there?' said the patriarch.

'Mrs. So-and-so.'

'Oh ay, that's her fairm is't? I've often haard o' her but I've never seen her. The fairm's a bit aff the ro'd, but losh, man, I wis never up at e' tap o' e' Glen!' The farm I wished to visit was certainly not three miles from where we then stood.

Now such an experience is absolutely true; it is indeed becoming rare, but it was not at all uncommon in the times of which I have been writing. Away down in Galloway, in the secluded parish of Carsphairn, the isolation was so complete, that my cousin assured me that the following incident was strictly true. A shepherd's lassie one day came running into the lowly cabin to tell her mother of an entirely novel sight. So secluded was the spot that the poor children had never seen another grown-up man than their father. So the artless lassie called out: 'Oh, mither, here's a thing like feyther comin' up the ro'd !'

Let me give a few more illustrations of this extreme rusticity and Arcadian simplicity, from my notes. The stories are legion of the whimsical mistakes made, for instance, by raw country lassies on first going to service. There is the case of the girl who mistook silver forks for 'spunes a' slittit doon the back'; a case, which came under my own notice, of a lassie cleaning the silver butter - knife on the knifeboard; of Donald mistaking the zebra in the Zoo for 'a tartan cuddy,' and the young elephant for 'a muckle ingy-rubber coo, wi' a tail at ilka end.' There are anecdotes by the dozen of Tam or Jock at the wax-works, of Meg or Kirsty at the telegraph station, and of Sandie or Peggy at 'the play,' but perhaps one of the most whimsical is that related of an old farmer, and which, I am assured, actually occurred a little north of Forfarshire, in my father's time. One old farmer, after paying his rent, had been asked in to dine with the laird, an honour now conferred for the first time. John had never been in such company, nor had he ever seen such grandeur. Now during the progress of the first course, he had conceived quite an affectionate attachment to the fine, big, solid silver

spoon, with which he had been ladling his soup down
his capacious maw. In fact he had confided to his
neighbour, an old dowager lady, who seemed much
surprised at the confidence, that it was a 'wyse-like
spune.' After carefully licking it clean, he laid it down
beside his plate, with a view to further service ; nor
would he allow the amazed and indignant butler to
remove it or even to touch it. The unsuccessful attempts
of the precise serving-man to take away the treasured
spoon had been giving much amusement to the observant
company. At length, when the sweets appeared, the
butler tried to tempt him to yield up the treasure, by
showing him a bright, clean dessert spoon, and whisperingly endeavoured to convey to the old farmer's intelligence, that the two spoons had quite separate and
distinct functions. But the obdurate old fellow was
proof against all the butler's blandishments. The good
champagne, too, had put him quite at his ease. He
evidently had made up his mind 'to stick to a good
thing when he had it' ; and at length he fairly convulsed
the quiet observers of all this comical by-play, and
nearly caused the bland butler to explode, by saying
very emphatically : 'Na, na, ma man, it's nae eese'
(use) ; 'ma mooth's as big for pudden' as it is for
kail.'

Another specimen of the ludicrous lack of a due
sense of proportion, or comparison, in the rustic mind,
is afforded by the anecdote told of two worthy cronies
who had gone up to London during the Fisheries
Exhibition, from Fittie (Foot Dee), Aberdeenshire. It
was the first time in their lives they had ever been over
a score of miles from home ; and among other places

L

they visited was the venerable and magnificent Abbey of Westminster, during the celebration of some great function. While gazing open-mouthed at the impressive pageant, with the strains of the solemn organ pealing down the sculptured aisles, the thoughts of one of the Aberdonians had evidently gone back to his native village, and he had been instituting some sort of mental comparison between the abbey and the village kirk. Turning to his companion, he said with delicious simplicity : 'Losh, Geordie, min, this clean beats Fittie a' tae Buff!'

Another Aberdonian utterance was equally naïve, but perhaps a little disconcerting, as being liable to some misinterpretation. An eminent physician, hailing from the granite county, had returned on a visit to his native parish. A poor man of his acquaintance being seriously ill, the doctor, whenever requisitioned, had attended him gratuitously, and had been very kind. Some little time, however, having elapsed without any summons for the exercise of his professional skill, and hearing that the patient had breathed his last, the worthy doctor went to call on the widow, and asked her why she had not sent for him as formerly. Whereupon she replied : 'Oh, ye see, sir, I wanted my man to dee a naiteral deith.'

As illustrating the difference now existing in this luxurious and conventional age, in the bringing up of children, and the plain diet of the former age of rural simplicity, I may instance the following. It was told me by an engineer residing in Liverpool, whose mother, a worthy dame of the old school, lived in Montrose. He had sent his two boys north during

the holidays to see their 'grannie,' and the boys were
of course accustomed to the modern *régime*. The dear
old lady had made special preparations in her simple,
primitive way, and wishing to give the 'laddies' a treat,
she had prepared with her own hands, a good substantial
currant dumpling, which, indeed, constituted the whole
of the repast. On putting the smoking, sonsy dish
before the two English-bred lads, she asked with a fine
assumption of careless unconcern :—

'Wull ye hae a bittie dumplin', lathies ?'

'Yes,' said one, rather loftily and superciliously,
'I'll take a little bit after dinner.'

'Efter denner, ye monkeys ?' said the irate grannie,
all her old Scottish susceptibilities at once aroused.
'Hech ! this is a' yer denner.'

It was not always safe, though, to presume too much
on the apparently Arcadian simplicity of these homely
country folks. A good instance of the schemer being
discomfited is the following :—

A pawky Forfarshire weaver had his home invaded
one day by a lusty truculent-looking beggar, who pre-
tended to be deaf and dumb, and went through a long
course of exaggerated pantomime. The shrewd old
wabster looked at him with a grim, quizzical expression.
Next he took up the long, thin, sharp knife with which
he was wont to trim the thrums. Then putting on an
angry expression, he shouted to his wife : 'Kirsty,
Kirsty, bring ben the shairpen-stane ; there's a dummy
here wi' lots o' bawbees, an' naebody saw him come
in.'

The impostor took to his heels ; his deafness was
cured.

Another instance of the comical naïveté of this simple old class is an anecdote recorded of one Peter Reid, a celebrity of Govan. Peter had a dispute with one of his humble cottar-tenants, who refused to pay his rent, pleading as a set-off that certain goods had been destroyed by rats, with which the premises were infested. Peter summoned him before the sheriff, but that functionary gave the case in favour of the tenant. Another Govan crony meeting Peter, remarked to him : ' Weel, Peter, I see ye've lost yer rat case.' Peter replied : ' Losh, man, gin the shirra had ta'en the same view o' the case as I did, I wud hae won 't.'

For quiet, rustic, good-natured philosophy, however, few instances, I think, could better the following :—

An old farmer whose wife had died bethought him after a time that he would again try a chance in the matrimonial lottery. He accordingly set his mature affections on a lady who was almost the direct antithesis of his first wife. He proposed, was accepted, and got married. An old friend and neighbour, whose ideas of housewifely excellence were of a very homely and practical character, moved by a natural curiosity, came to see the new mistress of his friend's establishment. He began at once to subject her to a very searching catechism as to the virtues of herbs and simples, the treatment of ' yowes' at lambing time, and other such recondite rural matters. The replies being from a town-bred woman, were apparently not of a very satisfactory character, for some short time afterwards, when taking leave of his old crony, he said :—

' I divna think muckle o' yer new wife, John.'

˟ John philosophically responded : 'Hoots, man, fat ails her ? She's jist God's handiwark, ye ken, altho' mebbe she's no jist a'thegither His maister-piece.'

A pure specimen of the raw Bœotian, however, must have been that old Deeside shepherd, who on his first visit to Aberdeen, looked with awe and amazement on the great expanse of ocean. Viewing the scene from a height near the city, he spied a stately clipper letting down fold after fold of her snowy canvas as she slowly glided out to sea. This novel sight struck him with added wonder. One of the ship's boats was being towed at the stern, and this seemed to astonish the guileless Corydon, even more than the heaving billows or aught else. Turning to his companion he gave vent to his wonderment in this fashion : 'Losh, Jess; arena the works o' natur' most wonnerfu'? bless me, even the vera ships hae little anes.'

Another somewhat different estimate of the ' works o' natur'' was that of the shepherd whose poverty of expression prevented him from rendering his feelings into words. He was lying on the braeside with a companion on a fine summer afternoon. The fair, fertile straths and valleys lay extended in beautiful amplitude beneath them. On either hand the majestic heather-clad hills rose range on range and tier on tier, till their crimson crests seemed to touch the fleecy clouds that threw here and there a soft shadow on the sunny slopes, where the sheep lay blinking in the hazy heat. It was a scene of wondrous beauty. The dull soul of the country clodhopper even, was stirred within him. He felt the beauty of the prospect. It stirred vague senti-

ments within him ; it whispered poetic images to his
mind ; but, alas ! he lacked the faculty of expression.
Still the beauty of the vision was on him ; the compulsion of poetic thought forced him to make some audible
confession of what he inly felt. If he were only gifted
now ! But, alas ! he was only a poor hard-worked farm
loon. But speak he must. So, taking his short, black
'cutty' out of his mouth he addressed his drowsy companion thus : ' Eh, man, Jock ! arena the works o'
natur' jist—jist—jist DEEVILITCH ? '

As an instance of the quiet, pawky, Southron humour
of the purely rustic sort, take this :—

A lanky, dishevelled shepherd having been to a fair,
had managed to get quit of his charge, the flock having
been sold, so he determined to indulge in the luxury of
a shave. He had never sat in a barber's chair, and he
thought he would just for once undergo the operation,
to see what it was like. He had a good stubble of
nearly a week's growth, and he fancied it would be nice
to go back to his sweetheart with a smooth, trim chin,
at all events. So he entered the barber's shop ; and the
barber, taking his measure at a glance, told off, as it
was a busy day, one of the improvers to operate on the
Arcadian tyro. The improver had not been further
improved by sundry potations, and moreover his razor
was about as blunt as his own manners. He fairly
lacerated the poor shepherd, taking off almost as much
skin as hair. The poor victim bore it as meekly as one
of his own sheep would have borne the shears, and at
length, when set free from the encompassing sheet, he
gravely marched up to the mirror, then reached out his
hand for a jug of water and took a mighty gulp,

with which he distended his mouth, and then spat it out in the basin. The master barber had been eyeing this strange procedure, and with natural curiosity inquired ' What was that for ? '　' Oh,' said the shepherd, ' I wis jist tryin' if ma mooth wad haud in.'

CHAPTER IX

RUSTICITY OF THE OLDEN TIME (*continued*)

The two ploughmen at Alloa—A simple magistrate—The laird
and his henchman Donald—Primitive dentistry—A rustic
dancing-lesson—Dancie Fettes—A Paisley apologist—A testy
farmer to his dog—The chief engineer's present—The D.D.
and the cuddy.

IN continuation of my remarks in the last chapter anent
the present age of universal travel, when men 'move to
and fro upon the face of the earth' as restlessly as Satan
himself, and when they have developed a certain Satanic
sharpness and precocity withal, such an instance of more
than Bœotian simplicity and ignorance as the following,
may hardly be credible. The story goes that 'twa
country Jocks,' regular 'hay-seed cousins' as an American would call them, men of the class I have been
describing, who had never been far from their native
parish, and knew little outside the rude if simple philosophy of the bothy, found themselves on one holiday
at the primitive little semi-marine town of Alloa on the
Forth. After gaping and gazing at all the unwonted
sights, their wonder reached its acme when they strolled

down to the muddy strand, and saw for the first time
the phenomenon of the tides, and discovered that the
water was salt. An old barge had been careened, and
was now stranded high and dry on the bank, with its
keel shorewards, and a plank led from its weather-beaten
bulwark to the sward, close to the feet of our two unsophisticated ploughmen.

Never having seen such a homogeneous mass of wood
in their lives before, and in their innocence mistaking it
for some natural product of some prehistoric forest perhaps, the more daring of the two, itching for a closer
scrutiny, cautiously crept on hands and knees up the
plank, and then viewing the sloping deck, with its great
gaping main-hatch yawning wide and gloomy, he nearly
fell off the plank in his astonishment; and with eyes
wide distended, and in awe-struck accents, he communicated to his chum on the bank the marvellous dis-
covery he had made, in these words : ' Losh, Geordie,
she's boss.'

' Boss ' is a good expressive word, signifying hollow,
empty. I have heard it used by an old Scot in a colonial
legislature, criticising a member of the opposition.
After a rather frothy speech the old fellow grimly said :
' Eh, sirs, but he's terrible boss.'

The simplicity of the ploughmen is equalled, if not
excelled, by that of the Glasgow bailie before whom a
case was being tried, in which the plaintiff sought to
recover damages from a defendant neighbour for alleged
carelessness in opening the door of a cage and allowing
a valuable ferret to escape. The worthy bailie had
never heard of a ferret, and did not know what sort of
a beast it could be, but the allusion to ' a cage ' seemed

to throw some glimmer of light on the suit. Assuming a wise air, he addressed the parties thus : 'It was nae doot wrang of you, sir, to open the door o' the cage ; but ye was wrang too, sir,' turning to the plaintiff ; 'for what for did ye no clip the brute's wings ?' Case dismissed.

This reminds me of another instance of bucolic simplicity on the part of a Highland bonnet-laird, of whom it is related that, having occasion to leave his ancestral home—a heather-theekit bit o' a biggin'—on some legal errand, he found himself for the first time in his life a guest in the home of one of the great chieftains of his name. As fitting to his descent, being lineally of chieftain's blood, he had chosen to accompany him on his travels one of his retainers—the only one almost, in fact, he had left. Donal' for the occasion was dressed in full clan costume, but at home he generally filled the less ornamental but more useful *rôle* of general-utility man —looking after the sheep, castin' peats, ploughing the sour bit of arable land on the laird's ancestral holding, and such like tasks. However, the story goes that at last the laird, accompanied by Donal', was shown to his bedroom. Now the room contained one of the old-fashioned solid mahogany four-post bedsteads. The canopy was a magnificent catafalque sort of an affair, draped with velvet and rich brocade, and the laird, who had never before witnessed such a magnificent structure, perhaps not unnaturally fancied that the highest position he could attain, was also the most honourable. So, with Donal's assistance, he climbed up on the top of the canopy, and there made the best dispositions he could, for the enjoyment of a night's rest. Donal', honest man, with the natural imperturbability of a true Hielantman, turned in, on to the bed, nothing loath, and was soon wrapped in slumber and a warm pair of blankets. By and by the laird, who was far from comfortable on his elevated perch, began to feel the cold, and he envied the sleeping Donald, whose melodious proboscis made it quite manifest to the laird that Donal' at all events was able to sleep. Cautiously peering over, he hailed his henchman, and having gained his hearing said: 'Od, Donal', if it wasna for the honour o' the thing, I wad fain come doon an' get in aside ye.'

By and by, so the story goes, Donal' and the laird reached Edinburgh. Being 'on pleasure bent,' yet withal 'of frugal mind,' the laird had engaged but a single room for himself and faithful attendant, and after a day's sight-seeing they retired to their apartment. With a due regard to the distinction of rank, and to maintain his dignity, the laird took up his position in the four-poster with possession of the pillows; but not wishing Donal' to spend as cold and comfortless a night as he himself had done on the canopy on a previous night, he told his man to put his head at the foot of the bed. So they disposed themselves 'heids and thraws' as the saying is. Presently the laird, being mellowed with a good jorum of toddy, and yielding to the genial warmth and comfort of the well-furnished bed, said in rather a condescending, patronising tone : 'Weel, Donal', an' hoo div ye like sleepin' at my feet?' To which Donal', with most matter-of-fact independence, replied : 'Ow, fine, laird! Hoo div ye like sleepin' at mine?'

Another instance of this rusticity comes to me. On

the Clyde, opposite Renfrew, nestles the village of
Yoker. One of the best-known worthies of the village
was Jeems Hervie, the proprietor of the smiddy. To
his vocation of blacksmith, he added that of amateur
dentist and blood-letter, and was often called on to
exercise his skill in both these accomplishments. One
of his patrons, an old woman, for whom the burly
Jeems had drawn a few teeth on odd occasions,
happened to be in Glasgow one day, and she was
'tormentit to deith wi' the teethache.' Seeing the
notice in a dentist's window, 'Teeth extracted,' she went
in, submitted herself to the skilful operator, and in a
trice, with wonderful dexterity and gentleness, she was
relieved of the aching molar. She asked the fee.

'Two-and-six, ma'am.'

'What?' said she. 'Hauf a croon? An' it sae easy
dune? Auld Jeems Hervie wad hae pu'ed me a' throw
the smiddy for saxpence!'

My fellow-passenger on the *Orotava*, Mr. M——, gave
me another most humorous rendering of an experience
which befel a young friend of his once in a secluded
rural district somewhere in the south of Scotland. I
wish I could reproduce it with the quaint drollery and
genuine humour Mr. M—— infused into his narration.
His informant was spending a holiday in this quiet
neighbourhood, and during one of his evening rambles
he heard a peculiar, crooning, lilting sound interspersed
with comments and commands, as of one addressing an
assemblage, and which seemed to proceed from a large
barn-like building close by. Seeing the glimmer of a
light through certain chinks, he sauntered up to the door,
pushed it open, and peeped in. A strange sight met his

eyes. One which formerly, however, in my young days might have often been seen in the Mearns.

A row of buxom lassies in short goons and wincey kirtles, hair neatly snooded, and feet, arms, and head for the most part bare, looking the very picture of rustic health and comeliness, stood in line opposite to a row of young ploughmen and farm hands, with hair well creeshed, faces shining with soap and hard towelling, and looking, sooth to say, much more rustic and awkward than the bouncing lassies confronting them. At the end, midway between the opposing rows, sat on an upturned bushel-measure, a dapper little weazen-faced character dressed in threadbare dress suit, with white stockings and dancing pumps on his dainty, delicate feet. The dress coat was of blue cloth adorned with brass buttons, but it sat well on the precise, ruddy-cheeked, twinkling-eyed little dancing-master.

His sharp eye at once noticed the intrusion of a well-dressed stranger, and he at once said : 'Oh, come awa' in-bye, sir! Ye're very welcome. I'm jist pittin' my pewpils through their dancin' lesson. We're jist at a bit kintra dance, an' I aye like tae start the beginners wi'oot the fiddle.'

A sharp tap with his cane on the bushel, brought the lads and lassies to 'attention,' and then in a chirpy staccato sort of croon—the noise which had at first attracted the visitor's curiosity—he began lilting to a well-known air, a continuous stream of instructions, explanations, encouragements, chidings, expostulations, and odd comments, all in rhyming cadenced time to the lilt he crooned without cessation—somewhat after this fashion :—

Up lads, noo !
      Ta teedleum ta toodleum.
Up lassies, too !
      Ta teedleum ta toodleum.
Taes in a line noo !
      Ta teedleum ta toodleum.
Lat ilka ane boo !
      Ta teedleum ta toodleum.
Toots, Jean Gibb, ye're a' wrang, you !
      Ta teedleum ta toodleum.
Ye're a' richt noo !
      Ta teedleum ta toodleum.
Set till ilk ither noo !
      Ta teedleum ta toodleum.
Turn roond about noo !
      Ta teedleum ta toodleum.
First frae tap noo !
      Ta teedleum ta toodleu
Doon the middle noo !
      Ta teedleum ta toodleum.
Stan' back, Jock Tamson—you !
      Ta teedleum ta toodleum.
Jine haunds noo !
      Ta teedleum ta toodleum.
Poussette tae ither noo !
      Ta teedleum ta toodleum.
Back tae places noo !
      Ta teedleum ta toodleum.
Toots, yer a' wrang thegither !
      Ta teedleum ta toodleum.
Tam Wilkie, ye're a gowk !
      Ta teedleum ta toodleum.

And so the old mannikin, with wonderful vivacity, proceeded, his keen eyes taking in every detail, noting every
fault. With pungent, caustic, quaint interpolations the
whimsical scene went on, and at length, perspiring, laugh-
ing, with hoydenish interchange of rural coquetries and
farmyard *plaisanterie*, not of the most refined kind, this
most original rehearsal concluded. It was said, however,

that the old fellow was really a most efficient dancing-master, and in this comically quaint and original way, turned out, if not Terpsichorean prodigies, at least passable dancers.

Of a somewhat similar old character known as Dancie Fettes, who used to teach dancing in the Howe o' the Mearns in my young days, accompanied always by his son who acted as assistant-master, it is related that on one occasion having partaken of a very poor 'scrimpit tea' at the table of a notoriously parsimonious and stingy housewife, he very pawkily remarked to his son, after they had left the inhospitable dwelling : 'Aweel, John, if we're no nae better we're no nae waur.' As a bit of typical Scottish philosophy this is hard to beat.

The vague distrust of giving a direct reply or com-mitting oneself to a positive statement without seeing fully what the result may be, which is a very common characteristic, even now, of the rustic Scot, is well shown in the following incident. The man was a stolid-looking fellow, and he was giving evidence in some police-court case. The cross-examining attorney was one of those sharp terrier-like 'limbs of the law,' whose very look sometimes bothers a witness of this rustic type, and he began by rather imperiously asking the man : 'Where were you born ?'

There was absolutely nothing in the question. It was merely one of the stock kind used by a lawyer while he is making up his mind as to his line of attack. The poor witness, however, had an instinctive idea that this man was hostile. His native caution and suspicious-ness were fully aroused. He perspired freely, blushed furiously, and not exactly seeing the object of the question, or what it might be preparing to lead up to, he fenced a bit, by saying in a vague, uncertain sort of way that 'He cam' frae the Sooth.'

'Yes, but where were you born? In Dunfermline?'

'Na, sir, I jist cam' frae the Sooth.' He evidently thought this was a safe non-committal answer, and he would do well to stick to it.

'Yes, but what part of the South? Dumfries? Berwick? Ayrshire? or where?'

'Oh, I jist cam' frae the Sooth, sir.'

This was really too much for the attorney. He began to rate him in no measured terms, demanding a categorical reply. The poor clown, now more than ever convinced that there was some deep design against his personal safety in this persistent, pitiless probing, but seeing no help for it, blurted out in desperation : 'Weel, sir, tae tell ye the plain truth, I wis born in "Paisley"'; then with intense earnestness, turning to the presiding magistrate, he sought to minimise the import of the awful admission by saying : 'But, as sure's deith, yer honner, I cudna help it; I cudna help it.'

The following is deliciously rustic and characteristically Scottish. An old farmer mannie in Midlothian, was driving a calf into Edinburgh to the butcher, and was accompanied by his young dog, which, in his untrained eagerness and zeal, kept bark, barking at the heels of the terrified and silly calf. At length the incessant barking, and consequent mad, zigzag rushes of the dazed calf, fairly exasperated the poor perspiring man. He testily addressed the over-officious dog : 'Hoots, ye gowkit brute, what are ye bowf, bowfin' at? It wud be wyser-like if ye'd gang an' fesh (fetch) a barrow.'

My good old friend 'M'Kendrick, chief engineer of the s.s. *Orotava*, as humorous and kindly a Scot as ever broke a bannock, told me a most ludicrous incident of which an old uncle of his, a small farmer in one of the southern counties, was the hero. The steamer had called in at Colombo, and Mac had purchased various trifles and nicknacks from the Cingalese traders that swarm aboard, displaying tortoise-shell, ebony, ivory, and other curios. Among the commonest of these are models of elephants made of ebony, designed for letter weights, or mere mantelpiece ornaments, and M'Kendrick had purchased two fine large specimens as a present from foreign parts to his old uncle. When the vessel arrived at London, Mac made up the parcel and wrote to the old gentleman that he was sending him two Ceylon elephants as a present, and he was to call at the railway station for them. You can imagine the poor old farmer's amazement. He knew nothing of ebony ornaments. Mac had never thought there was any need for being minutely explicit; but he learned afterwards from a cousin, that the receipt of the letter inspired the following outburst: 'The deil's in the fallow. Is he gaun clean gyte? Twa Ceylon elephants! Od, bless me, they'll kill ilka beast aboot the ferm.' Of course the mystery was eventually cleared up, but the mistake is still kept up as a good joke against the simple old man.

The late Thomas Constable used to tell the following story with admirable effect, and through the great courtesy and kindness of his son, I am able to reproduce it here, just as the kindly old publisher used to tell it himself.

Mrs. Macknight, *loquitur*. She is telling the story

M

about her husband's colleague.   Half the humour con-
sists in the excellent imitation of the dear old lady's
voice which Mr. Constable used to render with inimitable effect.   Thus ran the tale :—

'Ye'll hae heard tell o' Dr. Henry? He wis an
aix'lent man Dr. Henry.   Deed ay! but he wis nae
great gun o' the Gospel.   I min' yae day, when he wis
on his w'y to the kirk, there cam on an' awfu' doon-
pour, an' the doctor was jist dreepin' wat ; an' there wis
yiu o' the congregation that see'd him, an' he said—an'
it was geyan smairt tae—"Aweel, aweel! he'll be dry
eneuch whin he gets intae the poopit."   Eh! but he wis
an aix'lent man!   There wis yae day, whin he wis in
the vera middle o' his sermon, an' whin he wis fair
muvit his ain sel' by whit he wis sayin'—ay, an' he
wad daud the cushions sae as maist to blin' the precentor whiles.   Weel! whin the stoor begoud to clear
awa', he sees a wumman i' the middle o' the kirk
dichtin' her een twa or three times wi' her naipkin, an'
syne boo doon rael affeckit like.   "Weel," thinks he
tae himsel' (that's Dr. Henry, ye ken), "I maun fin' oot
whit pairt o' my discoorse has produced this effeck—I
maun e'en speir at Maggie hersel'."   So whin the morn's
morn wis come, he maks his w'y to the wee bit hoose
whaur Maggie bided.   An' whin he gangs in he says :
"Guid mornin', Maggie.   Hoo's a' wi' ye the day?"
"Oo brawly, sir.   Hoo are ye yersel'?" says Maggie.
An' syne she dichts a chyre, so's it suldna syle the
minister's black claes, ye ken.   An' then Dr. Henry
he sits doon, wi' a look o' dignity quite peculiar tae
himsel'.   "An'," says he—that's the minister tae Maggie,
ye ken—"I've aye observit, Maggie," says he, "that

ye're a vera reg'lar attender at the kirk." "Aweel, I'm sure, sir," says Maggie, "that I dae nae mair than my duty in that respeck!" "That's vera true," says Dr. Henry—that's the minister tae Maggie, ye ken—"but 'deed it's no ilka yin that dis their duty, Maggie. But I've observit, Maggie, that ye're no only a very reg'lar attender at the kirk, but that ye p'y parteec'lar attention to my discoorse. Indeed, I observit yesterday at the forenune's diet that there wis yae pint o' my discoorse that seemed to hae a parteec'lar effeck upon you Maggie, an' so I've just come this mornin' to learn frae yer ain lips what pint it wis, Maggie." "Ah weel, sir," said Maggie—that was Maggie tae the minister, ye ken—"I really culdna tell ye that, sir." "Oh, but I maun hear it," says Dr. Henry. "'Deed sir," says she—that's Maggie to the minister—"ye maunna be angry wi' me; but indeed I culdna tell ye that, sir." "Toots, wumman, but I maun hear it," says Dr. Henry. "Weel, sir," says Maggie, "if ye maun hae it —but indeed ye maunna be angry wi' me, sir!—I'm but a puir lane weeda' wumman. Whan the guidman wis leevin', ye see we hed a bit gairden, an' we keepit a cuddy—an' I wad gang wi' the cuddy to the toon an' to the market, an' sell a'thing oot o' the gairden, an' syne I'd come back, an' eh, sir, but we wis rael happy thegither. Weel, sir, the gudeman's deid, an' they've stown awa' the cuddy, an' it's been sair times wi' me; an' weel, sir—'deed ye maunna be angry wi' me, sir; but whan your vyse reaches a certain pitch, sir, it aye pits me in min' o' my puir cuddy; an'—an' (sobbingly), 'deed, sir, ye maunna be angry; but—but—I canna help it." '

CHAPTER X

OLD-FASHIONED SERVANTS AND SERVICE

The kindly relationships of the old time—A tactless guest in Glenesk—Modern precocity—John Macrae—The old Highland
keeper—Outspoken criticism—Robbie and the railway—Sandie
and the French *bonne*—A pawkÿ butler—Old Andrew's caution
about the cabs—A matter-of-fact Abigail—Deeside candour—
One from the Antipodes—Jock and the reid herrin'—A quaint
definition—Personal good fortune with servants—Length of
service and fidelity—Illustrations—Old George the gardener—
Lessons to be learned from such humble records.

WE constantly hear nowadays and on all hands that
the fine old faithful breed of servants has died out. It
would seem as if faith in disinterestedness had fled—as
if mutual trust and confidence between master and man
had taken flight. I think, however, it may be taken as
a solemn truth that wherever confidence has been lost,
it is mainly because it has been betrayed. It is a plant
of tender and of slow growth, and a rude breath or
nipping chill can easily stunt it. Any long-continued
cold draught will assuredly kill it. It would perhaps
not be altogether profitless—I am sure it would be
interesting—to hear what the servants have to say about
the fine old courtly and considerate breed of masters
and mistresses. For one thing, the modern apostle of

Progress, who is not uncommonly too, the Cassandra-like croaker and prophet of evil, fulfilling a Janus-like function, telling us the past was bad but the future is likely to be worse, is opposed on principle to the use of the good old phrase master and man, or master and servant. I was once taken soundly to task by an eloquent ex-member of Parliament in Australia, who had been asked by the chairman of a large public meeting to propose a vote of thanks to me for a lecture I had just delivered. My subject had been 'Servants and Service.' I had tried, according to my lights, to give the true ideas, the real, essential, underlying principles of all true service : how both the rendering and the accepting of service implied no one-sidedness, but that the compact was a mutual one. But my friend, who yet hoped to climb back into Parliament by the help of the working-man vote, waxed eloquent in withering indignation at my daring to use the obsolete and discredited term Master. With fine scorn he declared he would own no master. 'There were no masters or servants nowadays. I should have spoken of employer and employed.' What sorry fustian ! It is this persistent degradation of the fine, old, kindly community of interest, the human contact involved in the old ties, the warm sympathy and mutual trust and interdependence that was so much a feature of the old *régime*, both in the house, the store, and the workshop, that made the connection so lasting and so strong. The mere cash nexus, which is the only one that our modern demagogue or our purblind political economist will recognise, is as brittle as glass, and as inelastic as a withered stick.

The meanness of some of the ill-bred parvenus who

have risen from the ranks, and their want of tact, are
very quickly noted by the servants. There are no
keener observers than the oftentimes despised occupants
of the servants' hall. Among the old-fashioned class
of Scottish servants, too, there was often a rare delicacy
and a keen sensitiveness, that coarse - grained people
could scarce realise. I heard up in Glenesk an instance
of such coarse-grained maladroitness on the part of a
well-to-do gentleman, whose name was withheld, which
exemplifies how utterly inconsiderate and 'shabby'—
using the word in its Scottish sense to signify 'mean'—
even an educated man, occupying a good public position,
can be. On one occasion he had taken possession of the
rooms at a secluded home near the loch, occupied by a
fine stalwart farmer and his dear old mother, who,
in her young days, had seen service in my father's
manse. The party had been welcomed with true
Highland hospitality. For fully three weeks they
occupied the best rooms, turned the usual quiet routine
of the humble home completely topsy-turvy, and at
the end of their stay the stupid man crowned his selfish
and inconsiderate conduct, by actually offering to the
dear old dame, the lordly douceur of—what think you,
gentle reader ?—a whole half-crown ! As the stalwart
host said afterwards, in telling the story to a
friend : 'We wantit nothing, sir ; the man was welcome
for his very name's sake ; an' if he wished to pay for
what was freely-rendered hospitality, that was for his
own sel' to conseeder. But dang the man, tae offer my
old mother hauf-a-croon. Toots, toots, sir, it was a
puir, puir thing to do.' It would have been far better
to have offered nothing at all.

A rather whimsical illustration of the fact that the question of service has two sides however, is illustrated by the following incident. An Aberdeenshire 'loonie,' applying for a situation, was requested to bring a 'letter of character' from his minister or schoolmaster, and return with it in the afternoon, when, if all was satisfactory, he would likely get the vacant position for which he was applying. Two days passed, but there was no reappearance of the boy. At length the shopkeeper, who had been really attracted by the lad's bright appearance, happened to meet him in the street, recognised him instantly, and at once asked him 'why he had not come back with his certificate of character.' 'Weel, sir,' replied the precocious juvenile, 'afore gettin' hame, feth, I got *your* charackter—an' AH'M NO COMIN'.'

Among the old type of servants—those of the Caleb Balderstone and Andrew Fairservice order—there was none of that sleek obsequiousness, that exaggerated deference, that inordinate mock humility which is demanded from domestics by the parvenus and *nouveau riche* that arrogate to themselves the 'chief places in the synagogue' of our modern social fabric, at watering-places and other fashionable resorts. The old-fashioned Scottish servant was a man, not a flunkey. He was allowed to have feelings and opinions of his own, and he or she was frequently not at all backward in showing the one, or freely expressing the other; but always at the back lay great loyalty and affection, and a sincere, honest regard for the master's honour and the best interests of the family.

Numberless instances of this trait might be cited. The best stories of the kind have doubtless been told already, but there is such a strong element of living, human interest in these old-fashioned relationships and mutual attachments, that one may well be pardoned if he can add a few more pebbles to the already goodly cairn of servant stories, heaped up by past wayfarers and pilgrims in the path of Scottish story and reminiscence.

As an example of the frank, independent spirit of the old-time servant, and their fearless, ready outspokenness, so different from the silky, fawning, oriental obsequiousness of the typical modern flunkey, let me give a couple of instances detailed to me by a douce Highlander, John Macrae, head gamekeeper to my cousin George, at The Retreat in Glenesk. John himself has been a good many years with his generous master, and, indeed, every year as the grouse season comes round, one may safely predict that the same honest, pleasant faces may be seen, both in kitchen and on the moors, rendering loyal and faithful service to a kind and considerate master. Here, in fact, is exemplified what Shakespeare (in *As You Like It*) calls—

> The constant service of the antique world,
> When service sweat for duty, not for meed !
> . . . not for the fashion of these times,
> Where none will sweat but for promotion,
> And having that, do choke their service up
> Even with the having.

I was taking a cast for salmon one fine day early in August down by the pool of Keenie, on the North Esk, while waiting the arrival of the grouse-shooting contingent, and John was in attendance with the gaff. He comes from Strathconan, and had many a quaint story of

Highland life to tell me, while he also indulged in much shrewd questioning about my wanderings in the East, and life in Australia. Gradually the conversation drifted round to the subject of service. John spoke with evident feeling and real attachment of his present master, my warm-hearted cousin George, and I enjoyed some very shrewd and racy criticisms on one or two of the other keepers in the district, and a very correct and pawky estimate of the characters of several of my cousin's guests. John did not probably know that he was in reality being interviewed by an ex-journalist, yet such was the case. I am not, however, going to betray a confidence so pleasantly and innocently given.

One or two of his reminiscences about an old head keeper in a Highland establishment, a regular old retainer, under whom John had graduated as a gillie, were very characteristic, and bear on the subject at present under discussion.

On one occasion, at the opening of the shooting season, the old fellow was accosted in a patronising style by a pursy, fussy, self-important egotist, who was evidently no great favourite. In reply to his condescending inquiry after the old keeper's health, came the following unaccommodating reply :—

'Oh, ah'm fine, thank ye. But, save's a', *ye're* sair failed, and far owre fat.'

To another Cockney guest, with whom he had toiled nearly half a day to bring him within fair shooting distance of a lordly stag, only to see the tyro sportsman make a most palpable and humiliating miss, he was equally frank and direct. The young man, instead of honestly admitting his own inaccuracy and inexperience, began to make a minute and ostentatious inspection of the rifle with which he had made such a miss.   Donal', with a very sour, disgusted expression, watched this affectation for a moment, then dryly said, with a strong Highland accent—

' Iss the riffle goot, sir ? '

' Oh yes ! ' was the forced admission.

' Och, then, you pe no goot.'

My cousin David, now a Shetland laird, has evidently learned the old Glen secret of securing the attachment and the ' constant service ' of these humbler retainers, on whose goodwill and fidelity so much that is sweetest and most homelike about home life really depends.   At any rate he has been fortunate in having had few changes in his *ménage*.   One old servant, Peggy, has been with him over twenty years.   His *factotum*, however, is the Robbie already mentioned, a Shetlander, who under a somewhat pawky assumption of extreme simplicity really hides keen observation and much shrewdness.   One is never sure how far Robbie's acts and utterances are the outcome of pure innocence or sly artfulness. At any rate he is devoted to his master ; is industrious, willing, honest, and faithful to a degree.   It may illustrate his simplicity if I relate his earliest experience with the railway, when first he visited the South with his master, now some two decades ago—for he has never been in any other service but the one.   He was but a simple-minded rustic, never having been beyond the narrow confines of Shetland.   They came to Aberdeen by boat, and at the Granite City the party had, of course, to take to the train to get to Edinburgh.   The train was just about to start, and one of the young ladies

said : 'Come, get in now, Robbie, we are about to start.'
Poor Robbie betrayed his verdancy, but his true delicacy
at the same time, by saying : 'Na, na, Miss ! it's no for
the like o' me. I wad like tae tak' an ootside saet an'
see the kintra.'

David tells me, too, a characteristically professional
view of things taken by an old shepherd of his father's.
It so happened that some friends of high station—
'quality folks of high degree'—had been paying a visit
up the Glen in the old hospitable days, which I have
tried to describe in *Oor Ain Folk*. In attendance on the
lady was a fat French *bonne*, and she betrayed her
Parisian inclinings and Gallic ways by a variety of
affectations, and played off her little coquetries on the
lamb-like shepherd swains whom she met in the old
farm - kitchen. A picnic had been organised to visit a
favourite spot at the top of the Glen, which involved the
climbing of a pretty high hill, whence, however, a magnificent view rewarded the climbers for the rather steep
ascent. The buxom *bonne* was made over to the care of
my young cousin David, and old Sandie the shepherd.
Sandie was very undemonstrative, very matter-of-fact,
and utterly proof against all feminine blandishments—of
the Parisian type at all events. All the pretty attitudes
and pouting *moues* and captivating affectations of the
bonne, could not hide the plain unaccommodating facts
that the day was hot, the climb was steep, she was
heavy, and Sandie had to exert all his strength to haul
her up the hill. At length he paused to wipe the
beaded perspiration from his bald head, and with a keen
professional eye, having gauged the plump proportions
of his fair, fat, and frolicsome charge, he said admiringly

to David : 'Eh, Dauvit man, she's in graund order for winterin'.'

An instance of the Caleb Balderstone type is that related of the old butler, who, thinking the guests were sitting rather long at table, and that the cellar would proportionately suffer, gave the company rather a strong hint by gravely announcing, to his hospitable master's mortification : 'If ye please, sir, the kerridges are a' yokit, an' ah'm thinkin' the drivers 'll be wearyin'.'

The same fearless independence and kindly *aplomb* characterised the utterance of the somewhat spoilt old butler who had been sent to order a cab for 'Maister Walter,' a young barrister, who had been dining at the house of his rich uncle. Old Andrew, the butler, had been 'preein'' on his own account, and what with liberal tastin's of the fruity port and old claret, corrected by a modicum of mellow whisky, he was in that confidential stage when all that is kindly comes to the surface. Master Walter having known him ever since he had any recollection of his uncle's house, and being moreover a favourite with Andrew, the old fellow was disposed to be genially effusive. Helping on the young man with his coat in the hall, and receiving the liberal tip which accompanied the slight service, he waxed gushingly familiar and confidential. Beckoning Mr. Walter with a mysterious forefinger and a solemnly inscrutable nod, he drew him aside and whispered to him :—

'Maister Walter (hic), I've kent ye ever since ye was that heich,' holding his hand at a very unsteady height from the floor. 'An', Maister Walter (hic), ye sud aye stick tae the yae drink. Eh, man, I ken a' aboot it. But noo, Maister Walter, jist a wird (hic) o' caashion.' Then, very solemnly : ' Man, whin ye gang ootside, ye'll see twa caabs (hic). Tak' the first yin, the ither yin's no there.'

One of the most delicious of the old servant stories, however, is that told of an old valetudinarian laird on Tweedside, whose faithful and devoted housekeeper was a matter-of-fact, unromantic Abigail, of an intensely practical turn of mind. She was just a perfect example of the type we have been considering. Like many aged invalids, the somewhat 'peekin'' laird was always anticipating his own speedy demise. ' Ah, Nancy,' he said one day, coming over an oft-repeated querulous deliverance, ' I'm thinkin' that it canna be lang noo ; I'm jist feelin' as if this vera nicht the end wad come.'

' Weel, indeed, laird,' said the unemotional Nancy, ' if it wir the Lord's wull, it wad be rael convenient, for the coo's gaun tae cauve, an' I dinna weel see hoo ah'm tae fin' time tae 'tend on ye baith.'

The uncompromising bluntness of the old school is well illustrated, too, in the anecdote of the Deeside farmer's-man, Jock, while it also displays that trait of pawky cunning which is not less truly characteristic.

A gentleman ' frae the Sooth ' had just purchased a horse from the farmer, and after the price had been paid over, not before, Jock was asked to accompany the purchaser to hand over delivery of the animal. On the way to the field—or as it is always called thereabouts 'the Park '—the stranger gave Jock a handsome douceur and began questioning him about his recent purchase.

' Ye'll ken the horse weel aneuch, Jock ? '

' Hoot, ay, I weel a' wat div that ! '

' But you think I've made a good bargain, do you not?'

'Weel,' said Jock, with a fine air of candour, as if the gratuity made it incumbent on him that he should discharge his conscience, 'I maun tell ye he his jist twa fauts.'

'Oh, indeed! and what might they be?'

'Weel, jist, he's nae vera guid tae tak' oot o' the "Park."'

'Oh! rather hard to catch is he? Well, that perhaps would not matter much. He might not have much run of a park now, with me. But what is the other fault?'

'Weel, sir' (very dryly), 'he's jist nae vera muckle eese (use) fin' he *is* ta'en oot.'

Of course everything in connection even with the best and most faithful of the old type of servants was not absolutely idyllic. There were bad specimens then as well as now, and trials of temper were no doubt frequent, so long as carelessness, untidyness, laziness, and impudence were likely to be manifested. So, if the servants were outspoken and unsophisticated, the mistress or master was no less emphatic, and used plain blunt directness of speech if it were required.

Here is a servant story from the Antipodes which I think may be new to home readers. It is told of a quick-tempered Scottish emigrant serving-woman in a colonial hotel, where no doubt the manners and the language were rather rough. The poor girl had little time to herself, and had to move about pretty quickly at meal-times to supply the wants of the hungry legion who used to 'rush' the long dining-room — the word 'rush' being used in gold-diggers' parlance. There happened to be staying at the hotel a spurious sort of decayed gentle-woman, who gave herself intolerable airs, and aped gentility, though possessing none of its consideration for others. She was constantly giving extra trouble to poor over-worked Mary by coming in after the meal was well over, and then rather imperiously demanding hot viands, hot plates, etc. One day Mary sent word by her little girl that dinner was ready. The would-be fine dame, wanting to finish her novel, sent back a lacka-daisical reply to keep dinner for her, as she was not ready. Mary in the vehemence of her irritation blurted out: 'Oh, tell her to come to her denner at aince, or she can gang to h——, whichever she likes.' Presently in comes her ladyship fuming and flouncing, and haughtily asked Mary 'if she had had the impertinence to tell her little girl, that she, Mrs. R——, might go to Hades.' 'Weel, weel,' said Mary, 'I'm sure if I did, there wis nae great hairm, for, if a' stories be true, the vera best o' quality folk maistly a' gang there.'

Of the order of bothy stories, several of which I have given in *Oor Ain Folk*, the following is rather a typical specimen. It is told of a parsimonious old farmer in the Mearns. He was so notoriously stingy that ploughmen shunned his farm, and would not take service there. His usual course was to offer an advance of some ten shillings on the usual hiring fee, and having secured his man, he proceeded to take it out of him, by feeding him so badly as to provoke the unfortunate fellow, after a more or less prolonged probation, to throw up his situation in disgust. By so doing he of course forfeited his wages, and the cunning old hunks of a miserly farmer thus secured a certain amount of service for nothing. On one occasion, however, he met his match. The new man had been engaged at a more than ordinarily liberal fee, and tackled to his work with a will. He was not long however ere he discovered the character of his new master. Morning, noon, and night he was regaled with the saltest of 'reid herrin's.' Remonstrance was of no avail. Jock was told there was nothing better for him; but as he did not wish to throw up his place in the middle of the term and forfeit his wages, he met cunning with cunning. The fields he had to plough extended upwards in a long incline from a bright sparkling burnie which was the boundary of the farm. Jock seeing how the land lay, in more senses than one, ceased grumbling at his thirst-provoking provender, but as soon as he found himself nearly three-quarters up the hill, and at a good distance from the 'burn,' he made excuse to stop his team, and would then saunter slowly down the field to the burnside, where he slaked his thirst, and then leisurely resumed his interrupted task. This did not suit the avaricious old farmer at all, but on venturing to remonstrate, Jock met him with such an apparently guileless, open, good-humoured face, and pleaded his awful thirst, that the farmer was taken rather aback.

'Man,' said Jock, 'I've an awfu' drouth on me. I'm thinkin' it maun be thae reid herrin'.'

'Ay, an' div ye no like reid herrin'?' queried the farmer, hoping to pick a quarrel with his man, and thus force him to leave. But Jock was too wary.

'Oo ay! I like naething better nor reid herrin',' said he. 'Dinna cheenge the reid herrin' for me. I like them fine, but, ye see, sir, they aye like to be soomin'.'

Jock's diet was changed to something less drouth-inspiring, and he managed to stay on till Martinmas.

I have heard many curious definitions, but the following, I think, deserves to be recorded for its quaint, unconscious humour.

The mistress of the farm was wont to question the boys on Sunday afternoon, upon the morning's sermon in church. The subject for the day had been moral responsibility, and young Geordie, whose chief duty was to keep the craws from the standing crops, was asked to define 'responsibility.' 'Weel, mem,' said the unsophisticated Geordie, 'it's when yer troosers is hadden up wi' yae button an' a preen.'

I have myself, both in India and Australia, been exceptionally fortunate in winning the attachment of faithful friends, among all classes of workers. In India my body-servants were loyal and devoted to a most touching degree, and a sincere affection subsisted between us on both sides. In Australia, we have had very few changes in our domestic establishment, and one faithful maid has been in constant, unbroken, and loyal service with my wife for twenty-one years. In my business as a merchant I have a host of loyal and affectionate co-workers, many of whom have never had another employer than myself in the Colony, since their leaving the dear old country.

Writing to Sydney friends I noted the same thing in connection with many of the places I visited, and the people I have known in the old land. Drawing a contrast between England and Australia I said, *inter alia:* It is true that in some matters of social legislation, in law procedure relating to transfers of property, in the recognition of individual rights and in other notable respects, we are in advance of England, but the old

N

motherland is by no means the drowsy, stagnant, un-progressive centre some of our 'Domain howlers' and professional preachers of secession seek to proclaim. It is indeed most stimulating to the intellect, to note the changes and mark the progress in this old land, that thirty years have made in almost every department of human activity, and especially in all that pertains to cor-porate action and the sphere of municipal management.

The zest is heightened, too, as one sees side by side with this modern activity of county council—this sleep-less vigilance of boards of health—this splendid industry of numberless other boards formed for the furtherance of advanced modern ideas, which are all making in the direction of improving the conditions of massed human life in great cities—how persistent are some of the old habits and institutions, and what a stability and perma-nence one finds underlying even all the most whirling evolutions of change. One's sensations and perceptions are continually being sharpened on this whetstone of striking contrast. You read of mass movements in great industries, which on the surface almost presage revolution. You get into quiet converse with the units of the mass, and you are amazed to discover habitudes and associations which tell of a deep, abiding conserva-tism, and which enables you to find the key to many of the chambers, if not all, of that English orderliness and love of constitutional propriety which is at once the envy and the desire of many other peoples.

Just let me give a few illustrations in respect of the relations of master and servant alone. In this old-fashioned but most comfortable hotel, which has been my pleasant headquarters in England (Morley's, Trafalgar

Square), we find that one old factotum, 'George' (such a character as Dickens would have loved to depict), has been for wellnigh forty years a servant attached to this one establishment. 'Frer,' one of the old waiters, and a few others have been over twenty years in the same employ. Emma, the head housemaid, has been eighteen years. Many of the waiters, porters, maids, and servants generally, have been over ten years in the house. In the house of one dear old lady in Edinburgh, with snowy hair and all the graces of the old courtly *régime*, though advancing years have dimmed for ever the light of her gentle eyes, we found that the kitchen servants had been some score of years in the one service. The housemaid, who had accepted service when the young married couple started housekeeping, is now the honoured, faithful companion, having never had any other mistress during her long life. The old gardener had died in harness, after wellnigh a lifetime of devoted loyal service. The story of his attachment and devotion was very touching. When over seventy, and rendered very frail by his weight of years, he expressed a wish one day to be permitted to 'go home to lay down his bones' as he expressed it. He had a brother and some relations in Banffshire, and the strange homing instinct had come over the old man. The longing for home, which the Germans so beautifully call *Heimweh*, had come upon him. His gentle, white-haired, old mistress said : 'Well, George, I had thought that only death would part us now!' The old man knew perfectly well that his race was run, and touchingly assured his honoured mistress that indeed it was just that messenger that had come to call him. It was a correct premonition. He went home to the old, early, earthly home, that after the lapse of over half a century had still such a tender compulsive power to draw him thither. In a couple of short months the faithful old servant had exchanged the labour and the toil of earth, for the rest and the perfect service of the Master's home above.

At Helensburgh we found another instance of this touching community of kindly feeling. In one pleasant home there, the maid had been twenty years in the one house. In the lovely home of my only surviving aunt I found still remaining, old servants whom I had known in the same service in the old farmhouse thirty years ago, and on the estate several cottages, cosy and comfortable, in which dwelt the shepherds and other old servants whom I remembered from my boyhood, and who are now being loved and rewarded for wellnigh a lifetime of honest, faithful service.

In my own brother's house at Reigate he has servants —they may well be called friends—who have numbered more than a score of years in the one employ. Indeed, in some of the busy eating-houses of London, and in many of its clubs, one of my travelling companions tells me, he has been accosted by old servants whom he has met for the last ten or a dozen years during his various visits, still faithfully filling the old posts of trust. In many of the warehouses and shops of the city such is also the case.

I paid a filial visit to a sequestered nook near the old ruined castle of Edzell, nestling 'neath the budding beech and horse-chestnut trees, shadowed by the swelling Grampians, and within hearing of the murmurous ripple of the running river, winding amid the graceful drapery

of birch and hazel. There rests the honoured dust of a
faithful minister of the Gospel in the quiet God's acre,
amid daffodils and daisies, and the sweet scent of lilac
and golden furze. And almost in the shadow of the
recording granite, at the feet of his old master, rest the
remains of a faithful old servant of the type I am
describing, and on the stone is carved a tribute which to
me is eloquent of loving affection and loyal attachment.
Thus reads the simple statement : 'Here lies the body of
George Ferrier; for thirty-eight years the faithful servant
of the Rev. Robert Inglis, of this parish,' etc.

Surely such records as these may well have their
value in this epoch of change and clashing interest, in
this turmoil of warring tendencies and class antagonisms,
and such a lowly stone and such eloquent instances as I
have given of mutual trust and attachment between
master and man, may well set even the brassiest bell-
mouthed agitator thinking, and may well bring pause,
while we consider whether after all, there may not be
better methods of reconciling conflicting interests and
assuaging class antagonisms, than the truculent methods
so dear to the stirrer up of strifes.

I have heard several pretty warm orations in Hyde
Park ; I have passed through several borough towns
while a heated party fight was being waged ; but I have
nowhere heard such rabid and ridiculous fustian as is
often chronicled in the Australian papers, as being ranted
by some of our so-called Australian leaders of labour.
The reform of abuses, the onward march of enfranchise-
ment, the removal of unjust restrictions, and the better-
ment of the toiler, are not hindered one whit by calm,
dispassionate advocacy ; and the working men here in

Great Britain, so far as I have as yet been able to observe, would seem to conduct their propaganda with an ever-present sense of self-respect, and with a dignity and moderation which I most fraternally commend to my working-man friends at the Antipodes.

I must say that some of the reports of proceedings during recent strikes in Scotland, have caused me to modify the opinions I have herein expressed. It is most touching to me, to see the ill-advised loyalty with which masses of working men will stick to their (too often self-elected) leaders; and sadder still to see how these so-called leaders repay this splendid fidelity, by the most wanton and suicidal misdirection, the most utter fatuity, and the wildest misrepresentations. This has been very apparent in the late ill-advised and ill-directed Scottish coal strike.

CHAPTER XI

I THINK that surely by this time I have adduced
evidence enough to confirm the main portion of my
thesis, that my fellow-countrymen are not so devoid of
humour as some gainsayers have affirmed ; but I come
now to a class of examples which even more forcibly
and directly go to show how exuberant and how pungent
is this delightful, subtle quality—'the saving grace' of
social intercourse, as one writer has termed it. I still
prefer to let the illustrations speak for themselves. No
learned or laboured explanation or analysis is required ;
but, to be sure, humour is akin to many of the finer
human emotions ; it can only be appreciated where there

is reciprocity. The soulless curmudgeon who hath no latent gleam of kindly humour lurking in his eye, over whose heart-strings no wandering finger-tip of delicate humour hath ever swept, and in whose memory there linger not the echoes of some rippling melody of laughter, may lay down my humble book at once. I have nothing that he can assimilate. I will be to such an one, but as 'a vain babbler.'

But come thou, dear reader, of 'the moist and merry eye,' the fair rotundity of middle age, the mobile lip, and eke the nose and cheek of warm and healthy hue, in which the network traceries of ruddy life's-blood run like the delicate marbling on a pippin's dainty skin; ye whom the sun hath kissed, whose chests expand as ye drink in the fresh, life-giving air of Scotia's heathery hills, and who can laugh an open, honest laugh, not 'from the teeth outwards,' but from the generous centre of your being; come ye, the hearty, frank, warm-hearted, open-handed, whole-souled 'brither Scot,' and let us, with what appetite we may, enjoy together still a little more, the varied feast, with which many a sunny soul in the days bygone, hath refreshed my spirit, in climes afar, in regions strange, and amid companions and conditions stranger still.

No collection of Scottish anecdote would of course be complete, without a few of the multitudes, that have for their theme or leading inspiration, the national drink. I have of whisky stories 'goodly store,' and those that illustrate the kindly, social side of Scottish hospitality and neighbourly communion are innocent and enjoyable enough; but just as there are elements in the ambrosial compound itself, which are dangerous and even poisonous, if present in excess, so there are among the countless Scottish stories current, many that are coarse and base, and only appeal to what is bestial and degraded in those who hear or tell. Before proceeding to the few whisky stories, however, which I have chosen to select, I would like to adduce a few instances, and only a very few, of the shrewd, sly cunning, of a certain very common class of old-time Scotsmen, often accompanied by an eccentric, wayward, irritable temper—what we call 'thrawn' or 'cankert'—and the exact counterpart of which is very seldom met with, in any other nationality.

As an instance of what I have in my mind, take the direct, uncompromising bluntness of the old farmer who possessed little sentiment, but took life in a strictly economical and business-like way. An acquaintance happened to have called at the farm one day on business, and was rather surprised to receive an invitation to stay to dinner. The visitor, who knew the frugal habits of his host, amounting, in fact, to downright stinginess, replied that 'he would stay with pleasure, only he was afraid he would be giving a great deal of trouble.' Just here came in the solid, uncompromising bluntness and directness of the Scot. Perhaps already repenting of his unwonted cordiality, the farmer ejaculated : 'Dod, min, it's no the trubble, it's the expense.'

A good illustration of the dry, pawky sort of humour, is that given concerning a village blacksmith, who was frequently annoyed by the petty meannesses of just such another parsimonious farmer as the last I have quoted, and who lived in the neighbourhood of the brawny son of Vulcan. The farmer was in the habit of dropping in promiscuously at the smiddy, and getting small jobs done by the smith, for which he never offered to pay, never even asked the smith to 'share a gill wi' him,' but was always profuse in the empty reward of voluble acknowledgments. 'Oh, thanks, thanks! Thank ye, Tam! Mony thanks t'ye, Tam, for that!' And so on. One winter morning, when Tam happened to be pretty busy, the farmer made his appearance with 'a ploo couter' (plough coulter) in his hand, and evidently expecting that he should have instant attention given to the petty piece of repair which it wanted. The smith, however, went on at the bellows, and paid no attention to the demand made on his time. Instead, he began to expatiate on the merits of a splendid game-cock which he had recently acquired, and with such effect that the farmer said: 'Losh, man, but I wad like unco weel to see the bird.' 'Ay, man,' very dryly responded Tam, 'ah'm sorry I canna lat ye see him; it's clean oot o' ma pooer.' 'How's that?' said the farmer. 'Weel, ye see, sir, I tried feedin' the puir brute on thanks, but it dee'd.'

Here is an instance of sly exaggeration, almost Yankee-like. Two cronies in Auchterarder were one day disputing as to who remembered the most windy day. One of the worthies said 'he minded its bein' sic a win' that it took the craws to come from such and such a field, three 'oors to flee hame to their wud,' only about a mile distant. The other said: 'Hech, man, ah've seen't that windy that the craws hed tae *walk* hame.'

As an example of quiet, dry humour, the following, told by old 'Red Brown' of Paisley, a fine old Scotsman, well known to the fraternity of commercial travellers in the south of Scotland, is worthy of a place among my *omnium gatherum.*

'I mind,' he said, 'a story o' auld Wullie Millar, wheelwricht an' spindle-maker at Riccarton. He had been laid up for a conseederable time, an' whin he was gettin' convalescent, the meenister met him one day an' gey an' pointedly asked Wullie, hoo it wis that tho' he wis able to be in at Kilmarnock on the Setterday, yet he wis absent frae his place in church on the Sawbath. Wullie wis a wee bit annoyed, an' answered very short. "Weel, meenister, ye see, it's jist this w'y. When I gang tae Kilmarnock, I can get what I want; but when I gang tae the kirk I hiv tae tak' what I get."'

On the same occasion of Wullie's first visit to Kilmarnock after his long illness, he met the provost, who stopped to have a chat with him. During the rather prolonged colloquy which ensued, the Kilmarnock grave-digger, who was desirous of having a word with Wullie on some business of his own, came up, and, not wishing to disturb the conversation, he kept hovering around Wullie, trying to catch his eye. He circled round several times, getting closer and closer, latterly, in fact, almost rubbing against Wullie's coat-tails. The convalescent's patience at last got fairly exhausted, and, quite misunderstanding the reason of the poor sexton's attentions, he turned sharply round, and snapped out: 'Dod, min, ye needna stan' there measurin' me. I'm no deid yet, an', forbye, we dinna bury in Kilmarnock; we hae grund o' oor ain in Riccarton.'

For a pithy-telling illustration I fancy, too, the following would be hard to beat.

A gentleman from the south had been offered a shooting in the Highlands for the season; but before finally concluding the bargain, he decided to take a drive out himself, so as to personally inspect the place. Accordingly he hired a vehicle, or, as it is always called in the north, 'a masheen' (machine), and on the way, finding the driver a pleasant, pawky, communicative fellow, he asked him point-blank 'what sort of a place he considered the shooting to be, to which they were driving?' The reply was certainly original, but emphatic. 'Weel, sir, if the deil himsel' was tethered oot there a haill nicht, an' ye war tae meet him i' the mornin', ye wad say "Puir brute!"'

One of the most excellent examples of shrewd-witted cunning that I have come across yet, however, is a story told me by my friend Mr. J. B. Wood in the backblocks of Australia. It so tickled my fancy, and was so capitally told, that I asked Mr. Wood to write it down for me. He is one of the jolliest 'companions of the road' it has ever been my good fortune to meet, and hereby I render my acknowledgments for many, many a pleasant hour he has enabled me to pass.

'A noted poacher,' he writes, 'Chay Black by name, was being tried before the sheriff in my native town, in one of the southern Scottish counties, the offence being a flagrant poaching escapade. Chay had been seen in broad daylight by the keeper to clip a salmon; but on being pursued, his fleetness of foot had enabled him for the time being to make good his escape. He was, however, subsequently apprehended and brought to trial. The case seemed very clear and simple, and the evidence was going dead against Chay, when he humbly asked the sheriff if he might be permitted to ask the witness a few questions. Permission being granted, the clever rogue began operations, a certain catchiness in his speech adding a quaint drollery to his questions. Addressing his enemy, the gamekeeper, amid the breathless silence of the crowded court, he said : "Noo, Wullie, mind ye're on yer aith ! Hoo far micht ye hae been awa' when ye saw me clip the saumon ? Mind ye're on yer solum aith !" he earnestly repeated. "Weel, mebbe something better nor a hunder yairds, Chay," responded the complacent keeper. "Noo, Wullie," said Chay, suddenly assuming quite a severe judicial manner, "cud ye tell the difference atween a pike an' a saumon at that distance—mind ye're on yer aith— jist seein' it whuppit oot o' the watter as ye saw me dae on Setterday ?" Wullie visibly winced. It was evident he was perplexed, and after some hesitation he very reluctantly confessed that he could NOT distinguish between the two fish named, at such a distance under the circumstances. A bright light beamed in Chay's hitherto anxious eyes. He turned round with a confident air to the sheriff, and with apparently deep feeling exclaimed : "So help me, God ! My lord, it WIS a pike ! As shure's deith, ma lord, it WIS a pike !" Amid yells of laughter, in which the sheriff was forced to join, the case was dismissed.'

This, too, is pawky, but I have seen it in print.

Two farmers were bargaining over a horse. Said the one : ' It's a guid horse, I'll say that ; but tae be honest I maun tell ye it his gotten yae wee bit faut : it's gi'en tae rinnin' awa' wi' ye.' 'Oh, weel,' said the other, 'if that's a', it disna sae muckle maitter. Man, the last horse I hed wis gi'en tae rinnin' awa' withoot me.'

But even more quaint and humorous is the following delightful bit of homespun criticism by an old Deeside farmer. He had been down to Edinburgh, to attend the meetings of the General Assembly, and on his return a lady of my acquaintance asked him :—

'Weel, John, and how did ye like the speeches in the General Assembly ?'

'To tell the honest truth, mem,' said John, 'I thocht them vera like ma wife's tea.'

'Ay, an' what like's it, John ?'

'Jist vera waik an' vera war-r-r-m, mem.'

Possessed of the same quality of grim, dry humour is the following, which is vouched for as a true anecdote of 'the Iron Duke,' and I am told it possesses the merit of not having previously been published. At any rate, it is new to me. It would seem that a worthy Shetlander, who had not succeeded so well as he could wish in his bare native isle, wrote a letter to the Duke, stating his position, etc., and begging him to kindly keep him in mind if he knew of any easy or comfortable appointment, with good pay attached.

To this the Duke replied in characteristic fashion.

'Field-Marshal the Duke of Wellington presents his compliments to Mr.——, and begs leave to say, that if he knew of any such situation he would certainly apply for it himself.'

My next is an instance of the grim querulousness very characteristic of many of our aged cottagers : a sort of revolt against the very idea of dependence ; an impatience of anything savouring of patronage or conventional constraint. I am told this feeling is dying out; that the old rustic independence is on the wane. Certainly in my young days there was an absolute horror of anything like parish help, or even organised charity. Now, I am told, it is becoming more and more the custom to look to Government for everything. The dole of State relief is counted on as a right, not spurned as a stigma. In this I do hope I am misinformed. Certainly thirty years' absence from one's native land may excuse me if I have too readily given credence to such a report; but if it be true, if the old vigorous self-reliance and almost fierce protest against eleemosynary help is dying out, then so much the worse for Scotland and the proud supremacy of her children as a race, pre-eminently, of self-reliant, energetic, and independent men and women.

But to my story.

A good lady of the fussy, imperious, attending-to-everybody's-business-but-her-own type, had called on a lonely old fellow of the old-fashioned sort : one who was too proud and independent to accept the dole of promiscuous, shallow benevolence, and who had just enough—bare, no doubt, but sufficient—for his simple wants. The old man resented as an impertinence, the brassy, inconsiderate, fussy familiarity of the visitor, and he feigned to be hard of hearing. The self-constituted inquisitor was not however to be baulked. She fairly bored the poor old man with a multitude of questions about his means, his health, his diet, the state of both his soul and body, and at length she got on to the subject of his age. The old man parried several of her queries, and the energetic philanthropist had not tact or delicacy enough to see that the subject was distasteful to her involuntary victim. At length she fairly annoyed him by repeating for the third or fourth time : ' But you have not yet told me your age.   How old are you?' Up flashed the old protesting fire, and the old fellow snapped out : ' 'Deed I'm auld eneuch nae tae be sic a feel (fool) as tell you.'

The same esteemed correspondent who gave me the above, sends me another illustrating the good-natured drollery of the Deeside folk.

A ' rag-man ' was passing by a farmhouse in the neighbourhood one day, and seeing the mistress asked her :—

' Ony rags the day, gudewife ? '

' Ou ay,' she replied, ' plenty o' rags, but we're nae freely deen wi' them yet.'

Up our glen I know a quaint character, named Jeems, who serves the good Glen folks in the dual capacity of postmaster and as proprietor of the only store of which the secluded neighbourhood can boast. As may be easily imagined, the stock is neither very extensive nor varied, but such as it is, it seems to suffice for the few wants of the customers. Jeems is one of the old-fashioned, independent, taciturn, blunt sort, and many of his traits and sayings have been told to me. It would seem that he does not look with much favour on the annual irruption of summer visitors. They are too exacting and fastidious ; they have too many wants : they ask for all sorts of outlandish things that the Glen folk would never imagine ; and if truth must be told, Jeems does not put himself one bit out of his usual way to cater for their custom. So it is perhaps that outsiders take advantage of the opening so presented, and store-carts and pedlar's-carts with all sorts of wares make frequent visits to the Glen during the tourist season. One day a fine lady who had apartments near the post-office, sent her maid across, to try and get a loaf of bread at the shop. They were to take their departure on the morrow, and from some slight miscalculation they had allowed themselves to run short of bread. Now Jeems knew all about their contemplated move-ments as well almost as they themselves did. They had never patronised his shop before, and he knew that now they did it only on the compulsion of necessity. His conduct, therefore, affords a whimsical indication of his mental attitude towards these interlopers, as he doubtless considered them, as in his dry, slow, solemn style, he handed over the loaf, and said to the girl : 'Ay, ah'm thinkin' we'll no be gaen tae be bathered wi' your fowk muckle langer.'

Another day two dressy young dames came into the shop, and looking about, they began to make audible comment with that loud, vacant flippancy and utter want of consideration for any one else's feelings, which is so surely an evidence of vulgarity. Said one : 'Deah me, what a wetched shop ! And what an out-of-the-way place this is !'

Old Jeems, who had been stooping behind some packages, suddenly popped up his rather grim visage, and in his most deliberate manner said : 'Ou ay, it's nae doot a geyan oot-o'-the-w'y place this ; but we're judges o' gude breedin' for a' that.'

Bravo, Jeems !

A capital illustration of the extreme, punctilious

o

regard for absolute accuracy which is so truly Scottish, was also told me in relation to Jeems.

There had been some discussion in his hearing about the presence of salmon in the Esk, and as a resident he was appealed to. Jeems, in his ponderous, solemn way said bluntly : 'There's been nane seen this sisson.' 'Oh, but,' said the interlocutor, rashly venturing to contradict, 'I hear there was one hooked only last week down at Keenie.' Again came Jeems's grim and emphatic statement : 'There micht hae been ane hookit, but there's been nane seen.'

A fine instance of the indomitable spirit of manly independence possessed by the older generation of humble Scotsmen comes to me from a valued correspondent, Mrs. Rhind of Aberdeen.

A Morayshire laird, one of the Gradgrind order, said to a poor old shoemaker on his property, whose presence was an offence to him because, Ahab-like, he coveted the possession of his wee bit hoosie and haddin'—his ostensible reason being that he wished to rid the place of paupers—'I'll ruin you, sir, if you do not quit my property.'

'Na, na, laird,' replied the undaunted souter, 'ye'll no manage that as lang as bairns are born barefit !'—in allusion to his trade ; and then, as if by an afterthought, he added : 'But mebbe a mercifu' Providence 'll pit you aneth the sod gin that time.'

While on this subject, a whimsical illustration of the effect of a single ejaculation comes to my mind, and I may be permitted to jot it down. A celebrated female lecturer on Woman's Rights found a bumper house awaiting her appearance in the City Hall, Glasgow, one night.

Wishing to impress her audience with her first few words, and fix their attention, she stepped well forward on the platform, stretched forth her right arm, and rather melodramatically exclaimed : ' Why was I born a woman ? ' (Pause.) ' Why am I here to-night ? ' (Another pause—solemn silence.) Then a small, wicked keelie (street urchin) in the back gallery utterly spoiled all the effect, and sent the audience into convulsions of laughter, by piping out in a thin, reedy treble, ' We'll gie'd up ! '

To a well-known traveller I am indebted for the following. One night in the commercial-room of a leading hotel in one of the northern towns, 'the boys of the sample bag' were exchanging confidences, and, as is not uncommon, the talk became decidedly professional. One callow youth began to brag very pronouncedly about the large orders he had that day taken. A quiet, pawky, old fellow in a corner, in the same line, and one of the Nestors of 'the road,' knowing the youth to be wildly exaggerating, good - humouredly said : ' Toots, toots, man, ye ken ye've din naething like what ye say.' The youngster evidently felt very keenly the implied snub, and angrily retorted, ' Oh, I suppose I'm a liar then ! ' The old fellow convulsed the room, and completed the discomfiture of the green hand, by giving a dry chuckle as he produced his snuff-box and replied : ' Weel, that's nae muckle tae brag aboot aither.'

Talking of 'leears' reminds me of a good golf story which I am sure I have read somewhere, but where I cannot remember. I have found it in my note-book however, and here it is.

Two well-known professional golfers were playing a

match. We shall call them Sandie and Jock. On one side of the golf course was a railway, over which Jock drove his ball, landing it in some long grass. They then both hunted for a long time for the missing ball. Sandie wanted Jock to give in, and admit that the ball was lost, as a lost ball meant a lost hole. Continuing to look around, Jock slyly dropped another ball, and then coming back cried: 'I've fun' (found) the ba', Sandie.' 'Ye're a leear,' said the imperturbable and plain-spoken Sandie, 'for here it's in ma pooch.'

I find among my notes, a good example of punning humour recorded of a well-known accountant of one of the old-established banks in Edinburgh. He generally used to walk to his office accompanied by a neighbour friend, whose city office was close to the bank. The new head-office of a rival bank had just been completed—a handsome, pretentious building adorned with figures of beautiful statuary, supposed to represent the apostles. By comparison the more ancient bank building was a dwarfed, mean-looking structure, and the friend, intending a waggish bit of raillery, said to the accountant: 'Man, what a sorry-lookin' biggin' that is o' yours. Look at the graun' new bank there, that's a wyse-like bank noo! An' they've gotten the twal' apostles, tae!' To which came the dry but witty rejoinder: 'Oh ay! the apostles are a' vera weel, but I believe mair in the prophets!' (profits).

But one of the wittiest puns of which I have any original record, is in connection with a pair of the old Montrose worthies—Provost ——, and dear old Adam Burness, whose genial face and warm-hearted, cordial manner I can never forget. He was very good to me when I was a wild and thoughtless callant. Mr. Burness was one of the leading solicitors in the quaint 'gable-endie' town, and was moreover in close blood-relationship to our famous national poet, the immortal Robbie Burns. The worthy Provost was an extraordinary character : self-educated, vigorous in mind and body, utterly careless of conventionalities, and brimful of a robust, humorous intelligence, he was yet occasionally led away by his undoubted readiness of wit and wonderful glibness of speech, into the most extraordinary oratorical outbursts, which were not always remarkable for correctness of grammar or strict regard to the recognised rules of rhetoric. If one is privileged to possess the acquaintance of some of the old residents, one may occasionally hear illustrations such as I have tried to jot down from time to time.

The particular instance to which I have alluded, was on the occasion of the unveiling of the fine statue to Joseph Hume, M.P., the veteran Radical, who was a native of Montrose. The old Provost, after a grand speech befitting the occasion, at length concluded his address by saying : 'Leddies an' gentlemen, I will noo unveil this beeyootifool statute.' Old Mr. Burness with ready wit was heard to dryly remark : ' Richt to a T, Provost ! richt to a T ! '

Another specimen of the worthy Provost's oratory is told me in connection with a complimentary dinner given by the townsmen, to a certain medical man who was held in great esteem, and whose identity I may veil under the cognomen Dr. Scott. The Provost had to propose the toast of the evening, and he always used the broad, Angus dialect, which much enhanced the

raciness of his quaint deliverances. After a few opening
remarks, and wishing at once to focus the attention of
his audience on the worthy object of his eulogium, he
dropped into the Socratic method, and in vigorous
accents he asked : 'Gentlemen, fan we're born intil
this warl' fa div we sen' for ?   Why, for Dr. Scott !
Fin we have the teethache or the mizzles or the
scarlet fivver, fa div we sen' for ? For Dr. Scott, of
coorse !'   And so he enumerated pretty nearly every
disease incident to humanity, and amid continuously
increasing applause and bursts of merriment, which
the worthy man took as a compliment to his own
eloquence, he proceeded perspiringly to perorate
thus :   'An' when, gentlemen, we "shuffle off this
mortal coil" and descend intill "the dark valley o'
the shadow of death," fa div we sen' for ?' and a
tumultuous and unanimous yell, thundered in answer
from the now fairly convulsed audience—'Dr. Scott, of
course ! Dr. Scott !'

But even more delightfully ludicrous still, was the
only preserved remnant of an oration pronounced by the
Provost in presenting a handsome watch to one of the most
respected ministers of the town, given by his congregation and the townspeople, in recognition of a long career
of public usefulness.   The worthy and eloquent magistrate had evidently thought it behoved him to drop into
a somewhat scriptural style on such an occasion.   The
exquisite humour of these situations was always accentu-
ated by the Provost's constant habit of jerking his right
thumb over his shoulder after every outburst of
eloquence.   Each period was rounded off with this
peculiar jerk of the thumb, and each jerk was generally

the signal for an outburst of ' Hear, hears ' from the wags among the bankers and lawyers of the ' ancient gable-ended toun.'

After gradually warming to his task, and encouraged by the generous applause which greeted each sonorous sentence, he said : ' May this magneeficent watch, sir (jerk), be handed doon as an heirloom to posterity (jerk ; Hear ! hear !), an' may generations yet unborn rise up and say, " Watchman, what of the nicht ? " (jerk ; tumultuous applause). May it not only, sir, be your monitor in time (jerk), but your guide throw the coontless ages of a lang eternity !' (jerk). Here the applause became positively deafening, and the gratified orator, beaming with complacency, turned to one of the bailies sitting near and whispered : ' Fu am I gettin' on, Bylie ? ' ' Oh, fine, Provost, fine !' ' Ay, min, an' it's a' vairbittem !' (verbatim). The good old soul meant ' extempore,' but it was perfectly understood, and served the purpose just as well.

But with all his eccentricities of speech, the worthy Provost was a vigorous, useful, public-spirited character. He was one of a fine old breed that seem to be dying out now. He spared not himself, but gave generously of his time, his talents, and his means, to the service of his generation and the advancement of his town. He counted public honour and the recognition of his towns-men, sufficient reward for all his voluntary service. The cash nexus, as I have said, is the sole seeming incentive to public usefulness nowadays. Our members of Parlia-ment, our town councillors and mayors, all are learning to clamour and look for the sordid pelf and filthy lucre, in respect of services that should be voluntary, and are about as honourable as a man can assume, seeing they are representative, and should be the guerdon only of a stainless reputation and the general esteem and confidence.   How long will it be, I wonder, before our very churchwardens, elders, deacons, and Sabbath School teachers, will want to be paid for their services as well ? As it is, the choirs in many places actually expect and look for, pay for praise, and palm oil for psalmody.

Let me conclude this chapter by another presentation speech, though not so ornate as the good Provost's of Montrose.   It, too, was on the occasion of a presentation of a handsome drawing-room mantel-clock and two candelabra to a much-respected clergyman.   The ruling elder was deputed to perform the honourable ceremony, but being 'no orator as Brutus was,' but only a plain, blunt Scotsman, he came quickly to the point, saying simply : 'Weel, sir, here's the knock (clock) an' twa caunles, an' may ye never be exalted abuve meesure.'

CHAPTER XII

ODDITIES OF SPEECH AND OLD-TIME BLUNTNESS

Fondness for 'lang-nebbit' words—A queer illness—How a Scottish
lady acquired French—How the minister learned foreign languages — A clerkish mistake — A pulpit intimation — Queer
phrases among the fisher folk—Strange place for a 'Dissenter'
—The 'Calvinistic battery'—Further examples—Instances of
pithy Scotch—Deeside dialect—How Pharaoh died—Grades
in the fish-hawking business—The miller of Ashbogle—An
anecdote of the old minister—A horse-dealer's estimate of his
own profession—A wife's blunt injunction—How he knew
his sweetheart's name—Peter Ruff the coachdriver—Tam
Dick of Dunedin—'Speerits' an aid to digestion.

ONE rather strange peculiarity of the old-fashioned
rustic folk of the north, which I have frequently come
across in the course of my observations on Scottish
character, and of which I have noted a few typical
examples in the present chapter, is the tendency to use
and often totally to misapply, pretentious terms and
phrases, when the terse, pithy, native Doric would far
better fulfil the purpose intended. Perhaps this is not
exclusively or characteristically Scottish. It is a tendency of the bucolic mind in all nationalities, and it is
difficult to say whence it arises. There is probably the
innocent conceit of trying to appear more learned than

one really knows oneself to be, a sort of harmless
pedantry which is not confined to college dons and
learned professors. There is, too, an element of courtesy
in it—a desire to express oneself to a stranger or a
superior in the most choice and fitting language. You
will see that this is so, if you observe that the occasions
on which these 'lang-nebbit wirds,' as the country folk
term them, are used, are generally when the peasant is
talking to the minister, or the laird, or to some social
superior; and may there not be also in some cases a
very natural confusion of ideas, between sound and
sense, which is common to the unsophisticated and im-
perfectly educated of all nations? At all events the
foible is a very human and a very common one, and no
better illustration can be adduced than that old, old,
well-worn one, of 'the blessed unction' which was supposed to exist in the use of the sesquipedalian word
'Mesopotawmia.'

A funny example is that in which a young clergyman,
meeting one of his parishioners whose husband had been
for some time ill, made kindly inquiries for him, and
the conversation which ensued was something after
this fashion :—

'Is it true, what I have just heard, that John has
been ill ?' he asked.

'Oh, sir, he's been taen vera badly, sir !'

'Indeed ! I'm sorry to hear it. What is the matter ?'

'Weel, sir, the doctor says he's got a *catholic* in ilka
e'e, forbye *population* o' the hert.'

I doubt if even the apocryphal Mrs. Malaprop in
her wildest flights could transcend that 'derangement of
epitaphs.'

It is not a whit worse than one I find recorded in my notes of a very worthy, hospitable soul—a rich farmer's wife in Angus, who in later years became just perhaps a little spoiled by prosperity and a trip to the Continent, and affected the use of a vocabulary which I am sure she did not wholly understand. She dearly loved to tell her gossips of her continental experiences; and on one occasion, being pressed by a waggish caller to relate her adventures, and asked how in the world she managed to get on with the foreigners, seeing she did not know the language, she nearly upset the gravity of the circle by saying very mincingly : 'Oh weel, ye see, we jist *declined* aneth the shade o' the trees ilka mornin' an' *pursued* the Dickshonar'.'

But not less amusing, was the remark made by a well-known trader of Montrose, called from his business of china merchant 'Pigger' Mitchell—'pigs' being the Scottish synonym for crockery. As the story was told to me it would seem that the worthy dealer's eldest son was receiving lessons in modern languages from a Mr. Campbell, one of the ministers of the borough. A somewhat inquisitive and incredulous critic in converse one day with 'Pigger,' raised a doubt as to the competency of the clerical tutor, but 'Pigger' emphatically vindicated his learning by saying : 'Oh, nae fear but he's competent eneuch. Man, he gings ilka year to the Continent tae pick up the *deealogue*.'

My brother furnishes me with a not less ludicrous instance afforded by one of his clerks, a young fellow fresh up from the country. At a pleasant outing given to his staff at his Reigate home, it became necessary to *improvise* a table for some part of the *al fresco* repast, which had been provided on a princely scale. The young fellow, full of zeal, and anxious to air his best company words, bustled about with some planks he had found, and said : ' Oh, sir, we'll sune *impoverish* a table.'

Here is a note which illustrates the rather peculiar idiom in which English gets spoken by people who are more accustomed to speak 'ta Gaelic 'in its purity and richness. A Highland minister wanted to intimate from the pulpit that a certain probationer, not very brilliantly endowed with intellectual gifts, was to preach, and this is how he made the announcement : 'Maister R—— will endecvyour for. to try for to preach ta Gospel next Sawbath Day.'

My esteemed friend and correspondent, the Rev. James H——, already quoted, has given me quite a number of curious instances of this love for sounding phraseology and 'lang-nebbit words.' He ministered at one time among the quaint and deeply interesting fisher folk on the East Coast about the latitude of the Mearns, and it was quite a common experience to find these somewhat primitive people using regular 'jaw-breakers' when the simple, terse Scottish idiom would have been much prettier and more expressive.

For instance, he writes me that one day during his visitations, he entered a humble dwelling ; but I shall let him proceed in his own words : — 'Mrs. Guthrie, a carter's wife, was sitting by the fire, and rocking her body to and fro as if in pain, when I called upon her one day. She had her left hand wrapped up in flannel. I asked her what was the matter with her hand, and she replied : "Weel, sir, I dinna a'thegither ken, but I'm some thinkin' it's jist completely *disannulled*."' What on earth she meant to convey by such a ' blessed word ' as that, Mr. H—— did not know, and probably the poor bodie did not very clearly know herself. She may have probably meant disabled.

'On another occasion,' he writes, 'a worthy deacon of mine in the fishing village of Inverallochy was reproached with inconsistency of conduct in that he had allowed his boat to be launched before his proper turn, it being the habit to take down the small fishing-boats from the beach in rotation. My friend, in justifying himself, afterwards said : "The blame was not mine, sir ; it was the crew's. What could I do when sax great big, stoot, *carnal* men got hold of the boat and ran her doon intill the sea."

'I have found,' pursues Mr. H——, 'among these simple, warm-hearted fisher folk, a strange love for big words and sounding phrases. A fisherman one day telling me of a presentation that had been made to a certain popular "curer," in recognition of his liberality, said, with evident unction : "We *compromised* and *representated* him wi' a gold watch."

'Mr. W——, a minister I knew in the north,' he continues, 'was going through the same village of Inverallochy, in which the houses are all very much alike, the gables all facing seawards. Meeting a fisherman he said : "I am looking for ——'s house, but really the houses are all so much alike here that I'm fairly puzzled." "Yes," interrupted the resident, "the hooses are very *unanimous*."'

Another instance comes to me from Stirling. An old

wifie was asked by her minister 'hoo her man wis the day.' She answered : 'Oh, 'deed, minister, he's no vera weel. Ye see he's got a *Dissenter* in's inside.'

Another, very much akin, is as follows :—A worthy crofter had been afflicted with a slight shock of paralysis, and there being no doctor within convenient distance, the good minister of the parish visited the poor man, and producing an old galvanic battery of which he happened to be possessed, he applied it to the patient with some apparent considerable advantage. Next day a neighbour called to inquire for the sufferer, and asked the gudewife : 'Well, how is your husband to-day ?' 'He's no vera weel,' was the reply ; 'but I'm houpin' he'll sune be better. The minister's been giein' him a shock wi' the *Calvinistic battery*, an' it did him a lot o' guid.'

Of course this was a pardonable mistake, though whimsical enough. It was like an old servant of ours, who used to refer sometimes to the '*anniversity* of her mairritch,' and always spoke of a certain convalescent hospital as the *convalashun infirmity*—meaning, I suppose, infirmary.

Of the same curious category, however, as some of the above must have been the extraordinary phrase of a stolid, phlegmatic old Scotsman of whom I find I have a note. He was gazing on Niagara for the first time, and he had stirred the spleen of the voluble guide, by his non-betrayal of any wonderment or emotion whatsoever. At length the guide irritably ejaculated : 'Wal, strainger, don't you seem to thenk this rather a wonderful sight ?' 'Weel, no man,' said the imperturbable North Briton, 'I canna say I see onything vera won-

nerfu' aboot it! If the watter wis rinnin' up the ither
w'y noo, it wad nae doot be somethin' mair oot o' the
virnack'lar.'

What in the world the man meant by the use of such
a word in such a connection is a puzzle, unless explain-
able on the assumption that he was addicted to this
strange weakness for out-of-the-way phrases and 'lang-
nebbit wirds.'

But this extraordinary trait, of which I could give
many more examples, were it at all needful or profitable,
is all the more incomprehensible seeing how rich and
racy and expressive is the Scottish 'virnack'lar' itself.
Thousands of examples at once present themselves—
'greetin',' 'girnin',' 'pechin',' 'dawtie,' 'wimplin' burnie,'
'trachle,' 'bairnie,' and so on. But a few illustrations
by way of contrast may perhaps best illustrate my
meaning.

My father used to gleefully quote the reply of, I
think, a relation who had married a douce, humdrum,
good-looking shepherd. During some vicissitude of
their humble fortunes they had started a small butcher's
shop in a remote north-country township during the
tourist season. The goodman was waiting, in the little
bit shop one day, when an English-speaking damsel
came in, requiring a pound or so of suet. This was
clean beyond the amateur shopkeeper's scholarship; so
calling 'but the hoose' to his better-educated and
keener-witted spouse, he drawled out: 'Fat's sooet,
Nauncie?' 'Hoots, jist creesh, ye gowk!' came back
at once the perfectly understandable reply, in the
broadest vernacular.

And to 'creesh ane's loof' instantly suggests itself as

a thoroughly Scotch expression, though quite a foreign phrase to the ordinary Southron.

A quaint instance of the Scottish idiom which speaks of 'lacking' or 'being without' a thing, as 'wantin'' it, comes from a valued correspondent. 'Our inspector of schools,' he writes, 'was examining a class of small children the other day, and put the question : "What is a widow ?" Silence reigned for a few minutes, then a shrill little voice piped out the exquisite Scotticism : "A wife wantin' a man, sir." '

Quite as good in its way was the reply of a little fellow to his teacher, who had in the reading lesson come on the sentence : 'There are occasions for inquiring into the faults of every one, from bailie to beadle'; and wishing to test the intelligence of the class, he asked the meaning of the word beadle. Instantly the little fellow replied : 'Please, sir, it's—a—a—a stick for champin' tauties.'

Here is another example, from Mrs. Rhind, of the use of the word 'to win,' meaning to reach, or to get to. The minister of S—— asked one of his parishioners, whose mother was a notorious scold : 'Weel, Jock, an' hoo's yer mither the day ?' 'Oh, she's brawlies, sir. Ye see, sir, I'm thinkin' the grace o' God's in my mither's hert, but I'm sair dootin' it's never *won* the length o' her tongue.'

Here is a curious instance of the quaint and little-known Deeside dialect. Said a lady, whose school children had been playing among a farmer's turnips, and had been punished for the transgression : 'John, I hope the children have been behaving better ?' 'Ou ay, mem. They hinna been blaudin' ma neeps sae bias feerious as they eest tae dee.'

Another of the same is the following :—'How are ye the day, Kirsty ?' said a lady to an old wifie in Cromar. 'Thank ye, mem; I'm jist gielies i' ma helth, but I'm jist bias wi' a sair hoast.'

One eager little lassie, near Brechin, amused me the other day. She had dropped on 'a warm corner' in wild fruits evidently, for her face was 'skaiket up t'ye lugs,' as she would have put it, with rasp and blae-berry stains. Meeting some of her comrades, she breathlessly communicated the gleeful fact of her good fortune, by shouting out: 'We've been tae the Tyler's Widdie (Tailor's Wood), an' we're fou up t'ye mou.'

Let me be permitted to transcribe yet another from my notes, although this, I think, has already appeared in print.

Socrates excelled in the art of asking questions because he put them in words easily understood. An English clergyman and a Lowland Scotsman examining an Aberdeen school, failed because they did not adopt the Socratic method. 'Would you prefer to speir the boys, or that I should speir them ?' asked the master of the school. The Englishman having been told that speir meant to question, desired the master to proceed. He did so, and the boys answered many questions as to the exodus of the Israelites from Egypt. 'I would like to "speir" the boys,' then said the clergyman. 'Boys, how did Pharaoh die ?' Not a boy answered. 'I think, sir,' said the Lowlander, 'that the boys do not under-stand your English accent; let me try what I can make of them.' Then in the broadest Scotch he asked: 'Hoo did Phawraoh dee ?' Again a dead silence. 'I think,

P

gentlemen,' said the master, 'you canna speir these laddies. I'll show you how to do it.' Then turning to the scholars : 'Fat cam' to Phawraoh at his hinner end ?' 'He wis drooned !' at once answered the boys. The master then explained that in the Aberdeen dialect 'to dee' really means to die a natural death ; hence the perplexity of the boys, who knew that Pharaoh did not die in his bed.

A quaint illustration of another localism, is given in a report of a very interesting lecture, which I read with much delight, delivered, I think, in Edinburgh by the Rev. Alexander Wallace.

'Two of the genus known as Newhaven fish-women having happened to meet one day in the streets of Edinburgh, commenced a gossiping conversation, and were about to separate, when one of them, suddenly remembering a small piece of news, exclaimed hastily to her companion: "Eh, wumman, did ye hear that Janet Forsyth was deid ? " "Janet Forsyth, Janet Forsyth ?" mused the other, endeavouring to recall the name to her recollection. "Janet Forsyth ! na, wumman, na ! Wis she in the haddie line ?"—the two speakers themselves happened to belong to this elevated and aristocratic class of the fraternity. To which interrogation the first speaker answered .somewhat indignantly, and evidencing a lofty sense of superiority to the lowly Janet : "Na, na, wumman ! Na, na ! puir feckless body, she ne'er got abune the mussel line o' business."'

It is quite certain that if 'the gude auld braid Scots tongue' lent itself to directness and force in expression, the old-time folks, like the Apostle to the Gentiles, 'used great plainness of speech.' They were not afraid to express their meanings in language which could not be misunderstood. There was little of our modern niminy-piminy mealy-mouthedness about them, and it is just possible, as I have pointed out elsewhere, that what we may have gained in elegance and style, we may have lost in sincerity, directness, and force. What thus appears quite coarse, almost brutally so, in fact, to us, did not so appear to the older generation. The surviving examples of the unstudied bluntness of our forefathers, if rightly viewed, are simply so many evidences of a more primitive and less sophisticated state of society ; and without at all wishing to revive archaic and un-polished expressions, one often does wish that in high places as well as humble, there was more of the old courage and outspoken honesty in attacking abuses, and withstanding the encroachments of insidious evils, introduced often under 'very high and lofty patronage.' It does seem to me, in short, that in our modern life we are far too apt, as a people, to magnify and exalt mere worldly success, to bow down and worship mere wealth and outward show, and to lay less stress on the possession of the inward graces and homely virtues, the 'elevation of thought and feeling,' that often accompanies and in large measure compensates for the lack of material wealth or outward adornment.

As an instance of this direct bluntness, with just a touch of what to our more sophisticated ears would be deemed coarseness or vulgarity, let me give an extract from the letter of a friend of mine now in New Zealand. It gives a graphic glimpse of the old-fashioned farm-house life, with its unceasing industry, its primitive ways, and that dash of hard, dry humour, which we have been endeavouring to illustrate.

Ashbogle is a quaint little nook in the valley of the Deveron, some three miles from Turriff. The miller was Auld Chairlie Grieve, known up and down the whole country-side as 'The Mullart o' Ashbogle.' He was a fine typical specimen of the old-fashioned Aberdeen farmer. One of his most notable characteristics was his constant habit of being up with the lark, and often indeed ahead of that early chorister. Winter and summer alike, in glint or gloom, he was stirring before cockcrow, and by 4.30 A.M. he would be up and away, making the round of his farm, and be back again before the rest of the household were awake. To waken these was the old miller's next task, and his grandson writes : ' He would invariably come to the stair-foot and cry out each name, in a voice that made the walls ring again. My father and uncle were prone to indulge in a "lang lie" if they could manage it. On the particular occasion to which I allude, the old man bellowed up the stair to them: "Get up, you twa lazy loons ; gin ye lie muckle langer ye'll ROT !" "Na, na !" was the drowsy reply of my uncle, with a dash of quiet humour ; "we turn whiles."' This was in allusion to a common operation of the farm, namely the proper preparation of the compost heap.

I was recently told a story of my own father, the good old minister, which well illustrates this hearty, pawky humour, with just the requisite dash of pungency in it.

A would-be fine lady, at a certain dinner, affecting to be slightly indisposed, although her appetite was of a

very robust character, when asked by my father, who
happened to be carving one of the fowls, what he could
help her to, said in an affected, mincing manner, by way of
a joke : 'Oh, 'deed, minister, I'm no vera weel the day,
but ye micht jist gie me a leg, an' a wing, an' a bittie o'
the back.' My father took the good dame literally at her
word, for of all things in the world he hated affectation
most, and when helped as she had jokingly desired, she,
with a simper and a giggle, said : 'Oh, Mr. Inglis, but
ye've jist gien me cairtloads.' The large helping,
however, as my father fully expected, was not long
in disappearing, and noticing the empty plate, he said
in his hearty way, with a humorous twinkle of quizzical
banter in his eye : 'Noo, Mistress Jackson, jist back
in yer cairt for anither load.'

A good example, too, of this blunt outspokenness is
furnished by the reply of a well-known horse-dealer in a
northern district to his minister, who had frequently
pressed him to allow himself to be nominated for the
eldership. The minister knew the horse-couper, as he
would be called in 'The Mearns,' to be a man of substance, and possibly this fact weighed more with him
than high spirituality or moral worth. The couper
most probably had the higher sense of the responsibility
of the office, and he constantly gave the minister evasive
answers, till at last the worthy cleric demanded flatly
a sufficient reason for his constant refusal. He certainly
got it plump and plain. Looking him straight in the
eyes, the horse-couper replied : 'Toots, sir, hoo can a
man be an elder an' sell a horse ? '

Blunt enough, too, was that wifely injunction to a
rather stupid husband on the occasion of the christening

of their first child. The sharp goodwife had all her wits about her, but the blate shepherd may have been a bit disconcerted by his unwonted surroundings. At any rate when the minister asked the usual question whether he was the father of the child, the poor man stood open-mouthed and unresponsive, till the partner of his hearth and home smartly nudged him and said in an aside, loud enough for half the company to hear: 'Can ye no boo, ye stupit eedit?'

My friend the Rev. James H——, several of whose stories I have already given, tells me yet another, which was narrated to him by Sir Alexander Anderson. It illustrates the uncouth bluntness of the 'fisher fowk,' and a phase of Scottish rural life which perhaps happily is becoming much softened. One of the rustic swains had gone to the village 'to gie in the names' to the session-clerk on a Saturday, so that his banns might be published in the church on the morrow. Some feeling akin to stage fright, however, had possibly possessed him suddenly, as when he stood before the spectacled official he had clean forgotten the Christian name of his intended bride. The clerk unceremoniously packed him off to the house of the bride to get the required information. On the way a sudden flash of illumination lit up the dark chamber of memory. He recollected the name, and at once hastened back to complete his errand. The session-clerk, however, knowing full well that Tam had not had time to go all the way to the bride's home, was a little surprised and just a wee bit sceptical when Tam gave in the name as Bell. So he asked him rather sharply: 'How do you know that her name is Bell?' 'Oh,' was the blunt reply, 'I ken her naime's Bell weel eneuch, because she his a muckle B on the breist o' her sark.'

Much has been written illustrative of the old profanity and swearing habits which were formerly so common, but which happily are now much mitigated. One such is told of a notorious character known as old Peter Ruff, the driver of the Perth coach. On one occasion when he had been indulging in a more than ordinarily turgid torrent of profanity at his horses, a worthy minister seated beside him on the box, and who was naturally much shocked, ventured to remonstrate. ' Peter,' he said, ' ye shouldna sweir like that, man ; ye should try an' emulate the patience of Job.' Very gruffly, and with a terrible oath, came the query : ' Whatna —— coach did Job drive ? '

Peter was undoubtedly a coarse, brutal fellow, though unquestionably a good whip, and he only illustrates what is a very common failing among half-educated and ill-balanced natures. Let one of these lob-sided characters manifest any dexterity or pre-eminence in one particular line, and his self-conceit at once makes him think that he is equally eminent in everything else. In coach-drivers especially, nowadays, this is a very common fault. Because they can drive a coach well, they therefore seem to think that they are thereby relieved from any necessity to be pleasant spoken, to study their employer's interests, or to approve themselves ordinarily civil and polite. It is the old, old truth which Shakespeare with his wondrous intuition and observation has recorded. Some clown ' dressed in a little brief authority ' goes ' off the handle,' and makes an ass or a beast of himself. One often finds instances among callow gardeners and gamekeepers.

Now Peter the coach-driver was simply a vulgar ruffian, apart from his undoubted excellence as a whip, and he had not even 'the saving salt of humour' to make his profanity approximately interesting. He was not like another famous swearer at the Antipodes, about whom I have an entry in my note-book, which may perhaps fittingly be introduced just here. Tam Dick was a well-known oddity in the truly Scottish town of Dunedin, New Zealand, and he was noted no less for his wooden leg than for his powers of swearing. It was the delight of the Dunedin boys to torment Tam for the purpose of hearing him indulge in this most reprehensible propensity. Perhaps my readers have never heard a colonial bullock-driver swear? If so, they have no idea what really scientific, wholesale swearing is. Tam had been a bullock-driver, and was a past master in the art. On one occasion puir Tam had trusted his wooden leg to the treacherous support of a rotten piece of roadway, where some recent excavations had been but newly filled in. In an incautious moment he had stepped from the safety of the side walk, and in a twinkling the wooden leg had plunged down to the very hilt, and Tam in vain tried to extricate himself. There he was, spinning round like a '"chafer on a pin,' and of course he was soon surrounded by a crowd of mischievous and unsympathetic boys. Their jeers and laughter, as may be imagined, did not tend to improve Tam's temper. He made desperate efforts to extricate himself, but the tenacious clay held his prisoned wooden member fast. Then Tam began cursing. As was said by a witness in a celebrated police-court case, 'Tam swore at lairge.' The more the boys laughed, the deeper and louder swore puir prisoned Tam. Just then who should come up but the kindly, venerable old Doctor S——, the well-known minister of the High Church, who has just lately gone to his reward. Hastening up in his kindly way to help Tam out of his difficulty, he yet could not refrain from administering a deserved rebuke for the terrific torrent of profanity. Addressing Tam, who at once had subsided into the mildest form of objurgation, he rebuked him for the reprehensible exhibition of swearing he had just exhibited; but Tam with ready wit, with a clever knowledge of the good old doctor's love of humour, and with a really quick adaptation of the subtle shades of casuistry that he thought might readily appeal to the doctor as a theologian, turned the edge of the old divine's indignation, by saying with an assumption of *bonhomie :*—

'Toots, doctor, I wisna swearin' frae the hert, ye ken, but only frae the heid.'

'Ah, Tam, Tam,' said the mollified doctor, 'if I served ye right, I should be *sweir* (loath) to help ye oot.'

Yet one more story of the old-fashioned outspoken bluntness, and then I take leave of that part of my subject. An old gentleman who was of a very stay-at-home disposition, and detested ceremony, had found it incumbent upon him, in the discharge of some obligation of kinship, to attend at rather a stately, formal dinner at a house where there was a good deal more grandeur than comfort, according to the view of our homespun friend. At the fish course he put his hand to the side of his mouth, and whispered behind it to the grave liveried functionary behind him, 'Speerits.' The placid, well-bred menial took no notice. Again came the whisper

of distress — a little louder and hoarser this time—
'Speerits.' Still no response from the sphinx in plush.
The host, however, divining the difficulty, addressed the
footman, and asked him to bring Mr. So-and-so some
spirits. This naturally turned the eyes of the whole
distinguished company on our unfortunate bonnet-laird,
and seeing that he had made a deviation from the usual
placid procedure of a fashionable dinner, he sought to
excuse himself, by saying apologetically to the lady
presiding at his end of the table, the sister of his host,
what was no doubt a perfectly unnecessary piece of
information, but just the plain, honest truth : ' Ye see,
Miss Erskine, if I dinna hae speerits efter ma fush, I'm
aye gien to bock.' This simply meant that the poor man
desired to take a reasonable, and no doubt, in his case, a
necessary precaution against flatulence or indigestion.

CHAPTER XIII

WHISKY STORIES

Grouse shooting : its delights and surroundings—A disquisition
on whisky—'No the whisky, but the Here's t'ye !'—The true
path to lasting reform—Jimmy Dewar the toper—The two
farmers and their toasts, etc.—A lax teetotaller—Why the slow
boat was preferred—The twa gills—A deceptive measure—A
natural gill-stoup—A drinker's heaven—A cautious reason for
sobriety—A temperance testimony—A drouthy Dundee man's
dream—A dry commentary—The minister rebuked—The
humours of whisky—'No sma' dry '—A trick of the yill trade
—A professional estimate—Janet and the minister—Perfect
content.

SOME of my readers who may have followed me thus
far, have doubtless at one time or another participated
in the thrilling seductions of grouse shooting. I am
looking out as I write, over the Birks of Ardoch. The
mottled flanks of the great Glen hills come rolling down
into the Esk valley in all directions. The river is in
spate, and above the susurrus of the whispering breeze
of morn, which just lifts the birch leaves and makes
them glisten like plastic silver in the caressing sunbeams,
I can hear the hoarse, gurly roar of angry water, churning
and fuming among the granite rocks and boulders that
so thickly strew the bed of the stream, and impede its

onward, headlong rush. The water is black and angry to-day, and down the hillsides, as if in answer to that surly summons from the parent - stream, every runnel and sheep-track has become a brawling torrent, and the tawny-coloured element is brattling breathless down the hill, foaming over craggy buttress, leaping over stone and boulder, burrowing under mossy swell, and streaming with mad impatience over heather bush and sedgy tussock in its eager rush to outpace its gathering kinsmen, and mix in the heaving, seething 'meeting of the waters,' in the rocky channel of the Esk below.

The trailing mists caress the mountain peaks. Mount Keen with his conical top has not yet doffed his night-cap. Broad Battock stretches behind me swathed in sleepy sheets of curling vapour, on which the hot sun is now beginning to lavish his consuming ardour. The heather will be in full bloom by another week ; but a forerunner of the coming crimson glory already mantles many a swelling pap of the rounded ranges, and the shadows chasing each other over the heights and long - drawn slopes, alternately soften and again enhance the glory of colour and changing hue, with an exquisite embellishment that mocks the most cunning artist's brush. The fresh air fills each cranny with its life-giving flood. It is inspiriting as wine or whisky. Ah ! whisky ! That brings me back again to humble, plodding prose.

I promised you some whisky stories, did I not ? And I began this chapter too by a reference to grouse shooting. We were driving on the hill yesterday. The ground was wet and sloppy at the butt behind which I sat, watching for the birds. The hillside was like a sponge. The wind, for August, cut keen, and chilled the heated frame—heated by a toilsome plunge through tangled heather and spongy moss, up Battock's hoary flank. My butt is No. 1 at the extreme end of the line. Different this to the line of elephants on the Koosee Dyaras. Below me sits my cousin George, wiry, keen, with a look of the eagle about him, which thirty years' active life in South America has perhaps not tended to subdue. Next to him my cousin David, grizzled now and lined to what I remember him when we made that famous march to Ballater in the year—what was it? Ah, me! how the long procession of the years lengthens out as I try to recall that wild excursion. Here we three meet again in the same glen, after more than thirty years of severance and perilous adventure and arduous toil, and, thank God, some solid reward for it too, and a full survival of the old kindly affection and mutual trust.

How still it is! Nought but the sough of the cutting wind; the plaintive bleating of some distant sheep; a plover's melancholy cry; the twitter of a restless ouzel who flits from rock to rock at fitful intervals, setting my nerves on jar, and making me clutch my gun in the momentarily recurring belief that here come the expected grouse at last. Down the hill, still further, I can just discern the gray suit of one of the kindliest natures and most genial gentlemen who ever tramped the heather. He hails from distant Cuba, and every one dubs him 'the General': I suppose because he is a general favourite, for, bar his moustachios and imperial, there is nothing now aggressively military about him. Yet there was a time when the Spaniards

in Cuba knew what metal entered into the composition
of our wiry friend. Well he knows the difference
between the shot gun and the Remington. I can see,
too, the top of a head which surmounts some six feet of
Scottish - Australian brawn and brain. That is my
Australian chum, the Harper of our party. Further
down, but hidden by an intervening knoll, are two
London solicitors, and another Sassenach who is the
most promising 'colt' of the lot — all dead shots and
gallant gentlemen, but sadly given to drink cider at
lunch. Just fancy the degeneracy of the age! Cider
among the Grampians. What next, I wonder?

Bless me! will the birds never come? Cider? Ah,
that reminds me—I have a flask. Good! What is in
it? Whisky? Better still.

No sound yet of the distant beaters. No sudden
rush yet of impetuous wings. No startling 'birr-a-birr-
a-bic-bic-bic,' that sets the blood madly bounding in
one's pulses, and brings the ready gun to the receptive
shoulder. No! All is quiet. Some of the party, I
verily believe, are half asleep. I am getting drowsy
myself. The flask! the flask! What, ho! the native
wine of the country to the rescue? I unscrew the top;
I have filled a little into the metal cap; when, hark!
from George comes the cry of 'Mark covey!' and with
a rush and a swoop the ruddy beauties are upon me.
Alas! my hands are full. My gun lies idly on my
knees. Is it to be grouse or whisky? Oh, d——
Tut! tut! this will never do! What, dam the whisky
of Scotland? 'Tis impossible, sir! It cannot be done
—Sir Wilfrid Lawson and all the yards of blue ribbon in
the world to the contrary notwithstanding. It simply

cannot be done, sir ! You might as well try to dam
Niagara, or even Chicago, but Scottish whisky ? No,
no ! give up the vain attempt.

Hark, now ! The cries of the distant beaters. Gun-
shots ring out piff-paff-puff, down the line. The packed
coveys come hurtling down over the butts, here in
swooping battalions, from the midst of which you see
the wounded drop and the feathers fly, and then, bird by
bird ; and you can see the swift flight suddenly arrested
and hear the thud, as the feathered quarry bounds and
rebounds on the heathery knoll. What sensations ! what
moments of rapture, all too brief ! Ah ! the glory and the
beauty of it, slaughter though it be. The environment
of glorious scenery, the free, fresh air, the thrilling
excitement, the perfect companionship, and — well —
perhaps, just like the mustard with the sirloin, or the
oil with the salad—the dash of whisky !

You see, dear reader, I cannot exclude it. For twelve
chapters I have tried to avoid it. There has been here
and there a brief allusion to the potent liquor, just like
a stray, solitary grouse at the butts, but now my whisky
stories, 'an' ye want 'em,' can be on ye in packed coveys
and battalions.

The fact is, my friendly publisher, when he first
did me the compliment of looking over my mass of
collected notes, ventured to hint in the mildest manner
that I had 'too many whisky stories.' So I have
been trying all the time to steer clear of the seductive
subject, but you see it will not be forbidden. And
after all I am only a chronicler. I do not myself
make these whisky stories : I only set down without
malice and without bias, what I have picked up 'of

unconsidered trifles,' and if Sir Wilfrid on the one hand, or say James Greenlees on the other, chooses to evolve a cut-and-dry hypothesis, or some intricate philosophical deduction as to the habits and tendencies of the Scottish people from these memoranda, let them do so. The people themselves are the final court of appeal, and I must endeavour so to select and narrate my material, as to preserve, at all hazards, my own character for sobriety and impartiality.

I make no secret of the fact, that so far as Australian politics are concerned I am a pronounced Local Optionist without Compensation. I adequately, I think, recognise the peculiar elements and dangers in the whisky trade ; it is one that in the public interest should be under close and wise regulation ; but I recognise, too, that until human nature is very much altered indeed, it is hopeless to expect to 'make men sober by Act of Parliament.' The 'abuse' is the danger. The 'use' will continue in spite of all legislation, especially if the liquor is good and cheap ; and some queer arguments might no doubt be drawn even from that apparently simple remark. I confess, however, as I think I have mentioned in *Oor Ain Folk*, to always having had a certain sympathy with John, that genial possessor of a pronounced hiccup, and a rubicund proboscis (also pronounced), who on being taken to task by the minister, who said he could not see what seduction lay in whisky, to make it such a potent tyrant as in John's case it seemed to be, volunteered the breezy, complacent statement, which really expresses a profound philosophic truth : 'Ah, minister ! it's no the whisky ; it's the Here's t'ye !'

In other words, whisky has its social side as well as

its repellent, disgusting, bestial side. And most of the best Scottish stories connected with the national beverage, are illustrative of the social and humorous side of the national character. Besides, it must be remembered —and there is great comfort for the teetotallers in this —that the standard of moral judgment as to drinking, has been immensely raised since the days of our grandfathers. It needs not illustration. Every book of Scottish reminiscence is full of proof that this is so; and this is the true way in which all lasting reform must come. Oh, I wish our strike leaders and stirrers up of strife between class and class would recognise this. It is not by force but by reason; not by hasty enactment, but by slow, steady, patient, persistent moulding of public opinion that progress is made. When public opinion is ripe, then comes the enactment, and it being already part and parcel of the popular conscience, a ready submission is at once given, and every citizen himself becomes a willing policeman, to see that the law is observed. The divine plan is 'line upon line, precept upon precept, here a little and there a little,' until at last the broad, comprehensive change is made; and it becomes when founded thus on a people's reason and conscience, as strong as steel and as enduring as adamant.

For instance, such men as Jimmy Dewar were as common as domestic hens in Scottish villages in my young days. Their devotion to whisky was open, unabashed, unashamed. It was treated as a sort of amiable weakness, a laxity, a 'failing,' in Scottish parlance, for which the self-indulgent victim was to be pitied and petted rather than to be scouted and reprobated. But now, open debauchery has to 'hide its 'minished head.' Glaring, greedy drunkenness of the swinish type has to keep to its stye. It must no longer flaunt itself openly in the village streets. And why? Is it because police supervision is better organised and more effectively sustained? Is it because inns and public-houses are in better hands and are better administered? These and other reasons may possibly explain something of the change, but the real reason, I take it, is because of a vast change in public opinion, notably, too, from a very salutary and marked change in the manners of the upper and educated classes. Position and wealth and culture have tremendous responsibilities, and much of the hoggish dissipation of a former rude age among the common people, was simply due to its being a too faithful reflection of the excesses and licentiousness of the upper classes of society. The national conscience is now, however, more finely strung. Public sensibility is quicker to perceive 'the rank offence' of what was, in sad truth, a great national reproach. The change is no doubt due in great measure to the efforts of the Temperance party. May its power increase, may its influence spread, may its earnest workers be encouraged; but may, too, the appeal and the work be ever accompanied by that true temperance which depends on the righteousness of its cause, and the ultimate triumph of every wise and patient appeal to reason and conscience, rather than to force and passion and prejudice.

But we are keeping Jimmy Dewar waiting. Well, Jimmy was just such a confirmed tippler in one of our northern towns, as was very common fifty years ago. The ever-growing indulgence in his favourite vice had brought him down from a position of comparative affluence to great penury. He had 'drucken awa' hoose an' launds an' a gude bizness,' as one of his neighbours comprehensively said, but undeterred by all his losses, unabashed by all his reverses, unwarned by all the sad evidences of his debasing thraldom to a vicious habit, he still continued to prostrate his very manhood at the shrine of Bacchus, with all the fervour and constancy of a confirmed devotee. One day as he was about to toss down another jorum of his favourite poison, one of his mates, with a slight gleam of imagination working a temporary compunction in him, as he momentarily contrasted the sad, blotched wreck before him, with the trim, well-to-do master-workman of the olden time, said: 'Eh, man, Jimmy, ah'm thinkin' that stuff's jist been yer ruin.' 'Ou ay, min, so my wife says,' said the case-hardened, unabashed toper. Then came the glint of natural, rugged humour, which even under such circumstances could not be wholly repressed. 'Od, she says I've drucken a hoose! Feth it (hic) maun hae been a thack yin (thatched one), for I've never gotten the stoor out o' ma mooth yet!' and so saying he quaffed off his gill to see if that would help to lay the 'stoor.'

So common were the drinking habits of the former generation, so few were the intellectual resources, that it is abundantly on record, that much as the Russian peasant is now with his vodka, so formerly was the farmer in Scotland with his toddy, and the working rural classes with their raw whisky. My father used to instance the case of two phlegmatic, stolid, hard-drinking farmers, who used to meet alternately at each other's houses night after night, and sit simply soaking in, the regularly recurring 'browsts,' till they were saturated and almost brimming over. The only conversation used to be the challenge of the one, 'Here's t'ye, Mucklo Tulloh!' and the response, 'Thanks t'ye, Burnsaggart!' varied the next time by Burnsaggart, or 'Bunsie' as he was commonly called, taking the response to his neighbour's initiative, thus : 'Here's t'ye, Burnsaggart!' 'Thanks t'ye, Muckle Tulloh!'

This finds its complete parallel in the story related of the two Scotch skippers at Penang, who used to meet in each other's cabins nightly while their ships were being stowed, and used to continue their stolid debauch far into the night. They only had the two toasts, and on these they rang the changes, with unvarying fidelity to the etiquette of the period. The one was, 'The toon an' trade o' Leith.' The other was, 'A' ships at sea.'

A capital instance of the esteem in which good whisky was held, is afforded by the experience of old Mr. Fallon of Albury in N.S.W., a leading *vigneron* there. He had made many expensive and laudable attempts to make a good Australian champagne, and on one occasion had invited a numerous and representative company to taste the wine and give their opinion upon it. Among others was an old Scotchman, the popular and well-known captain of one of the P. and O. boats. He was a very outspoken, matter-of-fact type of his class, and he did not take much pains to conceal his poor opinion of the Australian champagne, which, truth to tell, was in regard to this particular sample just a trifle tart. Mr. Fallon seeing this, said : 'Ah, I'm sorry to see, Captain M——, that you do not seem to be over favourably impressed with the result of my experiments.' Being thus challenged, the old sea-dog at once said : 'Weel no, Maister Fallon, I cannot say I am, an' wi' your permission I wad fain synd ma mooth wi' a waucht o' oor ain auld naitional drink, for ye see ah'm no great judge o' THAE SOOR KINDS.'

It must surely have been a better brand which caused the old farmer's injunction to the attendant Hebe, at some dinner where he had for the first time been introduced to 'the foaming nectar.' At any rate he said whisperingly to her : 'Noo, lassie, whin yer daein' nocht else, jist be aye poorin' oot some mae o' this sma' yill tae me.'

Very pawky, too, was the reply of an old keeper in the north to a query of my brother. The old fellow was known as Peter Barrahashlin, and was quite an oddity. One day my brother asked him in jocular mood : 'Noo, Peter, tell me the truth—was ye ever fou ?' Peter replied : 'Weel, sir, I hef nefer peen drunk, put I'll alloo I may haf peen sometimes a leetle fou-lish '— with the accent strong on the first syllable.

How strong an influence towards moral obliquity is the potent potion, and how insidiously it leads the partaker towards a facile and dangerous casuistry, is evidenced by the following temperance anecdote. An old fellow who had taken the pledge, but whose practice it was shrewdly suspected did not keep pace with his profession, was twitted one day by an acquaintance, who expressed some indignation at a laxity which would allow of the infraction of a solemn pledge. 'Ah !' said the old self-apologist with a moist sigh, 'I jist whiles pits a wee drappie i' the boddom o' the tum'ler, jist tae warm the gless like ; bit, ye ken, I never drinks doon tae the whusky.'

A friend, of whose sudden death I have heard since writing these lines, told me a characteristic story of one of 'oor ain fowk' of the dry, drouthy order.

My friend Mr. L—— was desirous of getting down to Geelong from Melbourne on some urgent business, and having just missed his train, was told he had time still to catch the boat. Accordingly he hurried off to the wharf, and seeing two boats, he selected the larger and finer-looking one of the two, and as it almost immediately warped off and proceeded on its way, he inly congratulated himself on having made a wise selection.

Presently, however, somewhat to his chagrin, the other boat, having now started, began to overhaul them, and after a while it rapidly made up to and passed them. Mr. L—— remarked to a quiet-looking, dried-up sort of a fellow-passenger, who from his bonnet and general appearance he took to be a 'brither Scot': 'Dear me, I thought this was the fastest boat!'

'Oh no, sir,' was the response in broadest Doric, 'that yin startit ahint us, but she'll get in hauf an 'oor aheid o' us.'

'An' why did ye no gang by her then?' asked Mr. L——.

'Oh!'—with a pawky leer—'this yin's a saxpence cheaper, an', ye ken, I can get a gless o' whusky wi' that when we get in.'

This is very like the story of two old bodies in Tain, who lived by making straw mats, known as *basses*. Once a week they used to come in to Tain from Kilmure to buy their boll of meal, which they used to wheel out again to Kilmure a distance of six miles. One day, one of the bailies ventured to gently remonstrate with them

for this extraordinarily needless toil, pointing out that
they only got the meal a sixpence cheaper in Tain.
'Ah, bailie,' was the reply, 'but ye see we get the
twa gills wi' the saxpence on the w'y oot.'

Being on whisky stories reminds me of a quaint
saying of Robert M——, a fine farmer of the old
school, who was tenant of Leuchlands, near Brechin. In
the booths at the markets there used to be a small glass
in common use known locally as 'a wee Donal'.' Old
Mr. M—— held these in abhorrence, and was partial
to the good old-fashioned pewter gill-stoup. His par-
tiality was manifested thus on one occasion. Having
ordered the drink, the attendant Hebe prepared to cir-
culate the small glasses, but Mr. M—— in stentorian
tones shouted : ' Hoots, lassie, jist gie's a gill; ye ken
fat yer doin' wi' a gill, but as for thae d——d Donal's,
ye dinna ken far ye're gaun ava' ! '

Under somewhat similar circumstances, in the same
locality, another impatient, drouthy farmer was kept
waiting what he thought an unconscionable time for the
drink he had ordered. Rather sharply he called out to
the lassie, bewildered with many orders, and asked her
what in the world she was doing.

' Hech, sir, I'm lookin' for the gill-stoup ! ' she said.

' Hoots, 'umman,' was the instant reply, ' come awa'
wi' the bottle ; never mind the stoup ; my mooth jist
hauds a gill.'

In further illustration of the change which has come
over public opinion in regard to drinking habits, it
would, I daresay, not be possible for a minister nowadays to speak to his flock as it is reported an old-time
minister did some time early in the century, when he

was fencing the Communion Table. 'My freens,' he said, 'you would all like to go to heeven; but what kin' o' a heeven wad ye like to go to? Well, I'll tell you. You would just like the Cromarty Firth to be bilin' watter, the Black Isle to be loaf sugar, an' the Beauly rinnin' whisky, an' ye wad jist brew an' drink, an' drink an' brew, to all eternity.'

That was perhaps not an outrageous exaggeration of the then popular vice. One may chronicle with honest thankfulness that 'sweeter manners' and more temperate habits now prevail.

Mr. John T. Clough, a genial old acquaintance of mine 'on the road' in Australia, has sent me a few very good illustrations of some of the salient features of Scottish character. Some, I regret to say, would scarcely bear repetition outside the walls of the 'commercial smoking-room,' but the following are worthy of being recorded :—

The first is a capital illustration of Scottish caution. *Scene*—A favourite 'howf' in one of the large Lowland toons. *Time* — Setterday nicht. *Dramatis personæ* — Three drouthy cronies, whose appearance amply testifies to the sincerity of their attachment to the national beverage. One of the three is being pressed by the others to partake of another dram; but to their undisguised amazement he refuses. They redouble their invitations, and one exclaims : 'Losh, man, An'ra, ye surely dinna mean to say that ye'll no tak' ony mair the nicht; and you no half slockened yet? It's pairfectly rideeklus. Toots, man, yer haverin'; ye maun hae anither dram.' Andrew, with a deep sigh of regret, responds : 'Weel, no the nicht, billies; ye see I've jist shiftet ma lodgin's, an' ah'm no vera weel acquent wi' the stair yet.'

It might have been Andrew of whom the following is told :—

'A worthy worshipper at the shrine of Bacchus,' writes Mr. Clough (you see how thoroughly Scottish he is, in that he bestows the commendatory adjective on the drouthy knave !), 'had been persuaded by his minister (it was in a Galloway parish) to eschew his bibulous proclivities and sign the pledge. He had kept it with praiseworthy fidelity for some short time, and the minister was so pleased, that, having arranged for a temperance meeting to be held in the school-house, he determined to exhibit the new convert as one of the triumphs of the occasion. Meeting Andrew, therefore, the good minister insisted on taking him on to the platform along with other leading lights, and, after much hesitation, Andrew consented. The night came, and with it a crowded audience thronged the school-room— for the change in Andrew had been the current topic of conversation in the parish for some time. The minister delivered the usual introductory address, and alluded with pardonable gratulation to the fact of Andrew having now become a pledged teetotaller, a changed man, etc. etc., and announced that no doubt their reformed friend would be glad to say a few words anent his experiences.

'After much coaxing and hand-clapping, and the usual popular methods of encouraging a modest speaker, Andrew got to his feet, looking red and uncomfortable, and after clearing his throat, began : "Dear freens, ye a' ken me (cheers). Weel, I've been tectottle for the better feck o' a fortnicht " (great cheering).

' *Minister* (aside)—"Gang on, Andrew, tell them how ye feel."

'*Andrew* (continuing)—"Weel, ma freens, dod, tae tell ye the truth, I dinna feel muckle the waur o't ! (Hear ! hear !) I'm thinkin', sirss, the noo, that I've already saved as muckle i' the fortnicht as wad mebbe buy a coffin !" (Hear ! hear !) *Minister*—"Gang on, Andrew, ye're doin' grand !" *Andrew* (desperately)— " Dod, ma freens, as sure's deith, I dinna ken what tae say neist, but ah'm thinkin' if I'm teetottle for anither fortnicht, I'LL NEED IT !"'

Such an unlooked-for *dénouement* was, no doubt, an unwelcome surprise for the minister, but there is such an air of sophistication and strained humour about the story, that I am inclined to think it is a weak fabrication of the enemy, designed to have a sly dig at the tee-totallers. Quite as much, but only from the opposition side, might be said of the following, which appears too neatly put together almost, to be natural—too cut-and-dry altogether, too much of the goody-goody, namby-pamby order to be real. However, as I am sworn to hold the balances even, let it be told, as it scores against Boniface, although it has already been in print.

The tale goes that a labourer at the harbour of Dundee lately told his wife a curious dream which he said he had experienced during the night. He dreamed that he saw coming towards him, in order, four rats. The first one was very fat, and was followed by two lean rats, the rear rat being blind. The dreamer was greatly perplexed as to what evil might follow, as it has been understood that to dream of rats denotes coming calamity. He appealed to his wife concerning this, but she, poor woman, could not help him. His son, a sharp lad, who had heard his father tell the story, volunteered to be the interpreter. 'The fat rat,' said he, 'is the man 'at keeps the public-hoose that ye gang till sae aften ; an' the twa lean yins are me an' ma mither.' 'An' the blin' yin ?' asked the father. 'Oh, the blin' yin's jist yersel'.'

The next is evidently from the whisky side. A rather self-complacent teetotal lecturer at the end of a glowing peroration in favour of total abstinence, and with just possibly a slightly inflated sense of his own social importance, after mentioning several notable names whom he claimed as belonging to his own persuasion, he patted himself on the breast and pompously said : 'I myself also am a teetotaller.' A bibulous-looking old hag close to the platform simply convulsed the audience by saying quite audibly : 'Puir craetur, he jist looks like yin.'

Rather an ingenious rebuke is contained in the following, told of a Highland minister, who found one of his parishioners under the vicious influence. Next day he called to rebuke him for his evil excess. 'It is wrong to get drunk,' said the minister. 'I ken that,' said the unrepentant sinner, 'but I dinna drink as muckle as ye dae yersel'.' This was carrying the war into the enemy's country with a vengeance, and the minister no doubt looked as astonished as he felt. 'How do you make that out ?' he indignantly asked. 'Weel, sir,' said the pawky Scot, 'divna ye aye tak' a gless o' whisky an' watter efter denner ?' 'Yes, certainly,' assented the minister ; 'I take a glass of whisky and water after dinner, but merely to assist digestion.' 'Jist that,' said Jeems. ' An' dinna ye tak' a tum'ler o' toddy ilka nicht when ye're gaun tae bed ? ' ' Yes, to be sure,' again assented the minister, ' but that's just to help me to sleep.' ' Aweel,' proceeded the imperturbable Jeems, ' that mak's jist fourteen glesses i' the week, an' gey near saxty ilka munth.   Noo, ye see, I only get pyed my waages ilka munth, and if I wis tae tak' saxty glesses fin I get pyed, I wad be deid-drunk for a week.   Ye see, minister, the only differ atween the twa o's, is jist that ye time yours better than I dae.'

Here are a few good whisky stories which my good friend Mr. M.—— gave me on board the s.s. *Orotava*, and as they were all new to me, I hope they may prove fresh to many of my readers.   The first illustrates in characteristic fashion, the hold that the drink habit gets on its votaries, and the frank unconsciousness of any sense of shame in the victim.

Drouthy old carle to publican on a Sunday morning :—

' Tammas, can ye gimme a hauf mutchkin ? '

' Eh, man, ye ken it's the Sawbath Day.   I can gie ye nane the day.   Besides, I gied ye hauf a mutchkin awa' wi' ye last nicht.'

' Hoots, man, did ye think I could sleep wi' whusky i' the hoose ? '

The next shows the social *camaraderie* of whisky drinkers.

Two cronies, unco fou, of the ' Tam o' Shanter and Souter Johnnie' type, are shauchlin' along together, each trying to uphaud the ither, when at length the fouest of the twain fell heavily to mother earth, and there he lay.   The other tried in vain to raise him.   He could with difficulty maintain his own balance, and at length, with a muddled sense of the claims of boon companionship, said, suiting his actions to his words : ' Aweel, Sandie (hiccup), I canna lift ye ; but (hic) od, man, I like ye that weel, I'll jist (hic) lie doon aside ye.'

Of much the same conduct is that related of a poor, drucken, doited bodie in the Saut Market, who, after vainly trying to maintain his swaying balance, at length fell prone in the syver or gutter, which at the time happened to be well flushed with water. The cold water awoke him to a dim sort of consciousness, and by some association of ideas he evidently imagined himself in the water, and began striking out vigorously with legs and arms like a man in the act of swimming. Just then the policeman came up and grabbed him from behind ; but he, still under the influence of his dominant idea, struck out all the more vigorously, and bawled out : ' Never mind me ! I can soom. Help them that canna soom.'

He must have been of the same kidney as the old toper of whom it is told, that being surprised by a friend one day lying on his face at the burnside, greedily drinking the pure fresh water, he was asked :—

' What's that yer daein', Tammas ? '

' Oh, I'm makkin' toddy.'

' Hoo's that na ? '

' Oh, ye see, I hed the whusky last nicht.'

There used to be a well-known ' howf ' at Alloa, near the pier, kept by a Boniface named Harry Rutherford. One day a friend of mine heard the following pithy colloquy between two rather dingy loungers on the pier. Said the one :—

'Come awa' intae Hairry Rutherford's, Tam, an' I'll gie ye a drink o' sma'.'

'No thank ye,' responded Tam rather cavalierly; 'no the day. I'm no sma' dry.'

Tam's complaint was evidently deeper seated than anything that mere 'sma'' would alleviate.

Talking of 'sma'' I remember hearing a reminiscence of an old commercial traveller that lets a little light into the doings of the unsophisticated and immaculate licensed victualler. It seems he had sold a 'line' of bulk porter to an old landlady who kept a well-known House of Call, and on his next visit he was assailed by the old lady with indignant protests and denunciations concerning the quality of the last supply of porter.

The weather had been warm, and he fancied there might just be some little thing wrong which he could remedy, so as she said she could not sell it, that no one would drink it, etc., he requested that it might be shown to him. The old lady, evidently in a very bad temper, snappishly refused, telling him she had no time to spare. Her little niece stood by, and the traveller, not wishing to lose a good customer, said: 'Oh, do not you bother; but let your bit lassock come wi' me, and I can see then what's wrong.'

Away they accordingly went to the cellar, and on drawing some of the porter, it frothed up terrifically, and he at once thought he had hit on a solution of the trouble. 'Oh,' said he to the lassic, 'ye stupid little jaud, this porter's a' richt. It only wants some sma' yill mixin' intill't.'

'Hech,' said the lassock, unconsciously disclosing her auntie's trade secret, 'I never saw her pit mair sma' beer intae ony porter that ever cam' intae the hoose afore.'

In fact, the old bodie had overdone it.

Just another, while I am on the topic. How true it is, and how natural, that we all adopt standards of comparison suggested by our own environment! This is rather whimsically illustrated by the anecdote told of an old publican or inn-keeper at Loch Lomond, who used invariably to classify his customers according to their drinks, if he had occasion to speak of them. Thus, being asked if he knew 'Sir Somebody So-and-so,' he would reply with unctuous *empressement* as he rubbed his fat hands together:—

'Ou ay! a fine fallow that—a graund fallow—champagne ilka day, him! Ay, champagne ev-ery day, sir.'

'Yes! An' d'ye ken So-and-so?'

'Yes,' with an airy complacency; 'yes; a dacent sort o' man him. Indeed a vera dacent sort o' man. Port an' sherry, sir. Ay, jist that, port an' sherry, port an' sherry.'

'Ay! An' So-and-so. D'ye ken him?'

'Ou ay, sir, weel eneuch! A puir sort o' craetur, sir. Bottled yill, man; jist bottled yill.'

This is quite on a par with the nomenclature of the old minister, who used to speak of claret as puir washy stuff, fit for English Episcopawlians an' the like; or brandy as het an' fiery, like thae Methodists. 'Sma' beer' was thin an' meeserable like thae Baptists; and so on through the whole gamut of drinks and sects; but invariably he would finish up by producing the whisky bottle, and patting it would exclaim: 'Ah, the rael Auld Kirk o' Scotland, sir. There's naething beats it.'

One of the favourite punning old stories that used to be told round the glowing peat-fire in the old farmhouse up the Glen was the following. It affords a quaint glimpse of the old spinning-wheel days and the prevalent apologetic temper towards the national failing. The minister comes off second-best, and Janet the drouthy, has decidedly the best of it in the encounter of wits.

Old Janet was a regular 'hard case.' She had indeed 'broken bounds,' and become such a perfect nuisance with her ever-recurring drinking bouts that at length even the easy-going neighbour folk were moved to protest, and after many warnings and expostulations they at length took the extreme step of appealing to the then all-powerful and much-feared authority, 'the minister himsel'.' Janet was 'named' to the minister in a much more than Parliamentary way, and in the hope that his official monitions might have some effect on the hardened old toper. How he succeeded in his mission is evident from the following colloquy, which I have heard from dear, red, loving lips, many a time, 'to keep the loons quaiet.'

After passing the usual good-day to the blear-eyed old crone in the reeky, close cabin, which was all Janet had for a habitation, the minister began diplomatically by saying :—

'Ay, Janet, I hear ye've been reelin' ' '—meaning 'reelin' fou,' a common expression for being tipsy.

'Aweel, sir,' said the quick-witted Janet, purposely misunderstanding him, 'we maun aye reel efter we spin, ye ken.'

'Ah, but Janet, that's not what I mean. I hear ye have been drinking, and that without measure, too.'

'Na na, sir, ye've heard wrang. A' the little 'at I drink's aye measured, an' weel measured tae.'

'Ah, Janet, evasion ill becomes ye. Do you not know where drunkards go to?'

'Hoot ay, sir, brawlies that. They jist gang whaur they can get the best drink an' the maist for their siller.'

'Na, na, Janet,' said the good man, solemnly shaking his head ; 'they go where there's weeping and wailing and gnashing of teeth.'

'Aweel, aweel, sir,' said the hopeless old reprobate, 'let them 'at his teeth, gnash teeth, but, as for me, I hinna haen ane left i' my heid for mair nor thretty years.'

Janet was too evidently in 'the bond of iniquity,' and the minister had 'to confess that he could make no impression on her. She must have been just as hopelessly obdurate and unabashed as the reeling Bacchanal in Edinburgh, of whom the following is told by a very precise, trim, elegant banker of the old school. He was leaving the bank one evening, spotlessly neat as usual, and delicately drawing on his gloves, when suddenly with a 'staucherin'' lurch he was run into by a regular Silenus, almost overflowing with his favourite tipple. The disgusted and outraged banker with icy politeness said very testily to the leering sot :—

'My good man, what *do* you want?'

Instantly came the happy, hiccuping reply : 'Want? (hic). I want naething ! (hic). I'm as fou's I can haud.'

But I must turn off the whisky tap although not nearly exhausted, for, truth to tell, it is not a very elevating or even an amusing subject.

R

CHAPTER XIV

SCOTTISH COMPLACENCY

The national conceit — Shakespeare as a Scotsman — The complacent meal-man—The self-satisfied captain—' A mairchant ' on good terms with himself—Professional complacency—A near shot—Sir Robert Hamilton's story—A novel reason for church attendance—'The salt of the earth '—' As ithers see us ' — Awful ultimate fate of a Scotsman — The colonial version.

I HAVE referred more than once to the strong sense of individuality which the old Scottish training was designed to strengthen and develop. The hard, frugal home-life nurtured the sturdy virtues of industry, persistence, thrift, patience, and determination. The parish school and university between them, helped on the mental and intellectual faculties in much the same direction. The path of learning was a hard and thorny one ; ' the race ' was very much ' to the swift ' and ' the battle to the strong.' Success then, and indeed the very effort to achieve it, not unfrequently begot rather a hard, steely disregard of the struggles of others, and a corresponding self-satisfaction and a complacent appreciation of one's own powers and performances. Humorous instances of this have been cited often enough, but in the whole texture of the national character there was always a healthy mental appraisement. The Scot took stock of himself and of others in a frank, manly, independent way. It is well expressed in the exposition which I once heard a dear old Scottish minister give of the apostolic injunction to 'think soberly' of oneself. He pointed out, I thought very quaintly, yet with good reason, that 'Paul, no doubt, wanted to caution Timothy against being too priggish and conceited, but "soberly" meant, at the same time, that he was not to be unduly retiring and stupidly mock-modest. In fact he was to have a good, honest, reasonable, and fair conceit o' himsel'.'

The extreme was to be avoided, and in self-appraisement as in most things else, the happy mean is to be aimed at. There can be little doubt that envious detractors have not unfrequently magnified and distorted this perfectly legitimate attitude of mind on the part of Scotsmen in 'comparing themselves with themselves,' or with others, and so an abundant crop of stories has sprung up and been chronicled, in which rather the caricature of my countryman's self-complacency, as well as of his caution for instance, his thrift, or his patriotism, have been distorted and quite misrepresented.

One rather laughable instance at once suggests itself to my mind in illustration of this traditional self-sufficiency and proverbial 'gude conceit' of the typical Scot.

It happened in a mixed company in some public room, and a discussion had arisen between two of the guests, which soon became general, as to some recent speculations upon the authorship of certain of Shakespeare's plays. The old, old arguments as to 'the Baconian' and other theories had been stated, and at length a general laugh of a derisive sort had been raised, by a young traveller in a jocular sort of way, stating that 'there were not a few, especially from "north the Tweed," who on the strength of a few scattered allusions in *Macbeth*, for instance, actually advanced the absurd hypothesis that "the divine William" must certainly have been a Caledonian.' A saturnine-looking, sallow, lantern-jawed individual in the corner, who had hitherto preserved a stolid silence, suddenly interposed, with an acid sort of tone in his voice, and with not a little indignant heat, saying in broad Doric: 'Weel, gentlemen, I can see naething to lauch at in such a supposeetion, for ye maun alloo that the abeelity displayed wad fairly warrant the inference.'

That is an example of what might be called the broad, impersonal, national conceit. The Rev. John S—— of Edinburgh tells the story of a northern Scot who had gone to market to sell some meal, which illustrates the personal and particular possession of the same quality by some of 'oor ain folk.' The poor man had stood in the fair all day, but had got never an offer for his meal. At last, as evening fell, he left the market feeling not a little dejected. On the way home he called at a 'howf' by the wayside and ordered a gill. He slowly quaffed the distilled balm and felt not a little cheered. It seemed somehow to resuscitate him considerably in his own good opinion of himself. He ordered another. This made him quite buoyant. He became comparatively cheerful, and from being gloomy and taciturn he passed into the communicative stage and began to detail his day's experiences to the landlord. After he had finished the second gill his usual normal self-sufficiency would seem to have been quite restored, as he wound up by a burst of self-assertion in this fashion : ''Deed ay, they'll find the grunds o' their stammicks, afore I'll offer them *my* meal again.'

Poor Sandie's self-complacency, however, was perhaps not so pronouncedly smug, as that of an old ship captain of whom I have heard. An intending passenger of some pretensions to good birth and high station, and who had himself rather an exalted opinion of his own importance, had called at the ship to see the accommodation, and had been shown over the cabins by the chief steward. The would-be magnate had passed comments on the fittings, asked minutely about the cuisine and attendance, and so on, and was just about to ask what sort of a man the captain was, when that worthy himself appeared on the scene, beaming with his usual self-complacency, and the steward did the necessary introduction, saying : ' Oh, here's the captain himself, sir.'

' Haw—captain,' said the lofty one, ' I have just been looking ovaw—haw—your ship—haw—and I am rathaw pleased with her—aw ! I think the cawbins—haw—are woomy and clean ; and I was thinking that—aw—I might do worse—aw—than take a voyage—aw—with you—aw.'

Smiling with gratified complacency the captain thus responded :—

''Deed ye micht dae far waur than that, sir. The ship's weel aneuch nae doot. But ye see, sir, ye'll hae ither advantages. Ye see, I'm no like some cawptains. 'Deed no ! I dinna keep masel' tae masel' like some. An' I jist try to treat my paissengers as my equils.'

The innocent sort of rustic complacency arising from a continually indulged self-confession of superiority in a narrow, restricted circle where a man meets little opposition, and competition is absent, is amusingly shown in the incident I am now about to relate. A famous London merchant, whose ships sailed the seas of every quarter of the globe, and whose transactions were of great magnitude, embracing dealings with almost every known port of any consequence, had taken a shooting away up in the north, and being a man of active mind and very practical, he delighted to throw himself energetically into any movement around him of a public or beneficial character.   Some agitation had arisen over some local matter—roads perhaps, or the local school, or some other thing—and the rich merchant from the big house strolled down to the meeting which had been convened to discuss the subject.   There was much division of opinion, and many foolish suggestions were made.   The speech which most commended itself to the amused man of millions, was that made by a little keen-looking man, very wizened but very vigorous, and he enforced his arguments with good language and apposite illustrations.   The city merchant exercised his rights as a resident and ratepayer, and he, too, rose and made a strong, forceful, direct speech in support of the line advocated by the little weazen-faced mannie, whom, on inquiry from the neighbour sitting next him, he found to be the local sweetie and snuff seller, or, as any trader of the sort, no matter how small, is called in this part of the north, 'the village merchant.'   After the meeting the two orators of like opinions met, and the village huckster, gratified at the support he had received from such an eloquent and distinguished-looking stranger, manifested another Scottish characteristic, namely, that mixture of caution and curiosity which leaves its holder no rest till it has been satisfied; and after exchanging ordinary greetings the rustic asked the great commercial luminary :—

' Ay, an' fat micht you be noo, na ? '

' Oh, I'm a merchant.'

' Yea, na ?   Od that's gey na !   Ay, ay ! an' so ye're a mairchant, are ye ?   Weel that's queer too, na ! for ye see I'm a mairchant masel'.   But ah'll be thinkin' ah'll be a bittie better nor you.'

' Indeed ! How so ? ' said the much-amused capitalist.

' Ow, ye see, I hiv the post-offish as weel's the chop ' (shop).

The national complacency when it takes a professional bent would seem, however, even to survive a translation from a narrow, restricted sphere into the broader environment where competition is keener and opportunities for comparison more frequent ; at least one might judge so from my next dive into my notebook.

A Scottish gardener who had been filling a good situation in England, had gone north to his native place for a holiday.   Perhaps he was suffering from a slight attack of *Heimweh* as our German cousins call homesickness.   At any rate, while enjoying the caller air of his native hills he had been asked by an old crony : ' Ay, an' hoo div ye like thae Englitchers, na ? '   The calm, deep, abiding, ineffable sense of lofty, patronising superiority that shone through the answer was, I think, simply delicious from the Scottish point of view.   ' Oh, weel, I canna tak' it upo' me to say onythin' parteec'lar agin' them, for they've been vera guid tae me. But, efter a', I maun alloo that if ye want the like o' a gair'ner noo, or a minister, or onythin' o' that kin' that requires heid wark, ye've aye to come farrer north.'

It was not absent even from the pulpit if one may judge from the complacent, unctuous sort of way in which one worthy clergyman in the north used to include in his prayer, when Her Majesty was residing near by, a petition for her most gracious Majesty under the designation of 'Oor illustrious neebor noo residin' in these pairts.'

Nor is it confined exclusively to the old. The youthful Scot is fully possessed with the same sublime self-satisfaction, which is quite impervious to all assault and is equal to every fortune. My friend Major Hannay is responsible for the following naïve example of the truth of this.

As a boy he and his brother had been out with the head keeper rabbit shooting. They had a rustic lad with them who was working the ferrets, and ladlike was dying with eager desire to handle a gun and be allowed to have a shot at a real live rabbit. There had been a pause while the grizzled old keeper had been lighting his pipe. He had given the lad Johnnie the gun to hold. Just then the ferrets turned out quite a bevy of bunnies. The eager lad could not restrain himself. The coveted gun was in his grasp. Up it went to his shoulder, and he let fly at the scampering rabbits, bang! bang! but, alas! he missed the rabbits and destroyed a good patch of turf instead. The old veteran, pulling and puffing at his obdurate pipe like a half-started steam-engine, said very dryly, wishing to abash and reprove the lad : 'Ay, John, ye wir mair nor twa yairds aff'n that yin.' To which John, still aglow with the rapture of having actually fired a shot, complacently rejoined, much to the old keeper's disgust : 'Ou ay, ah kent ah wisna *far* aff'nt.'

The quality would seem, too, to survive even expatriation and transplantation to a foreign strand. Of this, Sir Robert Hamilton, the late able Governor of Tasmania, gave me a good illustration at the Mansion House dinner on St. George's Day, where I had the good fortune to be seated next my genial and gifted friend. He was good enough to compliment me on the success of *Oor Ain Folk*, and the conversation turned to the topic of Scottish characteristics. He narrated an experience which befel him on one occasion in Melbourne. He had been the guest of Sir Henry Loch at Government House, and a special concert had been arranged in honour of the distinguished company then gathered as guests of Sir Henry. For the honoured visitors a reserved circle had been set apart, and when the seats were filled, Sir Robert, who is an old Aberdeen University prizeman, and a patriotic, observant Scotsman, noticed with, I am sure, a very pardonable pride that with a single exception (and he was Welsh) all the other high dignitaries present as specially honoured guests were his fellow-countrymen. There were two Governors ; the Premier, Mr. Duncan Gillies, now Agent-General for Victoria ; Mr. Nimmo, Minister of Lands ; Sir James M'Bain, President of the Council, and one or two others whose names I forget. It was on a Saturday night, and Sir Robert had, perforce, to leave for Tasmania very early on the Monday. He wished to make a call of

ceremony on a dear old Scottish lady whose husband
held very high office in the State, and who indeed had
borne the chief part in getting up the musical entertain-
ment in honour of the visitors; and there was no help
for it but to call on the Sabbath afternoon.   He did so,
and was received with a certain amount of stiffness by
the good old lady, who in a peculiarly dry, matter-of-
fact, frank, Scottish fashion contrived to let her titled
visitor understand that she did not approve of Sabbath
visits.   The Governor, however, was too practised a
diplomatist to allow this feeling long to linger, and
immediately went on to speak of the delightful and
successful concert the previous evening.   Knowing, too,
the old lady's fervid patriotism and her intense nationality, he proceeded to express the delight he had felt in
seeing so many high and responsible offices filled by her
fellow-countrymen.   The fine old dame began to thaw at
once.   The allusion evidently much mollified her, and
when Sir Robert detailed the result of his previous
evening's observation as to the occupants of the seats of
honour, she remarked in the broadest Aberdeen Doric :
'Ou ay, Sir Robert, there's mebbe no sae mony o's
as ye wad think, but what there are, are a' o' the vera
best oot here.'

The sense of self-importance may, of course, and
often does, become a fault; but when it takes the
whimsical shape of making a man think himself of such
sufficient importance as even to influence the humours
of his Satanic Majesty, it may perhaps be counted something abnormal even for a Scotsman.

It is told of a hardened old reprobate, who had long
ago been given over by minister and 'neebors,' and

even by his own family, as a hopelessly incorrigible case, that one morning, when the rest of the household were preparing for church attendance, he astounded his wife by saying : ' Weel, Janet, I've been thinkin' I'll just gang wi' ye tae the kirk this mornin'.'

The poor wife scarce knew what to think. She scarce dared to indulge in the sweet hope that her hard-hearted ' man ' was at length softening and yielding to good influences. So very tremblingly, and with almost a greetin' gratefulness, she said : ' Eh, An'ra, but that will be nice ; but what's garred ye cheenge yer mind the day ? '

This was a very unwise move on the part of the wife. It roused An'ra's obstinacy and his self-importance at once, and he extinguished the good wife's grateful anticipations by saying : ' Weel, I think I'll gang for yince, jist to vex the deil.'

Now it is only in accord with the first instincts of unregenerate human nature that this complacent assumption of superiority should awaken envy and even strong antagonism. It is not in the nature of things that others in whom the same ' good conceit of themselves ' is well developed should tamely submit to this calm and, it must be confessed, irritating subordination of themselves, this cool relegation of themselves to an inferior place. They cannot see why they should be classed in a second-hand category or catalogue, as it were, nor why Scotsmen alone should be looked on as ' the elect,' the ' salt of the earth,' the peculiarly ' chosen people,' as most Scots, even unconsciously to themselves, very often complacently assume. Thus it is that we have the picture of Scottish character

occasionally painted on the reverse side, and this feeling
of restiveness is really the source and the reason of the
many stories that possibly less-privileged peoples love to
tell at the expense of Scottish faults and foibles, if such
can be said really to exist.   I speak now, of course, as a
Scot.

I must say, however, in justice to my countrymen, that
very few indeed of them ever take these seriously.   They
are so assured, so convinced of their own superiority,
that these 'weak inventions of the enemy' only provoke
a smile, and in the more genial natures evoke hearty
laughter.   Some have even been known to turn the
tables on the adversary by giving some clever, unexpected
twist to the apologue or parable that was supposed to be
turned against themselves; and I could give some note-
worthy instances of this experience where 'the biter has
been bit.'   But it would be unfair in me, a thorough
Scotsman, albeit one of the humble and retiring order,
to unduly boast over our exceptional advantages, and so
out of the kindliest consideration for those of my readers
who may not be of 'the chosen people,' I will mercifully
desist.   I think it only fair, however, to give one or two
examples of the sort of sorry stuff that is sometimes
vainly supposed to tell against the superlative and
transcendent merits of the true Scot.

But to be serious.   That the onlooker sees most of
the game is no doubt a true saying, seeing that he is in
a position to take a less prejudiced and broader view of
the varying 'chances and changes' which to a participant
in the fight may often be seen only from a partial or
purely personal standpoint.   So it is that outside criticism is generally so valuable, and though Scottish self-

complacency is, as a rule, serenely indifferent to censure, it is always interesting to hear ourselves described

As ithers see us.

Indeed, we quite welcome the criticism; whether we profit by it or no is quite another matter.

For that reason the American's estimate of our national character is worthy of record. A discussion had arisen as to the relative vices and virtues of the partners in the great British firm, and while some were vaunting certain salient features of Irish nationality, and others belauding the essentials of English character, a tall American chimed in with his epitomised sort of summary of the whole. And thus he delivered himself :—

'Wal I guess it's some'ut like this. S'posin' there wus three trav'lers in a railway kerridge—an Englishman, an Irishman, an' a Scotsman; an' s'posin' the train come to its destination, how wud them three act?'

He paused for a reply, and none being forthcoming, he proceeded :—

'Wal I'll tell you. The Irishman, I guess, 'ud jist step right out an' go slick on his way, mebbe whistlin', but at any rate pretty spry, and not carin' a darn about anythin' or anybody. Wal, now, the Englishman 'ud be more deliberate. He'd be perfectly calm and cool and methodical. He would arrange his wraps an' pick up his bag, and he would start off in a ruther consequential and very self-possessed manner. Arter that, last of all, the Scotsman, more deliberate still, would stretch hisself, and pick up his wraps and bag; but before leavin' the kerridge he'd look round to SEE IF THE OTHERS HAD LEFT ANYTHIN'—YOU BET!'

Let us take another. One of the many waggish stories which are told at the expense of 'oor ain fowk' by outsiders who cannot understand our deep love of a country which to them seems so bare and uninviting, is the following. I naturally tell it with a Scottish bias, and must disclaim all responsibility for its seeming irreverence.

A poor Scot having died, so the tale goes, his soul at once, following the usual course, as I assume, though the original says differently, winged its flight *upwards* till it arrived at the portals where Peter keeps the keys. After knocking, the reverend janitor came to the wicket, and demanded the name of the soul that knocked so loudly. 'Sandie Macphairson,' was the reply. Peter with some irritation bade Sandie begone, saying 'the place was jist pairfeckly fu' o' Macs already, and Sandie maun seek ither quarters.' The observant reader will see that Peter spoke with a decided Scottish accent, which, one may take it, is reasonable presumption of the antiquity and respectability of the auld Scots tongue. Hearing this reply, down sank the soul of Sandie till it 'fetched up' bump on the roof of his Satanic Majesty's dominions, and here the summons was sharp and imperious. Satan happened to be in a particularly bad temper, and with some asperity demanded who knocked so loud. 'Sandie Macphairson,' was again the response; whereupon Auld Clootie with many an oath bade the wandering soul begone, saying that he would harbour no Scotsman in his dominions, for the only one that had ever gained an entry had by his superior ability and cleverness nearly got up a successful revolution, intending to depose Satan, and take the rule of the kingdom into his own hands. 'So,' said Satan, 'I'll have no Scotsmen here; they know too much. Ye must try elsewhere.' You will observe this was said with a perfectly pure English accent.

The poor bewildered soul of Sandie, finding no resting-ing-place, began to shudder with a sense of baffled hopes, and at length said to itself: 'Eh, but this is awfu'. I suppose I'll hae to try the half-way hoose.' And so again directing its flight upwards, it tried for admittance at the gates of Purgatory. But here, too, it met with no better success. It was denounced as a schismatic, and possessed of too much independence; and so at length the naked soul was left in blank isolation, confronting the blackness of the universal void. An agony of despair swept the shuddering nonentity of the thrice-rejected wraith, and recognising the utter horror of the awful and only alternative that remained, he whispered in hoarse accents of icy despair: 'Gude Heevens! is it possible? I'll hae to gang back to Glesca.'

An evident paraphrase of the foregoing, is the version which is current in the back-blocks of Australia. The leading idea is of course the same, but the treatment is localised, somewhat thus. The Scottish wayfarer, or superintendent of the station, or shepherd or swagsman, as the case may be, when he presents himself in the morning at breakfast, is at once commiserated on his wan and dejected appearance. He is asked if he is ill? if a snake has bit him? if his whisky flask has run out? and so on. He responds with faltering accents, betokening much distress and mental disturbance, that the cause of his woe-begone aspect is 'a vera bad dream' he has had. He relates that the dream was so vivid and realistic that it has made a deep impression on him which he cannot shake off, and so on ; whereupon, according to the inventive genius of the narrator, come all sorts of humorous local allusions.

'Dear, dear!' says one, 'what was it ?   Did ye dream all the sheep were dead ? '

The Scotsman is supposed to shake his head and say : 'Waur than that.'

'Bless us ! Did ye dream there was another drought?'

'Waur than that.'

'What ! not bush fires ?'

'Waur than that.'

'Not that you were bushed ? no water ? horse dead ? tucker-bag empty, and no help within fifty miles ?'

'Waur than that.'

'What then, in Hivven's name, did ye dream ?'

'Eh, mon, I dreamed I was back again in Scotland.'

And that is where the laugh is supposed to come in ; but it is all envy—pure envy, and nothing else.

CHAPTER XV

The introduction of steam to an indigo factory—The first sight of a locomotive—Instances—The old sheep-farmer's experience—The porter's correction—Legs *versus* locomotive—Circumventing the ticket-collector—A pawky stationmaster—'Ower big for his place.'

OF all the agencies that have been at work in this busy and wonderful century to break down old traditions, peculiar customs, and quaint institutions, none perhaps have been so potent and subversive as the varied applications of the powers of steam and electricity to human use ; and of these the now common and everyday-used railway and telegraph have been the most productive of change. We are so accustomed now to the universal presence of these accessories to our daily life that it is difficult for us to imagine a state of society in which they were non-existent. And yet if we go back for but a brief half-century, we are landed in the primitive period, as it now appears to us, of the days of stage-coaches and emigrant sailing-ships. We can scarcely realise now what it must have been to our immediate ancestors to have had no railways or telegrams, no daily

S

newspaper, no well-organised postal service and quick
interchange of intelligence with the ends of the earth.
Only fancy having to go back to the days of tallow-
candles and oil lights, when there were not even lucifer
matches or wax vestas! How little we think of what a
volume of change in daily comfort and the easedom of
modern conditions is implied in the existence of such a
firm as, say, 'Bryant and May,' for instance. What
would we do now if we had to revert to the use of the
old goose quill instead of the steel pen, the dirk or
dagger in lieu of the knife and fork, or the cumbrous
flint and steel instead of the humble but handy pocket
match-box? And yet the century has seen these and
a thousand equally significant changes, which have
affected and modified mental and even moral conditions,
quite as much as they have merely physical.

This, however, is so self-evident on the slightest
reflection, that it is unnecessary to insist much upon it;
but having picked up several anecdotes bearing on the
introduction of railways into Scotland, and as these to
some extent exemplify the manners and customs and
attitude of mind of many of the rustic folk of whom we
have been speaking, they have a certain interest, and
may not inappropriately find a niche in these random
jottings.

I have seen the introduction of a steam-engine for the
first time, into the then secluded indigo-planting district
of Chumparun, one of the beautiful corners of the great,
fertile, populous province of Behar, in India. I shall
never forget the afternoon when, everything being completed, the machinery all accurately fitted and in perfect
order, our old manager, 'Hoolman Sahib' as the natives

called him, got up steam to test the engine. From far and near the villagers in thousands, had come to see the start of this wonderful, mysterious (*kull*) engine, of which they had heard such varied and marvellous reports. It was said 'to feed on fire, to vomit smoke and steam (*bhāf*), to do the work of a thousand coolies, and to scream louder than a whole line of elephants,' and so on. Well, the eventful day had at last arrived. Round about the indigo vats of Seeraha, the head factory, there must have been at least some ten or twelve thousand natives of every age and sex and condition of life assembled. The polished piston rods and glittering brasses of the engine shone spick-and-span in their glossy masonry and plaster-setting of *pucca* work. The furnace, fed with dried stalks of the refuse indigo, roared and gleamed fitfully as the doors were thrown open with a resounding clang from time to time, while the attendant sprites fed the fiery monster with fresh fuel. The bellowing volumes of smoke came rolling heavily from the tall chimney-stalk, and the vast assemblage of untutored natives looked on with gathering wonder and open-mouthed astonishment and awe. The hissing steam began to come in angry, short, puffing jets from here and there a loose joint, and from the rim of the safety-valve ; and at length, as the crucial moment arrived, and the gauge showed the requisite pressure, Butler, our engineer, helped by some of the European assistants standing by, put their shoulders to the metal, and the massive fly-wheel began to revolve, the wonder and the amaze reached their culmination. Just then, whether unintentionally or in mischievous design, 'Hoolman Sahib' turned on the escape-valve, and the shrill steam-whistle for the first time woke the echoes of the startled Chumparun air. We Europeans shouted a lusty shout of triumphant congratulation, but the effect on the unsophisticated natives was simply indescribable. With one ear-piercing shriek or yell of dismay, the pent-up breath of the congregated thousands seemed to find a simultaneous vent. And then commenced a wild, tumultuous, mad rush of frenzied fear and unreasoning dread. Women and children were upset and trampled on; barriers and hedges were broken and trampled flat; the poppy crop, most precious and sacred of growing stuffs, was flattened to the ground; men threw their garments from them, and flew as if the destroying furies were at their heels; and but for a few of the regular old servants of the factory, and ourselves, in a few moments the precincts of the place were utterly deserted by the panic-stricken crowd.

Now I do not mean to say that our Scottish rustics were as unsophisticated and simple as these poor Behar peasants, and yet it must have raised strange thoughts and surmises in the breasts of simple ploughmen and shepherds in these northern straths and glens, when the snorting locomotive for the first time tore past their doors, and obtruded itself on their hitherto restricted and uneventful experience.

I have given already the true experience of my cousin's servant Robbie, who, seeing the train for the first time, wished to 'traivel ootside, so as to see the kintra.'

Another old fellow, when he saw the first locomotive and rattling retinue of carriages go tearing past, until it entered a tunnel on ahead, was almost petrified with fear ; and describing the phenomenon afterwards in the smiddy, he said that 'a great muckle beast wi' reid een (red eyes) an' a bleezin', reekin' horn, cam' roarin' up the strath, but when it saw me,' he said, 'it gied a terrible scraich, an' ran intill a hole i' the hillside.'

This may possibly be apocryphal, but I have often heard my father tell the following as a veritable fact, although I rather fancy I have already told the story in another book :—

One old woman near Brig o' Dun, when the first passenger train went tearing through to Brechin, seeing the sparks flying from the engine, and the long row of carriages with their windows and doors, through which the lamp lights were gleaming, called out to her gudeman : 'Losh, An'ra, look here ! Michty me !' but here's a smith's shop run awa' wi' a raing (range) o' cottar hooses.'

Another good railway story is that of the old fellow from the Mearns who had gone to Lanark market with a flock of sheep for sale. Having disposed of his charge to good advantage, he was strongly urged by his son, who had accompanied him, to take the train back, as it would save them two or three days' tedious journey. The old man had never mustered up courage or resolution enough, to adventure on 'thae michty mischancie inventions o' the deevil,' as he called the railway trains. He looked on them as utterly subversive of the good old order, and imagined that perpetual accidents were certain to occur if he were rash enough to trust his precious carcase on board one of them. However, the younger man persisted, and as a youthful daughter was about to be married, and they desired to be home as

early as possible on that account, and also as there were
evidences of an approaching heavy snowstorm in the air,
the old man at length yielded to the importunities of his
son, and with much misgiving and many fears on his part,
they got safely seated in one of the old-fashioned third-
class carriages, which, as some of my older readers may
remember, were quite open at the sides, and about as
comfortable as modern cattle-trucks. However, away
sped the train.   The snowdrift came on thick and
furious ; the shivering passengers wrapped themselves in
their kindly, sheltering plaids ; and occasionally a faint,
ambrosial perfume of whisky would hover for a moment
round the carriages.   Thicker and thicker fell the snow.
The wind had risen, and in every cutting through which
the snorting engine plunged, lay great piled-up wreaths,
through which it became ever more and more difficult
for the train to push its way.   At length, just as the
train had reached the neighbourhood of the old man's
farm, it plunged into an obstinate, unyielding drift,
and with a scream and a sudden jolt it came to an
abrupt stop.   The shock threw the old man and his son
clean through the open side of the carriage, and pro-
pelled them with considerable velocity right into the
piled-up bank of virgin snow.   The old man went
'kerslap' right in up to his waist, and though his plaid
protected him, and the snow was soft, yet his nostrils
and ears were corked tightly up with the snow, and for
a moment or two he imagined that all his forebodings
had been realised, and that he was a dead man.   However his son, who had also escaped unhurt, after a few
vigorous tugs at the old man's projecting legs, managed
to extricate his imprisoned parent, who, after clearing

his plugged ears and nostrils, and shaking himself like a water-dog, began to plod his way through the snow over the fields towards his dwelling, which was indeed not far distant. Of course he was welcomed with every indication of joy, and when he had got time to settle down, began to be plied with eager questions. The young bride-elect got on her father's knee, and after sundry caresses, began to vaunt the conveniences of railway travel. She pointed out the time it saved, and so on, and then asked her father if he did not now agree with her. 'Come now,' she said, 'is it not a great saving of time, father? Is it not quite safe and convenient, to say nothing of it being cheap?' The old man, with a vivid recollection yet fresh in his memory of his involuntary plunge into the snowdrift, very cautiously replied: 'Weel, Jeannie, I'll no deny that it is somewhat expedeetious; but, losh bless me, lassie, it's a michty oncannie w'y they hae o' lattin' ye oot.'

Quite as whimsical in its way is the absurd mistake of the unsophisticated railway porter, of which you may have heard. The train to the north had come to a standstill for some minutes at a wayside station, and a commercial traveller, whose limbs had become numbed with cold and his long journey, took advantage of the short opportunity, and bounding out on to the platform, began to pace briskly up and down to try and restore warmth to his half-frozen extremities. Passing a stolid-looking porter in his walk, he crisply remarked: 'Ah, this is invigorating.' You may imagine his amused surprise, when the old fellow hobbled after him and exclaimed: 'Na, na, sir; this is Invergordon.'

That reminds me of another railway-station story, which forcibly illustrates the dour doggedness and never-say-die tenacity of purpose, which is very characteristic of certain sorts of 'oor ain fowk.'

It was a piping hot day. The ripened barley 'hung its head,' drooping under the sultry, direct rays of the burning autumn sun. The whins bordering the road were brown with dust, and not a breath of air was to be found to stir the motionless leaves on the russet birken-shaws. A florid, perspiring farm-servant came plunging along the road leading to the station, hurrying as fast as he could to catch the afternoon train for Aberdeen, which if he missed, he would have to wait for nearly a whole day before he could get another. He had taken off his coat, and it hung on his hazel staff over his shoulder; his calfskin waistcoat was unbuttoned, and he carried his hat swinging in his hand. He was hot, dusty, tired, and ill-tempered. He knew he had barely enough time, but he hoped just to catch the train. Just as he came in view of the station, the long train hove in sight, the burnished engine slowed down, and the pedestrian redoubled his efforts and made a frantic rush, with his clothes flapping about like the duds on a tautie-dooly. Will he reach it in time? Will the dashed thing wait? Will the stationmaster not see him? The bell clangs loudly; the stoor flies from his plunging tread. He tries to shout, but his throat is dry with dust and drouth, and he can only make a choking, smothered yell. Alas! alas! just as he reaches the wicket-gate, the engine, as if in derision, gives a snort, and a hoarse, whistling shriek, and the train with an elusive speed glides quickly out of reach. Choking with rage at what he chose to fancy was a deliberate mockery, he shook his fist at the retreating train, and apostrophising the engine, shouted, as his Scottish dour determination asserted itself : 'Oh ! blaw, ye black deevil ! I can walk !'

Then there is that most pawky instance, also in connection with railway travel, which, I think, first saw the light in the inimitable picture-gallery of *Punch*, but which I cannot refrain from reproducing. *Scene* — Railway carriage. Ticket-collector: 'Tickets, please.' All show their pasteboard except one stolid, stupid-looking being, muffled in a plaid, and with his broad bonnet well drawn over his ears. He fumbles in all his pockets ; mutters, 'I'm sure I had it jist the noo'; and then asks the impatient official to go on, and by the time he came back he would no doubt have found the missing ticket. The collector bangs the door before any one can speak, and as he whisks angrily away, the gentleman sitting opposite our plaided drover says, with a good-humoured sort of surprised air : 'Why, sir, you have your ticket in your mouth. I saw you put it there when the train pulled up.' With a wink of fearfully portentous meaning the weather-beaten old sinner answers : 'Wheesht, man, I wis jist sookin' aff the date.' This experience, of course, relates to a much later and more sophisticated period than that of which I have been treating.

The next too, is modern, but is a capital instance of dry, pawky, ironic humour.

During a strike a few years ago (there were fewer strikes in the old days) among the officials of the North British Railway, much difficulty was experienced in finding well-qualified engine-drivers to maintain the necessary

train-service. Upon one occasion a young fellow happened
to be put upon a section of the line in Fife. One day
he ran some distance past a certain station, and upon
reversing the engine to put back, he went just as far the
other way. The stationmaster seeing him preparing
for another attempt, to the great amusement of the
passengers on the platform, shouted : 'Jist bide whaur
ye are, Tammas; we'll shift the station.'

And here is yet another instance of the same kind of
caustic, hard-hitting humour.

An auld wifie from St. Cyrus, a bright little fishing-
village on the Mearns coast, found herself not very long
ago for the first time at a railway station. Naturally,
her wonder and her insatiable curiosity were excited
by the unwonted surroundings. Being what is called
in that locality 'a cracky bodie,' she began to ply
the ticket-clerk at the office window with all sorts of
quaint and eager queries. He being a bumptious,
supercilious, young fellow, answered her rather
brusquely, and snappishly told her to 'Ask the porter.'
The harmless but inquisitive old bodie in reply to several
quite innocent questions, very natural in one undergoing
such a novel experience, received the same reply in an
even more impertinent and ill-natured manner, and her
dogged Scottish pugnacity began to be aroused. She
came of a class not easily daunted, and with the spirit
of 'The Mearns' firing her honest self-respect, she was
evidently not inclined to accept a snub from any one,
least of all from one whom she rightly judged was put
there, and paid to be civil, and to afford every reasonable information to the customers of the Company. A
considerable crowd, much amused at the old wifie's

manner and questions, had in the meantime gathered around, and the old woman, now fairly on her mettle, said to the uppish, supercilious official :—

'Ay, ma man, div ye ken fa ye mind me o'?'

'No, I do not,' snapped the bilious clerk.

'Weel, than, ye jist mind me o' the mannie that cam' tae sweip ma grannie's lum, an' stack i' the middle o't. HE WIS OWER BIG FOR THE PLACE HE WIS IN.' Amid roars of laughter from the crowd, the discomfited clerk banged down the window, as the train swept in, leaving the old wifie fairly victor in the encounter of wits.

CHAPTER XVI

Modern methods in treatment of the insane—Danger of overdoing
even philanthropy—The old-time village life—'Finla' of the
Gun'—Too literal an answer to prayer—'Jock Brodie'—
'Singin' Willie'—'Jock Heral''—'Gude, gude wirds'—Stories
of 'The Laird'—'Johnnie Maisterton'—A queer old parish
minister and some stories about him—A cautious Scot—A
tight place for Abraham—Rustic simplicity.

ONE other feature of the old village life which seems
almost entirely to have passed away, is the constant
recurrence in all the small rural communities of what
were known as 'Naiterals': poor, half-witted unfortunates, harmless enough for the most part, often keen-
witted enough in some respects, but in some one
particular, incurably silly and deficient. As a rule they
were treated with the utmost kindness and allowed
every latitude; and it said much for the kindly, humane
spirit of the old Scottish folks in regard to this saddest
of all afflictions—mental weakness—that this was the
prevalent feeling towards these poor beclouded ones.

So far as regards the treatment of the hopelessly
insane and imbecile, our modern systems are no doubt

like perfect Paradise, compared with the very Gehenna
of barbarity and rigorous repression which characterised
the asylums of the past cruel *régime;* but it is at least
open to question whether in our more enlightened and
better organised, and certainly much more expensive
and luxurious philanthropy, we may not be just
overdoing things to some extent. I suppose it is scien-
tifically possible to have too much even of a good thing.
And it sometimes seems to me that in some things, in
education for instance, in the treatment of disease, in
the management of the insane, in the regulation of
criminals, and in other branches of sociology, we may
not be in danger of making the system too complex and
too expensive, so that the machinery may be in danger
of breaking down altogether some day, by reason of its
very complexity and enormous cost. Signs, indeed, are
not wanting that the corporate common-sense of the
people is at last beginning to kick against the faddists
and extremists among our so-called experts, whose
expertness in piling up expenditure is very often in
converse ratio to the practical results achieved in dimin-
ishing the evils they attack.

The excision of useless accomplishments and mere
ornamental frippery from the curriculum of common
schools in some of the Colonies, and the substitution of
plain, sound instruction in the primary principles of
technical education is an evidence of this. The breaking
up of the barrack system in the training of waifs, or so-
called State children, and placing them out in the homes
of kind people, is another blessed evidence of a return to
saner and, I am sure, more successful, ay! and cheaper
methods; and I do not see why in these days of over-

taxation and grandmotherly government, the vital question of economy should not be more studied than it is. Certain politicians seem to think that the chief end and aim of legislation is to raise taxes and spend money lavishly. The highest statesmanship, surely, is that which follows the lines of best domestic and commercial management, namely, to secure the widest freedom at the least expense, and with the largest result in happiness, liberty, and progress.

In this light one might well ask why criminals, for instance, should not be employed, where practicable, on necessary public works, and be forced to earn their own keep; but the bare mention of such an apparently sensible proposal, is enough to send certain self-dubbed 'working-men representatives,' and demagogues of the rabid Protectionist order, such as we have in some of our colonies, into such a condition of froth and fury as might well cause apprehension on the part of onlookers, as to whether these apostles of modern blatherskite can bite as well as bark, in which case they might of course be dangerous.

The very mention of this genus brings me *naturally* and easily to the subject of this chapter, 'Naiterals,' or the poor, half-witted characters that were formerly a constant feature in our village communities. Even in the treatment of these poor unfortunates, we are in some measure revolting against this excessive centralisation which characterises the insane - asylum movement of modern times; and many of the very highest and best minds both among experts and laymen are, I understand, beginning to question whether it is the best and most humane thing after all, to immure such unfortunates as are not of the violent type of insane

patients, and whether it would not be better to revert
to the old-fashioned system, in which the burden of
maintenance of such afflicted ones rightly devolved
on the kinsmen themselves, and not on the general
community. In this as in other respects our so-called
Christian Socialism has simply been Communism run mad.
The true Christian Socialism, I take it, is that which,
while giving its proper value to the injunction to ' bear
one another's burdens,' never forgets that it is still more
strongly insisted on, that ' each shall bear his own
burden.' Philanthropy by proxy is just as barren and
unfruitful, unless in evil results, as religion by proxy.
The very kernel of the sturdy, robust, old-time Scottish
Protestantism was the invaluable recognition of this one
vital fact : that a man must stand or fall by his own
conscience, and he could not hand over the keeping of
his conscience, or the performance of his duty, or the
observance of his religion, to any vicarious agency
whatsoever, be he priest or presbyter, county council-
man or government inspector.

Many of these old-time village ' naiterals ' were quite
competent to perform many little domestic tasks ; some
could even assist in field work ; and, as a rule, all could
do a little to assist their relations in the duty of their
own maintenance. It seems, then, a pity that such harmless unfortunates should be dragged away from their own
kinsfolk, and saddled as a permanent burden on the State.
That is what is very largely done in the Colonies at all
events; and the records of our State Charity Departments
there show in too many cases, a callous disregard of some
of the most sacred obligations of kinship on the part of
wealthy and well-to-do citizens, who unblushingly allow

even such near relations as parents, to be quartered in
State asylums and benevolent institutions, and never
contribute, except under strong compulsion, one fraction
towards the cost of their keep.

But to our examples. I promise they shall be but
few. Many tales are told of a famous 'pairish eediot'
of Ross-shire who, from his constant habit of carrying a
battered old fowling-piece, tied and spliced with wire and
twine and leather thongs, and who fancied himself no
mean sportsman, was known far and near as 'Finla' o'
the Gun.' He was a strange, forbidding sort of being,
and one of his most pronounced crazes was a mania for
collecting all sorts of unsavoury objects, such as dead
crows, and other carrion. These he was wont to show
as trophies of his gun, witnesses to his ability as a
marksman. He chiefly lived by collecting, for sale to
marine dealers, bones, rags, tufts of wool, scrap-iron, and
such-like 'unconsidered trifles,' and his miscellaneous 'pock
full,' as may well be imagined, had not just the fragrance
of violets. One day some one had told 'Finla' o' the
Gun' of a dead horse among the heather, and away the
poor creature trudged to secure a ghastly treasure-trove
of bones. He got up to the carcase, over whose grisly
remains a mob of hungry dogs were growling and
quarrelling. 'Finla'' drove them off, and began to hack
the bones asunder and transfer them to his pack. The
dogs assumed a menacing attitude, but 'Finla'' addressed
them in tones of indignant protest, asking them to 'agree
thegither, as there was eneuch an' to spare for them a'.'

It was his custom to demand a lodgment wherever
he might chance to be at nightfall, but most of all he
affected the hospitality of the various manses in the

shire. No one ever thought of refusing him shelter, having pity for his infirmity, but he was not certainly a desirable guest at any time. Shortly after the Disruption, he happened to arrive for the night at the manse of, let us say, Birkhill. The old minister had vacated his charge, being one of the gallant band of Disruption heroes, and a new incumbent all the way from America, had taken up the duties of parish minister, in a newly raised *quoad sacra* church. The former minister, Mr. Fraser, had been a kindly, homely man, much beloved by his people, and he had always given a pleasant word to poor, simple-witted 'Finla' o' the Gun.' The poor, doited creature had come in, as was his wont, unbidden to the manse, and had dumped down his unsavoury pack of bones and rags, which very soon attested its presence by the aroma which it diffused around. Out came the new minister fuming and puffing, and angrily addressing the poor daft creature ordered him to 'take up his stinking bones and begone out of that.' Old 'Finla'' moved never a muscle, but said very quietly : 'Ay, man, but I thocht ye maun hae a gude smell, when ye smelt the stipend o' Birkhill a' the way frae America.'

To my friend, the Rev. James H——, of whose racy store I have already given some specimens, I am indebted for the following.

'Did you ever hear' he writes, 'of the parish idiot who was in the habit frequently of retiring to pray behind a worn, old sod-dyke? One day when engaged in his usual devotional exercise, uttering the words : "that if this sod wa' wis tae fa' doon upon him, it wad be nae mair than he deserved for his wicked deeds," some village wag of a fellow who had crept up to hear puir,

T

daft Jock at his prayers, pushed over a portion of the dyke on the top of the silly loon, whereupon the startled idiot exclaimed : "Save's a', sirss, it's an awfu' warl' we live in ! A bodie canna say a thing in fun like, but it's ta'en in earnest." '

Jock Brodie was another of these quaint characters, well known in Dumfries. One night he was caught red-handed in the act of stealing the minister's hens. The minister said to him : ' John, I did not expect to find YOU here, John !' Jock replied : ' Dod, I didna expec' tae see you here aither, sir.'

I remember, as a boy, another of these harmless imbeciles called 'Singin' Willie.' He used to frequent the fairs in Angus and the Mearns, and his craze took the form of decorating his clothes, and a stick he carried, with all sorts of shining buttons he could collect, and with scraps of gaudy ribbons. He tootled on his stick believing it to be a musical instrument, and croodled a peculiar sing-song chant all the while. He was apt to get angry if laughed at, or if any one sought to dispute his harmless idea that the stick was a band instrument. Otherwise he was perfectly harmless, and not a little picturesque indeed.

A certain John Herald, or, as he was locally called, 'Jock Heral',' was another of these queer characters whom I remember in my youthful days. His special haunt was the side of the road leading to the famous Brechin picnic resort, the old Druidical circle on the summit of Caterthun—a beautiful rounded hill, crowned now with a belt of young fir-trees, but in the dim ages long ago, with a weird circle of Druid stones ; and which forms one of the first tier of swelling hills which are the

outliers of the mighty Grampians where they post their
sentinels on the verge of fertile Strathmore. Jock was
always seemingly in a hurry; that is, if he thought he
was the object of your observation he would affect to be
very busy. His favourite expression then used to be as
he met you or overtook you: 'Aweel, aweel, here I am,
puir Jock Heral', jist takkin' lang staps tae save ma
shune' (shoes). His next advance would be, in seeming
hearty fashion, to proffer you the refreshment of a
sneeshin' from his snuff-mull. It must be understood
that you were really all the time the object of a series of
calculated crafty advances, guised under an aspect of the
utmost simplicity and purely fortuitous haphazard. It
was expected of you that in return for the sneeshin', you
were to leave a gratuity in the snuff-box. Jock would
not openly ask for it; 'work he could not, and to beg he
was ashamed'; but his comments on the visitors according
to their liberality were ofttimes amusing enough. Thus
if one accepted the sneeshin' but put nothing into the
box, he would say with a snort of contempt: 'Humph!
some naisty, weary wratches gaed up the hill the day;
they took a sneeshin' oot'n ma mull, bit pit naethin' in.
Na, 'deed no. Fa wir they, ken ye?' Suppose you put
in a threepenny bit, he would say: 'A gey gude sort o'
man yon 'at gaed by the day, na; div ye ken far he comes
fae?' He was always anxious to know all about the
visitors, where they came from and so on. But suppose
you gave the munificent sum of a sixpence, or the regal
largess of a shilling, then poor Jock would wax quite
eloquent in your praises, thus: 'Ay, ay, na; thon
wis twa fine, bonnie, wyselike gentlemen gaed up the
hill the day. Ah'm thinkin' they wad be fae the

nobeelity, na. Eh na, fa wir they, div ye ken?' and so on.

One of this poor afflicted fraternity at Kelso, on one occasion confided to a kindly sympathiser that 'his mither had said gude, gude wirds till him afore she de'ed.' 'Ay, Jock, an' what did yer mither say tae ye?' asked the kindly tolerant friend. 'Ah, she said gude, gude wirds.' 'Weel, what wir they?' 'Oh, she said, jist afore she de'ed : "Weel, God help ye, Jock, for yir a puir silly eediet."'

It seems to me there is a world of pathos in this simply silly reminiscence of poor daft Jock. God help the poor things! What an awful responsibility rests on those who have the care of such helpless and afflicted brothers; and what an awful reckoning will be demanded from those who have proved recreant to their trust!

Another quaint character I remember, who was a famous fisherman up the Glen, and taught me first how to cast a fly. He was of good family, and though he could not be classed with the naiterals, yet was he fatally weak in the matter of self-control where drink was in question. He was always called 'The Laird.' There was another oddity whom we called 'Daddy.' Daddy in his cups was a perfect fiend, and exhibited the ugliest traits. 'The Laird,' on the other hand, even if overtaken in liquor, seemed never to forget that he was a gentleman, and was always gentle and good-tempered. He spoke with a peculiar burr, and was an inveterate snuff-taker. On one occasion he told my father, who had been reasoning and expostulating with him after a recent outburst : 'Weel, Maister Robert, I was never sae drunk yet, but aye when I passed the schulic I gaed tae the back o' the hoose tae pray for the bits o' bairns.'

In one of his fits of depression he determined to drown himself in the burn. He confided this fell resolve to another half-doited, feckless creature who was with him, but with ludicrous *sang froid* he diverted 'The Laird' from his dread resolve by saying : 'Hoots, Laird, it'll be better tae wait till a warmer nicht.'

On one occasion he had fallen and hurt his leg, and my uncle poured out some spirits in a cup as an embrocation for the bruised knee, but ere he could interpose, 'The Laird' had gulped the intended liniment down, with the pithy remark : 'Hech, we'll jist lat it sipe doon tae the sair.'

When his mother died he was much affected. My grandmother sympathised most affectionately with him, and at the sight of his artless and sincere grief could not restrain her own tears. 'The Laird' suddenly looked up and with innocent surprise said : 'Hech, ye needna greet; she wis nae freens tae you'— signifying that tears were only permissible for a blood relation.

My dear old aunt tells me of one such character as we have been considering, who, though not a 'naiteral,' was looked on in Montrose as being 'some saft.' He went by the name of Johnnie Maisterton. A most amusing conversation is recorded as having passed between Johnnie and the reverend old incumbent of the Montrose High Church, Dr. Patterson. Johnnie's errand to the manse seems to have been to engage the services of the reverend doctor to marry him. Having asked for the doctor, and being ushered into the study, he awkwardly fumbled about and rather shamefacedly said :—

'A fine day, Maister Paitterson.'

'Yes, it's a fine day, John.'

Then there was an awkward pause, and again John rallied, and repeated his phrase—

'It's a fine day, Maister Paitterson.'

'Yes, John, but you wanted to see me.'

'Ay,' boggled John, 'but it's a fine day, Maister Paitterson.'

'Oh yes, there's no doubt of that,' a little impatiently assented the minister. 'But what is it you really want, John? You surely did not take all this trouble to come and tell me it's a fine day?'

John thus fairly cornered, at last blurted out :—

'Weel, ah'm sair needin' tae be mairriet, Maister Paitterson.'

'Oh, I see! Well, John, what's the woman's name?'

At this John bridled up and said: 'Dod, Maister Paitterson, ye wad like tae ken a'thing.'

'Ah but, John, I must know that. Ye ken I canna marry ye unless I know.'

'Dod than, sir, an' ye wull hae'd, an' gin ye maun hae'd, it's jist Della Carr, sir.'

'Well, John, when will I come?'

'Oh, ony time ye like, Maister Paitterson,' said John, with a breezy indifference to precise punctuality.

'Ah, but you must tell me the hour now, John.'

John at once pulled out his silver turnip, and consulting the dial said: 'Od, it's jist close upon twal, sir.'

'No, no, John. I mean you must fix the hour when I am to come to marry you.'

So at last the date and hour were arranged, and John

was preparing to take his leave, when he asked : ' But div ye ken far ye're tae come till, Maister Paitterson ? '

' No, John, indeed I do not,' said the minister.

' Aweel, ye hiv tae come doon to (naming a close), then ye ging farrer doon till ye come till an ootside stane-stair wi' twal staps. Ye ging up that, an' syne turn tae yer thoom haund.'

Then, apparently quite forgetful of the minister's sacred calling, he said rather wheedlingly :—

' Noo, Maister Paitterson, ye'll come awa' up wi' me tae Rob Process's an' get share o' a mutchkin.'

' Oh, no, John,' said the horrified doctor, 'I never drink out of my own house.'

' Dod, Maister Paitterson,' said John, very coaxingly, ' ye micht come ; my brither Davie's there, an' he's a fine boxer.'

But not even this added inducement could overcome the worthy doctor's scruples, and poor, soft, blundering, queer-grained John had to depart alone.

From the same charming, old-time, gossipy source, I gathered some items about a very eccentric parish minister near Montrose, who lived away back in the earlier part of the century, and whose oddity was so pronounced, as to make him a fit subject for inclusion in the present chapter. He had an extraordinary dread of wild animals, and one of the invariable petitions in his litany was, that they 'micht be presairved frae whurlwin's, whurl-pools, airthquakks, an' the devoorin' jaws o' wild beests.' Meeting the celebrated Indian missionary Dr. Duff one day at a Presbytery dinner, he asked during a pause in the conversation : ' Did ye ever see ony leeyons (lions), doctor ? ' And this being replied to satisfactorily, he later on took advantage of another pause to again ask, much to the amusement of his clerical brethren : 'Did ye see ony tcegurs, doctor ?'

At the Disruption time he was one of those who were 'almost persuaded' to give up everything 'for conscience' sake,' and come boldly out, 'not knowing whither he went,' from the same lofty motive ; but at the last moment his heart failed him. He had a nice manse and good garden, and in this, it would seem, he had planted a crop of potatoes which were giving promise of an abundant return. So the poor man ultimately withdrew from his protesting brethren, with the plaintive plea that ' he couldna leave his tawties.'

Dear old Mr. Munro of Menmuir, one of my father's stanchest friends, who is still the honoured and useful minister of an attached congregation, among whom he has ministered faithfully and fruitfully for more than half a century, told me, when I called at his cosy little manse the other day, an incident relative to this same eccentric bodie of whom I am speaking. 'It illustrates,'said Mr. Munro, 'the extraordinary narrow limited ideas of the old "Moderate" era.' The rustic parson I have been describing had been chosen to preach to Mr. Nixon's wealthy Montrose congregation in aid of some particular cause, for which special appeals were being made in all the churches. Our poor, simple, 'bit mannie' wound up 'a gey dreich sermon' by saying : ' Now I do hope that a special effort will be made on this occāāshun, and those of you who are wealthy, instead of giein' a ha'penny, can shurely gie a penny the day.'

But there is no end to the stories about Montrose odd characters. One good example of caution is that told of a man in the gallery of the Court, who, when the officer called out the name of a witness who was wanted, shouted out, ' He's gane.' ' Gone ?' said the presiding magistrate ; ' where has he gone to ? It is his duty to be here.' To which came the delightfully Scottish reply : ' Weel, yer Honner, I'll no commit masel' sae far as tae say whaur he's gane ; but he's deid, sir.'

It was of an old wifie, near Montrose, that the following is narrated. She had been hearing her grandchild read her Bible lesson, and the little one had pronounced the word age, hard *g* without the terminal *e*. Thus : ' And Awbraham died in a good old egg.' ' Na, na,' said the old dame, ' ye're surely wrang,. 'umman.' Then getting on her specs, she read the passage and said : ' Hech, lassie, but ye're richt ; but, losh bless me, he maun hae been sair crammed.'

From the same quarter we are told of the rustic damsel who had been to a concert, the success of which was the talk of the village next day. One of the girls who had not been present said to the one who had : ' Did ony o' the singers get an ingcore ?' The other replied smartly : ' Hoo div I ken fat they got ? They wir a' ta'en intill a roomie by theirsel's.'

CHAPTER XVII

STORIES OF HIGHLANDERS

The Celtic temperament—Difficulties of the English tongue to the
Gael—Examples of Gaelic-English—'News from Tulloch'—
An Australian illustration—Two Highland hotel anecdotes—
The Skye barometer—Old John M'Leod and the Oban porter
—Distinguished company—The first recorded eviction—A
mal de mer experience—A Highland grace, from *Blackwood*—
Curious marriage customs.

IN my peregrinations through many lands it has often
been my good fortune to come much in friendly contact
with our Highland cousins, the true Celt or Gael. Multitudes of good racy stories could be told of their
distinctive racial characteristics : of their quick, fiery
temper ; their intense clannishness ; their fierce, unfor-
giving hatreds ; their sly, pawky cunning, and quick,
versatile wit—much akin this in some respects to the
Lowland Scot ; of their proud intolerance of outside
dictation or interference ; of their most paradoxical
niggardliness and meanness over trifles, and their lavish
and unbounded recognition of the generous grace of
hospitality ; their high-minded honour where their word
or the repute of chief or kinsman is concerned ; their
suspicion and distrust of strangers, and open-hearted

response to true friendship and generous emotion ; their quick, warm, impulsive emotionalism, exhibited in their songs, their literature, their loyalty, and the fervour of their religious faith; but my taste has been more to present my scraps and notes on Scottish rather than on Highland humour and customs, and the scope of my unpretentious *omnium gatherum*, scarcely permits me to enter into abstruse ethnical questions. Before I close my somewhat random and disjointed gossip, however, perhaps some of my Highland gleanings may be found not altogether uninteresting, as they make no pretence to being anything more than chatty and familiar.

Many of the more common stories of the Lowland Scotsman about the Highlandman, turn on the quaint mistakes so often made by the Gaelic-speaking Celt, when first he attempts to express himself in the less mellifluous if more comprehensive Anglo-Saxon tongue.

For instance, I am assured that the following was overheard in Fraserburgh. Two hard-featured Celts 'over' from the West Highlands with fish for sale, are having a colloquy. Says the one :—

' Shon, hiv ye a spunk ?' (*Anglice*, a match.)

' No.'

' Aweel, she'll haf to use her nain.'

Another of the same sort is as follows :—

Scene—Top of Loch Maree coach. Vehicle is approaching Tarradale. Tourist (to driver)—' Splendid country this.' Driver—' Ay, ay ! and you'll haf peen here pefore ?' Tourist — ' Oh yes ; several times.' Driver—' Ay, ay ! there's nopody effer comes here at aal, tat hasna peen here sometime pefore already.'

The next is an instance of what sailors call ' made-up yarns,' but it illustrates the sort of Gaelic-English often heard in the Highlands. It has been before in print. Two Highlanders were standing on Tarbert pier watching the boats setting out for the fishing-ground, when Hamish remarked : ' She'll pe a gran' fast poat, tat skiff o' MacTavish's.' 'Ay, she'll pe so,' answered Dugald. 'Put she'll not peat Shon MacIntyre's whatefer.' ' Shon MacIntyre's ! ' contemptuously answered the other. ' She'll no haud a can'le to her, nor keep up to her forbye.' A heated discussion ensued on the respective merits of the two boats, and words might fast have come to blows, when a third son of the heather arrived on the scene, and the matter was referred to him for decision. ' Weel,' said Donald, with a look of wisdom that would have done credit to Solomon himself, ' if there'll pe ony difference, they're poth the same ' ; then, after a profound pause, he added, ' especially MacTavish's.'

This, though evidently bearing traces of southern manufacture, as I have said many do, is not an uncommon experience to any one who intelligently observes the workings of the untutored Celtic mind.

The ordinary Highlander or Celt of the lower social strata, as distinguished from the Lowland Scot, has the same whimsical, illogical propensity to make a blundering bull as his Irish cousin has. The Lowland humour is of a broader, mellower, more pawky, sly kind. The Highlander blurts out on impulse the first thought that flits across his brain, and not unfrequently involves himself in a paradox, or logical absurdity. For instance, here is another much similar to the foregoing, but undeniably genuine.

'What news from Tulloch?' queries one gillie of another whom he meets on the heather.

'Och, man, they buried old Sandie Macrae yesterday.'

'Did they? Py Cot! Well, well, I have seen the day when it wad hae ta'en twenty men to bury him; ay, and more too, mirover.'

Much akin to this was the remark of the West Coast fisherman who, on hearing the news of the death of some well-known acquaintance, said, with a solemn shake of the head: 'Ay, ay, an' so Kenneth Macintyre is dead? Cot pless me, but there's a lot of folk deein' shust noo that didn't use to tie pefore.'

I knew an old Highland squatter in Australia, whose dry, caustic wit caused many a hearty laugh at the discomfiture of those on whom it fell. A rather pompous globe-trotter, discussing the merits of Australia as a place of residence, in one of the clubs in Sydney, happened to say, in a very condescending, patronising sort of way, in the hearing of my old friend: 'Ya'as, Australia would be vewy nice to live in if you only had bettah society and plenty of watah.' 'Ay, man,' dryly responded old H——y, 'if ye only had that, I daursay ye micht manage to live wi' Auld Nick.'

The following is supposed to have been overheard in a Highland hotel:—

Tonal. Can you tell me what is petter nor a gless of whusky an' watter?

Tougal. Hooch, ay; I can that. Shust twa glesses.

And this is another of the same.

'What'll ye hae, Mr. MacTavish?'

'Och, shust whateffer is gaun, sir.   Your wull iss
ma pleesure.   I could mebbe tak' a pottle of porter
till ta whusky's procht pen ta hoose; 'deed ay, mirover.'

Here is one from far-off Skye, where now dwell some
of my dear old chums of the long-distant, indigo-planting
days; and with whom I am glad to think time and
fortune have dealt kindly.   Long may it be so.   Some
visitors to the wild and rugged isle, had been sorely
disappointed with the weather.   For a whole week the
landscape had been enveloped in a dense mist, and their
patience had almost become exhausted, waiting for a
break in the leaden sky.   The landlord took the matter
with much more composure.   The circling mists meant
for him simply a richer harvest from the Southrons.
The weather-bound tourists had noticed that the inn
barometer had never varied by one hair's-breadth,
although there had been incessant variations in the
weather; so in an idle hour, having nothing else to do,
they began to quiz the landlord about his weather-glass.
One said : 'Surely that is a very queer barometer of
yours, landlord?'   'Och,' said the imperturbable Boniface, 'she'll pe a fery fine parometer, whatefer.   *She'll*
no be movin' for a truffle (trifle), mirover.'

An old friend of mine, John M'Leod of Sydney,
known to a wide circle of admiring Scotsmen as 'The
Chief,' now, alas! gone to his rest after sore suffering,
told me a capital characteristic story of the apparent
innocence, yet deep, pawky guile, of the 'Hielantman,'
which amused me much, as the dear old 'Chief' told
it in his dry, kindly, Highland way.

Old John, after amassing a handsome competence in

the land of the Southern Cross, had taken a run home to see the splendour of the Northern Lights and the glory of the crimson heather once again, before his sturdy limbs grew too old for travel, and one fine day he found himself at Oban, talking in Gaelic with a weather-beaten old veteran named MacTavish, who followed the humble vocation of a street porter. The old Chief had quite won the heart of MacTavish by his use of the Gaelic, but the conquest was rendered still more complete by the offer of a gill and a sneeshin', both of which had been duly accepted and enjoyed.

Wishing to study the character of the rugged old Celt, John drew him out in conversation on a number of topics, and at last said :—

' Ye'll be kept pretty busy wi' the Sassenachs ? '

' Ou ay.'

' Do you find them good customers, now ? '

' Weel, they're vera close fistit, and vera curious too, sometimes, mirover.'

Then as a rather pronounced specimen of the genus tourist approached, dressed in loud check tweeds, *pince-nez* aggressively fixed on an accommodating snub nose, and redolent altogether of supercilious bumptiousness, MacTavish said :—

' Here's wan comin' up noo, an' you'll see hoo I'll hold ma own wi' this wan.'

Up sauntered the unconscious object of the Celtic scrutiny, and addressed the porter.

' Haw—portaw, does *The Chevalier* come in to her time ? ' looking at his watch as he spoke.

With a pawky look towards M'Leod, MacTavish replied :—

'Weel, sir, sometimes she'll pe sooner, and sometimes she'll pe earlier, and sometimes she'll pe before that too.'

Then turning round to M'Leod, he said in Gaelic :—

'Tidn't I gif him his answer that time ?'

The love of poetry and song, which is such a pronounced characteristic of the Gael, is well shown by the high regard in which, from the earliest times of even misty tradition, the vocation of the bard and the musician has been held. Celtic literature of course abounds with instances of this ; but among the common folk the same feeling is exhibited in the esteem with which the person and functions of the piper is invested.

One illustration may suffice. It was at a lowly Highland inn, in the days before Cook had revolutionised the art of touring. A rather uncommon party had penetrated into the somewhat remote district, and they had put up at the inn, and being of a frugal kind, they had grumbled somewhat at the pawky landlord's charges. The party consisted of an English rector and his four sons. All of these were clerics. The sons were full-blown curates, and all had a rather too openly pronounced contempt for the genus Gael, while they were not slack in exhibiting that characteristic which is supposed to be peculiarly Scottish, namely, 'having a gude conceit o' themselves.' The sturdy innkeeper did not seem, however, to be much awed by the quality and pretensions of his customers. When settling the score the bumptious old rector, after grumbling at the charges and the fare and the accommodation, said very loftily :—

'Ah, I suppose you are not accustomed to having such guests as myself and my four sons? Let me tell you, sir, that we are all clergymen of the Church of England.'

'Hech,' said Donal' very dryly, 'I dinna ken, sir, but I've maybe had mair distinguished company than yersel', sir. Last week we had nae less than Neil Mackay an' his fower sons, sir. Braw stalwart lads, sir; ay, an' ilka ane o' them was a piper.'

The mention of pipers reminds me of an anecdote I once heard of an old retired regimental piper in a northern town, who fancied himself no end of a composer. One day, speaking to a gentleman who had been praising his skill on the national instrument, he said very gravely: 'Ay, it's a peety but the mayor wad dee, an' eh, sir, but I wad compose a gran' lament.'

One of the best exhibitions of pawky Highland humour I heard from a professor of moral philosophy in one of our universities at the Antipodes. It happily and very forcefully illustrates the homely old fact, that there are two ways at least of looking at every question.

As it was told to me I give it. Two crofters in the West Highlands, during the very height of a wave of intense local feeling caused by sundry harsh evictions, were discussing the burning and vexed question of landownership. The one was a tall, brawny, typical clansman, freckled and weather-beaten, with craggy cheeks and unkempt yellow hair, tawny as a lion's mane, floating o'er his angular shoulders. The other was a weenie, wizened, alert-looking, dwarfish man, swart of skin, with keen, beadlike, sparkling eyes and

U

'tip-tilted' nose, to which ever and anon he conveyed liberal supplies of pungent 'sneeshin'' from an old, well-worn, horn 'mull.'   The big man was working himself up into a state of intense emotional excitement, smiting one big fist into the open palm of its fellow, and with tossing hair and flaming eye, declaiming against the exactions and cruelties and iniquities that were being perpetrated under the hated and out-worn feudal system of landlordism.

'I say it's a black, burning shaame,' he declaimed, 'that weemen and children shuld be turned out on the bare hillside to die like black game in the heather. I maintain, Tonal,' he cried, 'that there shuld pe no lantlords at aall whatefer.   Doesna ta goot pook tell us tat "ta earth is ta Lort's an' ta fulness thereof," mirover?'

'Weel, Tougal,' very dryly responded the other, after a capacious pinch of snuff, and betraying the downright contrariness and combativeness of the true Celt, 'I do not know that we would pe much petter off, mirover.'

'And how iss that, sir?' thundered the irate Tougal.

'Weel, ye see,' said the biblical Tonal, with a sly, smirking gleam of suppressed humour, 'we read tat ta goot Lort Himsel' had twa tenants, an', feth, *He evicted them.*'

Another of the extraordinary attempts of the Gael to circumvent the difficulties of the Sassenach tongue is the following possibly apocryphal dialogue supposed to take place on board the s.s. *Iona.*

Tonal loq., Tougal, wass you effer on ta *Iona* again pefore?'

Tougal. I wass.

Tonal. Tid you effer *see* ta *Iona* again pefore ?

Tougal. I tid.

The same two I suppose it must have been who quite beat the famous story in *Punch*, where the Highland victim of sea-sickness refused to discharge the contents of his o'erladen stomach on the valid plea—at least to a Highlander—that 'it wass whusky.'

Tonal, on this occasion again addressing Tougal, who is almost pea-green with *mal de mer*, said :—

'Fat do you no throw it up for, Tougal ?'

Tougal, with a vain attempt to look dignified, says : 'Na, na! she canna do that; she canna affront hersel' pefore these Sassenach!' pointing to a limp-looking, forlorn line of tourists, all casting their food to the fishes over the side of the pitching vessel.

'Ay, ay! an' fat do you mean by affronting your-sel' ?' said Tonal. 'Do you not see they are aal sick togither whatefer ?'

'Oich, oich!' moaned Tougal, with a desperate effort at regurgitation; 'put, you'll see, I only had parritch to ma preakfast, an' thae chentlemen are . . . Oich, oich! . . .;' but let us drop a veil on the subsequent proceedings.

One of the best and most characteristic touches I find among my notes on this subject, is one culled long ago from the racy and original pages of *Blackwood*. It is as follows :—

'Said the landlady : "I'm just perspirin' a' ower wi' shame an' disgrace that the cows hasna calved for ye to get crame to your parritch." In spite of the cows having been so disobliging there was abundance of

Highland cheer—towering dishes of scones, oatcakes,
an enormous cheese, fish, eggs, and a monstrous grey-
beard of whisky, ready if required; fumes of tobacco
were floating in the air, and the whole seemed an
embodiment of the Highlander's grace: "Och, gie us
rivers of whisky, chau'ders o' snuff, an' tons o' tobacco;
a pread an' a cheese as pig as ta great hill o' Ben Nevis,
an' may oor childer's childer pe lords an' ladies to ta
latest sheneration."'

On repeating this grace to an old hillsman of eighty,
leaning on his staff, he thoughtfully answered: 'Weel, it's
a goot crace, a ferry goot crace, but it's a warldly thing.'

Under the head of funeral customs I described a
burial in Badenoch. Before I close this chapter I would
like to chronicle a note furnished by a good lady friend
in Aberdeen, relating to some quaint marriage customs.

She writes me :—'A very curious old custom pre-
vailed in the Aberdeenshire Highlands more than a
century ago, which I do not remember ever to have
seen described in print. It was called "The
Send."

'When a couple were to be married, the custom was
for the bridegroom to send a party of his *unmarried*
male friends, with a married one at the head, to fetch
his bride to his home, and there they would be married.
She rode if the distance was long, or walked if it was
short, and it was customary for the young men of the
party to run a race, trying to see who would first reach
the house. When the bride arrived, a bannock and sometimes a cheese was broken over her head as she crossed
the threshold. She was then led to the fireplace, and
made to hang a pot on the crook, or turn a live peat, or

some such formality, signifying her entrance on domestic duties.

'A later proceeding was what was called "ridin' the brooze." The bride, having been married in her father's house, was escorted to her future home by a number of her own and her husband's friends on horseback. Several of them would then start on a race, trying which would be the first to reach the bridegroom's home.'

It is said that dreadful scenes of license and excess were not unfrequently the issue of this rude and primitive mode of marriage procession.

CHAPTER XVIII

THE SCOT ABROAD

Pride of country—Scottish generosity—The Struan Highlander—
A Sydney matron's experience—An Antipodean beadle—A
typical Scot in Calcutta—Characteristic stories about him—
A close-fisted Scot in Melbourne—A Sydney alderman—Two
new-chum Scots in Sydney—A disillusioned grazier—A robber
despoiled—'Walkin' on the Sawbath'—'Shooin' the cat'—
Angling in New Zealand—A pawky Scot in the East—An
engineer's estimate of classic music.

SUCH is the tenacity and persistence of the Scottish
national character that it has been truly said that of
all men 'a Scotsman becomes more Scottish when he
leaves Scotland.' Whatever truth may lurk in this
seeming paradox, it is unquestionable that wherever
you find the sons of Scotia, in Arctic winters or in
torrid heat, their nationality is not to be hid. Some
trick of manner or of speech 'bewrayeth them.' Indeed
they are not wont to 'hide their talents under a bushel';
and it is but expressing an acknowledged fact, and I
trust as a Scotsman I do it with becoming modesty,
yet with a perfectly legitimate pride, that they are rarely
found, in any appreciable number, filling menial or sub-
ordinate positions anywhere abroad.

What is often levelled at us as a reproach, namely our clannishness, is not clannishness in the true sense of the word, and in no sense can it be considered a reproach. Our detractors by the charge seemingly mean to convey that we are narrow in our sympathies, and selfishly exclusive in our somewhat restricted view of humanity as a whole. Now the clan idea has little existence in the feeling of travelled Scotsmen. The national feeling, if you like, which is a far loftier and broader thing, burns with a clear, steady, ardent flame that nought can quench. Less demonstrative than our Irish brethren, we are not less devoted to the national idea; and the common heritage we possess in our language, our literature, our songs, our history, and the exquisite natural beauty of our rugged country, serves to knit Scotchmen to each other all the wide world over in bonds of sentiment as elastic as silk, but strong as steel—only, our sentiment seldom runs away with us. It is controlled by reason, by habits of acquired reflection and logical deduction; and though the national sentiment may refuse to manifest itself at the behest of a counterfeit, no matter howsoever cunningly bedecked in national guise; or to forward some unworthy object, no matter howsoever plausibly disguised in Scottish colours; let but a genuine call be made upon it, for objects worthy and in unmistakably truly Scottish tones, and the response is prompt and generous beyond all dry calculation or formal exactitude. I have seen this proved over and over again in my thirty years' residence abroad. The Scottish sentiment is being constantly appealed to by spurious, base, designing tricksters; but what it is capable of in the way of real brotherly help, broad, loving charity, and cosmopolitan beneficence, the records of many a Highland and Caledonian Society—and they flourish in all the ends of the earth—could abundantly establish were the testimony needed.

An instance of this love of home, of one's 'calf country,' and of the halting Highland - English, just comes to me as I write. A Highlander in Australia, not long away from the peat - reek and the heather, had wandered into the bar of a country-town hotel in search of refreshment. Scanning the labels on the various bottles, his attention suddenly seemed to be arrested by one showy label which represented a clansman in full Highland dress in a very bacchanalian attitude, and the bold brand in big letters bore the legend 'Struan Blend.' At once the eyes of the exile brightened, ay, and they might have been seen to glisten with a suspicious moistness. He stretched out his brawny arm, and took an affectionate grasp of the bottle, then holding it at arm's-length, he affectionately apostrophised the name. 'Ay, ay!' he gasped with deep feeling, 'Stru - u - an ! Stru-u-u-an ! Do you know, tat wass ta fery place I wass nearly porn to, mirover ?' He meant that his birthplace was in the Struan neighbourhood.

The matron of one of our magnificent Sydney hospitals told me an incident which she thought eminently characteristic of the Scot, and I must just let the reader judge for himself. One of the *rarae aves* in the Colony, an old Scottish beggar-woman, called on the matron one day, and after hearing her tale of woe, the kind lady gave the petitioner some tea, sugar, and other little comforts, and to crown her benevolence added a bright new shilling, fresh from the neighbouring mint. Next day, beaming with smiles and radiant with self-satisfaction, the suppliant again presented herself, apparently expecting another course of the same treatment. 'But,' said the matron, 'didn't I give you a shilling only yesterday?' 'Eh, bless me, mem!' with apparently innocent surprise, 'but shairly ye didna think I wad pairt wi' that, did ye?'

And we can even find beadle stories at the Antipodes. As witness the note I find about 'Auld Jamie Simm,' a well-known identity in Auckland, New Zealand, and for many a year beadle and sexton of St. Andrew's Church there. Jamie kept up the traditions of his office with true Scottish fidelity, and was notoriously fond of the mountain dew, especially when he had not to pay for it. On one occasion, two of his patrons, who were wont to humour the old man, and enjoyed his racy and shrewd sayings (Mr. Whitson, a wealthy brewer, and Mr. Russell, a prominent merchant, and both typical Scottish colonists), had asked him into the club, and there they had regaled the old fellow with a dram. Jamie with deep feeling, ere he quaffed the national nectar, and with as much solemnity as if he were saying grace, said : 'Weel, Maister Russell, here's t'ye! Eh, man, there's you an' Maister Whitson, losh I'll be sweir tae bury ye.'

One of the best-known Scottish characters in Calcutta when I first went out to India in 1866, was an eccentric, wealthy old merchant whom I will call Stuart. He was in many pronounced respects a typical Scot, such as is often portrayed by the novelist. No man better knew how to get full value for his rupee, and withal he had a somewhat ostentatious pride, and was never better pleased than when he could indulge his love of display and magnify his own importance at little cost to his pocket. Perhaps the following true anecdote will better illustrate his peculiar disposition.

Once a year it was his custom to give a sort of annual dinner to his clerks and clients. He had a nice house and grounds, and was most hospitable in throwing these open to the office hands, and any planters or ship captains having dealings with the firm who might be in Calcutta at the time. The dinner was always a substantial one : plenty of fruits provided, viands well cooked, and of the best procurable materials the bazaars could supply; but old Stuart's heart failed him when it came to the drinks. Here his Scottish idiosyncrasy betrayed itself. When all the guests were assembled, Stuart would come in, with an assumption of hilarious, almost boisterous hospitality, and rubbing his hands, or perhaps clapping some junior clerk on the back, he would call out loudly and cheerfully some such oft-heard formula as the following :—

'Come awa' in-bye noo, lads, an' sit doon. That's richt, that's richt. I'm rael gled tae see ye. It's only yince a year that we a' meet thegither, an' I want ye to enjoy yersol's. Noo, what'll ye hae? what'll ye hae? Jist gie't a name. There's everything ye can mention. There's hock an' clairet, an' Burgundy, an' Saaterrn, an' Mosell, an' champagne. But'—— here he became if possible more jocose and boisterous, and rattling on before any one could interrupt, he would continue : 'but I'm thinkin' a' thae's fusionless an' unsatisfactory drinks. They're no guid for the stamack, lads, no guid for the stamack.

There's naething for the digestion like beer. Jist that.
A vera good idea. Beer's the thing. Boy!' shouting to
the bearer, and as if in perfect agreement with an
expression of the popular demand, though not a soul
beside himself had had an opportunity of uttering a
syllable; 'Boy, bring in the beer! Ah, that's richt,
that's richt!' And the white-robed waiters, the beer
being all ready cooled and close at hand, promptly
appeared with the old fellow's selected beverage. And
to do him justice there was never any stint of beer, and
even a 'wee Donal' o' whusky' to keep the beer doon,
if any one desired it; but the clairet an' champagne,
'an' a' thae expensive an' fushionless drinks,' were
never forthcoming at any of old Stuart's annual
feasts.

The old fellow's peculiarities were of course well-
known, and formed the theme of many a joke in
merchant circles in Calcutta. A friend of my dear
brother's, Mr. Evan Jack, tells how he once tried, out
of a spirit of pure mischievous fun, to trick old Stuart
out of a small forced contribution to the kirk. It was
in this way. In Calcutta the usual currency for the
kirk - plate is the ubiquitous, but, alas! now sadly
shrunken and depreciated rupee. But rupees are bulky,
and Calcutta pantaloons are often made pocketless,
especially one's Sunday suit. No Calcutta merchant
ever thinks of carrying current coin about with him,
least of all to church. So a custom has grown up of
using what are called 'chits.' That is, a pencil and
little slips of paper are provided, or a worshipper may
use his calling card. Any way, he writes down on
card or slip the amount of his offering, and next day

the church *chuprassee* calls round to the various addresses, and collects the several amounts on these chits, practically, in fact, I.O.Us. Now one day Jack noticed that old Stuart always came provided with coin, and invariably dropped in just one rupee, and· wishing to test him, he whispered as they were going out of church : 'I say, Stuart, lend me a rupee to put in the plate, will you?' At once Stuart's hand went to his pocket, and then, as if a sudden thought had arrested his first impulse, he said : 'Oh, never mind, man. I'll pit it in for ye, an' ye can let me hae't back the morn.' So saying he dropped in his offering, 'ONE RUPEE.' Sure enough his *chuprassee* duly applied for the coin at Jack's office next day. Poor old Stuart! to him might well have been applied the biting satire of the old clergyman, who, after having extracted a reluctant contribution from a rich, old, penurious hunks of a fellow, who parted with his coin with a sigh, saying, 'Ah, well, we can't take our money with us, can we?' responded somewhat savagely : 'No, sir, an' if ye could I'm feared it wad melt.'

Equally close fisted was an old Melbourne identity in the early days, who went by the name of 'Licht wecht Davie,' though his real name, I believe, was Sandie Young. He had at one time kept a shop in Leith Walk, but whether he had been sent out

For his country's good,

or had emigrated of his own free will I know not. At any rate he had a demoniacal temper, and indulged sometimes in almost maniacal outbursts, culminating in atrocious cruelties, which he would inflict on the hapless objects of his fury, should they perchance be weak and helpless. He was a miser, too, and altogether an unlovely character. The favourite drink at that time in Melbourne was some compound of frothy beer and other ingredients, and was known as a Spider. It so happened that this ferocious old fellow had been arrested for some horrid act of cruelty committed on a number of goats in Melbourne. Being possessed of pretty ample means, he managed to retain Sir Archibald Michie for his defence. The learned Counsel limited his efforts to procure some mitigation of what he felt was likely to be a severe sentence, as the cruelty could not be denied. Several witnesses to character were called, but in cross-examination by the Counsel for the prosecution as to whether they had ever known the prisoner to commit any benevolent or kindly act, each one replied in the negative. Not one benevolent act could be adduced, until at length one humorous fellow seemed to remember something of the kind, and on being pressed by Sir Archibald : ' You have known the prisoner perform a benevolent act ? '

' Yes, sir.'

' Well, tell his Honour. What was the nature of the act ? '

' Please yer Honour,' said the witness, with a smile, as he thought of the quip, and referring to the frothy drink just mentioned above, 'I once saw him save a fly from a spider.' Even Michie was convulsed.

I have already shown that the Scot does not change so very much even when he finds himself in foreign parts, and I venture to cull a few more illustrations of this from my note-book.

The following is related of a very worthy alderman of Sydney, as true-hearted and kindly a Scot as ever smelled peat-reek, but whose acquisition of a handsome competence, and advancement in civic and social dignity, had not tended to lessen his complacent satisfaction with himself. It was on the occasion of the visit of the Prince of Wales' two sons to the Australian capital. Our friend was a toon cooncillor, and the corporate body, led by the Mayor, had assembled to do honour to the two young princes. The worthy alderman had no idea of allowing himself to be overshadowed by any mayor; and so with the idea of ingratiating himself and being pleasant and complimentary, he pushed through the inner circle, interrupted the Mayor, who was making himself as agreeable as he knew how, and much, no doubt, to the disgust of that worthy functionary and to the amused surprise of the princes, he seized the hand of one of them, shook it warmly, and acquainted them with the important fact, that he 'had met their mother at hame.' This was kindly meant, no doubt. He simply wished to put the royal visitors at their ease. His little item of news, however, seemed somehow to fall flat; there was but a frigid response. The Mayor turned purple. Some of the aldermen swore softly behind their beards. Others stuffed handkerchiefs in their mouths. Our friend, however, was in no way abashed. He just blundered on, shook the royal hand heartily, and, still thinking of his first item, added the commentary, 'An a vera good wumman she is.'

I once overheard a little morsel of real Scottish in Sydney, between two new arrivals. The two poor fellows were clad in heavy homespun, and the time

was December, when the blazing sun in Sydney pours
down liquid fire, in comparison with the cold gray
northern climate, and every living thing feels as if it were
about to be almost scorched and shrivelled out of existence, during the sweltering hours of high noon. I had
just come out of the Post-office, and was standing in the
shady arcade that runs along the imposing front of that
majestic pile (the architect by the bye was a typical
Scot), when I heard the well-known tones of the auld
Doric, and at once became an intent listener.

One poor fellow, taking off his thick Scottish cap and
wiping the streams of perspiration from his flushed and
steaming face, said, with a grip on the *r*s that no one
but a true Caledonian could accomplish. 'Man, Jock,
but it's awfu' war-r-r-m here!' and then with a touch of
pathos, as he thought of the wintry fields and hills far,
far away, he added, with almost a sob : ' An' jist tae think
that there's fower fit o' sna' at hame this vera meenit.'

I am glad to say I got work for them both, and they
are now doing well in the land of their adoption,
' war-r-r-m ' though that undoubtedly is.

I heard the following at a Government House dinner
in Melbourne. I had the good fortune to be seated
next my genial and gifted friend Mr. Ellery, the
Astronomer Royal for Victoria. He told us that one
night at the Observatory, he had been showing the
wonders of the moon to a distinguished party, among
them being a fine old Scottish pastoralist, or squatter as
they are generally called. He had experienced many
vicissitudes during his long colonial career. He had
been harassed by truculent selectors, who had picked
the choicest bits out of his run for the purpose of

levying black-mail, or for the more legitimate purpose of turning the grazing lands into arable farms, but in either case quite an object of detestation to the Shepherd King. Then when financial troubles came on the Colony, the Government had tried to make up for the failure of their fiscal policy by rack-renting the graziers; so the old squatter, after looking long and intently through the great telescope, and noting the forbidding desolateness and aridity of the great lunar plains, as he yielded up his place to another of the party, and in response to Mr. Ellery's query as to what he thought of the moon, said, as he sadly shook his head :—

'Ach ! there's anither illusion gone.'

'What do you mean ?' asked the astronomer.

'Eh, man,' said the squatter, 'I have aye thocht that if ever I was fairly hunted oot here, between the Government and thae infernal selectors, that I micht find a refuge in the mune, if naewhere else ; but, losh man, I maun say that hope is gone ; FOR IT LOOKS —— BAD SHEEP COUNTRY.'

The same entertaining companion told me, at the same dinner, another characteristic incident of the early, lawless Melbourne days. The fine city was but a small bush township then. The site whereon now stands the palatial but possibly pretentious Houses of Parliament, was then an uneven, rocky, thickly-wooded hillside. Mr. Ellery, wending his way to his lonely dwelling rather late one night, was suddenly waylaid by two lusty footpads, who knocked him down, rifled his pockets, and indeed half-throttled him. Just then, looming close by, and but dimly discernible through the haze, Mr. Ellery espied the towering bulk of a tall, athletic friend of his, who had been a fellow-passenger and chum on the voyage out. He managed to yell out his name—a distinctly Scottish one—and to appeal for help. In a moment the burly and gallant Scot sprang to the rescue. In a trice the positions were reversed. One of the miscreants bolted like a rabbit through the scrub ; the other was firmly held in the strong, nervous grip of the rescuing Scot, and over they went, locked in desperate clench, rolling over and over down the steep, till they went souse into a narrow sort of rocky gully at the bottom of the gorge. Mr. Ellery's friend was on top, and quickly jammed his bruised antagonist into a jagged crevice with his knee, as if he were dumping wool, and being now joined by the prospective Astronomer Royal, they began to over-haul the thief and 'take an observation or two.' Pulling out a watch, the placid athlete asked Ellery if that were his. 'Yes,' said my friend. Then came a purse. 'Is that yours also?' 'Yes,' was the response, and it was handed over. Next came a handful of coin and a fat roll of notes. 'Are these yours?' 'No,' was the reply. 'Aweel, then, they're mine,' said the Cale-donian, as he coolly pocketed the salvage ; and then, with a parting kick, the baffled thief was ignominiously dismissed into the thickening darkness.

A shrewd old farmer in New South Wales, one of my New England constituents, James Swales by name, told me an incident of his own early career which affords a capital illustration of one phase of the old, pawky, Pharisaic attitude of mind as regards the observance of the Sabbath, which characterised the ordinary Scottish mind about the middle of this century.

As it was told me in Australia, I may be permitted to introduce it here.   Mr. Swales was a young Englishman who had crossed the Border and settled in Dunbar, where an opening existed for an energetic young fellow as a shopkeeper.   The provost of the town was also the local banker, and as Mr. Swales was a customer of the bank, the provost took quite a kindly interest in the young trader.   One day he sent for Mr. Swales, and after a few compliments, saying how pleased he was to see he was getting on so well, etc., he said: 'An' I'm vera gled to see, Maister Swales, that ye dinna negleck yer releegious duties.   Ye gang to the Wesleyans, I'm hearin'; but I maun caution ye, my frien', no tae gang oot walkin' for pleesure on the Sawbath; for if ye dae, ye'll loss a' yer custom.   Oor folk'll no' stand Sawbath walkers at ony price.'

My good friend Mr. M'Eachern of Melbourne gave me a graphic picture of the old Scottish domestic life and the strong individuality of the older generation, which I would like to give here.   His own grandfather was the subject, and the story lost nothing in being told under the starry splendour of an Australian night, with the shrill, strident chorus of the cicadas making the air ring with their almost overpowering clamour all around. The whole family had been engaged in the usual family worship one evening, and the white-haired patriarch was praying with much fervour, when the current of his thoughts was somewhat rudely disturbed by hearing the aged wife of his bosom utter a sharp, sibilant 's-s-shoo!' from the other side of the room.   He looked up irritably, paused, and then resumed his interrupted petitions. The sound was repeated—'Shoo! s-s-shoo!' sounded grannie's voice in a loud whisper. Again the old man paused, glowered at her rather indignantly, while every head was lifted from their chairs. Yet a third time, but more intense, came the disconcerting 'sh-sh-shoo!' And this time, following the direction of the old lady's anxious glance, directed towards the supper-table, he spied the cat taking liberties with the milk. Hastily picking up his Psalm-book, he shied it at the marauder, interpolating in his prayer a bald statement of fact, rather than a petition perhaps, as he grimly muttered : 'Toots, wumman, that's better nor a' yer shoo-shoo-shooin'.'

The aim would seem to have been as earnest and direct as the prayer, as my friend was always careful to explain that the cat was sent flying in true sportsman-like fashion.

Many a laugh has been raised at some of John Leech's inimitable fishing pictures and yarns in the pages of· *Punch*, but not one, I think, ever came up in humorous suggestiveness to an incident which I heard related of an old squatter near Timaru, in New Zealand, and which was vouched for to me as an absolute fact. There is splendid fishing in the rivers and streams in that part of the Canterbury Province, trout and salmon acclimatisation having been practised with much success. Well, an old squatter from the Mackenzie Country, who had amassed considerable wealth in pastoral pursuits, and who was named M'L——, had settled down at Fairlie, near Timaru, and found time hanging rather heavy on his hands. The bank manager, who was an enthusiastic angler, advised him to try the delightful art so dear to the gentle Izaak. Old M'L——

was a prosaic, matter-of-fact man, with little imagination, and very few ideas beyond mutton and wool. However, he had heard men go into raptures over details of fishing excursions, and knowing it to be fashionable, he resolved to try 'his 'prentice han'.' Procuring the necessary paraphernalia, he accordingly hied him to a favourite bit of water in the vicinity known as Silver Stream. Here he began his first attempt at fly-fishing. He had seen the banker and others at the sport, and he attempted to follow their example. Imagine the scene : a solemn-visaged, preternaturally grave-looking old gentleman, clad in black beaver, stiff stock, white waistcoat, black coat and trousers, standing as stiff as a poker, with his fishing-rod held at arm's-length in front of him, and his arms moving mechanically, as if he were sawing a log. Swish went the line, swash went the hooks on the water. Old Mac kept pumping away in this fashion without moving a muscle or altering the monotonous regularity of his movements. For some hours he had kept this up, and was inly coming to the conclusion that 'fushin' was a vera much over-estimated species of deevairshun.' Just then the banker hove in sight.

'Hallo, Mr. M'L——,' he said, 'what's this you're doin'?'

'Ah'm fushin',' came the reply in tones of solemn gravity, while the pump-handle process was continued with dogged pertinacity, and with all the regularity of an automaton.

'Have you caught any?' again asked the cheery banker.

With even an added gloom and relentless severity, came the studiously truthful reply :—

'Weel, no, I canna say that I hae gotten ony fush;
but I have heerd the awnimals plash on mair than one
occaashion.'

Talk after that of 'fishing all day and getting a
nibble.' Surely our New Zealander tops the record for
patience and matter-of-factness.

A first-class illustration of the sly, pawky, almost sardonic irony of the genuine Scot, is told me by my
cousin, the ex-Danish Consul at Singapore, and for a
long time a member of the Council there, relative to one
of the leading merchants, whom we will call Mac-
Farlane. Old Mac was what is commonly known as
'a dry old stick.' He was a leading spirit in the often
highly-fluctuating prices and speculative dealings in
such native commodities as cutch, gambier, indigo,
cloves, etc. One day a rise in cutch had been rumoured,
and a pertinacious bill-broker, keenly on the scent for
reliable information, had called on Old Mac with the
intention of trying to elicit what information he could.
Affecting an airy indifference, he passed the usual remarks about the weather and other social local topics,
and then began his fishing operations.

'I hear you are buying cutch, largely, Mac.'

'Div ye? Wha tell't ye that?'

'Oh, I hear there's a short crop, and that you have
"got in" well.'

'Indeed!'

'I suppose the out-turn really is short this year?'

But the wary old badger was not to be drawn. Suddenly assuming the lead in the conversation, he said:—

'Maister Broon, did ye ever hear o' a distinguished
poet caa'ed Dr. Watts?'

'What! Dr. Watts the hymn writer? Oh, yes.'

'Aweel, div ye mind o' a hymn that begins—

> 'Hoo doth the little busy bee
> Improve ilk shining 'oor,
> An' gethers honey all the day
> From ev'ry openin' floo'er?'

'Oh yes, I quite remember that.'

'Ah weel, ah'm no' that openin' floo'er the day, Maister Broon. Gude mornin', sir.'

My friend Harper also tells me a good story of an old Scottish engineer, who was proceeding to Calcutta, and happened to be a fellow-passenger with my friend as far as Colombo on one of the P. and O. boats, and with this I may fitly close my chapter. It happened that two of the most gifted musical artistes of the century were also passengers, and in the goodness of their hearts, to relieve the tedium of the voyage, they graciously consented to improvise a concert for some benevolent object, and of course it goes without saying every one was charmed,—with one exception perhaps. Old Ross was asked how he liked the music. Thus he delivered himself :—

'Oh, weel, the fiddlin's no sae bad, but as for that pianny playin', I jist canna thole it at ony price. Ye see my three lassies hae been deave, deavin' me ilka mornin' for three years wi' jist the same sort o' thing. I can not stan' this high strike sort o' thing ava.' Noo-adays ye never hear a dacent sort o' a tune that a bodie can unnerstan'—the like o' "Green Grows the Rashes," noo. This Eyetawlyin trash is jist a pairfeck scunner.'

CHAPTER XIX

THUS far, dear reader, have we strayed together,. following the devious path of my random recollections. I set out with the main intention of culling what sprigs and sprays of humour might be found projecting along our path, and I would fain hope we may have together gathered enough to make some pleasant decoration, and leave some sweet perfume in one or other of the inner chambers of thy imagination and memory. My task would be ill fulfilled indeed, however, were I to leave the impression that our Scottish race are but a people given to erratic and eccentric manifestations of humour, whether grim or pawky, bucolic or bacchanalian. These stories I have given are but the lights and shadows on the stream. At best they can but indifferently indicate the course of the current from the surface. The broad, deep volume of national life is not to be gauged by any such standards. The grave-eyed, pure-souled, tender-hearted, earnest, thoughtful men that form the fate and shape the destiny of a people, under Providence, are for the most part silent men. It is in deeds, not words, we read the story of a nation's life. And brushing aside all the excrescences and aberrations of mere mutable phenomena and temporary trivialities, could we for a moment look a little deeper into this noble and majestic stream of Scottish national life, and seek to discover some of its best constituents, we would find, I think, one of the strongest elements in its composition to be, and ever to have been, a deep, abiding, all-powerful loyalty to conscience, and a splendid faith in the divine government and sovereign power of God.

I have come back, after thirty years of sometimes weary working and much wandering on the face of the earth, to the beautiful old glen where many of my tenderest associations are gathered together, and I find even here among the swelling hills that time and chance have worked wondrous changes. It matters little whether the change is inward or outward. The place to me is no longer the same. The old generation has almost passed away. The little heather-thatched habitations have sunk into the soil with their former owners, and we have now trim stone and slate cottages of the modern type. The very hills themselves look to my travelled imaginings to be less lofty, the rivers to be narrowed, and the distances somehow shrunken, and I know that much at least of these changes is in myself and not in them. Well, is it not true that all these ' outward things that perish in the using,' this goodly-seeming outward show, are after all only ' the things that are seen,' and in their very nature and essence ' temporal,' evanescent, mutable ? But when I begin to inquire into the inner and real life of the people ; when I seek to get below the placid exterior, the ofttimes

assumed look of stolidity, almost stupidity; when I
probe into emotions and touch tender chords; when I
revive old associations and recollections, I at once begin
to find that I am in the presence of 'the things that are
unseen and eternal.' I find still existing the deep,
passionate love of country, and the honest, worthy pride
in the high name and good repute of her best men and
women who have played their part and gone to their
reward. I find a warm attachment for living, present,
kindly, earnest men and noble women. There is yet the
simple, social, family life, the sweet, neighbourly kind-
nesses, the broad, bluff, democratic independence of spirit,
and above and below and through it all, the old earnest
faith in the unseen, the willing recognition of the
sovereignty of God, and the ready obedience to conscience as the final arbiter in every court of moral appeal.

I find the pulpit teaching to be broader than I fancy
it was of yore. I find less sectarian bitterness and a
heartier accord on matters of common belief, and a
much more tolerant spirit existent in matters non-
essential. I am told the old bitter intolerance and
bigoted spirit still lingers among the Western Highlands,
and that in some parts the *odium theologicum* flourishes
in all its wonted rank and baneful vigour; but there are
indications that Christian unity is making headway, and
that the river of our Scottish religious life is not only
getting broader, but that it carries depth with it as well
as breadth. At a Free Church Bazaar the other day,
for instance, up the Glen, the fine, forceful, young Free
Church minister and his amiable, gentle wife, had the
loyal and active assistance of the kindly incumbent of
the neighbouring Episcopal Church and his comely,

genial consort; while the sister of the Established Church minister of the parish gracefully and efficiently presided over another of the stalls. And this I am told is by no means an exceptional case. Oh, if the Christian Church and Christian workers could only thus 'close up the ranks' and present a united front to the common foe, what a splendid 'advance along the whole line' might not be made, and what conquests achieved under that glorious banner which is inscribed with the golden Gospel letters, 'Peace on earth and goodwill among men'!

I have been struck, too, with the hearty, breezy, self-respect and independent bearing of the people. It is far removed from arrogance or assertiveness, although it must be confessed it is sometimes calculated to rouse antagonism, as in the case of a dear old Scottish spinster who certainly has a gude conceit o' hersel', and who was made the subject of a fussy, under-bred English lady's questionings in Liverpool a short time ago. The Englishwoman rather resented the calm air of conscious superiority assumed by the Scottish lady, and with some asperity asked her: 'Do you really think, Miss K——, that you Scottish are better than we English?' The reply was direct and emphatic: 'Certainly, madam, we are better born.' My cousin, Captain W——, who was present, said afterwards: 'You were rather hard on Mrs. A—— were you not?' The good old spinster at once said with naïve surprise: 'But dear me, Captain, you agree with me, do you not? I only told her the truth.' Well, without endorsing this estimate of the complacent spinster, we may remark that this trait is the direct antithesis of the sycophancy of the East, and in many

respects different from the manner of either the English
or the Irish peasant. There is never the volubility of
the latter, nor, to be sure, the same rapid play of wit.
We are not so impulsive. Our emotions are as strong,
probably deeper, but they do not manifest themselves so
readily. We are not so stolid as the English on the other
hand, and perhaps not so sectional and provincial; and it
seems to me, from what I must confess to be a very
cursory and inadequate observation—too partial and
casual for me to trust too much to it, yet from what I
have seen, I would be inclined to think that there is
more general and kindly contact between all ranks and
classes in Scotland than in England. There is not such
a wide disparity between peasant and pastor, for
instance, north of the Tweed, as between Hodge and the
rector south of the same stream. All classes mix more
freely together in Scotland : relations between mistress
and maid, master and servant, were formerly, and even
now in great measure are, I think, kindlier, more cordial,
more human in fact. Now, can this be due, as I am
inclined to think in great measure it may be due, to the
difference in the genius of the two opposite forms of
Church government, Presbytery and Episcopacy ? I do
not profess to be qualified to give any authoritative
opinion, but I would like to see the question worked
out; and I hope a champion on either side may be
induced to take up the interesting task, and show how
the systems relatively work in the development of
national character, and in their attitude towards the
masses and the classes in this and other respects. It
does seem to me that 'the hall' and 'the parsonage,'
the 'suburban villa' and the substantial tradesman's or

trader's comfortable home, are farther removed in kindly social sentiment and mutuality of interest from the labourer's humble cot in England than is the case in Scotland. 'Giles and Hodge' are not the same as 'Sandie and Jock' in their attitude towards their so-called social superiors. There is very little touching of the cap in rural Scotland, but a deal of manly and frank courtesy and delicacy. There is a frank, hearty, breezy, yet perfectly respectful consciousness of one's own worth, and an unconventional, democratic, yet perfectly natural and easy self-assertion, which I find simply delightful, and which is very like the open, manly, democratic equality we find characteristic of the best of the Australian peoples as a rule.

I believe this to be largely due to the genius and influence of the Presbyterian system. But I must hurry to a close. My book is not intended as a pretentious or comprehensive inquiry into the causes of national character. I have been content to be simply a chronicler of gossip about some of the more characteristic and salient manifestations of the humour of the kindly Scot.

Let me conclude with the earnest hope and prayer, that all true Scotsmen everywhere, all who love the dear old land of crimson heather and trailing mist, will seek to maintain and perpetuate the kindly nature of the 'britherly Scot.' Amid the clash of creeds, the war of classes, the hatred and estrangement and bitter feuds that rage among the nations, let Scotland's sons all the wide world over testify to the warmth of their love for their common country, the sincerity of their attachment to each other, their passionate loyalty to the principles of liberty in every phase of human effort or aspiration.

Let them cherish the memory of that noble roll of heroes, martyrs, patriots, and kinsmen 'who laid down their lives' for truth and righteousness and freedom; let them hold fast their heritage of civil and religious liberty, purchased by such precious blood; and 'let no man take their crown.' So, united, so, loyal to each other and to our glorious past, so, faithful to conscience and loyal to 'the God of our Fathers,' we shall take up the burden allotted to us, and bear no ignoble part in the coming strife, which indeed is even now upon us: that war to the death against sedition, disunion, and spurious socialism; against fell anarchy and chill materialism; against soul-corroding mammon worship, and the subtle poison of mere intellectual advancement, unaccompanied by the devout surrender of the will and spirit to the universal, immanent Father Almighty.

So mote it be!

THE END

Printed by R. & R. CLARK, *Edinburgh*

OPINIONS OF THE PRESS ON 'OOR AIN FOLK.'

' His powers of description are utilised in many good scenes of rustic life . . . many happy sketches of the natural beauties of the Braes of Angus—many anecdotes . . . both fresh and forcible.'—*Athenæum.*

' Really interesting and amusing; there are few of his own nationality who will not be deeply interested in parts of these "memories of manse life." The central figure is that of no common man, and it must possess an interest even for those who can claim no kindred with his country, and whose lines have been cast in far different places.'—*Saturday Review.*

' With such stories the volume sparkles. The student and historian of Scotland and Scottish manners in the first half of the nineteenth century will find it both entertaining as a sketch book and invaluable as a record.'—*Montrose Standard.*

' No more genial and entertaining book has been issued from the press since Dean Ramsay printed his *Reminiscences of Scottish Life and Character* . . . tells his stories with such gusto and felicity of language . . . written with great vigour and freshness . . . will be read with genuine pleasure and interest by all who can enjoy the native humour of the Scottish peasantry.'—*People's Friend.*

' Contains a vivid picture of humble manse life, and the struggles of the Disruption, and above all is full of " pawky " stories. He has been before the public already as " Maori," and should attract fresh readers by his new book.'—*Pall Mall Gazette.*

' Scots folk all the world over will feel that they owe a debt of gratitude to Mr. Inglis for the charming volume of reminiscences which he has just produced. It is sure not only of a welcome but of a perpetual resting-place on the shelves of even the most crowded library.

'Contains a store of admirable Scottish stories, many of them quite new to us, that can only be compared in quality to the classic collection of Dean Ramsay. . . . A great treat to all true Scotchmen.' —*Glasgow Herald.*

'A perfect treasure-house of good things.'—*Arbroath Herald.*

'Much that is of public interest . . . many pleasant glimpses of a rural Scotland which has vanished as completely as the Flood. . . . Many of his stories are fresh, pointed, and racy of the soil,' etc.— *Daily Free Press* (Aberdeen).

'Of value as a historical record of Scottish rural life during the past hundred years. No musty chronicle of dry-as-dust facts. Every page is brightened either by a vivid description of scenery, a comical anecdote, or a witty retort, and the reader must be a morose mortal indeed who does not enjoy the brisk humour of the narrator.'—*Dundee Advertiser.*

'Wonderfully graphic and realistic. . . . We are introduced to many fine types of Scotch character, many quaint customs and habits, and a diversified mass of amusing and out-of-the-way information,' etc.—*North British Daily Mail.*

'Bound to become a favourite wherever Scottish character and humour are appreciated.'—*Scotsman.*

'One of the best of its class we have seen. . . abounds in capital stories.'—*Westminster Gazette.*

'A very chatty and interesting book, and will be especially appreciated by those who can recall the condition of social life in Scotland in the thirties and forties.'—*Inverness Courier.*

'A delightful book. . . . It contains a very vivid account of the Disruption and Disruption times.'—*Christian Leader.*

'A storehouse of witty retorts, and full of shrewd observation and vivid pictures of a phase of society which has passed away.'— *Speaker.*

'But no mere isolated quotations can give an adequate idea of these manse-born memories of "Oor Ain Folk," with their simplicity and pathos, their sturdy independence of character, their unconscious heroism in humble life, their intelligence, their humour, and their strong individuality—qualities which have induced the successful politician of the Southern Cross to become the social historian of the "Braes o' Angus," and made the facts of Mr. Inglis no less interesting than the fiction of Mr. Barrie.'—*Daily Chronicle.*

'Contains so much sound moral teaching, and so much homely worldly wisdom, that no one can fail to be much profited by reading it ; whilst the salt of humour, with which it is plentifully sprinkled, makes it one of the most delightful books on Scottish life and character we have met with for a very long time.'—*Banffshire Journal.*

'He has written with an air of convincing earnestness, and a desire to present a faithful family record.'—*Sydney Mail.*

'Will be read by all, and Scotchmen especially, with pleasure and profit.'—*New Zealand Herald.*

'A book which all Scotsmen will warm to, and most English readers will enjoy : the former because it brings with it the perfume of the heather and the reek of the peat-fire ; the latter on account of the sketches it presents of a condition of society more primitive and picturesque than anything of the kind to be met with of recent times in South Britain ; and both because it contains one of the best collections of stories of Scottish wit and humour that has appeared since the well-known volume of Dean Ramsay.'—*Australasian.*

'As a sketch of Scots life and character, it may be classed with the best.'—*Presbyterian, Sydney.*

'It would be a mistake to regard "Oor Ain Folk" as a mere repertory of stories about pawky Scots, or as a sketch of an affectionate home circle. It presents to the reader a glimpse into a sequestered patriarchal existence, now much changed by the changes of our headlong time. It records many a shrewd observation upon contemporary men and manners. And this it does for the most part without affectation or parade, with geniality and sometimes with unmistakable tenderness. . . . Those who take up "Oor Ain Folk" will hardly leave it down unperused to the very end, and certainly few will be so dull as not to heartily enjoy its humour and its tenderness."—*Sydney Morning Herald.*

'The book is robust, above all things, in manly sentiment, and instinct with broad yet tender sympathy, while the fine strain of affection which animates the reference to "Oor Ain Folk" in the "auld hoose at hame" will awake responsive chords in many who are parted from the parental hearth. The book is wholesome and bracing, and though written with no apparent purpose beyond the telling of the homely life of a minister's house, the reading of the simple, kindly record, will exercise an influence greater than many books written with a purpose more apparent. . . . Each particular phase of character dealt with by Mr. Inglis is illustrated by apt anecdote, and of such there is a choice and ample store.'—*Sydney Daily Telegraph.*

OUR AUSTRALIAN COUSINS.

By 'MAORI' (THE HONOURABLE JAMES INGLIS)

AUTHOR OF 'TIRHOOT RHYMES,' 'SPORT AND WORK ON THE NEPAUL FRONTIER,' ETC.

OPINIONS OF THE PRESS.

'Of the book as a whole it gives us pleasure to speak in terms of warm appreciation. The author is demonstrably a diligent and keen observer. . . . It may be read as quickly as a novel; and, indeed, it is more interesting than are many novels. This brings us to what we deem to be Mr. Inglis's special gifts, namely, remarkably vivid and racy descriptive and narrative powers. He has a capital vocabulary, and a bright, frank, cheery, racy, graphic style which evidently carried him along easily and pleasantly in the writing, and has equally carried us along in the reading.'—*Sydney Mail.*

'The book will be found highly interesting, valuable, and entertaining. Even the faults do not seem out of place in an account of a young, vigorous, and expanding nation, proudly conscious of its abounding energy and vitality, and not indisposed to "bounce" regarding its wonderful progress and industrial achievements.'—*The Scotsman.*

'Mr. Inglis possesses one singular merit, not often to be found in writers upon Australia: he has the courage to expose abuses and to denounce their authors, as well as to praise the climate and to extol the riches and capabilities of the country. . . . He indulges in warmer hopes of its future than most authors, and describes its scenery and rural sports in the bright, fresh style which characterised his former volume, *Sport and Work on the Nepaul Frontier.'—The Athenæum.*

'It is the characteristic and recommendation of the work that it fulfils the promise of the preface. It is naturally and frankly written, with a good deal of the ease and unreserve of private correspondence, and its author is exceedingly outspoken with respect to the flaws in the political and social life and institutions of these communities. . . . It is written in a lively and entertaining style, and it contains a fund of information respecting these colonies, besides offering some valuable suggestions for the introduction of novel industries.'—*The Argus, Melbourne.*

'Besides describing the legal, commercial, and legislative aspects of Australia, Mr. Inglis depicts with a skilful hand some curious adventures he met with in the social world. . . . In his broad survey of the Colony he has not omitted to describe Australian forest and coast scenery, together with many of the interesting denizens of plain and river. His sketches of his shooting expeditions are vivid, picturesque, and useful from a strictly scientific point of view.'—*The London Standard.*

'Mr. Inglis has written a very pleasant and a very valuable book, not for colonists only, but for those at home who wish to know what our colonies are like. . . . The portions of his book that will most please the general reader are those devoted to descriptions of the scenery, animal life, and sports of the colonies. We have seldom read fresher, healthier descriptions. . . . The scraps of natural history, too, are all exceedingly interesting, as well as some of the tales about animal sagacity. . . . The book is full of matter that will delight the sportsman and naturalist, and about which there can be no doubt of any kind.'—*The Spectator.*

BOOKS PUBLISHED BY

DAVID DOUGLAS

10 Castle Street
EDINBURGH, *July* 1894.

A FOREGONE CONCLUSION.

By

W. D. HOWELLS

EDINBURGH
DAVID DOUGLAS · PUBLISHER

T. & A. CONSTABLE

AMERICAN AUTHORS.

Latest Editions. Revised by the Authors. In 1s. volumes. By Post, 1s. 2d.
Printed by Constable, and published with the sanction of the Authors.

By W. D. HOWELLS.
A Foregone Conclusion.
A Chance Acquaintance.
Their Wedding Journey.
A Counterfeit Presentment.
The Lady of the Aroostook. 2 vols.
Out of the Question.
The Undiscovered Country. 2 vols.
A Fearful Responsibility.
Venetian Life. 2 vols.
Italian Journeys. 2 vols.
The Rise of Silas Lapham. 2 vols.
Indian Summer. 2 vols.
The Shadow of a Dream.
An Imperative Duty.

By FRANK R. STOCKTON.
Rudder Grange.
The Lady or the Tiger?
A Borrowed Month.

By GEORGE W. CURTIS.
Prue and I.

By J. C. HARRIS (*Uncle Remus*).
Mingo, and other Sketches.

By GEO. W. CABLE.
Old Creole Days.
Madame Delphine.

By B. W. HOWARD.
One Summer.

By MARY E. WILKINS.
A Humble Romance.
A Far-away Melody.

By HELEN JACKSON.
Zeph. A Posthumous Story.

By MATT. CRIM.
In Beaver Cove.

By JOHN BURROUGHS.
Winter Sunshine.
Pepacton.
Locusts and Wild Honey.
Wake-Robin.
Birds and Poets.
Fresh Fields.

By OLIVER WENDELL HOLMES.
The Autocrat of the Breakfast Table.
2 vols.
The Poet. 2 vols.
The Professor. 2 vols.
Poetical Works. 4 vols.

By G. P. LATHROP.
An Echo of Passion.

By R. C. WHITE.
Mr. Washington Adams.

By T. B. ALDRICH.
The Queen of Sheba.
Marjorie Daw.
Prudence Palfrey.
The Stillwater Tragedy. 2 vols.
Wyndham Towers: A Poem.
Two Bites at a Cherry.

By B. MATTHEWS and H. C. BUNNER.
In Partnership.

By WILLIAM WINTER.
Shakespeare's England.
Wanderers: A Collection of Poems.
Gray Days and Gold.

By JAMES L. ALLEN.
Flute and Violin.
Sister Dolorosa.

** *Other Volumes of this attractive Series in preparation.*

Any of the above may be had bound in Cloth extra, at 2s. each volume.

'A set of charming little books.'—*Blackwood's Magazine.*
'A remarkably pretty series.'—*Saturday Review.*
'These neat and minute volumes are creditable alike to printer and publisher.'—
Pall Mall Gazette.
'The most graceful and delicious little volumes with which we are acquainted.'—
Freeman.
'Soundly and tastefully bound . . . a little model of typography . . . and the con-
tents are worthy of the dress.'—*St. James's Gazette.*
'The delightful shilling series of "American Authors," introduced by Mr. David
Douglas, has afforded pleasure to thousands of persons.'—*Figaro.*
'The type is delightfully legible, and the page is pleasant for the eye to rest upon;
even in these days of cheap editions we have seen nothing that has pleased us so
well.'—*Literary World.*

EDINBURGH: DAVID DOUGLAS.

SCOTTISH STORIES AND SKETCHES.

Oor Ain Folk : Being Memories of Manse Life in the Mearns and a Crack aboot Auld Times, by JAMES INGLIS. Second Edition. Crown 8vo, 6s.

'In its construction and general tone "Oor Ain Folk" reminds the reader of Dr. Norman Macleod's "Reminiscences of a Highland Parish," whilst it contains a store of admirable Scottish stories, many of them quite new to us, that can only be compared in quality to the classic collection of Dean Ramsay.'—*Glasgow Herald.*

Johnny Gibb of Gushetneuk in the Parish of Pyketillim, with Glimpses of Parish Politics about A.D. 1843, by WILLIAM ALEXANDER, LL.D. Eleventh Edition, with Glossary, Fcap. 8vo, 2s.

Seventh Edition, with Twenty Illustrations—Portraits and Landscapes—by Sir GEORGE REID, P.R.S.A. Demy 8vo, 12s. 6d.

'A most vigorous and truthful delineation of local character, drawn from a portion of the country where that character is peculiarly worthy of careful study and record.' —*The Right Hon. W. E. Gladstone.*

'It is a grand addition to our pure Scottish dialect ; . . . it is not merely a capital specimen of genuine Scottish northern *dialect ;* but it is a capital specimen of pawky characteristic Scottish humour. It is full of good hard Scottish dry fun.' —*Dean Ramsay.*

Life among my Ain Folk, by the Author of 'JOHNNY GIBB OF GUSHETNEUK.'

Contents.

1. Mary Malcolmson's Wee Maggie.
2. Couper Sandy.
3. Francie Herriegerie's Sharger Laddie.

4. Baubie Huie's Bastard Geet.
5. Glengillodram.

Fcap. 8vo. Second Edition. Cloth, 2s. 6d. Paper, 2s.

'Mr. Alexander thoroughly understands the position of men and women who are too often treated with neglect, and graphically depicts their virtues and vices, and shows to his readers difficulties, struggles, and needs which they are sure to be the wiser for taking into view.'—*Freeman.*

Notes and Sketches of Northern Rural Life in the Eigh-teenth Century, by the Author of 'JOHNNY GIBB OF GUSHETNEUK.' In 1 vol. Fcap. 8vo, 2s. 6d., 2s., and 1s.

Chronicles of Glenbuckie, by HENRY JOHNSTON, Author of 'The Dawsons of Glenara.' Extra Fcap. 8vo, 5s.

*** A book of humour and pathos, descriptive of the social, political, and ecclesiastical life in a Scottish parish fifty years ago.

'A genuine bit of Scottish literature.'—*Scottish Leader.*

Scotch Folk. Illustrated. Fourth Edition enlarged. Fcap. 8vo, price 1s.

'They are stories of the best type, quite equal in the main to the average of Dean Ramsay's well-known collection.'—*Aberdeen Free Press.*

Rosetty Ends, or the Chronicles of a Country Cobbler. By Job Bradawl (A. DEWAR WILLOCK), Author of 'She Noddit to me.' Fcap. 8vo, Illustrated. 2s. and 1s.

'The sketches are amusing productions, narrating comical incidents, connected by a thread of common character running through them all—a thread waxed into occasional strength by the "roset" of a homely, entertaining wit.'—*Scotsman.*

EDINBURGH : DAVID DOUGLAS.

LITTLE BROWN BOOKS.

Foolscap 8vo, Sixpence each.

The Religion of Humanity : An Address delivered at the Church
Congress, Manchester, October 1888, by the Right Hon. ARTHUR J. BALFOUR, M.P., LL.D., etc. 6d.

' We have called the pamphlet a sermon because it is one, though the fitting text, '' The fool hath said in his heart, There is no God," is courteously omitted ; and we venture to say that of all who will read it, not one per cent. ever read or heard one more convincing or intellectually more delightful.'—*Spectator.*

[A large type edition of this may also be had in cloth at 5s.]

Fishin' Jimmy, by A. T. SLOSSON. 6d. *'A choice story from America.'*

' A story from which, in its simplicity and pathos, we may all learn lessons of wisdom and charity.'—*Freeman.*

' A pathetic but pretty little story, telling the simple life of one possessed of a profound veneration for all things heavenly, yet viewing them with the fearless questioning eyes of the child.'—*Literary World.*

'Macs' in Galloway. By PATRICK DUDGEON. 6d.

Ailsie and Gabr'el Veitch. 6d.

Rab and his Friends. By Dr. JOHN BROWN. 6d

Marjorie Fleming. By Dr. JOHN BROWN. 6d.

Our Dogs. By Dr. JOHN BROWN. 6d.

'With Brains, Sir.' By Dr. JOHN BROWN. 6d.

Minchmoor. By Dr. JOHN BROWN. 6d.

Jeems the Door-Keeper. By Dr. JOHN BROWN. 6d.

The Enterkin. By Dr. JOHN BROWN. 6d.

Plain Words on Health. By Dr. JOHN BROWN. 6d.

Something about a Well : with more of Our Dogs. By
Dr. JOHN BROWN. 6d.

WORKS BY DR. JOHN BROWN.

Horæ Subsecivæ. 3 Vols. 22s. 6d.
Vol. I. Locke and Sydenham. Sixth Edition, with Portrait by James Faed. Crown 8vo, 7s. 6d.

Vol. II. Rab and his Friends. Fourteenth Edition. Crown 8vo, 7s. 6d.

Vol. III. John Leech. Sixth Edition, with Portrait by George Reid, R.S.A. Crown 8vo, 7s. 6d.

Rab and his Friends. With India-proof Portrait of the Author
after Faed, and seven Illustrations after Sir G. Harvey, Sir Noel Paton, Mrs. Blackburn, and G. Reid, R.S.A. Demy 4to, cloth, 9s.

Marjorie Fleming : A Sketch. Being a Paper entitled 'Pet
Marjorie ; A Story of a Child's Life fifty years ago.' New Edition, with Illustrations by Warwick Brookes. Demy 4to, 7s. 6d. and 6s.

Rab and his Friends. Cheap Illustrated Edition. Square 12mo,
ornamental wrapper, 1s.

EDINBURGH : DAVID DOUGLAS.

SCRIPTURE HISTORY, ETC.

Rev. John Ker, D.D.

SERMONS: FIRST SERIES. 14th Edition. Crown 8vo, . . . 6s. od.
SERMONS: SECOND SERIES. Fifth Thousand. Crown 8vo, . . 6s. od.
THOUGHTS FOR HEART AND LIFE. Second Edition. Ex. Fcap. 8vo, . 4s. 6d.
LETTERS: 1866-1885. Second Edition. Crown 8vo, ... 4s. 6d.

Rev. George Bowen, of Bombay.

DAILY MEDITATIONS. New Edition. Sm. 4to, ... 5s. od.
LOVE REVEALED. New Edition. Sm. 4to, ... 5s. od.

Thomas Erskine, of Linlathen.

THE LETTERS OF. Edited by Dr. HANNA. New Edition. Cr. 8vo, . 7s. 6d.
THE BRAZEN SERPENT, OR LIFE COMING THROUGH DEATH. Cr. 8vo, 5s. od.
THE INTERNAL EVIDENCE OF REVEALED RELIGION. Cr. 8vo, . . 5s. od.
THE SPIRITUAL ORDER. Cr. 8vo, ... 5s. od.
THE DOCTRINE OF ELECTION. Cr. 8vo, ... 6s. od.
THE UNCONDITIONAL FREENESS OF THE GOSPEL. Cr. 8vo, . . 3s. 6d.
THE FATHERHOOD OF GOD. Ex. Fcap. 8vo, ... 1s. od.

William Hanna, D.D., LL.D.

THE EARLIER YEARS OF OUR LORD. Ex. Fcap. 8vo, . . . 5s. od.
THE MINISTRY IN GALILEE. Ex. Fcap. 8vo, ... 5s. od.
THE CLOSE OF THE MINISTRY. Ex. Fcap. 8vo, ... 5s. od.
THE PASSION WEEK. Ex. Fcap. 8vo, ... 5s. od.
THE LAST DAY OF OUR LORD'S PASSION. Ex. Fcap. 8vo, . 5s. od.
THE FORTY DAYS AFTER THE RESURRECTION. Ex. Fcap. 8vo, . 5s. od.
THE RESURRECTION OF THE DEAD. Ex. Fcap. 8vo, . . . 5s. od.

Rev. Walter C. Smith, D.D.

THE SERMON ON THE MOUNT. Cr. 8vo, ... 6s. od.

Professor Blackie.

ON SELF-CULTURE. Fcap. 8vo, ... 2s. 6d.

Principal Shairp.

STUDIES IN POETRY AND PHILOSOPHY. Cr. 8vo, . . . 7s. 6d.
SKETCHES IN HISTORY AND POETRY. Cr. 8vo, ... 7s. 6d.
CULTURE AND RELIGION. Fcap. 8vo, ... 3s. 6d.

Professor Hodgson.

ERRORS IN THE USE OF ENGLISH. Cr. 8vo, ... 3s. 6d.

Mrs. M. M. Gordon.

WORK; OR, PLENTY TO DO AND HOW TO DO IT. Fcap. 8vo, . . 2s. 6d.

Rev. Archibald Scott, D.D.

BUDDHISM AND CHRISTIANITY. Demy 8vo, ... 7s. 6d.
SACRIFICE: ITS PROPHECY AND FULFILMENT. Cr. 8vo, . . 7s. 6d.

The Duke of Argyll.

WHAT IS TRUTH? Fcap. 8vo, ... 1s. od.

EDINBURGH: DAVID DOUGLAS.

SCOTTISH HISTORY AND ARCHÆOLOGY.

The Hereditary Sheriffs of Galloway. By Sir Andrew Agnew, Bart. Second Edition. 2 vols. Demy 8vo, 25s.

Celtic Scotland : A History of Ancient Alban. By William F. Skene, D.C.L., Historiographer-Royal for Scotland. In 3 vols. I. History and Ethnology. II. Church and Culture. III. Land and People. Demy 8vo, 45s. Illustrated with Maps.

Scotland under her Early Kings. A History of the Kingdom to the close of the 13th century. By E. W. Robertson. In 2 vols. 8vo, cloth, 36s.

The History of Liddesdale, Eskdale, Ewesdale, Wauchope-dale, and the Debateable Land. Part I., from the Twelfth Century to 1530. By Robert Bruce Armstrong. The edition is limited to 275 copies demy quarto, and 105 copies on large paper (10 inches by 13), 42s. and 84s. net.

The Castellated and Domestic Architecture of Scotland, from the Twelfth to the Eighteenth Century. By David M'Gibbon and Thomas Ross, Architects. 5 vols., with about 2000 Illustrations of Ground Plans, Sections, Views, Elevations, and Details. Royal 8vo. 42s. each vol. net.

Scotland in Early Christian Times. By Joseph Anderson, LL.D., Keeper of the National Museum of the Antiquaries of Scotland. (Being the Rhind Lectures in Archæology for 1879 and 1880.) 2 vols. Demy 8vo, profusely Illustrated. 12s. each volume.

Scotland in Pagan Times. By Joseph Anderson, LL.D. (Being the Rhind Lectures in Archæology for 1881 and 1882.) In 2 vols. Demy 8vo, profusely Illustrated. 12s. each volume.

The Past in the Present. What is Civilisation? (Being the Rhind Lectures in Archæology, delivered in 1876 and 1878.) By Sir Arthur Mitchell, K.C.B., M.D., LL.D. Demy 8vo, with 148 Woodcuts, 15s.

Scotland as it was and as it is: A History of Races, Military Events, and the rise of Commerce. By the Duke of Argyll. Demy 8vo, illustrated, 7s. 6d.

Studies in the Topography of Galloway. By Sir Herbert Maxwell, Bart., M.P. Demy 8vo, 14s.

Ogham Inscriptions in Ireland, Wales, and Scotland. By the late Sir Samuel Ferguson. Demy 8vo, 12s.

Ecclesiological Notes on some of the Islands of Scot-land, with other Papers relating to Ecclesiological Remains on the Scottish Mainland and Islands. By Thomas S. Muir, Author of 'Characteristics of Old Church Architecture,' etc. Demy 8vo, with numerous Illustrations, 21s.

Early Travellers in Scotland, 1295-1689. Edited by P. Hume Brown. Demy 8vo, 14s.

Tours in Scotland, 1677 and 1681. By Thomas Kirk and Ralph Thoresby. Edited by P. Hume Brown. Demy 8vo, 5s.

Scotland before 1700. From Contemporary Documents. Edited by P. Hume Brown. Demy 8vo, 14s.

A Short Introduction to the Origin of Surnames. By Patrick Dudgeon, Cargen. Small 4to, 3s. 6d.

Circuit Journeys. By the late Lord Cockburn, one of the Judges of the Court of Session. Second Edition. Crown 8vo, 6s.

Recollections of a Tour made in Scotland, A.D. 1803. By Dorothy Wordsworth. Edited by J. C. Shairp. Third Edition. Crown 8vo, 5s.

EDINBURGH : DAVID DOUGLAS.

OPEN-AIR BOOKS.

The Art of Golf. By Sir W. G. SIMPSON, Bart. In 1 vol. demy 8vo, with twenty plates from instantaneous photographs of Professional Players, chiefly by A. F. Macfie, Esq. Price 15s.

'He has devoted himself for years with exemplary zeal to the collecting of everything which a true golfer would like to know about the royal game, and the result of his labour is worthy of the highest commendation. . . . The prominent feature of the volume is the set of illustrations. For the first time, by means of instantaneous photography, are produced on paper the movements made by players with a classical style in the process of striking a golf ball.'— *Scotsman*.

Modern Horsemanship. Three Schools of Riding. An Original Method of Teaching the Art by means of Pictures from the Life. By EDWARD L. ANDERSON. New Edition, re-written and re-arranged, with 40 Moment-Photographs. Demy 8vo, 21s.

The History of Curling. By JOHN KERR, M.A. This volume has been prepared under the authority of the Royal Caledonian Curling Club, and has been compiled from official sources. Illustrated. Demy 8vo, 10s. 6d. Royal 8vo, 31s. 6d. net.

'The book is one of high value. It represents much work of learning and inquiry into an obscure subject, and it illustrates the character of the Scot and the social history of Scotland in a manner that is not the less instructive for being pleasing as well as scholarly.'—*Scotsman*.

How to Catch Trout. By THREE ANGLERS. Illustrated, 1s. & 2s.

'The aim of this book is to give, within the smallest space possible, such practical information and advice as will enable the beginner, without further instruction, to attain moderate proficiency in the use of every legitimate lure.'

'A delightful little book, and one of great value to Anglers.'—*Scotsman*.
'The advice given is always sound.'—*Field*.
'The most practical and instructive work of its kind in the literature of angling.'—*Dundee Advertiser*.
'A well-written and thoroughly practical little book.'—*Land and Water*.

A Year in the Fields. By JOHN WATSON. Fcap. 8vo, 1s.

'A charming little work. A lover of life in the open air will read the book with unqualified pleasure.'—*Scotsman*.

On Horse-Breaking. By ROBERT MORETON. Second Edition, 1s.

Horses in Accident and Disease. By J. ROALFE COX. Demy 8vo, Illustrated. 5s.

The Gamekeeper's Manual; being an Epitome of the Game Laws of England and Scotland, and of the Gun Licenses and Wild Birds Acts. By ALEXANDER PORTER, Chief-Constable of Roxburghshire. Second Edition, crown 8vo, 3s. net.

'A concise and valuable epitome to the Game Laws, specially addressed to those engaged in protecting game.'—*Scotsman*.

The Protection of Woodlands against Dangers arising from Organic and Inorganic Causes, as re-arranged for the Fourth Edition of Kauschinger's 'Waldchutz.' By HERMANN FURST, D.Œc., Director of the Bavarian Forest Institute at Aschaffenburg. Translated by JOHN NISBET, D.Œc., of the Indian Forest Service, Author of 'British Forest Trees and their Sylvicultural Characteristics and Treatment.' Demy 8vo, Illustrated, 9s.

Timbers, and How to Know Them. By Dr. ROBERT HARTIG. Translated from the German by WILLIAM SOMERVILLE, D.Œc., B.Sc., etc. Illustrated, 2s.

Iona. By ELIZABETH A. M'HARDY, with Illustrations by the Author. Ex-fcap. 8vo, 1s.

Iona. With Illustrations. By the DUKE OF ARGYLL. Fcap. 8vo, 1s.

EDINBURGH: DAVID DOUGLAS.